Lucky

Staci Stallings

To all those "prophets" who help fashion the stories
that flow from my heart and my pen.
Thanks for your insights—whether you knew the Holy Spirit
was speaking through you or not. And to the One Who
fashions every story upon my heart. What a joy and
honor to know Your touch is upon each one!

Kalin's mind scrambled to make sense of the huddled mass of agony that gazed up at him through glassy brown eyes couched in the middle of a face smeared with mud and mascara. He reached out and touched her arms to make sure she was in fact still alive. "Good grief, you're freezing." Without questioning it, he ripped off his jacket, pulled her forward gently, and wrapped it around her shoulders. It took another second for him to assess the situation further and come up with a plan of action. "We should get you inside."

"No!" The word tore through the night air around him. Her gaze drilled into his, pleading and wild. "No. I'm not going back in there."

The panic in her voice did nothing to calm the alarm racing through him. God, I need your help with this one! *"Okay. Okay. Then can you at least tell me if you're all right?"*

Chapter 1

"You look so beautiful," Danae Scott said, her voice barely a whisper as she gazed at Molly Emerson in the rounded mirror. Molly's gold-toned blonde hair was pulled up, letting soft curls cascade down her long oval face. Danae's own emerald green satin gown was no comparison for the soft white satin of Molly's. Fitted with a drop shoulder shawl, it flowed to the floor in a wash of hand-sewn pearls.

Molly turned from her own reflection and looked at Danae with a mix of happy gentleness. "It won't be long, and you'll be the one standing here."

Danae stepped back to examine the back of Molly's dress more to avoid eye contact than to adjust anything on the dress. "He hasn't asked me yet."

"He will." Molly turned full around to talk to her friend, dragging most of the dress with her. "It's only a matter of time now. Think about it, by next year he'll have his master's, you'll be teaching, you can move off together and have lots of little cousins for our kids to play with."

It was a nice thought, but even after seven years, it still seemed so very far away. With little enthusiasm, Danae looked at Molly and smiled. "How about we get you and Rick married first? You haven't even said, 'I do' yet."

Molly smoothed the shiny material over her stomach. "It's so hard to believe we're already here. It seems like just yesterday you brought him to the Golden Light."

"And it was love at first sight," Danae said as she fluffed out the train to check for hidden wrinkles. It was a story she had by now memorized—half because she had heard it so many times and half because she had lived it.

"Have you seen him yet?" Molly asked, her attention swerving back to her own life.

"Rick?"

"Yeah."

Danae laughed. "It would be a little hard to see him. I've been in here with you since we got here."

Molly half-turned to her friend, pleading in her green-blue eyes. "Would you mind going and making sure he got here all right?"

"I guess that's why they call me a bride's *maid*," Danae said teasingly.

"Very funny."

"Stay put. I'll see what's going on out there." With that, Danae left Molly and stepped out onto the inside balcony. The festive sounds below engulfed her.

"Is she ready?" Mrs. Emerson, the older, more dignified, version of her daughter asked, meeting Danae on the top step of the gently winding staircase of the stately old mansion.

Careful not to move too drastically, Danae readjusted the sleeveless bodice that wrapped around her chest like a tight rubber band. "She's dressed, but she's a little worried Rick might make a break for it."

Mrs. Emerson laughed. "He'd better not. Victor would probably shoot the poor kid."

"Well, that would be kind compared with what Molly would do to him." Danae crossed past Mrs. Emerson and started down the stairs. One hand held the banister; the other pulled her floor length skirt away from her shoes. "I'll be right back."

"Take your time, dear. Oh, and make sure Brandt got his cummerbund on right. I gave up."

"I'll be sure to check." Careful not to trip on the soft shimmering material at her feet, Danae descended the last ten steps of the picturesque antebellum estate that Molly and Rick had mortgaged their parents' lives to rent for their special evening.

It was strange how much a part of Mrs. Emerson's family Danae felt. After all the years she had been dating their youngest son, Brandt, she might as well have already been one of the family's daughters.

Molly and Brandt and the rest of the Emerson family had moved next door to Danae's family the summer before she went to kindergarten. Their trampolines and backyards had never been the same since. Hardly a day had gone by since that first one that one group of kids wasn't at the other's house. It was almost like they were one and the same family.

Elementary school plays, middle school band, high school parties, dances, basketball, football, and baseball. Every season, every day. They were always together. They even went to the same church—youth group and all.

~ Lucky ~

One without the other seemed incomplete, and so when it came time to choose a college, there had been very little choice involved. Molly went to Tennessee University in their hometown of Knoxville, Tennessee, and two years later, Brandt and Danae followed. The only one who had broken ranks was Nikki, Danae's older sister. She made it the first two years, but then following their mother's advice, she had hooked herself to a wealthy frat boy and followed him to Virginia. They were expecting twins at any moment.

It was now only a matter of time before Danae, true to the well-known expectations of just about everyone around them, hooked herself permanently to her own semi-wealthy frat boy—the one and only Brandtly V. Emerson II.

Making nearly no sound at all compared with the other human beings on the premises, she stepped through the growing crowd of wedding specialists. There were five for the cake and three for the flowers, four for the music and two for the photography. She slipped through the throng and at the door down the hallway knocked softly. "Knock. Knock."

There was a mumble from the other side.

"It's Danae," she said to the mahogany wood door. A beat and then she turned the knob. The door swung inward an inch. "Everybody decent?"

"Hey, Brandt, the ball and chain's here," Rick called when he caught sight of her. He went back to fumbling with his tie at the mirror.

"Ha. Ha." She scrunched her face. "I'm not here to see him anyway." She stepped into the spacious room, which was decorated in rich mahogany furniture with burgundy and gold accents, and closed the door behind her.

"Let me guess," Rick said, "Molly thinks I'm going to bail."

"No, she doesn't think that. If she did, she'd have picked you up at your place with her shotgun."

With a frustrated growl, he swiped his fingers through the tie. "Stupid thing."

"Here, let me help." Danae stepped over to him, and he turned to face her. The solid shoulders lined up with hers as the dark eyes and angled features perused her face.

His eyes snagged on hers just before he lifted his chin. "How's she doing?"

"A little nervous, but that's to be expected. How are you?"

The tie finished, his gaze slid to hers and held. "Only one thing could make today any better."

She shook her head. "Rick, we've been through this a million times."

His gaze dropped to the floor. "I know, I just—"

The snap of the door behind them sent them both scrambling backward. Brandt, taller than the two of them by a full eight inches, stalked into the room. The second he saw Danae, annoyance tramped across his darkly tanned features. "What? Did Mom send in the second string?"

Danae took another step away from Rick and put her hands on her hips. "You know, you've really got to learn to curb your enthusiasm."

He yanked on his tie. "When's the keg getting here? Then I'll be downright thrilled."

"First things, first." Danae looked back at Rick who was busy repositioning his jacket. "I was going to tell you the photographer is here, so I think they'll be ready to start pictures any time now."

"Ugh. The joy never ends," Brandt said. "Why didn't you guys just elope? It would've made this so much easier."

"We like to torture people," Rick retorted.

"Obviously," Brandt spat. "Well, at least Danae and I are going to be smart. It's Vegas all the way for us. Right, baby?"

"Yeah." Danae's insides curled over themselves, but she held what she was really thinking in a tight rein. She turned to Rick. "Where's Philip anyway?"

"He went with Molly's dad a while ago. I think they're checking on the reception set up across the way."

She frowned. "Then I'd better go get them rounded up, too." With two fists of green material, she hiked her skirt up and started for the door. "I should've worn roller skates."

"Tell Molly I can't wait to see her," Rick said, his voice softening.

"She'll be the one at the end of the aisle," Danae said with a soft smile. She reached for the doorknob.

"Danae," Brandt said suddenly.

"Yeah?"

"Tell Mom I forgot my cufflinks."

Danae exhaled. "Figures."

"What?" he asked with no small amount of annoyance.

"I'll tell her."

Considering she hadn't been chosen as maid of honor, Danae had wrongly assumed that the day would be a snap. All she would have to do was take a few pictures, walk down the aisle with Brandt, look happy, and walk back. However, what she hadn't adequately figured on was being the one and only person everyone else counted on to make the day run smoothly.

As she strode across the gravel and puddle strewn parking lot to the reception building, she wondered how Krystal, the vaunted maid of honor, had actually made it to two hours before the nuptials without doing anything to help.

It was Danae who had wrapped birdseed in tiny bundles of tulle until her fingers were stiff and red. It was Danae who had painstakingly assembled the centerpieces for the reception—green and cream curling ribbon and all. It was Danae who had gone with Molly to get her pictures made—just before she went with the guys for their tuxedo fitting, and now it was Danae who had to make sure there would actually be photographic proof of this happy day.

"Mr. Emerson?" she called as she stepped from the sunshine into the room lit only by pinpoints of what would have to pass as starlight. Three weeks of intermittent thunderstorms hadn't given anyone confidence that the reception could reliably be held outside, so they had opted to bring the outside in. To one side the band was setting up. Wires criss-crossed the floor in front of the stage in a gazillion directions. She stopped one of the caterers. "Do you know where Mr. Emerson, umm, the bride's father is?"

"I think he's back there," the young man said, pointing to one of the storage closets just beyond the sea of cables.

"Thanks," she barely mumbled. Praying she wouldn't trip over something and lay herself out in front of the six guys in the band, she strode over to the mess of cables, surveyed her options, and then seeing no other way to get to the door, she tiptoed ever so carefully into the melee, wondering how long it would take to get to the other side.

"Can I help you?" one of the band members called just as she got to the center of the snaking cables.

Danae stopped instantly. "I'm sorry. I'm trying to get the bride's father for pictures."

Another one of the band members, who was at the moment on the stage piecing the sound system together, threw the connection cord he was carrying to the floor. "Stay right there. I'll get him."

Obediently Danae stood stock-still right in the middle of the ocean of black. In ten seconds, the band member returned with two tuxedoed figures in tow.

"It'd be better to go around," the band member said as he guided the two around the far outer edge of the cables pressed up against the wall.

His shag-cut golden hair ended right at his chin line, and the black T-shirt on black jeans outfit he wore looked like he'd just climbed off a motorcycle.

"Danae, what're you doing over here?" Mr. Emerson asked, puffing his rounded frame out like he was upset about being interrupted.

"I'm sorry, but they're about to start pictures," she said, turning carefully. Realizing only then that she should've made her assault next to the wall, she began to pick her way back out of the cables, but out was much farther than she had realized it would be. She stepped and stepped again, holding her dress, fighting to keep her balance, and trying to avoid catching her shoe on anything that would send her crashing to the floor. But the farther she went, the farther clear floor seemed to be.

"Here," the band member said when he and his charges reached the outer edge of the cables closest to the outside door. He put his foot into the mess of cords and reached for her hand. She put her hand in his, hoping he wouldn't just yank her free. Under her hand his felt smooth, his fingers easily blending with hers. "Not a good idea in heels," he said with a light smile.

She took two more steps, and together they stepped out of the mass of black. "Whoa." She ran her hand down the soft green satin at her stomach and then over her carefully pinned and upswept dark hair. "I may have to turn in my bridesmaid card if they keep sending me on these kinds of missions."

The band member's gaze had never left her. Soft and gentle, he smiled. "I wouldn't worry about that. You look beautiful." It was then that she noticed his thick accent that had nothing to do with eastern Tennessee.

Heat rushed to her cheeks, and Danae's gaze slid down her frame. With her shoulders bared and the top of the dress beginning only at the top of her chest, she suddenly felt very self-conscious. She mumbled a thank you, slid her hand over her hair again, and retrained her attention to Mr. Emerson and Philip. "We'd better go. The photographer's waiting."

Kalin Lane had the impression that someone had just sucker punched him because suddenly there was a weird lack of air in the building. He stood barely six inches from the snaking cables as he watched her glide gracefully to the door with her two tuxedoed companions.

"Wow. Did you get a load of the knockers on that one?" Von, the wild-haired guitarist, said as he stepped up to Kalin's side. "I'd sure like to take a drive on those curves." He put his hands out as if he was driving a racecar and slid them side to side. He turned to the other band members. "Maybe this gig won't be such a bust after all, boys. With bridesmaids like her we could be in for a long night."

Catcalls from the others met his lurid tone.

"Let the games begin!" he said, leaning in to Kalin.

"Shut up, Von," Kalin said with a shake of his head as he reached down to retrieve a cable. "If you'd get your mind out of the gutter once in awhile, you might figure out that the good ones aren't impressed with junkies like you."

"Oh, excuse me. I forgot I was talking to the preacher man," Von said loud enough for the others to hear as he too went back to work. "Hey, everybody, the preacher man's giving us another sermon on the wantonness of our ways."

"You need a sermon, Von," Claude, the drummer, called from the back of the stage.

"I don't need no sermons. Just give me some good lines and that bridesmaid, and I'll be in heaven." Von mounted the stage. "Know what I'm saying?"

With the smallest shake of his head, Kalin pulled the cable in his hands over to the soundboard. *Lord, they are really trying my patience today. Thanks for telling me to ride out here on my bike. There's no telling when they'll get home tonight.*

For good measure, he said a little side prayer for the protection of every woman at the wedding. With the six members of Silver Moonlight, Kalin's most recently adopted musical family, on the loose, the women would need all the prayers they could get.

The garden was awash in spring color. The rains followed by two bright days of sunshine brought the blossoms out of every one of their hiding places. Breathtaking barely described it, Danae thought as she walked down the aisle toward Rick, who stood in the gazebo with the preacher. It really was too bad that she and Brandt were so meant to be. Rick would certainly have gotten more than a half-second look from her had the situation been different. She smiled at him, and his return smile told her without words that everything she felt in her heart was in his as well. Just before she turned, she thought about smiling at Brandt, but when she looked his way, his gaze had already slipped past her to the aisle beyond.

At the end of her journey, she took her place where she turned and watched as Krystal, tall, blonde, and curvaceous traced down Danae's steps to the gazebo. They had never been friends. They barely knew each other—not for wont of trying on Danae's part, but Krystal didn't have time for other women, she was too focused on the other half of the population. It was still a mystery to Danae what Molly saw in her former college roommate. However, she decided that now was not the time to try to sort all of that out.

When Krystal was finally in her place, the song ended and the guests stood. For several full minutes Danae had to use her imagination to make out what was happening because she couldn't see anything through the crush of bodies. It took no imagination whatsoever to understand the look of pure joy on Rick's face as he watched his bride coming to meet him.

Molly was right. Sooner than not, that would be Danae walking toward Brandt. That thought lodged in her throat making her cough softly. She pushed the thought to the back of her mind and slid her gaze to the picture that had come into focus when Molly stepped past the final guest. Her eyes sparkled with love and excitement as she gazed at Rick. At that moment everything that had gone before slipped into oblivion. From this moment forward Molly and Rick would be tied to each other forever, and for that reason alone, everything was right with the world.

"Oh, Danae, your dress is so gorgeous," Elaine Benton, Mrs. Emerson's best friend, cooed when she strode up, pink punch in hand. Her baby blue dress barely contained her stout figure. "Oh, Brandtly, dear." She reached a perfectly manicured set of fingers out for Brandt who was standing five feet away surveying the crowd with Philip, Rick's brother. Mrs. Benton took hold of Brandt and pulled him over to Danae's side. "I want to get a picture of you two."

Dutifully although he didn't really look at Danae, Brandt slid his arm around her from her shoulder to her waist. They both smiled as if this was the best day of their lives. The camera flashed, and Brandt immediately released Danae.

"You know, it won't be long, and it will be the two of you standing up there," Mrs. Benton enthused.

"Something to look forward to," Brandt said soft enough that only Danae heard it. She tried to smile at his joke, but it wasn't really meant for her.

"So, Danae," Mrs. Benton said, pulling her from his side at which point he gratefully faded back to Philip's side, "tell me about teaching. When are you going to be finished?"

"Oh, well, all I lack is student teaching in the fall," Danae said. Her gaze bounced around the reception area, searching desperately for an excuse out of this conversation.

"Now tell me again, what age are you planning to teach?"

Danae cleared her throat. "Elementary. K through fifth."

"I can see you teaching fourth grade. You would be a good fourth grade teacher."

"Well, I hope so," she said although she had completely removed herself from the conversation in mind and spirit.

"And Brandtly, what's he going to do again?"

Danae had to clear her throat again to get the words out. "Structural engineering. He's going to build bridges."

"Are you planning on moving when you get out?" Mrs. Benton asked with concern.

"Oh, well, we haven't really made any solid plans yet. It's all kind of up in the air—"

"Danae! Sweetheart, will you help us with these?" Mrs. Emerson asked, straining under three massive presents. "They have some more out in the van."

"Sure," she said, not really wanting to be the moving crew but thankful for the pretext to conclude the conversation.

"Oh, Elaine," Mrs. Emerson said happily when she had transferred the boxes to Danae, "we're so glad you could come!"

Wishing she had asked the seamstress to take another inch or so off the hem of the full-length skirt, Danae made her way through the guests to the over-flowing gift table. One thing was for sure, the Emersons had no lack of friends.

"Well, if it isn't Danae Scott," Marcia Turner, a friend from high school, said as she fell into step with Danae.

"Hey, Marcia, I'm headed to the gift table. Walk with me. Talk with me."

Marcia sipped on her punch. "Looks like you and Brandt are still shacking up."

"We're not shacking up," Danae said, wishing she had remembered how annoying Marcia could be.

"Too bad for you," Marcia said, and Danae sighed to keep herself from leveling this friend in wolf's clothing. "So, are you guys ever going to get married, or are you just going to keep stringing him along forever?"

"Funny, I thought it was the *guy* who was supposed to ask."

"So, what's he waiting for—a telegraph from Mars?"

Danae set the presents down and headed for the door Mrs. Emerson had come from with the gifts. "You're going to have to ask him that question. If you'll excuse me..." She purposely stepped through a knot of guests so that Marcia couldn't follow her. The closer she got to the door, the better it looked. Just leave. Would anyone really miss her? Probably not unless they needed some grunt work done.

She crossed out into the late evening sunset and found the van Mrs. Emerson had spoken about. It was indeed filled to the brim with gifts. Mr. Emerson stood next to it handing them out to the few helpers standing around. It took nothing to notice that she was the only bridal attendant in on this work detail.

"Oh, good, Danae," he said. He pulled one box out and handed it to her, and she barely managed to keep from dropping it. "I think this is some of the crystal so be careful with it."

Just as she nodded and turned to head back, he exclaimed, "Oh! And take this one too." With that, he stacked a second box at least the size but thankfully not the weight of the first on the top of the previous one.

Her ankles wobbled under the weight and the bulk.

"This should've been done yesterday," Mr. Emerson said to one of the others helping, "but Gail didn't want anything stolen…"

Danae picked her way across the gravel, past the guests who seemed not to even notice her presence. As she reached the door, she began to wonder how she would ever manage to get it open without dropping the boxes. However, just as that thought went through her head, the door burst open seemingly on its own.

"Whoa!" said the person who'd opened it. "Looks like you've got a handful there."

Her heart skipped through her chest although she hadn't caught so much as a glimpse at the owner of that voice. The accent was impossible to miss.

"Here." Without asking, he pulled the top box from her and held the door with his foot. "They've really got you working overtime today."

She laughed as she crossed in front of him. A whiff of his cologne sent her head spinning. "It's one of the hazards of the job." She had thought he would give her the box back once they were inside. Instead he followed her across the expanse to the gift table. Trying not to, she noticed the tattoo, peeking out from under the hem of his black T-shirt sleeve on his nicely rounded bicep. She couldn't tell what the artwork was exactly, and before she got too carried away trying to figure it out, she yanked her attention back to the task at hand.

"Looks like they'll be here opening presents for a month," he said.

"Let's hope not." She set her box down, retrieved his and set it down as well. "Thanks." Her hand slipped up to her hair and smoothed it back. "I was wondering how I was going to get that done."

He smiled at her, and for the first time she noticed how soft his hazy gray eyes were couched underneath that golden mane. "Done."

She laughed. "Well, thank you."

"Danae! We need you over here for pictures!" Mrs. Emerson called from the cake table.

Danae looked at him and smiled helplessly. "Back to the grindstone."

"Looks like it."

With that, she turned and strode over to rejoin the wedding party.

Kalin tried not to watch her, but it wasn't easy. She was mesmerizing. The dark hair, the soft brown eyes, the skin like crushed velvet—to his way of thinking, she could've just stepped off the cover of a magazine. He faded back into the wall and watched as she took her place next to the tall young man with the Ivy League features. Kalin's heart plummeted to his shoes as he watched the young man wrap her in his arms and plant a kiss on her forehead. He hoped beyond all rationality that what he was seeing wasn't the reality of the situation.

But when they stayed right at each other's sides, arms entwined, toasting and drinking their champagne, he couldn't deny it. They were together and not at all trying to hide it. He twisted the leather wristband at his left wrist. With a push, he forced himself to go back to the stage. It was stupid to even let his thoughts go anywhere near her. He didn't need a woman in his life. He could barely keep up with himself.

"Did you get it?" Von asked when Kalin made it back to the stage.

"It…?" Then he stopped himself. The extra strap he had set out to get from their equipment trailer. "Oh, no, man. It wasn't there."

Von spat an expletive and spun back to recheck the amp. "I could've sworn I threw an extra one in there."

"Here, you can use mine," Kalin said. "I won't need it the first set anyway." Quickly he unhooked his guitar strap and handed it across the stage to Von. The fewer outbursts they managed to have, the better. This gig was a favor for his manager's old friend. Upsetting the old friend didn't sound like the best career move in the world, and he'd made enough bad career moves that it was a wonder he was even on a stage anywhere in the world—much less one in the great state of Tennessee.

Chapter 2

"Danae, sweetheart, I haven't seen your mother all day. I hope nothing's wrong," June Avery, K Street's answer to the town crier, said as Danae reassembled the bride's table that had obviously been viewed by too many guests.

She repositioned the picture of Molly and then the collage of Molly and Rick. "No, Ma'am. Everything's fine. She's in Virginia with Nikki."

"Oh, I hope nothing's wrong with Nikki," Mrs. Avery said, obviously fishing for some juicy little tidbit to pass along to the rest of the neighborhood.

"No, it's just with the twins on the way, Mom took some leave time and went to help her out." Danae reset the photo album that laid out the lives of Molly and Rick in all their four-color glory.

"That's so nice," Mrs. Avery said. "Now remind me again, when are the twins due?"

"May 17, but the doctors don't think she'll go that long."

"Oh, I bet you're just bustin' to get to see them."

Danae fought not to wince. "Yeah, bustin'." Her gaze chanced across the crowd to the door. "If you'll excuse me…" Normally she didn't make a point of catching up with Brandt, but this was a dire exception. "Brandt! Hold up." As quickly as she could, she strode to his side just before he and Philip made it to the door. "Where're you going? The dance is about to start."

"We were going to grab a beer," Brandt said, not too kindly. "Do you mind?"

"Well, no, but—"

"Three minutes," Philip said. "Surely they can wait that long."

Tall, with all the cockiness that came with being 20, Philip had a way of doing whatever he wanted no matter if that messed something up for anyone else on the planet or not. Without waiting for her reply, they left her standing at the door. A small shake of her head accompanied by the tiniest of sighs, and Danae turned back to the merriment wondering how long this torture was going to last.

On stage, Kalin was busy going over the list of songs for the first set. He'd been with Silver Moonlight three months, and still it seemed they weren't quite in sync. He had the sneaking suspicion that the gear-slips had as much to do with the extra-curricular activities of the other members as it had to his being new, but they didn't see it that way.

"They said groom and bride, then attendants and parents, and then two parent songs." Kalin ticked through the list quickly. "Then we've got three songs, and they'll do the garter and bouquet."

"Whatever you say," Von said as if he was about to fall asleep. "You're the boss."

It was the standard insult, right after the one about being a preacher. He wasn't the boss any more than they were the employees. It was simply an alliance that seemed to be about to drive right off a cliff at any moment. Stuffing all of that and everything else down, he stepped over to the microphone and let his smile take over his voice.

"Good evening, folks. We're really honored to be here for this very special occasion. If the bride and groom would come forward, we'd like to honor them with a very special song."

Behind him the band finalized their preparations while in front of him, the groom stepped forward and turned back to wait for his bride. It was then that Kalin caught sight of the bridesmaid working diligently to pin up the final folds of the bride's dress, and a genuine smile traipsed through him. Finally the bride joined the groom on the dance floor, and oohs and aahs echoed across the space.

On the keyboard just behind and to the side of Kalin, Carson drifted through the intro. The twinkling of the lights around the floor made it almost look like the twilight outside. As the words approached and he looked beyond the bride and groom to the bridesmaid standing at the edge of the floor watching, he wished the weather hadn't scared the families indoors. There was something special about playing outdoors in a cool Tennessee evening breeze.

"Your love took me by surprise." The song slid through him with little need for his brain to pay attention to it. "Your love reminds me to be me. Your love helps me to be strong. Your love is what I've been waiting for..."

Danae couldn't concentrate on Molly and Rick. Her gaze went back to the door in annoyance as she folded her arms across her chest. If Brandt and Philip didn't get back soon, they were going to totally ruin everything. Of course, that wouldn't surprise her at all. They were good at it, but today of all days they needed to act like the adults they were supposed to be. Okay, that was probably asking too much but...

"Miss me?" Brandt asked right in her ear. Relief poured through her.

"Of course," she said, letting all the bad thoughts drift away from her. Maybe she was wound a little too tightly for her own good. "I'm glad you're back."

"I'm glad I'm back, too," he said.

For one moment Danae remembered why she had fallen so hard for him in the first place. He really could be very sweet when he wanted to be. She smiled up at him as he wound his arm around her waist.

"They look happy," she said, gazing out at the dancers as she laid her head against the muscle in his shoulder.

"I'm glad." In time with her, his body swayed. It felt so right having him there. If she could ever just quit being annoyed with him, their fairy tale was within grasp.

The song ended.

"We would like to present to you Mr. and Mrs. Rick Langhorne," the lead singer said, and his voice jolted Danae out of the daydream. Her gaze snapped not to the bride and groom but to the stage. Sure enough, it was him. He had added a blue and white plaid shirt over the black T-shirt and jeans. Without really thinking about it, her mind contemplated how that shirt would bring out the color of his eyes if she was close enough to actually see them. He flipped his hair back nonchalantly and retook the microphone. "And now if we could have the attendants and the parents join the happy couple."

Danae's feet followed Brandt, but her mind was squarely on the stage. Even as the music started and Brandt took her into his arms, she had to fight to stay in the moment and not daydream about the guy at the microphone singing to her instead of to a room full of people. Of course, it was a love song, and of course, it melted right through her. She let Brandt pull her closer mostly so she wouldn't have to worry about carrying on a logical conversation. Every other person in the room dropped away as she floated on the wings of his voice.

"So, when are you two going to make it official?" Rick's dad asked suddenly, slicing through the moment like a hacksaw.

With a jolt, Danae's head came off Brandt's chest, and her attention crashed back into the room.

"Oh, you know," Brandt said, "we're just waiting for the right moment."

"No time like the present," Rick's dad said, to which his mom made a hard right turn.

"Don't mind him," she said over her shoulder, "he's just ready for another party." They danced away.

Danae's insides somersaulted through her as she looked up at Brandt. He looked down at her, and for the briefest of seconds she thought their lives might change right at that moment.

"Good band they got," he finally said.

"Oh, yeah." She ducked, realizing she was being utterly ridiculous. "I wonder where they found them."

"I think Dad pulled in a favor from one of his agent friends in Nashville."

That startled her. "They're professional?" She stumbled on the words. "I mean they aren't just some band out of Knoxville?"

"No, they're the real deal. I think the lead singer even had a contract or something at one time."

The comment didn't totally surprise her, but it threw her "wondering machine" into full gear. "They're really good."

"Yes, they are," he said just as the song ended. They let go of one another to clap. He led her off the floor. "Well, now that that's over, I think I'm going to run go get a cold beverage. You coming?"

"Oh, no." Danae wrapped her arms around her middle. "I think I'll just stay and watch."

He shrugged. "Suit yourself."

No more than ten seconds later, she was once again standing at the edge of the crowd, wishing she could be anywhere else.

How many times Kalin had berated himself to keep his mind on his present mission, he didn't know, but by the time they broke for the bouquet toss, his mind was playing tag with her ghost. He'd see her for seconds, and then she was gone again. No rational part of him said that even looking for her made any sense; however, he couldn't help himself. The only clear way he saw of breaking the spell was to remove himself from the premises altogether.

"I'm going to go look for that strap again," he said to Carson. "Why don't you MC this thing?" He walked to the side of the stage, stepped down the two steps, and exited through the side door. The cool night beyond the reception area whispered to his ragged spirit. If only this life wasn't so insane… If only he had kept it together the first go-round, then he wouldn't be here, praying he could make enough to make it to the next gig. Why he let his first opportunity slip through his fingers, he would never know.

He rounded the corner of the building and realized there was a group of wedding guests standing there. Feeling like the hired help, he skirted the crowd and headed for the band's trailer. However, even trying not to listen, he caught the mention of her name, and his steps slowed.

"...oh, you know, Danae," one of the group's participants said. "It'll be a miracle if I get to lay her on our wedding night."

"Yeah, but she is fine!" one of the others said.

"Like that does me a lot of good," the first guy said.

Kalin put his hands in his pockets and ducked his head as he stalked by them. A step past, however, his gaze bounced up to the face, and he realized who it was—those Ivy League features would be hard to mistake.

"Maybe you could get her drunk," the other guy said.

"I'd have a better chance of laying her!" the first guy said, and the whole group cracked up.

He'd heard enough. Fists jammed into his pockets, Kalin hurried to the trailer and let it bang a little extra loud against the side. "Jerks," he said to the emptiness of the blackness beyond. Sure, it had taken him nearly ten years and more meetings than he wanted to count to get past being that immature, but now that he was past it, it just looked disgusting. Once again as he emerged with the strap in hand, he repeated his prayer for her from earlier.

God, I think this may be more serious than I thought. There are wolves everywhere tonight. Please keep her safe. She needs Your protection.

By the time Brandt made it back in, the band was well into their third set, and Danae had resigned herself to sitting in the dark and obeying orders when they showed up. The cake was now down. The photos safely out in the van. The presents packed up as well. If she had thought the guests wouldn't mind, she might well have started taking the lights down. It was only a matter of time before she would be climbing the chairs to do that too.

A sick feeling slid through her stomach when Brandt walked up behind her as she stood watching the dancers. She could smell the alcohol that seemed to permeate his entire being.

"Hey, love of my life," he said softly as he wrapped his arms around her. "Wanna dance?"

It should've been heart-warming. It wasn't. She could tell by the slur in his voice he was drunk, and that always meant one thing. One question. One suggestion. One argument. On the dance floor he crushed her body to his so that she had to turn her head to be able to breathe.

"Having fun?" he asked, bending to look at her.

"I guess," she said with no enthusiasm at all. "You?"

"That depends. You got anything special planned for me tonight?"

Revulsion coiled around her. "Dancing?"

"No, not dancing," he said in annoyance. Then he looked around at the others. "Well, not here anyway. I was thinking, Mom and Dad rented this place for the whole night. We could have our pick of rooms."

She pulled in a long breath that lodged in her lungs. "Brandt, we've been through this."

"Yeah, and I keep hoping one of these days, you're going to quit just saying you love me and start proving it." He lowered his mouth to her neck, and she took an awkward step backward which very nearly landed them both on the floor.

"Brandt, not here," she pleaded, looking around at everyone else.

He pulled his head back. "Then come away with me. Right now. That big old house is empty. Nobody will disturb us…"

"We've talked about this," she said, looking into his alcohol-dulled eyes. "I want my wedding night to be special—"

"This night could be special."

"No, Brandt. It's not the same."

The song ended, and he took one step back from her. "You're serious?"

She smoothed out her dress. "Yes, I'm serious."

His gaze could've melted steel. With a set of his jaw he shook his head. "Fine. Whatever you want, Danae. I just don't see what the difference is."

The next song started. Without even asking, he pulled her into his grasp.

"Then it shouldn't make any difference if we wait," she said, but he didn't choose to continue the conversation. Instead he withdrew into his own little pity-party shell like he always did.

Tears stung her eyes. Why did every serious conversation with him have to come back to this one subject? It wasn't like he didn't know what her answer would be—what her answer had always been. Yet he kept asking, kept suggesting, kept needling. She sniffed to keep the tears from falling. The harder he pushed, the farther the love felt from her heart, and it hurt to watch it go.

When that song ended, he squeezed her extra-tight. "I'm going to go help Phil with the keg."

"Yeah," Danae said, swiping at the tears that hadn't fallen. "You do that." She didn't watch him leave. She didn't have to. She could feel it. They had been friends for what seemed like forever. They had been dating for nearly eight years, but she wondered at that moment if she knew him at all—or if he knew her. Her gaze fell to the silver ring on her left hand. It had been a promise she had made to herself and to God. Going back on that promise now felt like selling a piece of her soul. She twisted the ring first to the right and then to the left. Her eyes closed as she pulled the decision through her spirit.

God, I don't know what to do. I don't want to lose him, but this just doesn't feel right. What am I supposed to do?

"Life gives as good as it takes, destroys as good as it makes," they sang from the stage. "Stay true to your heart's message, your soul's direction. You'll never get lost. You'll never lose track. You'll never give in. You'll never look back..."

Her gaze drifted heavenward, and she smiled at how quickly God could answer prayers. She wouldn't give in, and Brandt would get over it just like he always did. Life would go on, and someday it would be right. Through all of the turmoil of the day, peace rushed through her.

"Dance with me," Rick said as he approached her.

Her smile was real then. They half-danced, half-walked out to the floor. At the edge of the dance floor, he spun her under his arm and sang the next ten words for emphasis. She laughed at him, and his smile washed through her as she stepped into his arms.

"Happy?" she asked.

He took a breath. "Ecstatic."

"Well, I'm happy for you."

"Yep, looks like we both got what we wanted."

"Oh, yeah? How's that?"

"Well, I've got a woman who loves me, and you've got Brandt. So it's all good."

"Yes," she said, nodding. "It's all good."

The clock had wound around to past midnight-fifteen, and Danae was dead on her feet. Molly and Rick had left to a hail of birdseed and cheers. They truly looked like the happiest couple on the earth. As she walked back into the hall, the band was beginning its last set. She pulled her hands up to her bare arms. Spring was beautiful, but the Tennessee nights of April hadn't quite gotten the message to warm up yet. Coupled with the rain-cooled air from the previous week's thunderstorms, the weather could only be called chilly.

"Danae, where is Brandt?" Mrs. Emerson asked in a huff when she strode up. "I've been looking everywhere for him."

Danae surveyed the quickly thinning crowd. "I haven't seen him in awhile. Maybe he went back to the house to get the tuxedos ready." She knew that was the last thing he was doing. More likely he was passed out in the back of Phil's pickup, but she would spare Mrs. Emerson the gory details of that theory.

"Would you mind running over there to check?" Mrs. Emerson asked. "I really can't leave right now, and Aunt Patricia and Uncle Teddy will be leaving soon. He should be here to say good-bye."

How she was planning on finding him, Danae had no idea, but she reasoned if she was gone looking, it would give her an excuse to miss the relatives leaving as well. "Sure, I'll go check."

"Oh, thank you, sweetheart. You are so wonderful."

Ulterior motives and all, Danae escaped from the building and headed to the mansion. In the ebony darkness it looked very big, very dark, and very quiet. She wrapped her arms around themselves and considered looking for Phil instead, but that could take more work than it was worth. Doggedly she stuck to her mission. She would search the parts of the house she knew. If he wasn't there, it wasn't her fault.

Only two table lamps were on in the large living room when she opened the front door. The house was completely still and eerily devoid of life. Her gaze traveled to the winding staircase that led up to the second floor. She considered going upstairs to change. Her clothes from sometime before time began were still up in the bridesmaids' room, but she nixed that idea when she considered the grief she would catch if she were to go back to the reception in her street clothes.

Instead she turned her steps down the now nearly black hallway and headed for the groom's room. It was a good thing she had been sent on her mission to check on Rick earlier in the day. Now she knew exactly which room she was looking for—otherwise a cursory search would have involved many more rooms, and at the moment all she wanted to do was get out of this creepy old house and back to the crowd of guests.

Just as she got to the door, she heard a noise, and hope jumped into her heart. Maybe she had been right after all. Maybe the guys had just come over here to get their things ready to go.

"Brandt?" she said, knocking softly even as her other hand turned the knob. "You in there?" On the next push she was in the room. With one look, the world as she had always known it shattered around her.

Chapter 3

"Danae." Brandt grabbed for the sheets and blankets that were in a heap on the bed. "What're you doing here?"

For the breath of a second, her eyes widened on the scene. "I'm… I'm sorry." Stunned, she backed out of the room and closed the door behind her. An eternity of memories flashed before her as she stood there, holding onto the doorknob to keep from falling to the ground. Gasping for breath, she fought to get the image of Brandt entangled with Krystal out of her head. She slammed her eyes closed, willing the scene to go away, to not tell her everything that it just had.

A sound on the other side of the door jolted her body into motion, and in the next breath, she was running down the hallway for the front door. Air lodged in her chest making it impossible to breathe as she fumbled for the doorknob before yanking the front door open. From behind her, Brandt called her name, but it didn't register. Nothing was registering. Nothing was making any sense. The carefree sounds pouring from the reception on the other side of the garden sounded like the mind-twisting music of a funhouse.

Her feet were running, stumbling through the parking lot pockmarked with the few remaining cars and potholes. The scene and Brandt's voice dogged her every stumbling step. In the darkness she had no idea where she was going, only that she was going as fast as she could because stopping meant she would have to face the nightmare she had somehow fallen into.

At the other end of the parking lot, her foot stepped off the pavement, and body and soul, she crashed to the ground next to the front tire of one of the cars. The earth under her hands and knees was moist, and pieces of wayward gravel dug into her flesh. Whimpers of agony ripped loose from her chest and clawed through the still night air. Had anyone heard, they would have thought an animal, ensnared in a trap, was dying a slow, unimaginably painful death. That's what this felt like. No, it was worse. Death itself couldn't hurt this badly. Out of breath she choked on the tears, retching and coughing, fighting to find the air. Everything in her hurt. It was as if the entire world was screaming in pain around her.

When the first wave of agony subsided, she reached up to her nose and wiped it with the back of her hand. All energy gone, her body slouched against the tire as her mind relentlessly replayed that scene—that one snippet of time, ensnared in her memory and destined to haunt her forever.

Her lungs screamed for air as her shoulders quaked forward. She was nearly doubled over now, knees to her chest, face buried in the folds of the skirt that she clutched with both fists. How could she have ever thought she loved him? How could she have ever convinced herself that he loved her? That wasn't love. That was... that was... she couldn't even get the words to line up in her head right. Tears and anguish marched right through the line of them, whisking them away as if on river rapids.

Until that moment she had never thought she could hate anyone, but along with every other good thought in her life, he had taken that belief from her too. She arched her foot upward and slammed it to the ground, digging the heel of her shoe into the soft earth. Frustration and anger poured through her. She'd been a fool to ever trust him, to ever believe him, to ever think they could have a future together. Grief and hurt jammed into her throat, choking out the air until she was gasping again.

For that moment the only real thing in the world was the fact that her entire life had been predicated on a lie. A lie that she loved him. A lie that he loved her, and to her, that had to be the biggest lie of all.

"I think we're going to hang out here for awhile," Von said with a second meaning just beneath the words. "Carson hooked up with one of the caterers, and me and Claude are going to wait around for him and relax."

"All right. Then I guess I'll see you Monday for practice," Kalin said, not even sniffing at the bait. "You want me to take my equipment to the trailer?"

"Na, man, we'll get it," Von said, his words slurring over themselves.

Kalin took one final look at the remnants of the band and shook his head. "Then I'm headed on. Catch you down the road." With that, he turned, grabbed his jacket, and exited out the side door. He hadn't realized how much he had been sweating, but the second the night-chilled air found his skin, he remembered. He pulled the warm black leather around him, glad for the barrier against the cool breeze drifting off the mountains.

It would be a cold four-hour ride back to Nashville on the bike, but even so, he was glad he had decided to come on his own. Staying around while Carson made out and the others got stoned was not at all his idea of fun.

A departing car's headlights sliced across the parking lot, illuminating his bike leaning against a tree on the far side for a second. He turned his steps toward it. The darkness retook the parking lot as his thoughts slid back to the band. All he could do was shake his head again. He had been hounding his manager since the second gig he did with Silver Moonlight three months before to find him another band, any other band. He wasn't picky. True, he had been through two bands—if you could call them that—before the Silver Moonlight connection, but surely there had to be something a step up from a bunch of crackheads…

Just as he stepped off the pavement, he heard a sound that seemed wholly out of place. It yanked his attention from his thoughts. His face furrowed in concentration as he glanced back to the brightly lit reception hall wondering where the sound had come from. However, with his gaze distracted as he wound around the last car on his way to his bike, he very nearly tripped right over the sobbing figure huddled in the darkness.

"Oh, m…!" He stopped so short, his balance swayed dangerously away from him. In the next heartbeat fear and concern swept through every other thought. "What happened? Are you all right?" He stood for a moment to get his bearings and then bent down to assess the magnitude of the situation. However, when enough images pieced themselves together for him to realize who it was, the rest of life slammed to a stop. "Good grief! What happened? Are you all right? Did you fall?"

His mind scrambled to make sense of the huddled mass of agony that gazed up at him through glassy brown eyes couched in the middle of a face smeared with mud and mascara. He reached out and touched her arms to make sure she was in fact still alive. "Good grief, you're freezing." Without questioning it, he ripped off his jacket, pulled her forward gently, and wrapped it around her shoulders. It took another second for him to assess the situation further and come up with a plan of action. "We should get you inside."

"No!" The word tore through the night air around him. Her gaze drilled into his, pleading and wild. "No. I'm not going back in there."

The panic in her voice did nothing to calm the alarm racing through him. *God, I need your help with this one!* "Okay. Okay. Then can you at least tell me if you're all right?"

It was the most absurd question Danae had ever heard, and yet in it she heard his concern and distress.

"If I said, 'Yes,' would you believe me?" she asked, tilting her throbbing head to the side as if it weighed a million pounds.

"No," he said, apparently not seeing the humor. His gaze searched hers. "Do you mind telling me why you're sitting out here alone in the mud?"

She forced a loopy smile onto her face as she reached up and wiped her nose with the back of her hand. "Oh, lots of reasons."

His features fell in understanding. "You're drunk," he said with no humor in his voice.

She only snorted. "I wish. Maybe then I wouldn't remember my boyfriend making out with the maid of honor."

That statement pushed him back on his heels where he sat for several seconds just looking at her. Slowly he spun around and sat down on the soft ground beside her, his back pressed against the cold steel of the car's door. "So, how long have you been out here?"

Her head was swimming from the tears and the pain, and she let it thunk back into the car fender. "Long enough. You?"

"I just got here," he said softly. Then his gaze drifted over to her face. "But I wish I would've come sooner."

With a jerk she pulled her head back down and nodded. "Let me tell you, it was quite a show."

"I can imagine. So, you found them out here then?"

She sniffed that image away and wiped her nose with her wrist. "No, over in the house. This is just how far I got before I stopped." She sniffed again just as the sounds of someone walking to their car halted the conversation.

Her golden-headed savior, who really at the moment could well have been an angel for all she knew, held up his index finger to get her words to stop. She didn't talk. She hardly took a breath until the car three doors down started and crunched its way onto the gravel driveway. When it was gone, he looked at her.

"I'm Kalin by the way. Kalin Lane." He extended a hand to her.

With the last ounce of her strength she pulled her hand up from the warmth of his jacket and touched his hand. "Danae Scott." She sniffed again. It was a given that she looked a fright, but at the moment, she really didn't care. It was too much work to care.

~ Lucky ~

"So, Danae Scott were you planning to sit out here in the mud all night or did you have another destination in mind?" he asked, apparently not grasping the gravity of the situation.

She shrugged although with no strength in her shoulders, she barely moved the jacket at all. "Hadn't really thought about it." Her gaze took in the darkness stretching out before them. She let the air in her lungs out slowly, hoping she could keep from breaking down again. "I guess I really don't have much of a way to go anywhere."

His gaze slipped over her. "Why not?"

Dully she let her gaze find his. "I came with him this morning, so I guess unless I hijack his car, I'm on my own." *On my own*, the words dredged up a fresh wave of pain, and the numbness crumpled under a gush of hurt. She ducked her head to the side and clamped her mouth closed to keep herself from crying. However, keeping herself from breathing only made the gasp for air sharper. Tears and pain ripped through her chest as she fought not to remember. In one second there was nothing but raw emotion left as she relinquished control to the tears.

"Hey," he said softly. "Hey." His arm came around her shoulders, and she didn't have the energy to keep from collapsing into him.

"I was so stupid," she said, shaking her head and dragging the words through the tears. "I was just so stupid."

"Shh," he whispered. "No, he's the stupid one. Don't do that to yourself."

She raked in air through her nose, sniffing hard. With a self-conscious tug, she pulled herself upright again. "I should've just gone…"

Confusion slipped over Kalin's features. "Gone where?"

Another sniff as her anger turned inward. "He asked me to go… back to the house with him, but I didn't."

Fury crashed through Kalin as he sat, looking at her crushed and broken under the callous boot of a self-centered boy who was too stupid to appreciate what he had. "No, you shouldn't have to give up your values for someone to love you. Real love doesn't work like that."

For a second her gaze grabbed his, and he thought she was going to ask how he knew anything at all about why she hadn't gone. However, even that seemed to require too much energy, and her head fell again.

"I'm telling you, don't do that to yourself, Danae. Don't give up who you are to make him happy. All you'll do is make yourself miserable. Besides, anybody that would do that—"

The trail of words snapped in half as his ears picked up the sound of footfalls in the parking lot. He listened, trying to discern their destination, but instead it caught on the nearly inaudible conversation.

"I wish you didn't have to go back tonight, but since you do, I can take you," the male voice said, and Kalin's attention snapped to Danae when she gasped.

Instantly his senses went on alert. Where were they going? Which car were they intending to take? Questions and options rushed through him at break-neck speed. The footfalls stopped at the car next to the one they were huddled against. Kalin's gaze slid to her face, which was crumpled with anguish. Slowly, gently, he reached over and pulled her under his arm. If they found them, he was plenty prepared to do whatever need be done to protect her.

"You really don't have to," the sultry voice said, and Kalin had been in that conversation often enough to know that she was working a very well-rehearsed plan.

"I want to," the male voice said, and the sounds of them pawing one another tore a soft sob from Danae.

"Shhh." Kalin bent his lips to her hair.

"What about Danae?" the female voice asked, like a cat on the prowl.

"What about her?" he asked, clearly having more attention for his current prey than for his girlfriend.

"How's she going to get home?" she asked as the sounds of his ardor escalated.

"Danae's a big girl," he said, his voice thick with desire. "I'm sure she'll think of something."

With that, the verbal part of the conversation stopped, and Kalin closed his eyes, wishing he could make them both disappear. *Come on, God. She doesn't deserve this. Get them out of here.*

"So, am I driving, or are you?" the female voice finally asked.

"I'll drive," he said, "you can entertain me." With that, the car door opened, and amid one final flurry of passion, the door finally closed, the car started, and with a screech of the tires, they were gone.

For a long moment neither of them moved. Then a sickening thought hit Kalin squarely in the lungs. She hadn't moved, not so much as a breath in more than five minutes. Huddled next to him, she could well have been dead for all he knew. "Danae. Hey, they're gone."

It was like waking from a nightmare too horrible to comprehend. She pulled her head, neck, and shoulders from the protectiveness of his embrace and wobbled twice on the weight they brought with them. His gaze traced through her. "I'm so sorry," he said barely loud enough to be heard over the breeze.

"Yeah, well." She brushed the strands of hair that had fallen out of the pins from her face. There was a thought there to finish that sentence, and then it was gone.

Concern etched across his heart. "If you want, I could take you home." He glanced over at his bike and then back to her dress, not sure how he would accomplish that if she accepted. However, she shook her head slowly.

"I think I just want to sit here for awhile."

He considered that as he surveyed her. "Okay. Then we'll sit here for awhile."

Chapter 4

Awhile turned into much longer than Kalin had anticipated. The night was deepening, turning the mountains around them to ebony black. A panorama of stars arched above them.

"So, do you think God exists?" she asked, her voice tired and dull.

He reached over for a piece of gravel, picked it up, and spun it through his fingers. "Yes, I do. Do you?"

"Yeah," she said slowly. "At least I did. Until tonight."

His gaze drifted over to her. "Mind explaining that?"

She shrugged, sniffed, and wiped her nose with her hand. "I thought if you were good... you know, if you did what He said, bad things like this wouldn't happen."

Kalin snorted softly at that. "What, do you think He's looking for—a pay-off? Like you do what He says, and He makes everything in your life work out?"

After a moment of thought, she nodded. "Something like that."

He considered the question and her and then shook his head. "So, you're only good so He'll be good to you?" For a long moment she said nothing, so he continued for her. "Don't you think that's kind of selling Him a little short? I mean even crackheads pay for their stash before they smoke it."

A confused look slid over her mascara-streaked features.

"I pay you. You give me what I want. It's a deal. Any druggy on the street knows that game." Passion crept into his voice as the hard-fought peace he'd found flowed through him. "But God's so much bigger than that. Sure He wants you to be good, but He wants you to be good because you love Him—not because you're going to get some pay-off for the deal."

"Well then what's the point of Him giving us all these rules to follow? If He's not testing us, why give the rules?"

"Because He wants you to know where the guardrails are." Many nights sitting in dingy classrooms with a gaggle of other ex-druggies drifted through Kalin's mind. He slid around so that he was crossways to her. "Think of it this way. You're up in the mountains, and you're driving on a road you've never been on before. You've got your headlights on, but everything around you is completely dark. How do you know when to turn so you won't go plunging off the side of the cliff?"

"The arrows."

"And the guardrails," he said as real understanding poured into his spirit. Gently he laid a hand on the arm of his jacket, feeling her arm underneath. Her gaze swung up to his. "You know to turn when you see the guardrails."

Annoyance and confusion traced through her eyes just before she dropped her head. "But why put them up if people are just going to crash through them anyway?"

He didn't even have to think about the reply. It came on its own power. "Because it's not about other people. It's about you. It's about He loves you *so much* that He wants you to know where that cliff is on every single turn, and so He put the rules up—the guardrails—so you would know where that cliff is even if you've never been on that road before."

She sighed and let her head crack back against the car. "I feel like I just went off that cliff."

Gentleness washed over him as he looked at her. "No, you just watched someone you love go over."

She let her head fall sideways so she was now looking at him. "How'd you get so smart?"

A soft smile traced across his lips. "You go over that cliff enough times, you either learn or you give up. I guess I learned." His gaze stayed on her for a long moment, and then he breathed. "What do you say we get out of here? It's really getting cold." For emphasis, he ran his hand over his cotton-shirt-covered arm.

This time she didn't protest, so he reached up to the car door and pulled himself up. With great care he slipped a hand under her arm and helped her to her feet. Even when she was standing, one hand balanced on the car, he didn't let her go. "You got it?"

She tested her legs and nodded. When she picked her head up, she had to brush the hair out of her face. "I need to go back and change."

"Oh," he said, not having realized that was an option. "Back at the house?"

Again she nodded. He reached out to help steady her as they started across the all-but empty parking lot. His bike, their hiding place, and only two or three other vehicles remained. She sniffed a short, little, soft sniff, and his attention whipped back to her. "You okay?"

"I'm trying to be," she said.

"You're going to get through this."

"How can you be so sure?"

"Because I'm going to be right here to make sure you do."

As she slid the moisture and mud-stained dress to the floor, Danae asked herself what she was planning to do next. However, thinking beyond the moment she happened to be living at that second threatened to overload her brain sockets. So she concentrated on doing what she could do. She had washed her face in the bathroom first, so her skin felt prickly and cold. Her jeans and purple T-shirt were warm mostly because they weren't wet. She did miss the leather jacket, and a sad but grateful smile slipped through her spirit when she looked over at it lying on the bed.

Thank You, God for sending me an angel.

She didn't need a mirror nor more than the dim table lamp to take her hair down, so she didn't bother with either one. Instead she just trusted her fingers to find the bobby pins, which she removed. When they were all gone, she flipped her head over, raked her fingers through her mane, and flipped it back over.

Carefully she reached under the bed, slipped her socks and then her Nikes on. Real clothes felt better than they ever had. Wishing she could put the leather jacket back on, but knowing she couldn't, she slid her oldest jean jacket replete with rips and strings on around her. It felt good, but it didn't quite compare.

Seeing no other thing she needed, she rolled the dress up into a tight ball, stuffed it and the mud-caked shoes into her bag and walked to the door. Without even a single glance backward, she opened it and stepped through.

Wondering what came next, Kalin had found a semi-comfortable spot on the hardwood floor next to the banister poles to sit and wait. *God, I need You here. She needs You. Please be with her, and don't let his mistake rip her from Your side. Please give me the right words. Don't let me overstep my bounds. Keep Your hand on me, and guide me in what I should say and what I should do...*

The snap of the door yanked his attention upward, and when she stepped through that doorway into the soft, hazy light of the balcony where he sat, for one moment he wondered if someone else had been in there with her. A mass of beautifully undulating curls began at her head and flowed down several inches beyond her shoulders. The jeans hugged slim hips—not tight, but just enough to define them. Her duffle bag was slung over one shoulder, and his jacket was draped over her other arm.

"Much better," she said, barely breaking the stillness of the house.

He couldn't have agreed more. "You ready?"

"I don't think I have much of a choice." With a heartrending smile, she stepped past him to the staircase.

It took every ounce of sanity he had left to get his feet under him to follow her.

"So, where is it we're going anyway?" Kalin asked without the slightest hint that this side trip hadn't been on his itinerary. The night air around them was crisp as they made their way across the parking lot.

"Knoxville."

"Right on the way? Good deal."

She nodded, having suddenly realized that they had made it all the way out to the outer edge of the parking lot, and they'd already passed all but one of the cars parked there. She looked back to the others. "Which one is yours?"

The leather of his jacket made a whooshing sound as he picked his arm up to point sheepishly at the black motorcycle sitting in the darkness under the trees beyond the parking lot.

Her steps slowed but didn't stop completely. "You don't have a car?"

"A '79 Camero, but it wasn't supposed to rain tonight."

She felt his gaze find her face as his steps slowed. He hooked his hands in the back pockets of his jeans and looked back to the reception hall. "We could always go back and see if someone else could take you."

Her gaze followed his to the reception hall and then slid back to the bike. A fate worse than death vs. a fate worse than death. It wasn't an easy choice. "I… I guess I could try the bike. It is safe, isn't it?"

"Depends on the driver," he said without cracking a smile.

Her eyebrows shot up as she surveyed him, and she wondered if that was sarcastic or not. Only now did she see that the golden hair was chopped rather than cut evenly. It was as if the hairdresser wasn't sure which length it was supposed to be. When he flipped his hair back to look at her, she caught the faint glimmer at his ear, and panic slipped through her. Was he really somebody she wanted to be leaving with—on a motorcycle of all things?

~ Lucky ~

The confident look on his face swerved when he saw the look on hers. "Maybe we should just go back..."

God, I don't know what to do here. Help!

Her hesitation lasted too long.

"We should go back," he said, turning around, clearly understanding that she wasn't comfortable with this arrangement.

"I just..." she said slowly as her gaze swung from him to the motorcycle and back again, "umm, I've never really ridden... a motorcycle before."

Having taken two steps back to the reception hall, he stopped and turned to her. "It really is safe," he said softly, "but it's your choice."

She wasn't at all sure which made her more nervous—him or the bike. However, his seemingly sincere willingness to get her a different ride coupled with the genuine concern for her in his eyes melted her protests. "I guess it would be okay... this time."

He didn't move. "You sure?"

It took a breath to get her nerves steady. "Yeah, I'm sure."

Kalin couldn't help but think that wasn't the answer he should've been wishing for. As he started back for the bike, the thoughts in his head yanked the breath from his chest. *God, You know as well as I do I don't need this in my life right now. I don't need her out here looking all beautiful and vulnerable. I've screwed that situation up too many times in my life already. Remember?*

He left her standing at the edge of the pavement and walked into the darkness. Under cover of the branches, he yanked the bike up from its resting place on the bark of one tree. He righted the kickstand before giving the bike a solid push to get it moving in the soft earth. The earth gave under his foot, and he willed himself to stay on his feet. The last thing he needed at this point was to face-plant in the dirt with her watching. Shoulders hunched into the effort of pushing the bike, he glanced up to where she stood waiting on the pavement, and his confidence that said he was doing the right thing once again wavered. He put his head down as he pushed.

'And then the Holy Spirit will begin to believe you have changed. He will begin to believe that you will trust Him no matter what... that you will put every situation into His hands, that you will help those who need Him most,' the preacher's words from the previous week's sermon ran through Kalin's thoughts, *'and He will begin sending souls to you because He knows you will let Him work through you to help them.'*

Even as he pushed, he let his eyes go closed for a single moment.

How long had he been trying to do exactly that—to put his life in God's hands? The image of the church in Vancouver flashed through his mind. That night nothing seemed impossible because Jesus had seemed so close. But out here in the real world, there were times Jesus felt very far away indeed.

"I'm not sure about this," Kalin whispered to the night. "If this isn't a good idea, please show me the other options."

When he finally got the bike to the pavement and pushed it to her side, it felt like stepping off the sheer side of a mountain with no bungee cord. Walking onto a stage with thousands of screaming fans had never shaken his confidence the way the uncertain trust on her face did.

"Here you go," he managed to say as he yanked the helmet off its perch. "You can have mine."

She hesitated before accepting it. "You don't need one?"

"Won't be the first time." He took the bag from her hands, slung it over his shoulder, and mounted the bike. When he and the bike were ready, he looked at her, and she couldn't have looked more panicked had she tried.

With everything in him, he wanted to give her a way out. "You sure about this?"

In three short motions she nodded. Cautiously she approached the side of the bike as he reached down and flipped out the footrests. Straddling the bike and holding it steady, he turned to her and reached out to help her on.

"Plant that foot," he instructed, taking hold of the top of her arm to keep her balanced. "Then swing that one over..."

She did as he instructed, and in a matter of seconds, her body was pressed up next to his back. That feeling tore through him, and he had to concentrate on the bike and the details of making this work to keep his mind from wandering into territory he had long since sworn he would never go back to.

"Here's the footrests," he said, pointing to them. "Keep your feet on them, or you'll burn yourself on the muffler." He waited for her to find her footing. Wishing it didn't feel so much like a move on his part, he reached back for her hands. They were the softest he'd ever held. "Now just hold on like this." He took her hands and slid them under his jacket around his belt-line. Still praying some new option would show up, he let go of her and took hold of the handlebars. He inhaled another breath to steady his rushing nerves.

With that, he turned the key and hit the starter. The noise ripped through the still night air. He leaned the bike carefully to the right to put it in gear, and he heard her gasp and felt her grip tighten on his waist. He swiveled slightly to be able to talk to her. "Now, just relax. Let me do the work."

That was asking a lot of someone who was scared out of her mind, but Danae didn't get a chance to tell him that because with no hesitation at all he revved the engine, picked up his feet, and they were gone. The power of the bike underneath her swept the breath from her lungs. He slowed only a millisecond at the fence bordering the main road before he turned and accelerated to a speed she was quite certain she had never actually gone in her life.

As the deep ebony outline of the Smoky Mountains receded behind them, fear wrapped around her. He shifted gears effortlessly, and the speed increased. Despite her previous vows to keep a good amount of distance between them, her grip on him tightened as she slid her hands all the way around him and clasped them at his waist, pulling her chest to his back. The night air whipped by her. Darkness enveloped everything other than the sound of the bike and the solidity of his back.

At first she could hardly breathe. They rounded a turn and headed out for the highway. Then as the speed evened out again, she forced herself to focus on relaxing. It wasn't easy. However, slowly the fear began to lose its hold on her, and she almost started laughing hysterically at the absurdity of this moment. Never in her life had she done anything so crazy. No, to that moment every single decision had been well-thought-out, long-considered, and utterly safe. However, as they raced through the night, she couldn't help but think that flying itself couldn't feel this unbelievable.

The knowledge that there were only two things—a motorcycle and him—between her and certain death slid through her consciousness, followed instantly by the thought that stayed with her the rest of the ride home. *I never knew living could feel like this.*

Chapter 5

At the edge of Knoxville, Kalin slowed the bike and turned into the all-night truck stop just off the Interstate. They'd been riding for nearly two hours, and besides feeling like he needed to take a walk to get the monotony out of his head, he didn't know exactly where they were going now that they were in Knoxville. He pulled into a parking space and grasped the hand brake to stop their forward progress. With the fluid motion of having done it a million times, he put both feet down then leaned the bike slightly so he could put it in neutral.

He noticed there was no audible gasp from her this time. Two motions and the reverberating noise of the motor slipped into oblivion.

"Why're we stopping?" she asked, looking around in concern.

Careful not to wrench his tight shoulders too badly, he tilted his head to one side, then the other, and pulled the bag off his shoulder before tossing it to the pavement next to the bike. "Need coffee. Must stop." He reached back to help her off.

"We could've gotten coffee at my house."

Getting her off didn't seem nearly as hard as getting her on had. "That was the other problem." He swung his leg off the bike and straightened out his legs and then his jeans. "I needed directions." His gaze swept over the bank of windows lit softly in dusky amber. "Besides I'm starving." Then he stopped, realizing that she might not be. "But if you're ready to go now, I could always take you and pick something up—"

"You think they have pancakes?" she asked, sounding like a little kid as she pulled the helmet off and handed it to him.

"We could see."

She swept the bag off the pavement. "Then lead the way. I haven't had more than a couple mints in like hours."

It had something to do with the bike. Danae had no question about that. The feeling of pure freedom seemed to surround her in a way it never had before. It gave her a confidence she couldn't quite fathom. At the door, Kalin swung it open for her, and she walked in.

The place probably would've been jam-packed had it not been nearly 4:30 in the morning. Self-consciously Danae put her hand in her back pocket. She wasn't used to inhabiting truck stops in the middle of the night with leather-clad bikers by her side.

With very little conversation, the waitress led them to a booth at the back of the restaurant and laid the menus in front of them. Kalin picked his up and perused it. "You're in luck. Pancakes. Blueberry. Buttermilk. Looks like you get your pick."

Although some parts of her had vaguely registered hunger, Danae hadn't realized how truly hungry she really was. "I think I'll get some of both. Two heaping stacks of pancakes with lots of butter and syrup. Oh, man. That sounds like heaven."

Kalin looked up from his menu at her, and she couldn't quite read the expression she found there.

"What?" she asked.

Quickly he shook his head. "Nothing."

The waitress came then and took their orders. When she was gone, Danae pulled the little truck stop brochure from between the salt and the peppershakers. It was something for her fingers to do, and somewhere for her gaze to go. Neither of them said a word for the length of time it took her to read most of the front and back. Seeing no way to further that stall tactic, she put it back. "Huh." Her gaze chanced across at him, and her heart thudded forward. "So…"

He looked at her, and those gray-blue eyes looked both tired and nervous. "So…"

It became clear that having come this far, he didn't want to push her into anything—even conversation.

"You're from Nashville then," she finally said.

When he nodded, his hair slid down around his face. It was then that she realized how thin he really was. His hair made his already thin features look almost razor-like. Even his hands looked all fingers. "For about six months now." His accent danced across her heart.

"Really? You've only been there a few months, and you're already in the business? That's impressive."

He pulled himself forward and examined his long, thin hands.

"I'm sorry," she said, seeing she had made him uncomfortable. "I just… I mean they said…"

"No," he said with the slightest of smiles, "it's okay. I'm just… I'm trying to get things to work out. It gets kind of tough sometimes."

"So, you're not from here then?" she asked, hating how stupid that question sounded.

Skepticism jumped to his face. "Have you ever heard a native Tennessean talk like this?"

She laughed. "Okay, dumb question number one. Sorry."

His gaze couldn't hold hers. "No, it's okay. I'm from Canada. I just made it back—"

"Back?"

"Well…" Every word he spoke seemed to take monumental amounts of effort. He laid an arm over the booth back, clearly trying to look calm and collected although that wasn't at all what she saw in his eyes. "I was here about five years ago."

"You were here? What happened? Why'd you go back?"

The waitress picked that moment to bring their drinks, and when she was gone, Kalin downed his soda as if he was a man dehydrated in the desert. Danae waited until he set the red plastic cup back down and then pursued the conversation.

"Why'd you leave?"

He looked at her like he would've gladly been anywhere other than there at that moment. "My visa ran out. I didn't have a choice."

"Oh." She contemplated that information, not totally sure what to do with it. "Where you in the business back then, when you were here before?"

He pushed the material on his legs down nervously. "Yeah." He took a long breath. "Let's just say things didn't work out quite the way I thought they would."

"But you're back now… older and wiser."

"Older, yes," he said, and for the first time he cracked a tiny smile. "But wiser? I wouldn't go quite that far."

"Leaving something to aspire to, huh?"

His smile widened. "Yeah. Something like that." Then he looked at her quizzically. "How about you? What do you do in the great city of Knoxville, Tennessee?"

It would've been easier to talk about him. Her smile faded as life descended on her shoulders. "I'm in school… college." Her gaze bounced from the table up to his face. "University of Tennessee."

"Wow. That's cool. So, you're like what then? A freshman? Sophomore?"

She leveled a horrified look at him. "How young do you think I am?"

"I'm sorry. I just thought…"

"No." She reined in the offended tone. "I'm a senior." She took a long breath to stabilize the thought of her looming future. "After I get through this semester, all I lack is student teaching in the fall."

"Oh, so you're going to be a teacher." He sounded happy about that—just like everyone did.

"I guess so." She picked up her knife and spun it end-to-end.

The awkwardness left his demeanor as he looked at her, and he leaned forward and laid his forearms on the edges of the table. "You don't sound too thrilled about that."

She tried to look at him, but her gaze barely touched his face before it fell back to the table. She shrugged. "It's just one of those things I guess."

"What things?" he asked as though he genuinely cared.

"Oh, you know," she said, staving off the admission. "Gotta do something with your life."

"So I take it teaching wasn't your first choice."

She laughed softly. "More like 73rd. Right after being shot from a cannon at the circus."

"That good, huh?"

When she looked across the table, it took all of a second to decide that it didn't matter if she was honest with him or not. After tonight, she would never see him again anyway. "Mom says it'll be a good fall-back-on job. Plus, it's not something if you quit to have a family, you can't get back into. They always need teachers."

The waitress brought their food, but Danae had lost a good amount of her appetite. On the other side of the table, Kalin cut into his chicken fried steak with a vengeance.

"Well, if teaching is 73rd, what's 52nd?" he asked.

She laughed as she cut into her pancakes. "I don't know, NASA?"

"Controller or astronaut?"

"Controller," she said definitively. "Can you see me in a Space Shuttle?"

He smiled as he picked a forkful of mashed potatoes up. "Hey, you rode a motorcycle didn't you?"

"True," she said, pointing the tip of her knife at him.

"Okay, so what's 22nd on the list?"

For a moment she scrunched her face, thinking. "I don't know. Rock star?"

Interest descended on him. "Really?"

"Yeah, but seeing as how I don't play anything and I can't sing to save my life—I'm thinking that's not going to get me very far."

He laughed and sawed more meat off. "Okay, what's eighth on this list of yours?"

"Eighth? Hmm…" She cut a chunk off her pancakes, took the bite, and chewed thoughtfully. She took a drink to wash that down. "How about a big city crime reporter?"

His eyebrows shot for the ceiling. "Crime? That sounds a little dangerous, don't you think?"

"Ugh. I think it sounds exciting. You know, Perry Mason without the law books, figuring out whodunit and why. Sounds pretty cool to me."

Kalin, however, didn't look entirely convinced. "Well, you don't look like the criminal stalking kind to me, so what's number two?"

Her eating slowed as she realized that all but one slice of her pancakes was gone. She shrugged. "I'd always kind of thought about nursing."

"Nursing? Really?" He stopped eating to gaze across at her, and her pulse jumped into her throat with the intense interest in his eyes. "So, why didn't you do that?"

Again she shrugged as if it meant nothing to her. "Long hours, late nights away from your family. It just didn't seem very practical." With all the energy of a dead leaf, she cut the last two bites of her pancakes in half. However, they didn't even look appetizing anymore. Suddenly she was very tired, to the point of wanting to fall asleep right there. She laid her fork and knife down and sat back.

"So," he finally said after he took a drink of the soda the waitress had come to refill at some point, "that brings us to number one. You, Danae Scott, can now be anything you want to be… the world is your oyster. What is your number one?"

Her head felt like it weighed a million pounds. Her forehead started to ache even as she searched for a logical way to change the subject. She started to say something and then shook her head in annoyance.

"What?" he asked, his voice and eating utensils falling on the word.

The edge of her finger traced down her glass. She glanced up at him. "Promise you won't laugh."

"I promise," he said with no hint of hesitation.

She looked down and then back over at him. Once again she told herself that this would be the only time she would ever see him in her life, and she asked herself what possible harm could there be in just telling him? "A doctor," she said so quietly the sounds of the truck stop drown the words out. Her gaze flitted across the other empty tables.

"What?" he asked just as softly.

She cleared her throat and leveled her gaze on him. "A doctor."

His face registered only confusion. "Why would I laugh about that?"

Even her shrug took more energy than she had left. "Everybody else does."

As Kalin gazed at her, he could see the hurt deep down in her dark eyes. She had given up on her dream, and it was killing her. "So that's it then. You settle for 73rd and give up on what you really want just like that?"

She sniffed and then shrugged. "I'm one semester from finishing. What am I supposed to do—start over?"

"A few years compared with a lifetime of regret? Sounds like a fair trade to me."

Slowly she shook her head. "It's not that easy. I've got other people to think about."

"Like who?" He saw the list slide through her eyes, and he wished he hadn't asked.

She glanced at him and then dropped her gaze to the table. "It's just... reaching for the stars had never been my forte. It's probably better this way anyway."

"Why?" he asked, not willing to let her give up as easily as she seemed to be.

"What would I want to waste all that schooling and time for when in a couple years I'll be married and staying home with my kids anyway?"

"So, that's what you want then—the house, the husband, the kids?"

"Yeah." But she didn't sound at all convincing. "That's what I'm supposed to want."

That statement didn't sit well with him at all. "What you're supposed to want? What? That's what everyone else says you're supposed to want?"

She nodded without really moving her head. "Something like that."

Finally he understood why God had put her in his path. He laid his fork and knife down next to the plate so his full attention was on her. "You know what, maybe this is none of my business, but your dreams aren't about everybody else. They are about what God wants for your life. He gave you those dreams for a reason, and it wasn't so that you would put them aside and do something else."

Her gaze snagged on him. "But—"

"No." He cut into her protest. "Every 'but' is just the devil's way of trying to talk you out of what God wants for you. He's trying to tell you it's too hard, it's not worth it, it won't matter if you do something else anyway."

"But—"

"No," he said again. "Don't do that. Start that sentence with something else."

For a long minute she sat there. "Okay," she finally said very slowly, clearly searching for another way to start her protest. "If I go for it and it doesn't work out, what then?"

"Then that's a piece you needed for something else that's coming down the road."

"Huh?"

There was only one lump of potatoes left on his plate, but Kalin had forgotten all about his food. "Look. When I couldn't stay here, I thought my dream was over. I thought that was it—that I had to give up. But when I got back home, the music hadn't left. I tried some other things, but it wouldn't leave me alone. The practicing, the learning, the loving it with everything I had… it was all still there. I got so depressed trying to walk away from that dream I almost lost who I was altogether. But then at the bottom of the bottom, I told God I was tired of hurting so bad, and that if He wanted me to do something else then to please take the music away from me because I just couldn't take it anymore."

The memories bumped into one another as he sat there in that truck stop a couple thousand miles from where his life had turned around.

"So, I guess God didn't take the music away from you?" she asked.

"No." Kalin's gaze found her face. "He gave me… me."

Confusion slipped across the table at him. "I don't understand."

His gaze fell to the table. He'd never actually tried to put it into real words because nobody had ever asked him to explain it. "When I was here the first time, I wanted the dream so bad, I was willing to twist myself into any shape they wanted me to be. If they said it would only work one way, then I did it that way—whether that made sense for me or not, whether I felt like it was right or not." He closed his eyes as images from what seemed a lifetime before drifted over him. "I changed everything about myself to be what they said I should be. It wasn't until I went back to Canada that I realized I didn't even know who I was anymore."

"But how could you be someone you weren't?"

His gaze trapped hers. "How could you?" The point was made, and his spirit said it was time to go. He looked up at the clock on the wall. "Wow. It's after five. I'd better get you home."

Danae's mind was in so much turmoil she couldn't find a good reason to protest. She stood, followed him to the register, paid her half and walked with him out to the bike. Only then did she get a good enough look at their transportation to see that it was black with silver chrome. There was no windshield, and once again, she questioned her own sanity.

She accepted the helmet and handed him her bag.

"Okay, where are we going from here?" he asked, righting the bike and backing it out of the parking space.

When they had left Gatlinburg, she had figured they would go to her mother's house, but something about waking up alone in that house with Brandt's window in perfect view wasn't appealing. "You know where the campus is?"

"I think so."

"My apartment's six blocks to the north of campus on North 57th."

He was ready for her to get on. She let him hold her balance as she swung her leg across. It was strange, but this time the fear felt more like excitement. It might actually have gotten there had she not been so tired. She waited for him to flip the footrests out, and then she put her feet up and her arms around him. For as dangerous as this should've felt, it was the safest feeling she'd ever had.

"Ready?" he asked, twisting slightly.

"As I'll ever be."

With that, he hit the ignition, and the bike roared to life. She couldn't stop the smile. Smoothly the bike glided forward, slowed once as they approached the roadway, and then accelerated into the fading darkness.

It was only a mild problem to find her apartment, and they were in the parking lot just before five-thirty a.m. Kalin helped her off and went to hand her the bag as she took off the helmet. However, when she looked at him, her forehead furrowed in concern. "You're exhausted," she said as if she was stating a scientific fact. "You don't need to be driving."

"I'm fine," he said, shaking his head. "Don't worry about it."

However, the concern didn't leave as she glanced at the door to the apartments beyond. She handed him the helmet. "Why don't you come in? You could crash on our couch."

"Really, I'm fine." However, a yawn attacked him at the thought of catching a few hours of sleep.

"No, you aren't. I can't let you turn yourself into highway pizza because of me. Come on. The couch is safe. I'll even lend you a real pillow if you're nice."

"I haven't been nice?" he asked.

"My point exactly. You've done so much for me, let me do something for you... please?"

He surveyed her, considered, and finally decided it wouldn't kill him to get back to Nashville a little later. There was nothing waiting for him there anyway. "Okay, you talked me into it."

Chapter 6

It took less than ten minutes from the time they got into the apartment to the time he was asleep on her couch. After checking on him one last time, Danae climbed the stairs and fell into her bed. Tara, Danae's roommate, had gone home for the weekend, so Danae wasn't worried about who might find out anything. Not that it mattered. He was a friend, and hardly that. He was sleeping on her couch, a payback for the kindness he had conveyed to her. That was hardly a salacious set-up, and yet she made sure that not only was it perfectly innocent, but that it looked perfectly innocent as well.

When she had convinced herself that she shouldn't feel guilty about it at all, she fell asleep and didn't even have to dream for life to feel all right.

It was the creak of the front door opening that brought Kalin out of a dead sleep. For a moment and then another he fought to figure out where he was and how he had gotten there. Then his memory snagged on her, and he remembered everything. However, he hadn't put it all together quickly enough to save himself from coming face-to-face with a young lady he had never met before when he sat up on the couch.

"Oh!" she said, jumping just after she had closed the door behind her and then realized there was someone she didn't know in the room with her. Her short hair and long straight nose set off a face sprinkled with freckles. "I… hi." It was clear she didn't know what to do. "I'm sorry. How did you…?"

"Oh," he finally said finding his voice, "Umm, I came with Danae. I mean, I brought her home, and I was…" He glanced at the clock on the bookcase and realized with a start that he'd been sleeping nearly seven hours. His gaze went to the stairs. "I'm really sorry I scared you. I've got to be getting back. I'll just..." He pointed to the door as he stood and grabbed his jacket. With trepidation in her gaze, she slid down the wall away from the door.

"I'm really sorry," he said again as he skirted the opposite side of the room and got to the door. "Tell Danae thanks." With that, he slid into the jacket, opened the door, and fled.

He would've liked to tell her good-bye, but as he crawled onto the bike and put his helmet on, he decided it was for the best. They were two strangers who happened to meet in a muddy parking lot. It was one night, and now it was over.

Wanting only to put distance between himself and the tugging of her spirit on his, he revved the bike to life and headed back out to the Interstate. *Thank You, God for letting us meet. Please keep her safe for me. Amen.*

"Well, good morning. Or should I say good afternoon?" Tara asked when she looked up from the little four-seat dining table as Danae stepped from the bottom stair.

"Hi." Danae lifted the mane of hair off her face and pushed it backward. She glanced over at the couch and realized he was gone. "Did you...umm... was..."

"Yeah. He said thanks."

"Oh." The understanding that he was gone slashed through her, but she fought not to let it show. "Did you bring coffee?"

"It's in the cabinet."

Trying not to think or to make any sudden moves, Danae filled the coffeemaker and let the aroma fill the tiny kitchen. After the pancakes she hadn't thought she could ever be hungry again, but as the smells awoke her senses, she decided eating sounded like a very good proposition. She pulled the Frosted Flakes from the cabinet, poured some, added some milk, and grabbed a spoon. She had half the bowl eaten before the coffee was ready.

Bowl and cup in hand, she went through the little doorway to the dining/living room and sat down across the table from Tara. Liking the noise of the crunching, Danae ate without really paying attention to anything for several minutes.

"So," Tara said as she bent over her Calculus book, "how was the wedding?"

The wedding. It seemed like eons ago. "Fine."

"Fine?" Tara glanced at her. "Just 'fine'?"

Danae crunched some more Frosted Flakes and didn't answer.

"Umm... did I miss something?" Tara finally asked, concern edging the question.

"Like what?"

Tara gave up trying to look preoccupied. "Well, when I got here, there was a strange guy on our couch. I'm assuming he came home with you."

"Yeah... so?"

"So? So who was he? Where was Brandt? And why was this strange guy sleeping on our couch?"

Danae sighed and decided it wouldn't hurt to give Tara the basic outline. "His name is Kalin. He's a musician out of Nashville. I needed a ride home, so he offered." There were so many holes in that story that someone could've driven a truck through them.

"And Brandt?" Tara asked uncertainly.

That topic was much harder to face. "I don't think we'll be seeing too much of Brandt anymore..." Danae crunched the Frosted Flakes harder.

The pencil in Tara's hand clicked on the table. "You're kidding. What happened?"

It would take too much energy to lie, so Danae didn't even try. In as few words as possible, she told Tara about finding Brandt with Krystal and how everything from that moment on had been mostly a blur.

"Except for Kalin," Tara said.

Danae couldn't stop the slight smile. "Except for Kalin."

"Well," Tara said after a long pause, "I can't say I'm surprised."

Danae's gaze jumped to her roommate's defensively.

"No, about Brandt. You know he's never been on my top ten list."

Another list slid through Danae's mind, but she brushed that back. "Yeah, but you've never actually said it."

Tara shrugged. "Wasn't my business, but for what it's worth, I think you're better off without him."

Those words stomped across Danae's chest, and in the next breath loneliness filled their boot steps. "He wasn't that bad."

"Wake up, Danae. He treated you like dirt. I never could figure out why you put up with him in the first place."

Because I love him, her heart screamed. *Loved. Love.* The words battled for their place in that sentence. Her cereal was gone, so she stood. "I'd better go get my language arts project finished. Let me know when you're ready for dinner."

She didn't wait for Tara to protest. She took her dishes to the kitchen and put them in the dishwasher. Then she tiptoed back through the room so as not to disturb Tara. Once in her room, she considered crawling back into bed; however, the language arts project really did need some attention. She sat down at her computer and lost the thoughts of him and everything else in trying to explain how to teach conceptual understanding.

The trailer park was a bustle of activity when Kalin pulled into his little spot. His options upon returning to Nashville six months before hadn't exactly been numerous. He'd found the camper he now called home in a Shop/Swap/Buy magazine that cost 50 cents at the grocery store. The thoughts of those first few days back with literally nothing but a dream, the motorcycle, and a guitar to his name beat through his mind.

His trailer wasn't much to brag about, neither was the army-green '79 Camero sitting next to it. But to him they each represented giant steps up from being coked-out in the ally he'd finally pulled himself out of in Vancouver. He killed the motorcycle's engine and pushed it back with his legs next to the trailer. As he swung off the bike, his legs felt like he'd been riding forever, and he had to stretch them an extra time to get them to hold him up.

Without so much as a glance at his neighbors, he unlocked his trailer and stepped inside. Dishes from breakfast the day before were still in the sink. His now-cold coffee from the previous morning still sat on the foldout table. Not wanting to deal with anything resembling life, he threw his jacket onto the little two seat couch next to the table, pulled himself up into the bed over the hitch, and flat on his back, he folded his hands on his stomach. How life had taken the detour it had the night before, he wasn't quite sure. How he would ever get back to real life again was even less clear.

He rolled to the side and looked out the window at the neighbors to the east. The man was yelling something about how he'd worked all week and he deserved the chance to sit down and enjoy life for a change. Depression wafted through Kalin's chest. So much turmoil. So much commotion. So much hurt and so little hope. Tiring of that scene, he flipped over being careful not to whack his head on the ceiling as he had so often when he'd first moved in. The bruise was only now beginning to heal.

Through the other window, he could see the old man sitting in the afternoon sunshine. He didn't seem to be doing anything—just watching life go by in front of him. The wrinkles and the faded eyes spoke of a life filled with regret for days long gone. Kalin's gaze stayed on the old man. So many times he had lived with no thought as to where he was going or to how he was getting there. So many hours gone... wasted at the end of little white lines of a lie he had believed until they had almost destroyed his life. The demons seemed to hover over the old man's face—regret, remorse, loneliness, bitterness. They were all there.

Closing his eyes, Kalin examined his own spirit. There were times he felt free of the demons, and then there were the times he was sure they would find a way to get their claws into him again. *The waves*, he thought.

The words of some long-forgotten preacher slipped into his mind. *We all have waves in our lives. We all have situations that knock us around and pull our gaze from Christ. That's what life is best at, taking us away from Him. But it's when we look at the waves and take our eyes off Christ that they begin to take over our lives and pull us under. The waves are always there—even after you know Christ. Even after you believe He is there for you every single minute of every single day. That knowledge doesn't take the waves away, it just gives you a different perspective. If Christ is your destination, you have a new option. You have the choice to stop looking at the waves. Keep your eyes on Him, and the waves will never have a chance to take you down.*

The thoughts dragged him off the bed, and he grabbed the ancient Fender guitar that had never left his side through every descent into the waves he had taken. Sitting on the couch, he pulled it up to his knee and strummed. There was something about that simple motion, that simple act of bringing a little music into the chaos of the world that made his very life make some sense.

"Okay, God," he said to the empty trailer. "I'm officially taking my eyes off the waves. If this is the dream You gave me, then show me what to do." Two more strums, and a thought hit him. He looked at his watch. He would be hopelessly early, but he didn't care. He needed to say thanks in person.

"Where are you going?" Tara asked, when Danae reached for her coat at the bottom of the stairs.

"Church. Be back in awhile."

She left Tara shaking her head. It was a given that Tara didn't understand. Danae had met so few people who did, and even some of them she had her doubts about. It was like they were all pursuing the world with such a vengeance that they had no time to stop and remember Heaven. In fact, she had been guilty of that at times herself. However, it was in those times that her life had seemed to spin out of control—like this last semester.

With the wedding, there was always an excuse not to go. Parties to go to, shopping to do… Something other than the rock she had long ago set her life on. Well, that was over. It was time to remember what she thought was important, and it was time to make it important in her life again.

"God is busy right now," the preacher said as Kalin sat six rows back, wishing he had thought to clean himself up a little before going on this excursion. He was sure by the annoyed glances he was getting that he looked frightful. However, as those thoughts drifted though him, he recognized them for what they were—waves, intent on keeping his attention from understanding why God had led him here, so he discarded them and fixed his attention to the preacher who stood smack in the middle of the center aisle.

"God is busy building a house right now. But a house isn't just made of bricks. No, you've got to have all kinds of things—nails, wood, sheetrock, windows, doors… no one thing would make a house by itself. And so it is with us. If God has made you wood, don't try to be bricks because you think they are more important. Be what God made you to be.

"If you are a window, don't try to be a door, and don't resent someone else for being the door either. Be what He made *you* to be, and bless *them* for being what God made them to be. Realize that you have a special place, a special role that only you can fill. No one else can fill the place God has put you—no one! No one can be who God made you to be. And so it is with every single person.

"Think about it. The further from what you were made to be that you get, the more miserable you become. It's God's way of saying, 'Hey, you're on the wrong track.' And to my way of thinking, there are a lot of windows out there trying desperately to be doors."

Kalin's mind drifted to Danae sitting in the dim light of the truck stop. She had let the world tell her that God's dream for her was to be wood when God had really made her to be the nails. That's why she was so unhappy, why life seemed to be such a struggle. Concern for her life's path drifted over him. *God, please show her that she's not where You want her to be and give her the courage to be what You made her to be.*

"Understanding someone is like baking a cake," the preacher 120 miles away in Knoxville said as Danae sat six rows back, wondering why she had ever thought she could live without this piece of her life in place.

Snickers of disbelief swept the crowd.

"Stay with me here," the preacher said. "To bake a cake, what do you need? You need ingredients, right? You need flour and sugar and milk and eggs and coffee and bacon…"

People in the congregation started looking at one another in confusion as if they were wondering what he was talking about.

"Oh, you don't?" he asked clearly trying not to be amused. "You don't put coffee and bacon into your cakes?"

A few soft "no's" scattered the crowd.

"So it takes not just ingredients but the *right* ingredients to make a cake. You can't just throw any old thing in and it will taste good?"

A few more "no's."

"Okay, then consider this… why do we throw any old thing into our lives and expect them to taste good? And why do we allow our friends to throw whatever they want into our lives and expect it not to affect our cake?" His gaze swept the crowd. "But it can be even worse than that. We can choose our friends based not on the ingredients they have chosen to include in their lives, but sometimes we choose our friends based on how the cake looks on the outside. We base our decision on the icing when sometimes all that icing does is mask that they've made their cake with the wrong ingredients."

Danae's thoughts went to Kalin sitting across a table at the truck stop, and then they slid backward to him standing in the parking lot with her. She had looked at what was on the outside—not giving the ingredients he had shown her the very real importance that they deserved.

He wasn't just icing. He was the real deal. He'd been a friend when he didn't have to be. He'd taken his time to help her out, and he didn't even know her. *God, thank You so much for sending Kalin into my life last night. Please let every dream he's chasing come true. He deserves that and so much more.*

"Kalin?" His name snapped through the conversations around him, and he turned to it, sure it was meant for someone else. "Kalin Lane! Oh, my gosh! I can't believe it, man. What are you doing back?"

In the next second he was wrapped in a bear hug the size of Montana. His mind hadn't really been too grounded in the present, and so the reality of this someone being so happy to see him pitched him totally off track for a moment. When he stepped back from the hug, it took another ten seconds for him to register who this person was—the name and the face were simply too clouded in fuzzy memories that didn't even seem real.

"Kalin, man, it's me. Jesse. Jesse Ralston."

Shock jumped through Kalin's soul. "Jesse? Oh, my... Wow! Are you kidding?" He looked around as if Jesse had just dropped from the rafters. "Where'd you come from?"

"Question is: Where'd you come from? I heard you'd left the country." Tall and lank with wavy, jet-black hair that fell down over one eye, Jesse was the only person Kalin had ever met who seemed to love music even more than Kalin did.

"Forced exile," Kalin said, dropping his gaze to the church carpet as he followed the rest of the crowd out. "What are you up to these days?"

"We're doing some regional touring with an A-list." Jesse leaned in secretively. "Would tell you who, but you'd probably ask me for a job."

Kalin laughed. "Give me anything that pays, and I'm there."

Together they moved through the crowd, by-passing the preacher. Once out the side door, Jesse picked up the conversation. "So, you're working then?"

"Some. Just did a wedding in Gatlinburg."

"Ugh. The wedding circuit. I remember those days," Jesse said as though that was akin to death by water torture. "So, do you still kick a mean one on the electric?"

Kalin stuck his hands in his jeans pockets. "When I get the chance, but we haven't been playing many gigs that rock the house lately."

"Who's your band again?"

"Silver Moonlight. Who are you with?"

"Phoenix Rising. They're really a great bunch of guys—not the usual dregs of the earth like a lot of them."

"I hear you there." Kalin looked back at the church, surprised to meet anyone he knew there. "I didn't know you... you know..."

"Church?" Jesse asked. "Oh, yeah. Ever since my Granny Ralston could pound a Bible over my head. Fact, that's where I got started, singing in the First United Methodist Church choir. Choir robe and all."

Kalin couldn't really picture Jesse singing in a choir. On stage hammering his fingers across six strings was more like it.

"We ought to get together sometime," Jesse said, "rehash the old days that kind of thing."

"Sounds cool."

"So, you got like a cell number or something?"

"Yeah." Kalin dug through his memory for the digits. "Leave a message though, I don't always carry it." He gave Jesse the numbers, and Jesse promised to get in touch with him. With that, he signed off, and they went their separate ways.

~ Lucky ~

Regret and past mistakes traced through Kalin as he walked slowly across the parking lot. If only he had been given Jesse's life, things could've been so much smoother. Growing up with God, living where you could pursue whatever you wanted, getting the breaks at just the right moment, knowing what was real and what wasn't... It would've been nice. Then as if an angel tapped him on the shoulder, Kalin recognized that his gaze was once again rocking in the waves.

Determinedly he lifted his gaze from them. "There I go again, trying to be the door." He laughed and shook his head. "I'll get back. With You as my goal, how could I not?"

"Brandt called." It was the message lying on the table when Danae got home. She read it, took it, folded it, put it in her pocket, and went to finish studying.

Chapter 7

"Man, you need to turn that thing on and leave it on," Von practically screamed through the tiny second-hand cell phone the minute Kalin made the connection Monday morning. "How are we supposed to get in touch with you otherwise?"

Standing in his trailer over a sink of dishes and dirty dishwater, Kalin flipped the phone to the other ear. "Sorry," he said, dragging the two syllables out. "I was busy."

"Yeah, well, we're supposed to practice tonight. We're playing at The Roadhouse in Brentwood Friday and Saturday, and we sounded like crap at that wedding. Give me Nine Inch Nails any day. That ballad crap gets freaking old."

Although Kalin agreed in theory, this conversation was grating his nerves. "Where am I supposed to be for practice and when?" he asked, grabbing a pen. Silver Moonlight was more of a rag-tag band with no set anything. Their practice sessions moved almost as much as their performances did.

Von gave him the information and signed off with "Do not forget."

Like he had ever forgotten before. Of course, that said nothing for the other band members. They were about as likely to show up as to hit the lottery. Once Von hung up, Kalin checked his other messages. One was from a number he didn't know. He called it but found it was a wrong number. The next number in the list, he did know. He hit the Call button and waited for the chewing out he was sure was coming.

"Hey, Zane, what's up?" Kalin asked of his manager, Zane Wedgewood. Zane had been in the business so long that he had practically given up on ever seeing one of his clients hit the big time, so he quietly pulled the connection string network he had painstakingly built for 30 years to get "off-the-big-time" gigs for those who signed with him. His one and only shooting star had slipped from the radar screen five years before, and Kalin still felt guilty about that.

"Well, it's about time you check in... What do you think? I'm your mistress or something? You need to leave that phone on, Kalin, so I can get a hold of you when I need to. That's why I gave it to you, remember?"

More waves, but today Kalin was determined not to watch them. "I'll keep it on, Zane. What's up?"

He sounded perturbed even as he continued. "Mr. Emerson called this morning. He was really happy with the way things went this weekend."

A face drifted through Kalin's thoughts. "That's good, right?"

"Yeah, that's good. That's great. He's got some connections in Knoxville that could sure come in handy down the road."

Kalin nodded although Zane couldn't see him.

"So, we've got this gig with Silver Moonlight coming up this weekend..."

Opening the cabinet that had a salt and peppershaker but not much else, a thought occurred to Kalin. "Hey, Zane, did they say anything about being paid? I'm kind of running low."

"Paid? Yeah. He said he gave it to one of the band members. I figured that meant you."

Trying not to, Kalin sighed. "I'll talk to Von about it." That was a dead end street he didn't even want to go down. If the money had already transferred hands, the great accounting skills of Von Sabine had surely already been employed as well. Drugs 10,000; Kalin zero. He was getting sick of this game. "Listen, Zane, I know we've talked about this, but is there anyway you can scout out another band for me?"

"Kalin..." Zane said, sounding very tired.

"I know. I know, but listen, these guys are trying to pull me back to where I was when I left last time."

That image undoubtedly registered with Zane who had been the one that had dragged him to his first Narcotics Anonymous meeting two weeks before he had ridden out of town. That simple act of friendship hadn't been lost on Kalin.

"I'm telling you, the drugs, the women, the alcohol... It's just not me anymore."

"Listen, Kalin, I appreciate what you're saying. Really, I do, but you've got to face reality. There just aren't that many bands at your level where you're not going to run into that junk at every turn. It's just the way it is." He paused. "Unless you want to try the Christian route."

For a long second, Kalin considered that. "No, that's just not the way I feel this thing is headed, but please, Zane, please, can you make a few phone calls, see what else is out there? Please?"

Zane sighed. "You'll owe me one right?"

The statement slid through him like a knife. "Yeah, one more."

In his early days when he and Zane had first hooked up, they could both smell the contract. He was hot, and Zane was tired of being the second-tier manager no legitimate star wanted to hire. When they hooked up, it was like nothing could stop them. Then trouble hit almost as fast as the stardom had. In no time, Kalin was as likely to be stoned out when he stepped on the stage as sober. Even so, shows were lining themselves up in their path, and whispers of a serious contract and the big time began floating through the air.

All of the other band members—save one, were as into drugs as he was and thus were no help in keeping him together. They fed the addiction to fast drugs and fast women, sensing that he was their ticket to both. Then quietly the money started to become a problem. So he went to Zane at first asking for the money saying only, "I'll owe you one." Then it devolved into pleading, then groveling, and then demanding. In short, it got ugly.

Zane, being the good guy he had always been, lent Kalin the money—not realizing it was being lined up and snorted at an alarming rate. Before the final curtain fell on Kalin's life in the States, he was the richest homeless person in the world. Having been thrown from his apartment for smashing the place up one night for reasons he still couldn't really remember, he had called the only person who might still care. Zane.

The N.A. meeting that night was their first real fight, and it hadn't really ended until Zane watched his golden egg drive away on the bike, his Fender guitar strapped to his back two weeks later. So much about those three years was a total blur. He remembered being on stage, but to this day he could only name a couple of the venues. What he remembered most was the look of pure devastation on Zane's face when he rode away, an acrid "thanks for nothing" still burning on his lips.

If he lived forever, he would regret those words until the day he was in his grave. However, when he had walked back into Zane's office just seven months ago, having worked his way back by the grace of God, the old man was the personification of the prodigal son's father. The question of taking Kalin back as a client had never even come up—only how was he, why was he back, and how could Zane help. Zane had always said it was Kalin's talent that drew him, but Kalin knew it was far more than that. It had to be. No one put that much effort into someone else's talent—no matter how incredible it was.

"You still there?" Zane asked with concern in his voice.

"Yeah. Can you make some calls?"

"I'll do what I can."

Danae had tacked the message to the board above her computer just like she always did. She would call Brandt later. She kept deciding that even after looking at it so long, it was permanently burned into her brain. Tuesday passed and then Wednesday. The questions of why he had called and what he wanted to tell her drifted around in her brain, but she couldn't get curious enough about them to actually pick up the phone and make the call.

So, still procrastinating from studying for finals, which were only two weeks away, she picked up her Bible and flipped it open. Her brain told her there were other more pressing matters, but she needed something to hold onto, some reason to not let the world and all its problems run completely over her life.

Truly, truly I say to you; if you shall ask the Father for anything, He will give it to you in My name. Until now you have asked for nothing in My name; ask and you will receive, that your joy may be made full...

Joy? That was asking a lot. Peace maybe, but joy? In annoyance, she flipped to another page.

Be strong in the Lord and in the strength of His might. Put on the full armor of God, that you may be able to stand firm against the schemes of the devil. For our struggle is not against flesh and blood, but against the rulers, against the powers, against the world forces of this darkness, against the spiritual forces of wickedness in the heavenly pieces...

Be strong in the Lord? How was she supposed to do that when everyone around her thought she was insane for even giving Him time in her life? Brandt. Tara. Even Molly and Rick seemed more interested in everything other than God.

Ask.

Ask? She shook her head at the thought. She didn't even know what to ask for. Her gaze tripped up to the message on the board. If she asked Him to help her forgive, wasn't that saying what Brandt had done was all right? If she asked to be strong and keep him at bay, yet what God wanted her to do was to forgive and reconcile, wouldn't she even then be on the wrong track? Every suggestion of what to ask for was rejected almost as quickly as it came into her mind. Finally Kalin's face drifted through her. Sitting in the darkness next to that tire, his presence had settled her like nothing else had in years. She couldn't pray for herself, but she could pray for him.

God, he deserves everything good. Please be with Kalin. Open doors for him that he thought were closed. Give him what he needs to make his dream reality. This I ask in Your name. Amen.

She still didn't have any answers to her own dilemma, but she felt better all the same. She slid off the bed, grabbed her language arts book, and buckled into the task of studying for the last finals she would ever take.

It was a given that Von had used the money before Kalin even asked for it, and short of going to Zane to ask for more, he didn't have any other options. Scrimping by with the last half of a loaf of bread and ham that was starting to smell funny, Kalin made it to Friday night—barely. At The Roadhouse he threw himself into the music, hammering out riffs on the guitar as if he and the guitar were one and the same. The music poured through him as it never had before. His fingers moved as if on their own—up and down the neck of the guitar in perfect rhythm. He had decided as he ate the last piece of bread just before heading for the concert that he wasn't going to worry about it anymore. He was putting life and everything in it—including the music—into God's hands

God was in control now because the truth was if it was up to Kalin, the end of the road had just flown past the window. At 10:30 they took a break, and he set the guitar in its stand, exhausted from lack of food, lack of sleep, and lack of forward progress options. He swiped a hand through his hair which fell right back down over his face and grabbed the bottle of water that the bar had graciously given them.

"We'll be back," Von said to Kalin, the look of a junkie badly in need of a fix staring from his eyes.

"Don't take too long," Kalin said in exhausted annoyance. He stepped off the stage, into the edge of the crowd that had materialized at some point in the evening. Hands reached out to him, and he clasped them and let the praise waft past him. If they only knew...

"Mr. Lane?" a stout man the size of a barn asked when Kalin had made his way halfway through the bar with no real destination in mind.

"Yeah." He turned, flipping his hair out of the way as he did so.

The man stuck out a meaty hand. "Rhett Melbourne, I own Sevens in Nashville."

The bar name registered, the man's name didn't.

Rhett clapped a meaty hand on Kalin's shoulder as he shook his other hand. "Listen, son, we've been looking for a band that doesn't just do stage tunes to front our weekend line-up. You all wouldn't be interested, would you?"

In complete disbelief Kalin stared at him. "Permanently?"

"Well," Rhett laughed heartily. "Let's try it for a week or two, and we'll see how it goes."

"Oh." The thought was so good Kalin could've kissed Rhett right there; however, he knew the proper channels had to be followed. He took a small drink. "Well, I can't really make that kind of commitment myself…"

Rhett nodded. "I understand. I understand. How about this? You come over here to my table for a few minutes, and we'll exchange info. Then you can have your people call my people and set something up."

Nodding and hoping he didn't look completely ridiculous, Kalin followed Rhett through the throng. At his table there were several ladies and a couple of guys who were obviously out for a good time.

"Kalin, this is everybody. Everybody, this is Kalin," Rhett said to the group.

"Man, you play one awesome guitar," one of the guys said, extending his hand to Kalin.

"Yeah, it's like you're from another world," another guy said.

"Just Canada," Kalin said, not realizing that would be funny, but they all laughed.

"And a sense of humor too," Rhett said. "I like this guy."

At that moment Kalin's senses registered the well-endowed blonde who had conveniently sidled up to him in the midst of the conversation.

"Hi, I'm Lea," she said, her voice smooth.

"Kalin," he said, sticking out his hand to halt her advance.

"Here, Kalin," Rhett said, motioning for the others at the rounded booth to move over. "Have a seat right here. Oh, and help yourself. We've got enough food for an army."

He wasn't kidding. Food was second only to drinks at the table.

"Oh, I'm fine," Kalin lied.

"No, here," one of the girls said. "Somebody should eat it. It's too much for us."

Someone handed him a plate, and a glass of water materialized in front of him.

"If you want something stronger, we can get you that too," Rhett said.

"Oh, no. This… this is great. Thanks." As Rhett consulted with one of his people, Kalin took a small sampling of vegetables and crackers. It

~ Lucky ~

literally looked like Heaven.

"Now, who are you with?" Rhett asked, coming back to the table.

"Zane. Zane Wedgewood."

"You're with Wedgewood? Where's he been hiding you?"

With that, the information trade was worked out. Kalin shook his head. He couldn't believe his luck. Then he laughed to himself. *Luck nothing. Thanks God.*

When the phone rang on Saturday night, Danae answered it before she thought about not. Tara was out. That meant Danae was the receptionist on duty. She so seldom got calls, she hardly remembered it was her number too.

"Hello?" Danae asked, trying to remember where Tara had said she was going and wondering if it made any difference if she remembered.

"Danae."

Her own name slammed her back into the computer chair. All week she had thought she was ready for this call, but the second she heard his voice, her first thought was to hang up.

"Look, I know you're mad," Brandt said, his words tumbling over themselves, "but I wanted you to know I'm sorry. It was stupid, and if you never forgive me, I'll understand."

A frown dropped over her whole spirit. "What do you want me to say to that? Congratulations, you're an idiot?"

"Come on, Danae. Don't be like that. I said I was sorry."

"And that's supposed to make what you did all right?" Anger boiled in her.

"No. It's just... look, I was drunk. I didn't know what I was doing."

"And that's supposed to make it all right?"

"Come on, Danae. Cut me some slack. I get it. I crossed the line, and I'm sorry."

"You obliterated the line, Brandt. What do you want me to do—take you back after you trashed everything I thought we stood for? Sorry. I think you have the wrong number."

"Danae!" The name was sharp this time as if he had thought she would actually hang up on him. "Look, I know I messed up. I get that, but please, this last week without you has been the worst one of my life. I can't even concentrate on school. I've got all these finals coming up, and all I want to do is see you. Please... Don't throw away what we have because I was an idiot."

"What about Krystal?" The name raked up muck in Danae's chest.

Brandt cleared his throat. "She never meant anything to me, Danae.

She was just there, and things kind of happened."

"They kind of happened. Uh-huh."

"I didn't mean for it to go that far. We were just hanging out, getting to know each other, and…"

"You slipped, and she broke your fall?"

"Danae, please. I'm trying to apologize here."

She said nothing because every single thing she could think of was sarcastic.

"Look, I know I don't deserve for you to forgive me," he said slowly, "but I'm asking anyway. I know now what I want is you. You're all I've ever wanted. Please don't throw us away because I did something stupid. Please…"

She closed her eyes, wishing she didn't still love him so much, wishing all she saw when she looked at him was what Tara saw, but the truth was he was who she had given her heart to all the way back in high school. True, he had some things about him that weren't great, but so did everyone. Finally she sighed. "You really hurt me, you know that?"

"I know, sweetheart, and I'm really, really sorry. You just have no idea…"

"And you promise never to do anything like that again?"

"I swear that was the only time."

She sighed again. She had known she would take him back when she'd first seen the message. It was only a matter of time.

They were set up at Sevens starting the second weekend in May. That was great news. Even better was the fact that the previous club had paid Zane, so Kalin got the cut he was supposed to get. He used it to buy groceries and to put gas in his motorcycle. The car could sit there half a line from empty because he only used it when it was raining anyway. Thankfully the weather was holding out, so it was fill the motorcycle and pray that would get him to the next tank.

When he wasn't practicing with Silver Moonlight, he kept busy writing songs and practicing on his own. The break with Rhett was one he wasn't going to take for granted. Breaks like that were too few and far between. In his trailer, he pulled the Fender from its perch and set it on his knee. His thoughts traveled back to home in Canada to the day his father had first suggested lessons. They weren't poor, but money wasn't in great abundance either. To even suggest it had to have taken a real act of faith.

Kalin had done his best from the first minute he had bought this guitar second-hand at the flea market. He learned notes first, not because

~ Lucky ~

he could read them but because he could hear them. For hours in his room he would turn the radio on, tune it to the only country station he could ever find and replicate what they played. It was only after his first performance when he was ten in the local high school's talent show—on which had been displayed little talent and very little show—that his father had suggested getting him lessons.

In truth it was probably more so that he wouldn't embarrass them again, but it had worked. His teacher had a gaggle of guitars—electric, acoustic, 7-string, 12-string, bass—he even had a banjo that Kalin picked up and within three weeks was playing like Buck Owens. His teacher said he'd never seen anything like it, and he encouraged Kalin's somewhat reluctant parents to let him play "for real" with some other local guitarists when Kalin was 15.

From the very first time he held a guitar, music had been his life. He studied so he could play. He did his chores the second he got home so he could have time to play. The longest month of his life was his senior year when he had wrecked his father's car and was grounded from the guitar—even not driving didn't hurt as badly.

At first his parents were excited about him finally finding something he loved. Then they went through a stage where they tried to talk him out of it. Eventually they had accepted that Kalin wasn't Kalin without a guitar in his hands. And nothing had changed that in all the years since.

As his fingers danced over the strings with little direction from him, he thought about his parents. Moving to the states was the only logical step for someone who wanted so badly to play country music, but it wasn't without tears. A progression of minor chords slipped through him as he thought about the last time he had been home. By then his big break had slipped through the strings and right through his fingers. By then they had a cocaine-addicted son who was struggling just to get to the next minute without freaking out. But they never lost faith in him—or hope.

Even when he had made the decision to come back, his father had said, "Call us if you need anything. You know we're behind you."

He rocked his fingers back and forth on the strings, making them radiate with the music. He was going to make it this time—whatever it took, he was going to make it. He owed it to too many people to do anything else.

Chapter 8

"You know, for someone who's supposed to be studying for finals, you sure are finding a lot of other things to do," Tara said the next Friday when Danae came down the steps, obviously dressed for something other than studying. "Let me guess, Brandt just wouldn't let you say no."

Danae stuck her tongue out at her roommate. "Like it's any of your business."

"I didn't say it was," Tara retorted as she bent back over her Calculus book. "Far be it from me to say anything bad about the vaunted Brandtly Emerson. Heavens. That would be a travesty."

"Not listening," Danae said.

"Like that's news."

Resentment crept into Danae's spirit. What right did her roommate have to judge her relationship? She didn't know. She wasn't there the night Brandt had asked her to go steady. She wasn't there the day they had gone to the falls together. Brandt wasn't perfect, but who was? Funny how many times Danae had told herself that throughout the course of the past week.

"We're just going for dinner. Then I'll be back to study, so there."

"Hey, I'm not asking."

"Yeah, I noticed."

Brandt picked that moment to knock, and Danae opened the door. He swept her into his arms and kissed her soundly. Heat flooded her cheeks as she remembered being on the listening end of his ardor. When he let her go, she glanced back at Tara. "We'll be back."

Tara only waved without looking up. They walked out the door, down the hallway, and out to his car—a black-on-black Audi 500. He was so proud of that car, a present from his parents for his 21st birthday. It shone in the late evening sunshine. When they were in the car, he looked over at her with the look that melted her knees.

"So, did you miss me?" he asked, a wide smile stretching dimple to dimple.

"Of course." She returned the smile although hers wasn't nearly so wide. "Where're we going?"

"Some of the guys are getting together at Pat's Pub."

Confusion smashed into her. "I thought we were going to eat."

"We are, but I want to say a quick hi to the guys first. It won't take long." He backed out and then looked over at her. "Why, do you have something else to do?"

She thought about that question. "No, just some studying."

"You have until Thursday. What's your hurry?"

Her shoulders reached for the car's ceiling as she wound her hair around her ear. "Just didn't want to wait until the last minute."

He drove without reply. After the first several blocks, Danae looked over at him, and his profile skittered across her heart. He was good-looking. Up-standing. That was a good word for him. Another face drifted through her, and she closed her eyes, turned her head, and looked out the other window. She had been trying to forget that face for the better part of two weeks, still he was right there. A question ran through her mind, and she looked back over at Brandt. It was silly to even ask, but her heart said she had to at least try.

"You remember when I use to talk about being a doctor?" she asked softly, and his gaze traced over to hers.

"When you were eight?" he asked with a laugh. "Yeah, you were always chasing me around with that stupid stethoscope. I for one am glad you grew out of that stage."

She tried to laugh but couldn't. "It's been a long time since I've thought of that."

"So, why bring it up now?"

Her thoughts crashed into each other. "No reason. I've just been thinking."

"I try to do as little of that as possible," he said with another laugh as they pulled up to Pat's.

Happy hour at the Pub had never had the appeal to Danae that it seemed to have for Brandt. His friends were loud and obnoxious. He wasn't any better when he was around them. Stealing herself against the desire to run, she followed him to the door and slid through it behind him on his push.

In minutes they were sitting at the bar between Dan and Fagan. The worst two of the bunch.

"Hey, Danae, baby, you decided to join us for a change," Fagan said, leaning into her. His curly black hair stuck out in half a hundred directions. Although it was barely after 5:30, she could tell by the smell of his breath and the slur of his words he'd already had far too much to drink. "I thought you were too good for the likes of us." He put a hand on the back of her chair and twisted it toward him.

She didn't say anything, hoping he would get the message and find a different topic—or someone else to talk to. Finally he let go of her chair, and as slowly as possible she turned it with her foot.

"Well, Brandt, what did you think of that…" the rest of the sentence was one long rant punctuated with four-letter words and a harangue of insults to the entire structural engineering department. The gist was that Fagan was tired of school, the tests, the professors, the other students, the work… All of them he deemed worthy of the ultimate degradation of terms.

By the time Brandt joined in, Danae was wondering why she had agreed to this. The more they drank, the worse the language, the worse the language, the more self-conscious she got. Other patrons of the establishment began looking their direction, and she hated being with the group they were looking at.

"Like that's going to do any good," Brandt said, lifting his beer. The finish to that sentence was littered with gutter language. Danae looked at him as if seeing him for the first time.

The memories of growing up suddenly looked very pale and far away. That may well have been who Brandt was, but sometime between then and now he had changed—and not for the better. They continued spewing sewer spray for an hour while Danae excused herself to go to the bathroom, ran out to the car for her purse, and generally slunk as close as she could get to the bar so no one would realize she was with them.

Finally, mercifully, Brandt looked at his watch. He swore once more. "It's almost seven-thirty, man. We're going to have to take off."

"So soon?" Fagan asked. "We're just getting started."

"I know, but…" Brandt glanced at Danae. "I promised we'd be back early."

Again, Fagan's hand was on the back of her chair, and he spun it so she was facing him. Loathing crawled through her on the taunting look in his eyes. "Ah, come on, Danae! If you'd just loosen up a little and get toasted like the rest of us…"

She wanted to deck him, but she kept her fists at her sides. She slid off the chair and up to Brandt's side, more to get away from Fagan than for any other reason.

"No, you guys are just going to have fun without us," Brandt said as if his best friend hadn't just slammed her to the curb. Together, they walked out, but as they approached the car, Danae's alert system went up.

"You know, I could drive if you want," she said, looking up at him.

"What? You think I'm drunk?" Brandt asked with a challenge in his voice as he fumbled with the keys.

"You've been drinking. I haven't. Why don't you just let me drive?"

He scoffed at her. "You drive like a girl."

"I am a girl. Come on, Brandt, give me the keys."

"I can drive better stone-drunk than you ever could sober." He flipped the remote unlock button, and the car beeped to life. She followed him to his side of the car.

"Would you give me the keys? Please."

He swept them up and out of her reach. "My car. My keys."

"Come on, Brandt. I'm not having this fight right now."

"Well, if you'd get over yourself, maybe we wouldn't have to go through this every time." He added three swear words to emphasize his point. "I'm driving. Get in."

"But—"

He opened his door a crack. "You can ride, or you can stay here. Your choice." He swung the door open and got in.

With every fiber of her being, Danae hated this scene, and they were experts at playing it out by now. She always lost. She always got in, and she always wondered if this would be the time that they wouldn't both climb out alive. She smiled sadly at the couple standing at their car across the parking lot as she rounded the back of the Audi to get in. They'd been watching the scene. She wasn't sure who she was trying to convince that it would be all right—herself or them.

Angry and sullen, Brandt started the car, but he wasn't finished yet. "I don't know why you have to act like such a baby when I just want to go out and have a little fun. I'm so sick of you telling me what to do…"

"I'm sick of this too, you know." She reached back and put her seatbelt on. "You really get to be a jerk when you're with them."

"Whoa. Why don't you just tell me what you really think?"

"What I really think? I really think you should just take me home."

"I thought we were going out to eat."

"I thought we were too. Now we're not. Take me home."

Seething rage slid over his face as the car jerked out of the parking lot. He didn't even look as he squealed the tires and jumped into traffic.

"Hey!" Danae screamed, grabbing onto the door handle. "Jeez! What're you trying to do, get us killed?"

"You're the one who can't wait to get home."

"I didn't say in a casket!"

He twisted the wheel, sliding into the tiniest of spaces between two other cars.

Her grip on the door handle tightened. "Brandt! Stop it!"

"Shut up. I'm trying to drive."

She should never have gotten in; however, barring jumping out the door going 60 through traffic, she didn't have any other options. Instead, she held on, held her tongue, and prayed like she had never prayed in her life.

Remarkably he made it to her apartment, and without waiting for him to say anything, she jumped out.

"I'll call you tomorrow night," he said just before she slammed the door.

"Don't bother!" she shot back. The slam of the door rocked the car. She stomped up to the first door and swung it open with a yank. At her own apartment door, her fingers were shaking so much she could hardly get the door open. Once she was inside, she fought off the tears.

After a minute she pushed off the door and stalked toward the living room. Tara still sat at the table, and she looked up when Danae got to the kitchen door.

"That was quick."

Danae went into the kitchen and poured herself a glass of milk. Her stomach hurt too much for anything else. She took her glass, walked out to the table, and sat down. She took a drink and then another. Her gaze drilled into Tara.

"Why do I do that?" she asked.

"Do what?" Tara asked without looking up.

"Let him talk me into that... Let him get me into situations that I swore I would never put up with."

Tara's pencil tilted to one side as she gazed at Danae. "Is that a rhetorical question, or do you really want an answer?"

That should've been an easy question to answer, but Danae hesitated. Did she really want the answer, or was it easier to keep going and not have to face dealing with it? Her gaze slid up to Tara's face, and the choice drifted through her. "Yeah, I really want the answer."

Tara thought about that a moment and then sighed. "Okay, here's what I think... Now mind you, I'm no psychologist or anything, but I think you're scared of being left again."

The words brought anger and hurt into Danae's chest in a rush, but she kept her face still.

"I think you're willing to put up with a bunch of crap so he won't bail like your dad did," Tara continued although Danae wasn't at all sure she was glad she had asked. "Brandt looks real good on the outside. I mean he looks the part of the devoted husband, but he's manipulative and controlling, and all he cares about is Brandt. He flirts with anything wearing perfume, and it wouldn't surprise me if he hasn't slept with his share of them."

The longer the list went, the farther down in her chair Danae slid.

"You're a good front for him," Tara continued. "For his parents and everything. He figures as long as he's with you, they don't have to ever figure out who he really is. He's getting everything he wants, and he's just smart enough to make you think that everything that's wrong with you guys is your fault." Finally Tara shrugged. "Not that I'm a psychologist or anything."

"Well, you sure have your theory all worked out," Danae said, and there was a tinge of anger in her voice.

"Hey, you asked."

"Yeah," she said sullenly. "I did." She stood and trudged over to the steps. "I'll be up in my room."

"Don't study too hard!" Tara called as if it was a joke.

But it was no joke. As Danae collapsed on her bed, she punched the pillow. Was there anything in her life that was real? Anything that didn't at some point go back to a lie? She looked but found nothing. She thought about Tara's comment about Brandt making all their problems be her fault. If that was true, then he must be awfully good at it because she sure felt horrendous at the moment.

The gig at Rhett's was proving to be better than Kalin had dared hope. It was at least three steps up from The Roadhouse, which was a step up from where he had played prior to that. In fact, there was no chicken wire to be seen anywhere. The patrons seemed to be upper-middleclass, 20 and 30 year olds. It took three songs to get anyone on the dance floor, but once they were there, it was packed the rest of the night.

They played three sets, and when they got ready to leave, Rhett had come up personally to tell them it was a great show. As shows went, they couldn't get much better. Back on his bike, Kalin made his way to the trailer, thanking God sincerely for at least setting him on something that didn't resemble a sinking ship. Steady work. Steady money. It wasn't perfect, but it was a step up.

~ Lucky ~

After changing into his gray sweatpants and white T-shirt, he thought to check his cell phone, which was lying on the counter. Everyone gave him such a hard time about not turning it on, but the less he turned it on, the less chance that he would run up the minutes. He didn't have money to spend on airtime. Food, shelter, and the gas to get to and from work were over-taxing his finances. There was one message, and when he pulled it up, he closed his eyes as guilt poured through him.

It was late there, but the call had been received only 30 minutes before, so maybe they would still be awake. Punching two buttons he redialed the number and waited for someone to pick up.

"Hello?" the feminine voice asked. He loved that voice.

"Hey, Mom. What's up?"

"Well, it's about time. We were beginning to wonder if you'd dropped off the face of the earth!"

"Nope. I'm still here."

"You sure know how to scare your mother to death, you know that? I've been waiting for a reply for two weeks now. Where've you been?"

"Two weeks? You just called," he said in confusion.

"Your email, Kalin. You said you'd check it."

"Oh, yeah... I haven't made it into the library in awhile."

"Well, then don't tell me to email you and then forget to pick it up! I was this close to sending out the cavalry to look for you."

"Hey, Kalin," his father said, apparently from the other phone.

"Hey."

"How's it going? We haven't heard from you in awhile."

"Yeah, Mom was just telling me." He sat down on the little couch and leaned back against the side of the trailer before putting his foot up on the couch next to the trailer's other side. "So, how's everything?"

They talked about Canada, about his sister and her family, about summer coming up and his schedule. Finally his phone started beeping to let him know it would shut down any second. "Listen, guys, I've gotta go before this phone cuts us off."

"Be sure to check your emails from now on," his mother managed to get in before they had to sign off.

He laughed. "I will. I promise."

When the phone call ended, he hit the End button and then leaned his head back against the cold steel of the trailer. Loneliness seeped into his spirit. He missed them all so much. He hadn't seen his niece or nephew in nearly a year, and being without them made him feel almost as if he was completely alone on the earth.

Before the melancholy could settle over him permanently, he pulled himself up and hiked himself up onto the bed over the hitch. Tonight he would sleep, but tomorrow he would make it a point to go to the library.

The arrow on the computer screen went back and forth as Danae moved it absently in her hand. She should be getting something done. Something important like sleeping or studying, but she couldn't even clearly think what that something should be. Instead she sat, staring at Yahoo! and wondering what fabulous place on the world wide web would take her mind off Brandt and the other depressing thoughts swirling through her.

As the cursor slid across the screen, her time with Brandt wafted through the corridors of her mind. The more she looked, the more she saw the things that Tara had talked about. It was like she was them during the times he didn't want to be. She remembered the one date that she and Brandt had gone on with Tara and her boyfriend. To say that had been a disaster would've been putting it mildly.

Brandt found every possible opportunity to tell them all how wonderful he was. He had badgered Michael, Tara's boyfriend, so much that Michael had finally just given up and sat sullenly. The more Danae tried to help, the worse it got, and by the time they left, it was pretty clear that Michael and Tara would walk through flaming briquettes before they would subject themselves to another outing with Brandt and Danae. At the time she had thought it was just a clash of personalities. Now she saw it in a different light.

Her mind drifted past the actual date back into the car on the way home. Brandt had leveled every spitefully mean comment he could about Michael and about Tara. There didn't seem to be one thing he was impressed with, and the more he had talked, the more crushed Danae felt. She had genuinely liked Michael when he'd been at the apartment prior to the date, and she'd always considered Tara to be a really good friend. Since then, however, Tara mostly went to Michael's place. In fact, Danae couldn't remember a single time he had been to theirs since. It was easier that way. Danae had never really questioned that either—until now.

Fighting to get something other than Brandt into her brain, she chanced on a face that was fading slowly from her memory. Sitting at the computer, she had a thought, and for a moment she tried to talk herself out of it. However, it wouldn't hurt to just look. A click and she carefully typed his name into the little search box—with quote marks. It wouldn't work, but what else did she have to do?

The search pulled up references to 793 Kalin Lanes. Her gaze traveled through the first page of options and found one on number four that said something about "guitar playing." It was a possibility, so she clicked on it. It was one of those free sites, set up by a fan, but it had obviously not been touched for quite some time.

"He plays guitar like a dream!" the headline screamed. Danae clicked over on the link reading "Photos." It wouldn't be him, she was sure. The photos loaded into tiny little thumbnails, and she had to click on one to enlarge it just to be sure it was actually a person with very blond hair and not some fluffy white rabbit.

The second the picture came up, Danae leaned closer to the screen squinting her eyes to see better. It didn't look at all like him, and yet it was. Short, cropped hair the color of blonde baby fuzz capped his head. He was clean-shaven and reminded her of Dolly Pardon's old partner... what was his name again? Danae discarded that question. Off-handedly she clicked to make the next picture bigger. It was then that she noticed the rhinestone-studded jacket. It was horrid and made her wonder who had to tackle him to get that thing on him.

One by one she clicked through the pictures, mesmerized by them. They were all basically the same—taken from some ceremony of some kind. It was amazing how different he looked. Only his eyes were the same, and yet even they spoke a very different story than the one she had remembered from the wedding. She clicked back to the Home page and scanned it. At the very bottom there was a message. "If you want to email Kalin, here's an address I used once. He even wrote me back!"

Danae looked at the email address and knew it was further than a long shot. The site was ancient. He had probably changed addresses a hundred times since that fan had found him. However, the possibility that there was a chance that she could write to him and tell him thanks wouldn't let her click off the site.

Trying not to think about it too much, she clicked on the email address, typed a few lines, and hit send. It was crazy to even hope, but by then all she had to live on was hope. The rest of her life was an empty shell she didn't even recognize any more. She would just tell him thanks, and then she would find a way to rebuild her life with the tiny shards she had left.

Saturday morning, Kalin tramped out to the bike. He needed groceries, and he decided he could swing by the library on his way to the store. That way his mother wouldn't actually come down here and beat him. It was a joke they had because she had never touched her kids except to give them a hug. But Kalin smiled at the thought nonetheless.

He backed the motorcycle out and headed to the highway. Nashville was a nice place to live. Busy. Everyone always seemed to have somewhere important to go, so if you were going somewhere, it must be important. He debated which to do first and finally decided on the library. He didn't think they would appreciate him dragging bags of groceries up to the second floor to use the computers.

Trying not to appear too out of place in his scraggly jeans and old T-shirt, he walked into the library and climbed the stairs. He didn't look like what anyone would've thought of as a bookworm, so he kept his head down all the way into the computer area. Thankfully there were two free computers. He took the one by the wall and sat down, hoping he still remembered how to do this and what his password was.

He pulled up his free email host, typed in his username and password and then sat for a moment as it thought through the instructions. With his luck his account had been closed and his mother would have reason to beat him. Just before he smiled, it beeped, and a long list of messages appeared. He started down the first page, clicking delete as he came to each one without really paying much attention. The only one he cared about had a .ca tag on the end anyway. Then about twelve messages down, his attention snagged on a name. D_Scott.

His pulse leaped into his throat, and he sat up closer to the screen. It couldn't be. Could it?

The mouse shook ever-so-slightly as he fought to calm his racing nerves. He ran his other hand over the whiskers on his face as his gaze bounced across the screen. It wasn't her. It couldn't be, but then again, it wouldn't hurt to just make sure. A click and the message jumped through the ether onto the screen.

Hi. I got this email from a website, and this probably isn't even the Kalin Lane I think it is. But if you were at a wedding in Gatlinburg a couple of weeks ago, would you please email me? I'm the one you rescued in the parking lot, and I just wanted the chance to say a proper, "Thank you." However, if you have no idea what I'm talking about, please just delete this message and go on with your life. God bless.

He scrolled even after the mouse quit scrolling, but that was all that was there. He laid his chin in the palm of his hand and thought for a long moment. Not sure what to do, he sat back in the chair and let his hand flop to his mouth as he considered what he should do with the message from a ghost he had been sure was long gone. It was pretty certain no one else could've known enough about that night to send that email. Besides, the address was registered D_Scott. It almost had to be her.

He closed his eyes wishing he could just delete the message and pretend he had never seen it. She wouldn't write again. She would think it had been lost in cyberspace or that he wasn't who she thought he was. Either way, that would be the end of it. And yet. How many times had he thought about her since he'd left that apartment? How many times had he wondered how her life was going? How many times had she shown up in his prayers and in his dreams? And now, here she was—a couple of mouse clicks away, and he was going to go on with life as if he hadn't noticed?

More to the point, he had made a promise to be true to himself and to God no matter if it made sense or not. But this? This made absolutely no sense at all; however, to not at least acknowledge that he had gotten it would've been reneging on his promise, so finally he pulled himself forward, hit reply, and laid his fingers on the keys.

Officially they were down to three days of classes before finals, but most of those were show up and turn in your final project type classes. So, Danae had spent all of Saturday curled up with her Language Arts book studying for one of her two finals. Tara was downstairs, and it was a given she was studying as well. They had learned early on that they didn't study well in the same room, so Danae was by all accounts a prisoner in this room she had learned to call home.

Her computer was on, mostly for the company the whirring sound made. It sounded like progress even though she felt like she was making none. At ten minutes until noon another sound jangled through the whir, and Danae looked up from her book. Knowing it was the email but knowing also that she should concentrate on studying, she bent her head over the book again. However, her gaze slipped back up to the computer. Curious, she slid off the bed and walked over to it.

The black screen fuzzed to life with the motion of the mouse, and her gaze scanned the email list to the bottom. Lane_K jumped out at her, and heart, body, and soul she gasped. It was probably just the owner of the account telling her she was insane. Nonetheless, she slid into the chair, clicked on the message, and took a breath to steady herself against whatever the message said.

Hey, Danae. It was great to hear from you. It is me—although "rescuing you" might be a little strong. I didn't do anything anyone else wouldn't have. Are your classes over yet? I'm just at the library checking messages so don't be too surprised if I don't always write right back this fast. Things are pretty crazy around here. But anyway, it's me. Good to hear from you. God bless.
Kalin

Danae didn't realize she was no longer breathing. With a single click on the reply button, she was typing away, hoping he hadn't left yet.

After sorting through all of the messages and deleting most of them, Kalin buckled down to read the ones his mother had sent. There was one about someone's chicken coming into their yard, and one about his niece's piano recital, and one about his dad considering retiring. No earth-shattering news overall, but he was glad she had reminded him. He looked at the clock and decided after a quick note to his mother, he'd better be getting.

He clicked back to the Home page and was a half-second from clicking on Compose when he realized there was a new message at the top. D_Scott stared back at him, and a fear he hadn't realized was even there swept over him. He hadn't meant to encourage her. At least he hadn't thought he meant to encourage her.

Thinking he would just write his mother back and then decide what to do about D_Scott, he clicked the Compose button. However, his note to his mother was literally nothing to write home about. It was something along the lines of "I'm here. Thanks for writing." She wouldn't be thrilled with such a sparse reply, but his brain was too intent on wondering what reply Danae had made.

Against his better judgment when he sent his mother's email, he clicked on Danae's message.

*I'm so glad it was you! I thought somebody was going to think I was completely insane. I hope everything's great where you are. I've got two classes Monday and Tuesday. Then Thursday starts finals. I have one Thursday, and one the next Tuesday. Will be glad to have a break after that although I don't know what I'm going to do with myself all summer—dread next fall probably * grin * Tell music row Hi for me! Blessings, Danae*

Although it made no sense, he couldn't stop the smile that spread through his spirit. A friend. It had been a long time since he'd had anyone that cared other than his family. Not replying wasn't even an option.

She was studying again when his message came through. The second it jangled in, she sat up and clicked on it.

Things are GREAT! We got a new gig at Sevens. Weekends which is a lot better than wondering if you're going to have ANYTHING for weeks at a time. I've been praying so hard for this for so long, sometimes I wonder if He's even hearing me. But then again, in His time... I've just gotta keep remembering that (wish it was easier to remember sometimes!). So, I guess you're still pursuing Number 73. Have you given any more thought to Number 1? Peace, Kalin

Kalin had told himself he needed to go, and yet still he sat. Every minute or so, he clicked the refresh button hoping there would be a new message. He'd said three more times and he was leaving, but on the second try, a new message was there—three now perched at the top of his inbox. Sitting forward in the chair, he clicked on it.

Cool about the new gig! Hope that works out as well as you want it to—I'll be praying for you. And just so you know, He does hear you, but sometimes you're praying for X when what He really wants to give you is X-Better. So be sure to pray for what He wants instead of praying for what you want. It works better that way :) As for #73, well... That's kind of the path I took. I don't really see how I can turn back now. Blessings, Danae

He read it again and considered the last statement. She was going on with her life as if teaching was what she wanted to be doing. He should just let well enough alone. What business was it of his what she did with her life? He hardly knew her, and yet the Holy Spirit in him wouldn't let him let it be.

Danae hadn't even left her computer when the new message jangled in. With no hesitation whatsoever, she clicked on it.

Did He put you here to be wood or nails? Kalin

Confusion jumped on her, and she typed her reply.

Amusement sifted through him as he waited, and it didn't take long.

Huh?!

It was all the invitation he needed.

Like a cat swaying on a branch in the wind, Danae sat in the chair. First she wound a leg under her, and then she scowled at the screen, wondering what was taking him so long, and wondering also what in the world he meant by the wood or nails comment.

Her computer had barely jangled before she clicked on his message.

It's something my minister said the other day—about it takes all kinds of things to build a house—wood, nails, sheetrock, doors, windows. God's building a house, and He's using us to do it, only problem is we want to be what everyone else is or whatever everyone else says we should be rather than being what He made us to be. So if you were made to be nails, why are you trying so hard to be a window? Kalin

She let the chair back catch her as she fell onto it. Her spirit felt like someone had slapped her. He was asking the impossible—to go for a dream she had long ago passed up for "practical." She tried to think of a reply to explain that to him, but when she looked up, she saw the door, and the thought ran through her mind how funny and useless a window would be right there.

Kalin had never been a nail biter, but he was gnawing away for all he was worth. She either thought he was insane or that he had just obliterated the line between when you could tell someone and when you should keep your mouth shut. After all, it was her life. He knew so very little about it. Who was he to give her any advice?

When he hit the Inbox button to see if anything was there, the sight of the message tore sanity from him. Very slowly as if the computer might jump out and bite him, he clicked to her message.

I don't know... because I think being nails isn't possible?

His heart wrapped around that statement even as his fingers touched the keys.

Studying for finals was long forgotten. Danae was all but curled in the chair, waiting for his reply. She had never been that honest with anyone, and now she was wondering why she thought being honest with him was a good idea. The message jangled into her inbox, and she clicked on it.

All things are possible with God. Think about it. I've really got to run. Kalin

Chapter 9

The rest of Saturday Danae thought about what he'd said. Sunday she hardly listened in church, and the final Bible study of the year afterward was no better. "All things are possible with God" kept running through her mind—drowning everything else out. She'd heard that before, but it had never before pertained to her dreams, only to what she'd thought had to be done.

Sitting in class Tuesday afternoon for her last final, her mind wasn't on how best to teach language arts, it was too busy working through the idea that had shown up in the middle of the previous night. No one would understand. She wasn't sure she did, but the thought wouldn't leave her alone.

It took only the minimal amount of time necessary to finish the test. Truth was, she really didn't care. Number 1 was calling her name.

Leaving the Education Building behind, she strode across campus. "Don't think about it. Just do it," she kept telling herself. She knew if she thought about it too much she'd talk herself out of doing it.

By 3:15 it was done. She was signed up—a full course load for the summer intercession and for the whole summer. Biology. Anatomy & Physiology. Genetics. She had to be out of her mind, but she was so excited, she stopped off in the computer lab so she could tell him.

Kalin made it all the way to Wednesday before he gave up the fight to act nonchalant and like it wasn't killing him not knowing if she had written back or not. Climbing the library steps, he wasn't sure which would be worse—if she had written or if she hadn't. There was one computer left in the corner of the bookshelves, and he grabbed it. Telling himself this was no big deal and that it didn't really matter to him one way or the other, he went through the motions of pulling up his email account.

When his gaze scanned the list, his heart fell momentarily. Junk mail. Then, buried in the junk, he saw the D_Scott, and he had to take a breath to calm down.

"Jeez, Kalin," he said under his breath, "it's just an email."

But cool and smooth had flown away like a flock of scattering birds. He clicked over to the message.

I hope you weren't just saying that about all things being possible with God because I think I just did the impossible, and without Him, I must be completely insane. But insane or not, I'm going for Number 1 starting Monday morning. Biology 102. Man! This is like wanting to play a symphony but not knowing the first thing about music... What am I doing?! Danae

He couldn't have been happier if someone had just handed him a Grammy. The smile was etched on his face as he put his fingers to the keyboard to type back.

Tara had gone to Michael's for the evening, so Danae had the run of the place. Still she was sitting on her bed just like usual. She was trying to read a spy thriller she'd been wanting to read for two months, but her mind wasn't really on it. She wondered what he was doing—how life was treating him, where he was... "God, please let Kalin know I said thank you."

At that exact moment her email jangled, and she looked up at it. It probably wasn't him. She had been so hopeful for more than 24 hours, and still there was nothing. However, the thought that "maybe it was him this time" was too much to overcome. She slid off the bed, walked to the computer, and sat down. As she slid the mouse over the screen, her breath caught.

Excitement flowed through her as she clicked on his newest message.

If you want to learn to play a symphony, the bottom string is E. You don't have to learn the whole of music in one fell swoop. You just have to take it one step—one note—at a time. That's how you learn to do anything worth doing. Kalin
P.S. Did I tell you how proud I am of you?! You go, girl!

Excitement mixed with something she couldn't quite name surged over her. "Please, God, don't let him leave yet."

Trying to look like he was actually being productive, Kalin pulled a book off the shelf behind him and opened it on the desk. Every so often he would click to see if there was anything new. After the fourth click, his efforts were rewarded.

Glad to hear someone's proud of me because honestly, I'm scared to death. Danae

He almost laughed out loud. Shaking his head, he put his fingers to the keyboard.

She clicked on it the moment it came into her inbox.

That's why they call it "impossible," silly. If they called it "possible," you would believe you could do it! Kalin

The second her reply came in, he clicked on it.

Are you saying I can't do it? D

He took a long breath and let it out slowly. "Okay, God, how are we going to explain this?" He put his hand on his jaw line. For a long moment he looked at the screen, listening and thinking. Then his fingers began their reply.

If it was possible to will an email to an inbox, Danae was trying. The waiting was pure torture. The jangle of the email jolted her nerves.

I'm saying that you by yourself can't, but the phrase is "all things are possible with God." Doing it on your own is a recipe for disaster. The awesome thing is He doesn't require you to do it on your own. He wants you to let Him do it with you—through you. And when you start letting Him do it through you, you can't lose! Kalin

A verse from Sunday's Bible study floated through her mind.

He clicked the message.

If God is for us, who can be against?

He laughed out loud at that.

She clicked the message.

You got it! If He gave you the dream, don't you think He will also give you all that you need to make that dream come true? We need to work on this trust thing, girl!

The reply was back to him in no time.

Trust? I feel like I'm about to jump off a cliff into the dark! How much more trust do you want me to have? Danae

Haven't you ever heard that when you get to the end of everything you know and you step off into the darkness, one of two things will happen... either you will step on something solid, or you will learn... to fly! Kalin

Her heart soared away from her when she read that. Learn to fly, what a concept.

That's awesome! How'd you come up with that?

He shook his head as he typed the reply.

I'd love to take credit for it, but it wasn't me. It was something a lady on Oprah said one day when I was sitting on my parents' couch feeling sorry for myself. I've remembered it ever since.

You watch Oprah?

Somehow she couldn't picture that.

I used to watch it a lot when I had time and a television. Okay, I could've done without the shows about the latest, greatest handbags, but when she talked about spiritual stuff—and especially about going for dreams, I was right there. I probably needed it more than anyone who's ever lived...

Why you more than anyone else?

Kalin sat for a long time after reading that question. It wasn't that he didn't know how to answer it. It was more that he didn't know how to answer it and not show her how truly lost he had been. Closing his eyes, he stepped off his own cliff.

When you lose the only dream you've ever cared about—especially when it was so close you could reach out and touch it, it's not that easy to pick yourself up from the dust and go for it again. It kind of feels like banging your head against a brick wall.

Intrigued, Danae sat up straighter to type her reply.

Kalin's thumbnail was raw from him gnawing on it, but he couldn't help it. The nerves were making the rest of him do unusual things. When her reply came in, he had to breathe to settle himself before he could read it. His stomach felt queasy from the strain.

Going for it once is tough. Twice is unbelievable—especially when it was just yanked away like that. You must be tougher than you look.

He laughed at that and hit the Compose button.

Hardly. I'm just more stubborn than most :) I guess I figured there were a lot of people who had supported me, and I couldn't let them down. But crawling out of that hole was the hardest thing I've ever done—not that I'm out yet, mind you, but getting really honest with yourself about who you are and why the dream is important is a great first step. So is grabbing on to God and holding on for dear life! :)

Danae had never met anyone who so freely talked about God. Most of the time if anything it was, Why did He do this to me? and What's the point of trying? God's going to get you anyway. But this conversation felt very different—almost as if the thrusters of Kalin's existence came from God, and Kalin knew it.

She put her fingers to the keyboard and tried to get what was in her heart onto the ether.

To hear you talk about God sounds so different than everyone else. It's like He's a real part of your life—not just having to go to church on Sunday or something. Why is that?

Kalin breathed in the question as he sat in the library that had gotten much noisier in the past hour. However, tucked in his own little corner, the only thing that sounded noisy was his mind screaming at him that she was going to think he was a freak. Slowly he typed the words his heart said were true, but his mind said no one else would ever understand. Then he sat back and ran his hand over his chin just before he hit SEND.

I once heard that Mother Teresa said, "When you get to the end of everything else, and you lose everything, even yourself, that's where you find Jesus, and when you find Him, you finally understand that He is all you need." I can't explain it any better than that. K

Peace or something very much like it floated through her spirit.

I'm thinking that's a pretty good explanation. So I guess my next question is, can someone get <u>there</u> without losing everything?

I sure hope so because I wouldn't wish that on a dog! :) It was awful. No, it was worse than awful. Awful would've been miles of steps up. It was like one second I was six inches from everything and two seconds later it was all gone just like that. The worst part was waking up and not even recognizing myself. I mean literally looking in the mirror and having no idea who that was looking back at me. But I guess that's what it took to get my attention.

Her heart snagged on his sincerity.

Well, that would certainly get my attention! So you were so wrapped up in the dream that when it was gone, you were gone?

Kind of, but it was more than that. I'd given up myself trying to be what they said I had to be to get the dream. The more I did that, the more miserable I got, so then I started finding very unhealthy ways to stop feeling miserable. I didn't even realize how miserable I was until the dream was gone, and all that was left was the lies.

Lies like what?

As he read her reply, Kalin sat back in the chair. Honesty had a way of getting really honest if you weren't careful, and with her it seemed he was never careful enough. He breathed. It was all he could do. The truth was choking everything else out.

For longer than an eternity, Danae sat there. Something in her knew the answer to that question before she'd even asked it. She wondered how she knew, but the image of him flashed through her memory—the long hair, the ragged look, the earring, the tattoo, the motorcycle. It was what she had surmised about him almost immediately. He lived on the razor's edge of life, and that way of life always brought with it the kind of escapes that she had done everything in her power to stay away from her whole life.

In fact, she hadn't had two drinks in 24 years of existence—much less anything harder. In high school unless she went with Brandt, she didn't go to parties. Not because she didn't want to go but because she wasn't invited. When the others figured out her no really meant no, it was just easier to party without her.

College wasn't much different save for the two frat parties Brandt had talked her into going to. Now those couldn't even be called drinking. They were more like using liquor to play Russian Roulette. She wasn't playing, so that was the end of that. Even Brandt quit asking.

Now, here she was, face-to-face with what Kalin's life entailed, and she could clearly see the guardrail in front of her. He was wonderful, but nothing was that wonderful. Praying she was wrong about everything, when his reply came through, she clicked on it.

Oh, man, there were so many lies, it's hard to know where to start. There was the lie that I didn't look right, and the lie that I didn't act right. There was the lie that said how I sang was wrong, how I played was wrong. There was the lie that having money would solve everything. It didn't. It just brought lots of friends who were anything but...

There was the lie that I was some kind of superstar and the bad stuff couldn't get me. Then there was the bad stuff... It started out with us just drinking a few after the shows to relax. Then someone thought it was a good idea to smoke some weed. It progressed from there until bad turned into hell. Half the time I didn't remember the shows. I didn't remember writing music or playing or practicing. I didn't remember anything.

But there were always people around—everywhere. Someone was always there. I didn't want to be alone, and so I made sure I wasn't. Most of the worst of it I don't even remember. When I'd wake up in the morning and the memories were there, I'd grab the glass and cut some more lines. I didn't want to remember. I still don't.

Her heart ached for the pain scratched across those words.

He had no idea if she would even reply, but in minutes a new message showed up.

So what made you stop? What made you realize you were living a lie?

That was the one clear memory in the whole, sad mess.

The night I woke up passed out and homeless on my manager's doorstep.

Where were your friends?

What friends?

Good point.

No, the amazing thing is all I remember as I laid there, was wanting another hit. Just one more. I would've killed for it. I didn't care if I ever had a home again. I didn't care if I ever saw my family again. I didn't care that I had a contract two floors up waiting to be signed. I didn't even care if I never played again. All I cared about was how could I get more drugs and how long would that take.

When they talk about hell, you may not believe in it, but I'm here to tell you, there is a hell. I know. I was there.

How did it get so far out of control? I mean, you had it together enough to make it here, to reach for your dream and have it in your grasp. How did it go so wrong?

Kalin hadn't exactly ever thought about it in quite those terms. There was a beginning. What was it?

I think it was the moment I began to believe that what God had made me to be wasn't good enough. It was the moment I started trying to be the bricks rather than being happy He made me the wood. It was like what He said didn't matter. All I cared about was what the world said was important. I think at that moment I sold my soul to the devil.

And so you ended up trashing everything.

Pretty much. It's funny. What the devil offers looks so good on the outside, but on the inside it's nothing but a rotten, stinking mess. The bad thing is you can't even see that at first. It just looks so GOOD. You just want some so bad. But before you know it, he has you in his grasp. It happens so slow, you don't even realize it. One step. One step. One more, and all of a sudden you're in something and you can't even see the way out. Scares me to death to think about it now—how easy it is to look at that offer and not see it for what it is. I just wish I had known then what I know now. It all could've been so different.

And now?

He laughed at the very thought.

And now... I'm just happy for this minute because I know how easily it can all be taken away. I'm me—at least I'm learning to be. If you don't like who I am, that's fine. But I'm not going to change who I am, who God made me to be, so other people will like me.

Okay. So, who are you?

Once again he laughed.

Well, let's see... I'm a guy who loves music, who loves to get lost in it. I'm someone who may not know how to get where I'm going, but I figure I've got the best pilot around, so I'm not going to worry about it. I'm a guy who doesn't play by everyone else's rules. I would much rather make my own and go by what God says than by what the world tries to tell me. I'm a guy who takes life as it comes and lives it to the fullest. I try to enjoy every moment—whether it makes any sense to do that or not (and more often than not these days, it doesn't make much sense at all ;) I'm a guy who lives in a tiny little 5th wheel trailer, who scrapes by to eat, *who has given everything for a dream but who now realizes that some things are too precious to part with even when the world is laid out before you. I'm a guy who wants to do things right this time and not go through the guardrails again—because let me tell you, that is a scary ride down... Yep. That's pretty much who I am. You running for the exits yet?*

Ten seconds prior to reading the message, that was exactly what Danae was doing. However, the more she read, the more she wanted to know.

What about everything else—from before?

It took several seconds for him to formulate a reply to that one.

The things I can fix, I'm trying to fix. The things I can't, I'm trying to put in His hands. Everything else is a prayer I'm learning to live everyday.

It was so beautiful, it could've been a song. Then she realized it probably was.

I wish I could live like that.

You can.

How?

Stop believing you have to have all of the answers. You don't have them, but He does! Start trusting that His answers will always guide you to X-Better. (I love X-Better, by the way. I've been letting go of even asking for what I want and figuring He knows X-Better since you said that. Funny how many truly awesome things have started showing up in my life because of it.)

Like?

Well, you, for one.

That wasn't the reply she had expected. Just as she set her fingers to type her reply, a knock sounded on her door downstairs. Quickly she typed in her reply and then rushed down the stairs to get it.

I'm so glad God put you in my life. I don't think I deserved that!
  Oops. Someone's here. Gotta jet. Peace out, danae

The second hand wound around the clock on the wall as Kalin sat there, the message still on the screen. Had this been something he had seen coming, he would've swerved to miss it. But here it was. Here she was. Holding out a hand to his battered spirit, asking him to trust another human being again. "God, I don't know if I'm ready for this. How do I know I won't hurt her like I've hurt so many others before?" He wanted an answer to that question, but there didn't seem to be one.

Finally, he laid his fingers on the keys for one final reply.

Chapter 10

Danae took the stairs two at a time because she was high on life. At the door, she bounced twice in her sock feet wishing there was a possibility that it would be Kalin on the other side. However, the second the door was open, she wished she hadn't bother to answer it. "Brandt."

"Hello, to you too," he said with no warmth whatsoever.

She hadn't opened the door any more than a body-width. "What're you doing here?"

"Mom invited us over. Molly and Rick are there." His hands were on his hips, just hidden under the brown suede jacket. "So, can I come in or not?"

With everything in her, she wanted to tell him to leave. Her gaze chanced up the stairs, but finally she relinquished fantasy to reality. "Yeah, I guess."

The Tennessee breezes had never felt so warm. As Kalin crawled on his bike to head to practice, he looked into the brilliant blue sky scattered with clouds. "You know, God, sometimes I can't quite figure you out, and sometimes it's more fun not knowing what's coming. Please be with her, and keep her safe."

"Well, are you going to get ready or not?" Brandt demanded when he was in the middle of her living room. "They said to be there at five."

Courage and recklessness flowed through her. "Who says I'm going? You just show up here and expect me to drop everything?"

He snorted contemptuously. "Everything like what? Watching Oprah?"

Her heart slid through her chest on that name. "No, I do have things to do, you know. It's not like I sit here all day and twiddle my thumbs."

"Huh. You could've fooled me." He looked up the stairs. "Would you go get ready already? We're going to be late."

She hated this. Every single minute of it. Most of all she hated feeling like there was nothing she could say that would make him stop ordering her around. She folded her arms over her chest. "What if I don't want to?"

"Would you stop being such a brat? This isn't about what you want to do. Now, go change, or you're going to make us late." He looked at her with no question that she would do exactly as he had said.

Finally she exhaled her frustration. It wouldn't kill her to go see Molly and Rick. Maybe she would even get the chance to talk to Molly about everything. With that thought, she started for the stairs.

"Oh, and wear something better than those raggedy jeans you wore last time. They look trashy."

Climbing even as she fought not to hear his comment, Danae stomped up the stairs. How dare he come in here and order her around like a six-year-old? Who did he think he was anyway? And why did he find something to criticize every single time they were together? Why did she even care what he thought?

She threw clothes around in the closet like they were in a tornado. Finally she pulled out her brown pants and light tan top. They weren't trashy. Anger flowed through her veins. She didn't treat him that way. What made him think he could treat her like that?

She yanked the top on, pulled on the pants, and grabbed her brown leather clogs. At the mirror, she jerked her makeup from the side drawn and slammed it down. It didn't matter with him. He always won. Always. She didn't have the strength to stand up to him permanently. He always came back, and she always let him.

As she arched her face to put on her mascara, her gaze snagged on her own reflection, and she backed up as she stared at the girl in that mirror. When was the last time she had really looked at herself? It must've been a forever ago because as she looked, she couldn't remember ever seeing this person before.

This person didn't look like a girl anymore. She looked like a woman. She looked like a woman who hated life, who wanted to find a way out, a woman on the edge of the abyss looking down and just waiting to be pushed into it. Her knees buckled on that thought, and she sat down on the bed. Still she looked.

Those eyes were so haunted and sad—so wary. She looked down at her shirt and pulled on it. Did even it look trashy? She had never thought so before, but now she wasn't sure. Numbness took over her body as she pulled that shirt off and replaced it with another more tailored one from her closet. The white set off her dark features, and the buttons pulled in the material at the curve of her waist.

She dressed slowly—her fingers working the buttons more from memory than from the messages coming from her mind. Once she was changed, she stepped back to the mirror. Those eyes held her attention. They wouldn't let her go. In them was a silent plea, "Please, help me. Get me out of here!"

Brushing that thought away, she finished her make up and then grabbed the hairbrush. However, the eyes were back. How had she missed how sad and scared they looked? Haunted by the memory of them, she finished her preparations just as she heard him yell from downstairs.

"Danae! Are you going to take all dang day? You're going to make us late again!"

As she looked at her own face in the mirror, she sighed softly. "We'll get out. I promise."

"Oh, Hawaii was so beautiful," Molly said, fawning closer to Rick even as the mashed potatoes were passed around the table. "Wasn't it, honey?" However, she didn't wait for his reply. "We even got to surf! Rick about killed himself trying to get on the board. It took him like 25 tries to just get standing."

Rick shrugged. "Hey, it's harder than it looks." He passed the potatoes to Danae who took them wordlessly. She put some on her plate and passed it on to Brandt.

"And the lava flows!" Molly continued unabated. "Oh! They are unbelievable. Just miles and miles of nothing but black."

Danae could relate. She had never felt so lonely. Fighting to get her stomach to stop being so queasy, she ate slowly. There was no reason for her to join the conversation. Molly was a non-stop vacation reel.

An hour later just before dessert was to be served Brandt wiped his mouth with his napkin and laid it next to his plate. He cleared his throat, which brought Danae's gaze to his face.

"If I could have everyone's attention," he said solidly, and all the gazes at the table went to him as the conversation ceased. "I know you've all been wondering what's taken me so long. Well, tonight I want to put those thoughts to rest."

Danae was having trouble following this little speech. Her mind at some point had drifted away from the conversation and was busy flying down the highway on the back of a bike.

Concern slammed into her as Brandt exhaled once sharply, pushed back his chair, moved it to the side, and stood over her. Her gaze stayed on him as her mind struggled to figure out what was going on. At that moment everyone in the room gasped as he dropped to one knee next to her chair. Her eyes widened as she watched him remove a small box from his jacket pocket. Again he cleared his throat.

"Danae, you know I love you. Marry me."

"Oh, Brandt!" his mother exclaimed. "That's so wonderful!"

For the life of her, Danae couldn't get a single word out of her mouth. Without hesitation, Brandt reached out, took her hand, gently slid the silver ring off the finger of her left hand, and replaced it with a diamond one. She just stared at it. She couldn't move. She couldn't think. In the next second, it was like someone had hit the fast-forward button on life as everything around her flew into action.

She was being hugged. Why she couldn't clearly recall.

"Oh, Danae!" Molly screeched. "Look at the size of that ring." She let go of Danae to hug her brother. "Well, little brother, you out-did yourself this time."

"Congratulations, Danae," Rick said, enfolding her in his arms.

She tried to say thanks, but nothing came out. And then it was Mr. and Mrs. Emerson enveloping her in hugs she wasn't sure she would ever recover from. When Mr. Emerson broke the hug, he didn't let her go. Instead he held onto her arms and with the goofiest smile she'd ever seen, he said, "Welcome to the family."

The family? Those words sent nausea swimming through her. She already had a family, and that one was almost more than she could handle. What in the world would she do with another one?

"This calls for a celebration," Mr. Emerson boomed when he finished hugging Brandt. "Let's break out the left over bubbly from the wedding!"

Something of a cheer went up.

"Oh, and we can eat dessert in the living room," Mrs. Emerson said.

"Mom," Molly said in disbelief.

"Oh, just this once," her mother responded. "We're just so happy."

It seemed that everyone around her was "just so happy" too. For Danae, however, happiness was about 73rd on the list of what she was feeling.

Somehow Danae made it through the rest of the evening. She was sure the shock had something to do with it because without it, she would've run screaming from the premises. When they were in his car and started back to her apartment, Brandt glanced over at her, a big smile on his face. "Surprised?"

She tried to get her brain to function, but that didn't work as well as she would have liked. "Yeah, stunned."

He reached across the seat and ran his hand over her shoulder. "I knew you would be." His hand retook the steering wheel. "So, I was thinking. We graduate in December, how about a January wedding?"

The nausea was back.

"I... I don't know. This is all kind of sudden."

His smile widened. "Just think, by next year at this time, you'll be Mrs. Brandt Emerson. Man, I like the sound of that."

Danae couldn't even respond. Every word was smashing into the "NO!" screaming through her head. At her apartment, she genuinely felt like she might be sick. When he opened his door to get out and follow her, panic surged through her. "You know, Brandt, it's really late, and Tara was wanting me to go shopping with her tomorrow. Maybe it would be better if you just come over tomorrow night or something."

"You sure? I could give you a back rub."

The thought sent chills up her spine. "Yeah, I'm sure. Call me." With that, she slammed the passenger's door and ran to the apartment. It seemed that all the air in the world had vanished. She couldn't get a good breath in. Safely in her apartment with the door locked behind her, she looked around. Nothing had moved. Nothing at all looked different. But things had changed. With that thought, she raced up the stairs, ran into her room, closed and locked that door behind her as well.

Feelings she had thought had been long since dead and buried rose in her gut pushing everything else out ahead of it as she stood with her back pressed against the door. There had to be something, somewhere that would get her out of this nightmare, something real to hold onto... She looked down at the computer. Or someone.

Her intent was to send him a message—sort of an S.O.S. However, when the computer fuzzed to life, something even better was there to greet her. She clicked on his message wondering when he had sent it.

Danae, Who doesn't deserve whom here? I've come to the conclusion that you must be an angel sent down to keep an eye on me. :) You must be an angel. Because no other word fits. Thanks for listening to my ramblings. Thanks for making them seem important. I needed that. But most of all, thanks for being you... You're the best you God ever made, and I'm so very grateful He chose to send you into my life. Peace & Blessings, Kalin

Through the streaming tears, she put her hands to the keyboard, then thought better of it. She reached down and removed the ring. Without really looking at it, she laid it to the side, just out of her line of sight. Even as she began to type, she whispered, "Thank You, God so much for Kalin."

It was completely crazy to even go check, Kalin told himself Thursday morning as he climbed the steps of the library. She hadn't written back. It had only been 12 hours. Still the chance that there could be a message waiting on that computer for him had kept him awake most of the night.

His body tingled with the feeling of being truly alive again. He hadn't felt that way since the first time he had set foot on Tennessee soil some eight years before. Life finally felt right. True he didn't know where he was going, but he was really looking forward to the journey there whatever road it happened to go down.

On the second floor, he chose a computer in the back and had his email program up in no time. His heart surged in his chest when he saw there was a new message from her, and a smile danced across his spirit. Had he been anyone else, he would've thought himself insane, and yet insanity felt so good, he never wanted to leave.

Clicking on the message, he sat forward, eager to soak in her words. However, instead of a screen full of them, there was only one line.

I have news.

In a heartbeat all of the excitement was gone. "I have news? What does that mean?" he asked the air in front of him. Fighting to keep the lurking demons that had suddenly shown up in his thoughts away, he clicked on Compose.

She had been up half the night crying and the other half working out an escape plan. Brandt would never understand, and no was not an answer he was used to hearing. Curled next to her pillow much later than she should've been on a Thursday morning, Danae heard the jangle of the email and jumped out of bed so fast, she almost hurled herself onto the floor when her foot caught on the sheets. Catching her balance on the chair, she stumbled into it and grabbed the mouse.

The Lane_K message at the bottom was simply more than she could ever have hoped for. She clicked on it and held her breath.

Would you like to elaborate, or are you trying to drive me crazy? K

With all the horrible things running through her head, Danae sighed. "Oh, Kalin, you're not going to like this."

As he sat at the computer terminal, his hand twisted the brown leather band on his left wrist back and forth. He sent up a silent, desperate prayer that she was home, that she had gotten the message, and that she would write back. Otherwise, it was going to be a long, long day.

Holding patience to him, he counted to fifty and then to one hundred. Then he took hold of the mouse and clicked it. The screen took an eternity to load, but when it finally did, he took a breath to say thanks to God for answering this prayer. He clicked on the message and leaned forward, breathing to steady himself.

I'm engaged... I think.

"Wh...?" The message pushed him back in the chair. A scowl dropped over him as he reread the message. Engaged? No! With that thought racing through him, he put his fingers to the keyboard.

The jangle untangled Danae enough to let her reach for the mouse. She sniffed once, her head resting on her knees. She hadn't felt like this since Gatlinburg... But she shoved that thought away to read his message.

How do you be "engaged... I think"?

Her legs uncurled. Well, he knew now. Whatever damage had been done was done.

Kalin's body was locked on full-motion. He sat forward. He sat back. He couldn't get comfortable. She was engaged. The ramifications of that ran through his mind, and he didn't like any of them. How could she say yes to a guy like Brandt? He was a pretty boy, all glitz, no substance. Surely she could see that.

After waiting as long as he possibly could, he reached over and checked the messages. With no hesitation he clicked on the new one.

Well, he asked... I didn't exactly say yes. I didn't exactly say anything, but his family was there, and I guess they kind of assumed...

Fury and disbelief burst through him. Oh, this guy was smooth—ask with the family around, that way she couldn't say no. Another thought rammed into that one. His fingers flew over the keys as if they were guitar strings.

What did you go out with him again for? Wasn't one trip through the mud enough?

Her insides wrapped around that question, and the tears started sliding down her face again.

I know. It was stupid. I just... I just can't tell him to leave for some reason. We have so much history together, and our families are so excited about us being together... How can I disappoint everyone like that?

Kalin's protective nature surged through him.

How can you disappoint yourself like that?

He was right, and she knew it. The problem was, it just wasn't that easy.

I don't want everyone to think I've been stringing him along or something.

So you're going to base the biggest decision of your life on what everyone else thinks? That's a quick trip to disaster, Danae. Haven't you been listening to anything we've talked about?

I have. I really have. It's just... I know, it's not easy for you to say, and it wasn't easy for you to do. But I'm not you. I'm not that strong.

Kalin read that, and a thought occurred to him.

So what did lover boy say when you told him you were going to take pre-med classes this summer?

Never before had one sentence hit her so hard. For a full minute, she couldn't even bring herself to reply. Finally, it was defensiveness that gave her the energy to begin to type.

His name is Brandt, and I haven't told him yet.

Kalin had figured as much.

Why not?

Because I don't think he will understand.

The woman he loves wants to chase after her dream, what's there to understand?

Danae read that message once and then again. It sounded so logical. It sounded like the most reasonable thing in the world, and yet as she set her fingers on the keyboard, she could think of no reply.

He couldn't help but think he should've just left well enough alone, said,

"Congratulations" and moved on. However, Kalin's whole spirit was surging through him with a power that wouldn't let him do that. It wasn't so much that he was jealous. It was more that he was afraid for her life—maybe not physically, but emotionally, and mentally, and spiritually. If she tied the knot to that manipulative idiot, she would surely live the rest of her days in a nightmare too horrifying to contemplate. With the last breath in his body, he would do whatever it took to make sure that didn't happen.

"Come on, come on, come on," he muttered when there was no reply after the fifth check. "Where did you go?"

Finally in frustration he laid his fingers on the keys.

The jangle of the email jolted her from her thoughts.

You deserve better, Danae. X-Better, remember? Not X-Worse. Please write back. K

It took all of the sanity she had left to get her fingers to type the message.

I hear you. I really do, but I'm telling you... It's so complicated... Everything is just so complicated.

Kalin read the words and shook his head.

Do you love him? Does he love you? If so, then it shouldn't be complicated.

There was no longer any accurate answers to those questions in her. She looked, and she saw a lot of things—memories, fun, growing up together. But as those faded into more recent images, the love she had thought would be there was just a gaping hole. She laid her fingers on the keyboard.

You know, last night I looked in the mirror... And someone was staring back at me. I'm not sure I even know who she is anymore...

His heart wound around the hurt in those words.

Don't you think you deserve a chance to find out? Or are you willing to live your whole life not knowing?

She read it once and then again. Shaking her head, she typed her message.

I don't know. I really don't ... Listen, I've gotta go. Keep yourself out of trouble for me, okay? God bless... Danae

His spirit jumped forward when he read the sign-off. "No! Danae, don't go. Please don't go…" Like a wildfire out of control, his fingers rushed over the keys.

She heard the email jingle to life as she pulled her oldest sweats from the drawer. Despite what she had told Brandt, Tara had never said anything about shopping today. Right now, a shower and a long cup of hot coffee sounded really good. Everything else would have to wait.

Kalin sent the first message and prayed. Five minutes later, he sent a second message. By the time he was typing the third message, panic had set in. Even in her emails, she sounded so distant, almost numb. His mind flashed back to that first night by the tire. That was exactly how she had sounded that night.

Anger and helplessness crashed in the middle of him. His gaze checked the clock on the wall. They were due for sound checks at Sevens in thirty minutes. Frustrated, he anchored his attention to the computer screen and banged out one final message before he traced his way back out of the library.

"God, please help. She needs You. I need You. Please, Dear Lord… I'm asking…"

Chapter 11

Her hair hung down in waterlogged tendrils. In sweats and no make-up, Danae padded down to the kitchen. Just as she got to the door, Tara sat up from the floor in front of the couch.

"Good morning," Tara said happily.

"Whatever."

"Gee, someone woke up on the wrong side of the bed."

Danae went into the kitchen, grabbed the coffeepot, and poured herself a cup, not sane enough to even be thankful that there was some already made. Without bothering to get anything to eat, she stalked into the living room and over to the couch where she collapsed. For a long moment she sat and watched Tara cutting and pasting things in a large binder.

However, when Tara glanced over at Danae, Tara's eyebrows shot for the ceiling. "What happened to you?"

The creases of her eyelids narrowed as she stared at her roommate. "Does it matter?"

The scissors fell to Tara's knee. "Of course it matters. What's wrong?"

Danae took a sip of the coffee and considered which question to start with. "How do you know if something is right?"

Tara tilted her head in confusion. "Right? As in right and wrong?"

"Right as in, don't let it go, don't screw it up, hold onto it for dear life."

Interest sparked in Tara's eyes. "Why do you ask?"

Again she took a sip of coffee to forestall her answer. "What if I told you I signed up for some pre-med classes for the summer?"

"I'd say, 'Woohoo! Half the rent will still be covered!'"

Danae scrunched her face. "Be serious."

"I am serious. Do you know how hard it is to find a good roommate? I looked for three semesters, went through two roommates from you-know-where before I got you. You really think I want to go through that again?"

Danae's face scrunched farther. "Hey, drama queen. Hello. We're talking about me here. My life. Remember?" The scowl softened. "Okay, irrespective of how this affects your life, what do you think about me taking some pre-med courses?"

Tara considered the question. "Well, I guess it would come in handy if one of your kids fell off the monkey bars or something—"

In a huff, Danae uncurled from the couch and went to get more coffee.

"What?" Tara asked clearly not understanding what Danae was so upset about.

In the kitchen, Danae took as long as possible to fill her cup. Then she walked back out and over to the couch although she didn't go around and sit down. Instead she leaned her elbows on the back of it. "What would you say if I wasn't doing it in case someone fell off the monkey bars? What if I actually changed my major?"

Shock jumped to Tara's face. "But you're only one semester from graduating! Why would you want to do something like that?"

Danae took a drink and then shrugged. "Because I've always wanted to do it, and if I don't do it now, I might never get the chance to again."

Tara looked positively dumbstruck. "What did Brandt have to say about that?"

Annoyance careening wildly toward anger flashed through her. "Why does everything have to come back to Brandt? Can't I make one decision without him being in the middle of it?"

Obviously afraid she was stepping into a minefield, Tara gazed at her. "Not if your decision affects him like this one would. Have you told him?"

Danae shrugged. "I tried... kind of."

"Kind of tried? And what did he say?"

"That he was glad I'd grown out of that stage." She took another sip of coffee as the anger heated to a boil.

The phone in the kitchen rang, and Danae set her cup on the table on the way to get it. She picked the receiver up on the third ring and had just enough presence of mind not to scream her "Hello."

"Danae! Oh, I'm so glad I caught you, sweetheart," her mother said, the words coming in a rush.

She leaned her back against the wall. "I'm here. What's up?"

"Well, first of all... you're a new aunt!"

A half smile slid to her face. "So she had them, huh?"

"A little boy and a little girl. Oh, Danae, they are just so precious. The most beautiful little babies in the whole world."

"And the fact that you're their grandma has nothing to do with that?" The melancholy in her spirit began to lift.

"Okay, it might have a tiny, little something to do with it," her mother admitted. "She had them at six-thirty this morning." Her mother launched into a detailed description of which came first, how much they weighed, how Nikki was doing, and when the doctors said they could go home. If she left a detail out, Danae couldn't have said what it was.

"Well, tell Nikki and John congratulations," Danae said. "I'm really happy for them."

There was a pause in the conversation.

"So, that's our news," her mother finally said. "But I hear you've got some news too."

She sighed. "You heard, huh?"

"Joan called me this morning. I kept waiting for you to call, but I just couldn't stand it anymore! Twins and an engagement in one day? This has to be the best day of my life."

"That's great, Mom."

"So, Nikki was wondering when you and Brandt would be coming. She'll be home day after tomorrow, but I think it would be best if you get a hotel. I don't think she'll be up to overnight guests just yet."

"Oh," Danae said, suddenly seeing Monday staring at her from the calendar across the room. She ran her fingers through her wet hair to push it out of her face. "I'm going to be pretty busy all next week. I don't know if—"

"Danae Rachel Scott. This is your sister we're talking about here. This is a once in a lifetime event."

Annoyance punched through her. "Well, Mom, I've got a life too, you know. I can't just drop everything for days at a time. It doesn't work that way."

"Nikki wants to see you," her mother said in that semi-childlike voice that Danae hated. "You can't spare 48 hours for your sister? Besides Nikki is as excited as I am. We want to see the blushing bride-to-be."

There's a great reason. "I'll look at my schedule. Maybe I can swing a weekend trip." She didn't mention the fact that she might be buried in homework by then. It seemed easier not to.

"Well, I'm going to be here for three more weeks. Then I'm going to have to get back too. So don't take too long to fit us into your schedule somewhere." It was a dig, and they both knew it.

"I'll see what I can do."

The tiny radio seemed to radiate music. It was turned all the way up. The small amp next to Kalin's leg was throbbing with the riffs ripping through it. That song ended and another started. He barely missed a beat figuring out what key it was in. Up and down the neck of the electric guitar he had borrowed from the band's equipment, his fingers jammed themselves across the strings.

Forgetting seemed like a great idea at the moment. Drowning out the thoughts was the second best thing he could find to do. As thoughts of her tried to get in, he played harder. His foot stomped out the beat, bouncing the floor of the small trailer.

Why hadn't she written back? Would she ever? How could she marry someone who didn't love her in anything other than name only?

The questions pounded through his body. He could think of nothing else to do for her. If she wouldn't listen to him, who would she listen to?

As that song ended, he reached over and snapped the radio off with one twist. Suddenly the only sounds in the trailer were the nearly imperceptible whir of the amp and the intense ringing in his ears.

It was time to get ready for Sevens. He'd have to take the car to get the equipment back to the gig, and that required a stop to get gas. Five dollars at a time—it didn't take long to run out again. Sniffing back the thoughts of how she was, where she was, and most depressingly who she was with, he ran his wrist under his nose and stood. It was stupid to have gotten so wrapped up in her so quickly. He shook his head as more depressing thoughts ran through it. Finally, he leaned against the sink, turned on the water, and splashed some on his face.

When he looked up, the tiny cross his mother had given him just before he left shone back at him from the windowsill. "God, Danae's in your hands now. I've done all I can do. Please give the right words to whoever can get through to her."

"I take it Nikki's a mom now," Tara said when Danae hung up and walked back into the living room.

"You guessed right. I'm an aunt. Woohoo." She dropped onto the couch, spun so she could lie down, and put her forearm over her head. "Life is unbearably wonderful."

This time Tara stopped completely, pulled herself off the floor, and sat down on the coffee table. "Okay, that's it. What is really up?"

~ Lucky ~

"What makes you think something's up?"

"Hello. You're down here in sweats at two o'clock in the afternoon. Your sister just had twins, and you're acting like a jerk. This isn't you. What's going on?"

As her thoughts went to the night before, tears stung the backs of her eyes again. "Brandt asked me to marry him."

"Oh, here we go," Tara said in annoyance. She looked at Danae, all seriousness. "You told him to go jump off the first moving train he could find, right?"

"I didn't *tell* him anything. It's just… I was sitting there, and he asked, and all of a sudden everyone was congratulating us, and how could I say no?"

Anger dropped over Tara's face. "He asked you in front of the family?"

"I guess he wanted them in on it."

"Of course he did, Danae!" Tara launched off of the coffee table and paced to the other side of it. "When are you going to wake up? He is so manipulative he should win an award."

"I figured he thought it would be nice."

"Danae, honey." Tara leveled a grave look at her. "Don't you get it? He asked you with the family there so you couldn't say no. More pressure to keep up appearances. Plus, I'm sure the news has spread halfway to Mexico by now."

"Virginia," Danae corrected.

Horror split through the anger on Tara's features. "He called your mother?"

Danae shrugged. "His mom did. Same difference. She knows now."

"Oh, man. This really is bad." With a long sigh, Tara sat back down and ran her hand through her hair. "I'm sure your mom told you to run the other direction."

"She loves Brandt, you know that."

"I was being sarcastic," Tara said as if Danae should've figured that out. "So did he give you a ring and everything?"

"It's up in my room. I took it off last night. I don't know. Everything just seems to be out of place with this thing. It just doesn't feel right."

"Well, that's something."

"What's that?"

"That it doesn't feel right. Generally you jump into these things like it's the best thing that's ever happened to you. You've got to admit he's got you on a very short chain, Danae."

"I'm not on a chain."

"Uh-huh. Right. He says, 'Jump.' And you ask, 'How high?'"

"I do not."

"You do too. Have you ever stood up to him with anything really important?"

The fingers of one hand wound around the finger of her left hand. In the next instant she sat straight up, panic surging through her. "My ring!"

"I thought you said you took it off."

"No, my promise ring! He took it off to put the other one on." She had hardly gotten the entire thought through her mouth before she was climbing the stairs. She didn't want Tara eavesdropping on this conversation. In her room, Danae closed the door, and straining to hold onto the last of her sanity, she sat down at her computer.

She yanked the phone from its cradle and punched in the numbers in a quick-staccato beat. "Come on, pick up. Pick up."

"Yyyello," Brandt said in his maddening greeting.

"Brandt, this is Danae. What did you do with my promise ring?"

"Your…?" He sounded confused. "I… I threw it away last night after I dropped you off. I figured, you know, you didn't need it anymore anyway."

Her spirit was alternating between ache and anger. "You threw it away?" she asked in utter disbelief. "How could you do that? That was my ring."

"You've got a new ring now, remember? Oh, and Mom said January would be fine with her, but she said you'll have to step on it to get any decent accommodations."

Danae felt like she was being strangled. "I've got to go."

"I guess we're still on for tonight, right? Dinner at Dan's house."

"I'm not feeling very good. I think I'm going to have to pass."

"But I told them we'd be there. What am I supposed to do? Tell them, Danae thinks she's better than you?"

"I said I'm sick," she practically yelled. "However you want to tell them that is fine with me." With that, she did something she had never done in her life. She slammed the phone down. Winding her arms over themselves, she threw herself back into the chair. Tara was right. He was a jerk.

Her gaze dipped to the ring still lying on the computer desk. It was the first time she had really seen it. The diamond was huge—gaudy almost. She would've rather had something much smaller. A lot smaller with a lot more love behind it would've been fine by her. The marquee diamond was set in a silver metal. It wasn't even gold. She'd always thought it would be gold. She'd always thought so many other things too.

As she looked at that ring and thought of the empty-shell of a relationship it represented, a tear slid out of the side of her eye, and she wiped it with her sleeve. How did this happen? How was she suddenly engaged to a man she realized only now that she didn't even know?

The phone next to her rang, but she didn't bother to pick it up. Instead she reached for the mouse and slid it across the screen. At first she thought she must be imagining things, but as she looked closer, she realized there were in fact four unread messages marked Lane_K at the bottom.

"Danae!" Tara called from the bottom of the steps. "It's for you."

Courage swelled in her chest. She cracked the door opened a half inch. "Who is it?"

"Brandt."

"Tell him I'm not here."

"But he knows you're here, I just told him you were."

"Then tell him you were wrong. I don't want to talk to him." With that, she closed the door. Rebelliousness slipped into her spirit. She clicked on the first message he had sent.

Danae, please don't go. We can talk about this... Please don't go. Write back. Please...

She clicked back to the home screen as the phone next to her rang again, making her jump. She looked at it and then set her attention on the computer screen. She clicked on the next message.

I'm sorry. I know I shouldn't have judged you like that. It's just that you've got so many dreams and hopes to chase. I don't want to see you throw that away because it would be easier. This isn't easier. It's a trap, and sooner or later you're going to see that. Please write back... K

Tara tapped on her door. "Danae?"

Danae sniffed the tears back as she wiped her eyes on her sleeve. "Yeah?"

"You mind if I come in?"

She reached over and flicked the doorknob. Uncertainly Tara took a step forward where she stopped and leaned on the doorpost. "That was Brandt, and he didn't sound too happy."

Danae's gaze never left the computer screen. "Did you tell him welcome to the club?"

"He said you hung up on him."

"Well, he's perceptive. You gotta give him that."

Tara's gaze dropped to the desk. She reached down and picked the ring up. "This the ring?"

Danae barely glanced up. "That would be the one all right." Her thoughts slammed into her promise ring, now in someone's trashcan, and her heart flipped over. "He pitched my other one."

In shock, Tara's gaze snapped to Danae's face. "He threw it away?"

"He said I didn't need it anymore."

"No wonder you hung up on him." Tara laid the ring back down, pushed herself off the doorpost, and walked over to the bed where she sat down.

Absently Danae was reviewing the old messages Kalin had sent rather than reading the new ones. She wanted her full attention to read those, but it still felt like she needed his words to hang onto. It was strange how even out of context they could make her feel so much better about life and about herself.

"You know, this is none of my business, but if you go through with this marriage thing, who are you doing it for?" Tara asked.

Danae read the message on the screen, her heart reading it in a new light.

I'd given up myself trying to be what they said I had to be to get the dream. The more I did that, the more miserable I got, so then I started finding very unhealthy ways to stop feeling miserable. I didn't even realize how miserable I was until the dream was gone, and all that was left was the lies.

"Everyone's going to be furious if I don't," Danae said like a ghost. "They all think we're the perfect couple."

"What looks good on the outside isn't always good on the inside," Tara said softly. "Besides, you can't throw your life away because somebody else thinks it's a good idea. You've got to make this decision for you... for Danae. Not for Brandt. Not for his family. Not even for your mother. This is about you, about your life. About what you want for you."

The phone rang, but neither of them moved.

"You should get married because you love him more than life itself," Tara said as the phone rang again, "because he brings out the very best in you, because he thinks the things you value are important, because he thinks *you* are important." The phone rang, but Tara continued. "It shouldn't be because you're too scared to find something real or because he tells you that he loves you. If he doesn't show it in the ways that it really matters, it's not love."

The phone stopped ringing, and Danae knew as she looked at it that she had no more than 20 minutes to make up her mind and to get on solid-enough footing with herself and the world to do what she had to do.

She stood up and turned to Tara. "Thanks. I needed to hear that. And now, I need to think about it. Okay?"

Tara looked at her uncertainly. "You going to be okay?"

With three quick nods, Danae smiled. "I'm going to be just fine."

As if the other band members weren't milling about, Kalin picked up the acoustic guitar and sat down on the little stool next to the microphone. The equipment was set up, tuned, and sound-checked. His thoughts, however, weren't on being on stage in two hours. They were on her.

Melancholy chords melted into gloomy riffs of notes. Sadness permeated his spirit. Helplessness enveloped him. He closed his eyes and let the music fuse with the feelings until they became one and the same. How long he played, he wasn't at all sure, but as his finger made the last note vibrato through his soul, the sound of utter silence around him slid over his consciousness. When he opened his eyes, no one around him moved. They all stood stock-still staring at him.

He tried to smile as if he hadn't just been a million miles away. A clap at a time the pre-open workers broke into scattered applause. He smiled slightly, set the guitar off to the side, and breathed. She would be a part of him forever. At that moment he was sure of that and nothing else.

Waiting for Brandt to show up after she had changed clothes, Danae sat down at the computer and clicked on Kalin's third message.

Change is scary. If it wasn't, people wouldn't try so hard not to. But what's even scarier is staying in a place that makes no sense for you. Don't give up on yourself because change scares you. Believe in what's inside you. Listen to what's inside you. It's trying to guide you to what's real, to what's right, to what's X-Better for you. Everything else is a lie.

She heard the pounding on the front door. Like a serene lake with gently undulating ripples, she stood from the chair, picked up the ring, and put it in her pocket. "Holy Spirit, all I need is the words. I'm ready to reach for something more. Just give me what I need to not let him talk me out of me." She took a deep breath and opened the door.

At the bottom of the steps, Tara stood at the door, her hand pressed against it. "Go away! She doesn't want to talk to you!"

"Tara, let me in this door right now!" Brant yelled, the anger and bitterness biting right through the door.

Tara's gaze snapped to Danae who was descending the stairs slowly. "What do you want me to do?" Tara mouthed.

"Let him in," Danae said placidly.

"Are you sure? He sounds hysterical."

"I'm sure. Let him in."

Shaking her head in concern, Tara flicked the chain off, clicked the lock, and swung the door open.

Brandt burst through the opening—a man possessed. "Where is she?"

"She's right here," Danae said, and both gazes jumped to her on the stairs. "I guess this means you came to talk."

He turned to her, hands planted on his hips. "You darned right I did. How dare you hang up on me and then not pick up! That's rude, Danae. Not to even mention putting your roommate in the middle of all this." He looked over at Tara, who looked like she wanted to run.

"Tara, why don't you go on up to your room?" Danae said as Tara carefully closed the door to the outside on the fight she had just admitted in.

"Are you sure?"

Danae nodded and stepped down the final three stairs into the living room. Tara's eyes conveyed the message that she wasn't at all sure that was a good idea.

"Don't worry, I know how to dial 9-1-1," Danae said, and there was humor in the statement.

Concern poured through Tara's face, but after a long pause, she acquiesced to Danae's request.

The second after Tara disappeared up the stairs, Brandt turned his full fury on Danae as his hands fell to his sides. "What was that 9-1-1 crack about? What do you think I am—some kind of jerk who's going to beat you up?"

"I didn't say that," Danae said innocently. She stepped past him, walked to the couch, and turned. "It's just I heard you trying to beat down our door, screaming so the neighbors could all hear, and then yelling at Tara. I figured it's better to be safe than sorry."

"You really think I would hurt you?" Brandt asked, the bravado falling from his voice.

"Would hurt me? You already have hurt me, Brandt."

He took a menacing step toward her. "That's not true! I've never touched you! Not once!"

But she stood her ground. "Physically, no. But you've beaten me up in plenty of other ways."

"What other ways?" he asked with sarcasm dripping from the question.

"Like pushing me to be things I'm not."

"Like what?"

"Well, a teacher for one."

"Oh, come on," he said, throwing his gaze over his shoulder. "We're not going to go through that again."

"Only once more," she said without malice. "For me this time." Her gaze dug into him. "It was easy, you know. To follow you here, to sign up for those classes because you said that would be smarter. It was easy to hang onto you because I was too afraid to stand on my own. It was easy to let you make all the decisions for me because then I didn't have to make them for myself. But I've realized that nobody can make decisions like that for someone else. It doesn't work that way."

"This is silly. You're blowing this out of proportion."

"Am I?" she asked. "How would you know what's out of proportion for me? You don't even know me."

He put a hand on his hip in annoyance. "Danae, this is stupid. We've been friends forever, how could I not know you?"

She took only a breath to steady the statement in her head. "Because I don't know me." With that, she reached into her pocket and pulled out the ring. "I believe this is yours." She took the three steps over to him and dropped the ring into his hand, which he held out before he'd fully understood what she was giving him.

He looked down at it in confusion, which fell into concern. Then his gaze slid up to hers. "You can't be serious."

She took the steps backward away from him and hooked her fingers in her back pockets. "I am serious." For a moment she debated whether to finish the relationship off or to leave it an open question. Her heart tore in one long rip as she let the compass in her guide her words. "And I think it would be better if we didn't see each other anymore—"

Fury melted into disbelief and confusion. "Danae, you can't do this. You can't break us up like that. What're my parents going to say?"

"I'm sure they'll come up with something," she said, hearing the names they would call her even from this distance. "I'm sorry it took me so long to tell you, but it wouldn't be fair to you to keep living this lie. It's just going to hurt everybody in the end."

His face had fallen into a desperate sadness that Danae really hadn't expected. "Come on, Danae. We can work this out. This... whatever it is... it doesn't have to be the end of us. We can get you help."

What should've been anger only registered as long-buried understanding. "It's me, Brandt. It's who I am. You can't fix that. I can only be true to it and trust that it guides me where I'm supposed to be."

"If this is about the night of the wedding..."

Danae shook her head. "You're not hearing me. This isn't about you. It's about me. For the first time since I said yes when you asked me out when I was a freshman, this is about me. It's about what I want, and you're not it."

"But how can you say that? We've been together so long? Jeez! We've practically been married for the last seven years. My family loves you. I love you…"

"That's just it. You can't love me. You can't love something that's not real." Her gaze slipped over him. "Don't you get it, Brant? It's a lie. I'm a lie. I was too scared to find out who I really was, so I just went along with what everyone else said I was. But it's not real, and a lie is not something you can build forever on."

"So you're saying that's it then? Just boom and we're over?"

"That's what I'm saying."

He looked down at the ring. "Well, what if I say I can't accept that? What if I don't want it to be over?"

"It's not your decision. It's mine, and I've made it."

Chapter 12

Actually getting Brandt out of the apartment hadn't been easy. He had begged and pleaded. He'd even threatened to make a scene if she threw him out, but in the end with the Spirit guiding her, she had successfully gotten him to leave without one. Long minutes after the door had closed, Tara tiptoed down the stairs to find Danae sitting at the table staring into space.

"He left?"

"He did."

"And you didn't go with him?"

"Nope."

Tara walked around the table and pressed Danae's head into her stomach. "I'm proud of you, you know that? That couldn't have been easy."

Danae sniffed softly. "It wasn't, but he was probably the easiest one to convince."

Sitting down on her heels, Tara took Danae's face in her hands. "You did the right thing. You hear me? You did the right thing." With that she wrapped Danae into her arms.

They had decided to watch the evening movie. After popcorn and a little Ben Affleck, Danae was feeling much better. She still didn't have a handle on where life was going, but she knew she was glad that what she was leaving behind was now in her rearview mirror.

At ten o'clock they talked about nothing in particular until Saturday Night Live came on. By the time it was over, Danae was exhausted. Emotionally and physically.

"Well, if I'm going to be up for church bright and early, I'd better go get me some shut-eye," she said as Tara turned off the television, plunging the room into darkness. Two steps and Danae's shin met up with the corner of the coffee table. She let out a yelp. "Yeow! Ow! Ow! Ow! Dang! That hurt!"

Behind her Tara was laughing. "What did you do?"

"Ugh! Who moved the coffee table?"

"Apparently not you, or you don't have a very good memory. You okay?"

Danae limped to the stairs. "Besides the fact that I can't walk now?"

Tara laughed. "Yeah, besides that…"

"Yeah, I'm peachy."

They climbed the stairs together, and at the top said good night. Danae went into her room, flicked on the light, and sat down on her bed where she pulled the hem of her jeans up high enough to be able to see the welt forming on her shin. Putting her hand over it felt good so she did that for a moment. Then her gaze went to the computer, and she wondered if anything important had come in. "Important," of course, had come to mean "Kalin."

Even as she thought it, her heart filled her chest. Kalin would never believe this one. She limped over to the computer, sat down, wrapped her hand back around her shin, and moved the mouse to start the screen. The email program was still open. The last Lane_K message at the bottom.

It was strange how comforting that was. Clicking on it, she pulled herself forward to read it.

Danae, I'm not going to try to talk you out of anything because you know better than I do what's right for you. I'm also not going to stop being here for you—whatever you decide. A friend deserves that much, and make no mistake about it, you are my friend now. Just take some time to really think about what you want—not for me, but because you deserve that too. No matter what you decide, me & God think you're the greatest! Don't ever forget that. Friends, Kalin

Gratefulness to him, coupled with gratefulness to God for putting him in her life, flowed through her. She might never be able to repay him, but she had to start somewhere. She laid her fingers on the keys. Words seemed so inadequate, and yet that was all she had to give.

Kalin could feel his spirit nose-diving. No matter what he did, he couldn't get a handle on it. Every time he thought about her, for one half-second his heart grabbed for joy, but in the next half second it fell flat back on the floor. Playing helped to take his mind off of it, and so as he played, he poured himself into the music, letting the rest of everything go in the pulsating beat. His fingers were like kamikaze pilots jamming into the strings. The place was rocking so loud, no one could hear his heart breaking.

When they took a break just past midnight, Kalin's hands were shaking from the ferocity of his playing. He pulled the guitar off his shoulder and went to set it on the holder.

"Man, you look like you could use a stiff one," Von said, noticing Kalin fumble to get his guitar into the stand.

It sounded better than he wanted to admit. "I'm going to run out and see if I left my other capo in the car. This one is giving me fits."

Von looked at him knowingly. "Something sure is. You want us to deal you in on the fun after the show?"

Scratching the back of his head, Kalin ducked. "Uh, no thanks. I've got to be getting home right after we finish up."

"Well, if you change your mind…"

Kalin didn't wait for the end of that sentence. He pushed out the back door, realizing only when he was five steps out that it was pouring rain. Not wanting to go back although he knew he should, he ran through the downpour to the car, hoping he had thought to put the windows up. He hated driving with them up. It felt claustrophobic. Sure enough, both windows were down, and the rain was pouring in.

In two motions, he was in the car with the door shut. Quickly he reached over and rolled up the passenger window even as the rain pelted down on him from the other side. Just as quickly he turned his attention to the driver's side window and cranked it. It was then that he realized how much his arms ached. They hadn't hurt that bad since…

He chopped that thought in two. With both windows up, he laid his forearms on top of the steering wheel and then laid his head on top of them. Exhaustion slid over him. How would he ever have the energy to finish tonight? He knew he only had a few more minutes before he had to be on stage again, but all he wanted to do was leave. If he just didn't go back, maybe he could outrun the demons dogging his heels.

It had been years since he'd wanted something so badly. One drink. One line. To be able to forget for a moment.

But he knew that one was never one. He knew as well that it was a trap. He'd been there too many times to not see it. Yet he felt like he was falling, inextricably toward it. As if gravity was pulling him in the direction he had fought so hard to pull himself away from.

If he just hadn't let himself believe that he had a chance with her, he could've gone on with his life as if nothing had ever happened. If she just hadn't emailed, if he just hadn't answered… A hundred thousand if's. The worst part was, even if she didn't marry the jerk, there was no way she would give Kalin a second look. She was a doctor—or she would be.

Doctors were special people. They didn't hang out with ex-druggies who played guitars. They only hung out with sophisticated, up-and-coming types with fancy cars and bank accounts. He looked around him, and it hurt to be honest with himself about where he really was in life. He wasn't up-and-coming. He was sitting in a car that only ran some of the time, hoping he'd make enough tonight to buy groceries that would last for the next few days.

Even if by some miracle he could get her to notice him for more than a friend, it was a given that she deserved so much better. All he had to do to see that was look at where they met. She was in her friend's wedding at a secluded bed and breakfast in the footprint of the Smoky Mountains. It wasn't the sort of place where people who buy day-old bread because it's cheaper get married. The fact that she was the friend of someone that wealthy spoke volumes about her family's financial well-being.

How could he compete with that? How could he ever live up to that?

As he sat back, his hand twisted the leather cuff around his wrist until it began to burn. He had to let her go from his heart. Somehow he had to let her go. "God, please, help me…"

The knock on his window startled the thoughts from him.

"Kalin, man! It's time to play! Come on." It was Carson who had been sent out to retrieve him.

"Okay. Okay. I'm coming," he said, crawling out of the car. It was the last thing he wanted to do.

When Danae woke up at 1:32 in the morning, she squinted at the clock. She'd been having a dream. At first she really couldn't remember it, but then as she lay there, her mind began to play it back. It was a dark street, and there was something… no someone standing there telling her… What? She tried to pull it up because it felt so important.

"You can't have him. He's mine again," the voice from the depths of the dream rasped through her, and she sat bolt upright.

Kalin. He was her first thought, and instantly she knew he was in trouble. She jumped out of bed, raced to the computer, fuzzed it to see if there was anything there. Her heart thumped forward when squinting she saw nothing new. She stood, looking at Lane_K on the screen, her heart thumping in her chest. He was in trouble. Real, serious, spiritually-deadly trouble. Her gaze slid around her room as she tried to decipher her options, which weren't many.

She didn't even know where he was, but the dream and the feeling of terror for him were too real to ignore. Seeing no other option, she knelt on the soft carpeting by her bed.

"Oh, dear Lord, this makes no sense, but I really think Kalin is in trouble. I don't know why, but I think the devil thinks he's vulnerable right now. Please, dear Lord, please, send your angels to protect him. Send them in droves. He needs you, Lord. He needs Your help and Your protection. He needs You to stand between him and the forces of evil. Do not let them get near him. Keep them away. Help him, Lord…"

She had never felt more panicked in her life. The urgency didn't pass even after she had prayed, so finally she grabbed her Bible, flipped on the lamp on her nightstand, spun and sat on the floor. She opened the Bible, and let the words flow through her in one solid stream of prayers to heaven.

The crowd had thinned almost to nothing by the last call at just before two a.m. Waitresses in skimpy outfits criss-crossed in front of the stage bringing out the last rounds. Kalin bent his head over his guitar. He didn't need to look at his fingers to know where they were and where they needed to go, but he kept his gaze down lest his mind betray him with thoughts of other things. Those drinks and those girls promised so many things he'd thought he had learned were lies. He had thought they didn't bother him anymore, but now they were back.

At two, they played the last note, and in the next minutes the band was departing the stage.

"Jeez! Preacher man, you look like death warmed over tonight," Von said. "I'm telling you, I know something that can help. Me and some of the guys scored some good stuff. It'll cure whatever ails you. You're welcome to join us."

Exhaustion engulfed him. He was so tired of fighting it. His eyes fell closed, and he had to will them back open. That offer was whispering through him, telling him just once wouldn't hurt, telling him it would be all right just one more time.

Pain and fear surged through Danae again, and she redoubled her prayers. "Dear God, please be with Kalin. Please don't let Satan get close. Give Kalin the strength to turn away—no matter what." She lay flat on her back on the bed, looking at the ceiling. She had been awake for more than an hour, praying and listening to the rain. It drummed incessantly on her window. It should have been soothing, but it wasn't. Every time she closed her eyes, Kalin's face was right there, and she knew without knowing how that he was in trouble. Worry dug into her gut. "Please, God. Put Your hand on him and lead him to safety. Kalin needs Your help, Lord. Please, send someone to help him."

"I really think I'd better be getting home," Kalin said, sanity's tug clinging to him desperately.

"Oh, come on," Von said with a laugh. "We've even got a few girls lined up and waiting. Carson'll share. Won't you, Carson?"

Carson was already gone, but Von apparently didn't realize that. He put a bony hand on Kalin's shoulder as if they were best buds. "It'll be fun, hanging out. Besides, you look like you could use a line or two."

The way of the serpent is death. The phrase brought Kalin's senses back to him in a rush, and he shrugged off Von's hand.

"I'm going home. I'll catch your act tomorrow night," Kalin said, barely throwing the words over his shoulder. He grabbed his jacket and pushed out the back door into the downpour that continued unabated. Throwing the jacket on and then hiking the collar of it up, he ran for the car and dove inside. His lungs pulled in air in gasps. Had he just had a little less resolve, there was no telling where Von would be leading him right now. "Thank You, God, for getting me out of there."

He reached down to start the car, but when he turned the key, nothing happened. Once again he turned the key. "Oh, no, please. Don't do this to me now." He wrenched the key, willing the car to start. But it was deader than highway pizza. With the palm of his hand, he hit the steering wheel with a force that reverberated through him. For a second he looked back at the club door but dismissed that idea with a slow shake of his head.

Seeing no other option, he popped the hood and went out to assess the situation. Rain spattered off the hood as he lifted it. With his hands up on it, he stood, looking at the mass of cables and metal swathed in darkness, and he knew his half-semester in wood-shop fifteen years before wasn't going to help much. When the understanding that it was hopeless crawled through him, he leaned his head back so that the raindrops could splatter their cold fingers across his face. "Why me, God?" he yelled into them. "Why me?"

At that moment, a car's headlights sliced through the rain and over his car. Kalin turned to it, praying it wouldn't be anyone Von would hang out with as the car rolled to a stop parallel with his.

"Car trouble?" the voice from the driver's side asked. When he leaned down into the passenger's window, Kalin recognized Rhett.

Leaving one hand on the hood, he turned. "Yeah. It won't start."

"Well, I'm not much of a mechanic even when it's not raining. Why don't you get in, and I'll take you home?"

Kalin walked closer to the passenger's window, which was nearest him. "Oh, I couldn't ask you to do that."

"You didn't ask. Get in."

Standing in the pouring rain over a dead car out of pride seemed ridiculous. So owing someone else won out over pride. He went back to his car, slammed the hood, strode back to Rhett's car, and got in. The heater was on, and he had never been so thankful for warmth.

"Where to?" Rhett said as if he was the chauffeur.

"Olsen's KOA on Music Valley." He knew he was dripping on the soft, tan leather seats, but there wasn't much he could do about that.

With a nod, Rhett put it in drive and headed out of the parking lot. "I'm surprised you're not with your buddies."

"Buddies?" Kalin asked, the lethargy lifting. "Oh, the band? They're not..." He cleared his throat. "We just play together. It was a mutual thing. They needed a lead. I needed a job."

The look Rhett turned on him was one of skepticism. "With the way you play? You could get a job with any band in town. What are you doing hanging around with that bunch for?"

Kalin appreciated the compliment, but he shook his head. Some of the strands of wet hair followed his movement. The others clung to his face like vines on a fence. "It's not that easy. You've gotta have connections. People don't want to hire a no name. It's tough enough finding a band to front that has some kind of reputation."

Rhett turned through an intersection and headed out into the deepening darkness. "You want the reputation they have?"

"No, but Zane... well, he's been trying to find someone else." Kalin shrugged. "Nothing's worked out so far." His hand went to the leather on his wrist, and he twisted it. "Believe me, Silver Moonlight was not my first choice."

"So, you're not happy with them then?"

Kalin snorted. "No. But I'm stuck with them until something better comes along."

They pulled into the trailer park, and Kalin's stomach flipped over at the understanding that Rhett was about to see where he lived. Even Zane didn't know for sure how minute-to-minute he was living.

"That's it," Kalin said, pointing to the peeling gray of the little fifth wheel.

Wordlessly, Rhett pulled up to it and stopped. He looked out the front window to the trailer illuminated by the headlights. "You know, maybe it's none of my business, but you've got more talent and more sense than most of the people in this town put together. You've got to know that this," Rhett waved his hand at the trailer, "is only temporary. Just keep your head on your shoulders and keep working at it. Somebody's going to stand up and notice, and all this will just be a memory."

Rhett looked right at him although Kalin couldn't bring himself to look at the older man. "Take it from somebody who's seen some of the good and a lot of the bad in this old world, God's got a plan for you, Kalin Lane. You've got too much going for you for that not to be true."

The rain was beating down on the top of the car, and Kalin knew he should leave. However, sitting in that car felt like being in his parents' home, and for one more moment, he didn't want to let that go.

"I wish it wasn't so hard to remember that sometimes," he said softly.

"It's all a matter of where your focus is," Rhett said. He looked back out at the trailer. "If your focus is on the fact that you're holding on by your thumbnails to something that could be gone tomorrow, it's tough to remember that things could ever be better. But if you're focus is on the fact that your life has already been bought and paid for by Jesus Christ and that all He wants is to work through you and that if you just trust that, He will work miracles in your life for you and for others through you, then remembering becomes a no-brainer because you're not the one doing it anymore. He is."

There seemed to be no question in Rhett's eyes that Kalin would know exactly what he was talking about. Kalin wondered about that but was too taken with Rhett's words to say it. Besides, another thought had already overtaken that one. Kalin looked over at him. "How did you know I was stranded tonight?"

Rhett smiled peacefully. "I didn't." He pointed to the top of the car. "He did."

"But you were the one who came and got me," Kalin persisted.

Rhett laughed. "I didn't know I was coming back for you. I was already on my way home when I remembered my wife wanted me to bring her reading glasses that she'd left in my office. At first I thought, 'She'll get over it.' But something kept telling me I needed to go back." The story wound to a stop, and then Rhett glanced at Kalin. "The second I saw you standing out in the rain, I knew why He had me forget and why it was so important to go back. I guess you could say you were my assignment."

"Well, I'm glad you showed up because going back in to ask Von for help was not something I was thrilled about."

"And so God pressed me into service," Rhett said.

"Lucky you." Kalin glanced at him curiously. "Mind if I ask you something?"

Rhett smiled knowingly. "What's a guy like me doing owning a bar?"

"Yeah."

"Well, I love music. Never could play to save my life, but I just love it. And I love being around people who are having a good time. My daddy owned that bar until he passed on, and I decided that's what I wanted to do, too. I get to enjoy the things I love and let other people enjoy them too. Plus, I get to give a real shot to young musicians like you—just like I'd seen my daddy do all his life. If I told you some of the names he helped put on the map, you'd know 'em. It's what I love to do. It's where God put me."

"But it's a bar," Kalin protested. "It's not like it's..."

"Church?" Rhett asked when Kalin didn't finish the sentence.

"Well, yeah."

Rhett exhaled and sat for a full minute before answering. "Let me tell you a little something my daddy told me a long time ago. He said, 'Rhett, the Lord is where people invite Him in. It has nothing to do with being in a church. Sunday mornin's nice, but if you don't have Him with you the rest of the week, you're missing the point altogether. It's not about you going to visit Him once in awhile or even about you trying to fit Him in somewhere, it's about giving Him your life and seeing what He wants done with it. If you do that, you'll find God everywhere you look, in every single person He puts in your path—no matter where you happened to be.' You know what? My daddy was a smart man."

"So, you don't go to church then?" Kalin asked, getting even more confused.

"'Course I do," Rhett said. "You take a coal out of the fire and put it on the cold hearth, it's going to go out sooner or later. A man's gotta be in the fire, getting hot, so he can share that heat with the world around him. I go to church to soak up the heat, but I remember to take it with me when I walk out them doors."

The words spun in Kalin's head. He was trying to do that, and yet he'd always kind of wondered in the back of his heart if he was kidding himself, if the life of playing music could really coexist with a life of living with God.

"Do you really think God has a plan for me?" Kalin finally asked.

A small smile spread across Rhett's face. "I sure do. Think about it. You're apparently important enough for Him to have me up at all hours of the night, running around in the rain to get you."

Kalin laughed with him. "Well, thanks. I don't know what I'd have done without you."

"It wasn't me," Rhett said. "You thank Him, and we'll both be evened up."

As Kalin reached for the door handle, he nodded. "I'll be sure to do that." He jumped out of the car. "'Night. Thanks!"

Rhett waved once as he backed up out of the little driveway. Kalin noticed the car then. It was nice, fancy. Something a star would drive. He thought about Rhett and decided it couldn't have belonged to a nicer guy.

The rain had slowed to a miserable drizzle, and Kalin strode through it to his front door. Once inside he pulled off wet layer after wet layer. He didn't even want to think about how long he would've been out there had Rhett not come along. As he dressed for bed and climbed up onto the mattress, he thought again about what Rhett had said. Maybe his dream of making music and living with God weren't such strange bedfellows after all. Maybe God could use even his music, the kind of music he loved—though not called Christian—to make the world a better place. Maybe it didn't have to look a certain way or sound a certain way or have Hallelujah in every other sentence to be able to touch someone's life. Maybe the music God had given him had a purpose too.

He had never really believed that. He had always thought it was inferior in God's eyes. Now he wondered. If Rhett had taken what he loved and used it to help others, no matter if it was what the world thought of as Godly or not, wasn't it possible that he could do the same with his music? "Okay, God," he said to the darkness. "Whatever You've got in mind, I'm listening."

Chapter 13

Danae had no idea what time she had finally fallen asleep. It must've been sometime around 3:30 or so because that was the last time she had looked at the clock. However, the second she opened her eyes on Sunday morning, the sight of the lamp's light next to her brought the memories back with a snap. Still knowing it was all she could do, she closed her eyes. "God, please keep Kalin safe today. Hold him in the palm of Your hand, and lead him where he needs to go. Amen."

Although it was after 3:30 in the morning when Kalin had finally fallen asleep, he was up and headed to church by ten o'clock. He and the Big Guy upstairs had some serious things to discuss, and the coal story hadn't been lost on him. At the church, he slipped into a side bench and knelt down. His scraggily hair fell around his face, blocking out the rest of life. "Listen, God, I know You were looking out for me last night, and I know I wouldn't have made it without You. So, today, I'm breathing and waiting. Show me what You want me to do."

It took all the way to the end of the service for his first assignment to show up. As Kalin followed the crowd out, he noticed Jesse slouching up the aisle. His shoulders seemed to heave together as if he was lifting something very heavy. He didn't look like the Jesse that Kalin knew. For one moment Kalin's mind said he was the last thing Jesse needed to deal with today, but with a whack, he knocked that thought away from him. "Excuse me," he said to the ladies in front of him as he stepped past them. "Jesse!" He continued sliding through parishioners until he was nearly shoulder-to-shoulder with his friend. "Hey, fancy meeting you here again."

When Jesse looked at him, his face sallow and pained, Kalin's heart fell.

"Man, are you all right? You look horrible."

"I'm making it," Jesse said, but there was no enthusiasm in that voice.

Kalin considered taking that as a stay-out-of-my-business hint; however, the sadness pouring through Jesse's face wouldn't let him. "Is something wrong? Did something happen?"

It was clear that Jesse hadn't realized he was going to be asked, and for six steps he said nothing. Finally with barely a glance at Kalin, he said, "I got a call this morning."

"Is everything okay?"

Jesse took a ragged breath, and his eyes fell closed for a second. "They took my mom in for emergency surgery last night."

"Ah, man. Is she all right?" They walked by the preacher without really seeing him.

"Yeah, I guess so. Her appendix burst. Scared Dad to death. They said she's going to be fine, but…" Jesse shook his head, and the strands of wavy, long, black hair swung with the movement. "We were playing last night. I didn't get the call 'til this morning." He took a long breath to steady his voice. "I'll tell you, that's the hardest call I've ever gotten. I mean, she could've been gone like that, and I wouldn't even have gotten to say good-bye or nothing." Jesse sniffed although there were no tears.

"But she's doing all right now?" Kalin asked, his concern for his friend growing.

"Yeah. As well as can be expected, I guess. I just wish I was there, you know?"

"Where's 'there'?"

"Nevada." Jesse shook his head again as they stopped under the trees outside the church. "I really wish I could go and see her. Everybody else is there, but I just… It's already been a year, and I haven't been back." He breathed out slowly to corral the emotion in his voice. "But I can't leave. We've got gigs tomorrow night and Tuesday in Memphis, and there's just no way…"

The idea ran through Kalin's mind like a wildfire. He didn't know how to say it or if to say it. However, seeing Jesse in this state, all he wanted to do was help. "You know if they need a fill in guitar, it's not like I've got anything lined up the next two nights."

Jesse looked at him, and Kalin's courage faded.

"I mean, not that someone could just step in for the great Jesse Ralston like that, but…"

"You would really do that?" Jesse asked.

Kalin laughed softly. "Hey, you know me, I'll play for squirrels if they'll listen."

"But you don't know the songs."

Kalin shrugged. "So, I show up a little early, and we go through them. There can't be more than a couple. Right?"

"Four," Jesse said.

"And I'm sure you've got demos of most of them," Kalin said.

"They're on CD."

"Like I said. So I take the CD home, go through them on my own, show up a little early, run through them with the band. You go to Nevada, and everyone's happy."

"You think you can pick it up like that? It's only one day."

"Hey, Jess," Kalin said, leaning in. "This is me we're talking about here."

The memory of jam sessions that lasted well into the next day slid across the memories of the two men.

"I won't let you down," Kalin said. His memory slow-played through the end of the tape with Jesse. It was filled with more broken promises and lies than he cared to count. "I know that's probably hard to believe, but I'm not the idiot I used to be."

"You were never an idiot," Jesse said. "You just got caught up. It's easy to do when you don't have nothing else to hold onto."

"Yeah, well now I do." Kalin's gaze traveled back to the church and up to the steeple. Once again he thanked the Lord for pulling him out of the fire the night before. "So, what do you say? I'll do whatever you think is best." As he watched Jesse considered the idea, Kalin's mind said he should feel at least anxious if not downright agitated. However, all he truly felt was peace. Whatever Jesse decided, it would be the best—X-better—because it would be what God most wanted to happen.

"I've got the CD in my truck," Jesse said, and Kalin nodded. "Why don't you take it home, listen to it, see what you come up with? We can meet tonight, and go over it. If the band thinks they can make it work, then we'll do it. Fair enough?"

"More than."

When Danae got back from church, she checked her email box again. There were still no new messages, and she was beginning to get worried. As she sat down at the computer to type a new message to him, she sent up a prayer from the middle of her heart. "God, please be with Kalin. Please…"

It wasn't the electric guitar he should've used, but with his electric not to mention the amp back at Sevens and no way to get it home, Kalin had to settle for the Fender. He didn't have time to be picky. They were scheduled to meet with the band at five. If all went well, Jesse would be on the plane out to Nevada by nine. That left just four hours of practicing for the biggest audition of his life. He popped the CD in the little player and queued up the first song.

As it played, his fingers found the key first and then began picking out the notes. It wasn't a particularly fast song, so it wasn't too hard to tease out the guitar parts that added the filler to the rest of the band. He couldn't be sure that what he was playing was Jesse's part, but his mind recorded the music on his soul just the same. Never would he have thought that in this situation he would be able to relax. Yet that's exactly what was happening. It was like his mind opened up to soak in the chord progressions and the way the notes fit together. It was like playing a symphony he had never heard before.

Danae had done every single thing she could think of to keep herself busy all day Sunday. She cleaned her room, sorted her closet, prepared her things for the next day. She even made a trip to the grocery store after church for a new notebook and some pens. Her books would be purchased in the morning after the first class. It wasn't the best set-up, but it couldn't be helped.

When she sat down at her computer at four-thirty, depression dropped over her. He still hadn't written back. She had known that whatever it was, was bad, but she hadn't thought he would actually stop writing. "Dear Lord, please be with Kalin, wherever he is. Please guide him and give him whatever he needs today. Amen." With that, she typed out a short message and then went down to eat dinner with Tara.

"This is Kalin," Jesse said by way of introduction to the other members of Phoenix Rising. "Kalin, this is Rob."

Rob, a tall guy with dark hair and large hands, stepped from behind the drums to shake Kalin's hand. "Nice to meet you," he said in the deepest voice Kalin had ever heard. Kalin just nodded, intimidated into wordlessness.

"This is Orin." The base guitarist, a guy only a couple inches taller than Kalin with longish dark hair plastered to the sides of his head and sporting tattoos everywhere, didn't look overly pleased to be there but shook Kalin's hand anyway and then went back to working on his guitar.

"This is Adrian," Jesse continued as Kalin turned to a young looking

Spanish guy. "He plays fiddle and sings back up. He's our pretty boy. Don't get between him and the ladies, you might get trampled to death."

Jesse laughed at his own joke. Kalin shook Adrian's hand. He was obviously much younger than the others, maybe early 20's. He wore a cross on a chain at his neck just over the black ebony of his T-shirt, and Kalin had to push away the thought that no guy in Silver Moonlight would've been caught dead wearing a cross.

"Nice to meet you," Kalin said to Adrian who ducked his head shyly. The dark waves of his jet-black hair flopped forward.

The keyboard player, a guy who would've been menacing for his height and breath save for the easy smile, stepped up.

"Steve is over on keys," Jesse said.

"Glad to meet you, Kalin. We've heard a lot of good things about you."

Even as he shook Steve's hand and nodded, Kalin wondered what good things there could be. He didn't remember many, and he couldn't tell how Jesse could either.

Steve turned back for the keyboards and started making sure they were hooked up and working.

Finally Jesse turned to the last guy left. "And this, is Colton, our lead singer."

The lead singer looked like he could've just stepped off a hay trailer. He was just taller than Kalin but considerably heavier. The bent and mangled cowboy hat he wore looked like it had been chewed up and spit out by some kind of farm machinery. When he made it to Kalin, he swiped the hat off his head to reveal closely clipped blonde hair. He shook Kalin's hand firmly. "Thanks for coming on such short notice, man."

"Hey, don't thank me yet," Kalin said as his hand fell back to the two silver chains linked to the wallet in the back of his jeans. "You may want to throw me out once you hear me play."

Remarkably the others laughed. That was new. Von and his bunch usually just looked at him like he'd fallen off the planet Fluton when he tried to make a joke.

"Well, we'd better get started so Jess can make that plane," Colton said, replacing his hat and backing over to the microphone stand. He didn't pick up an instrument, so Kalin assumed that meant it was the band with a front. That was okay. He didn't mind not being the lead. He was just glad for the chance to play with someone other than Von and the crackheads.

The practice area was a converted garage at the back of one of the guy's house. Kalin couldn't remember which guy. His head was swimming with chords and words and fingerings—not to mention names. He grabbed the electric that Jesse had brought for him. His was still locked up across town at Sevens. This one was ten times nicer than his, the silver edging the sea green caught the light, sending it scattering in all directions. As the others tuned up and got ready, he pulled the strap over his shoulder, adjusted it, and ran through a couple of riffs he had memorized during his crash course in the Phoenix Rising repertoire.

His head was down checking out the strings, watching his fingers, listening for something out of tune when suddenly he picked up the understanding that the other noises around him had stopped. Heat rose into him as he glanced up only to find six awestruck faces staring at him. "What?" he asked without taking his fingers off the tuning key at the top of the guitar.

"Dang, Jess, you said he could play, but you didn't say he was good," Rob said from behind the drums in that booming voice that seemed to shake everything.

Jesse shook his head. "Man, them five years were good for your fingers."

Embarrassment dropped over Kalin, and he shook his head. "Could we go through the tracks like they are on the CD? That's how I learned them."

"Whatever you say, man," Colton said, staring at him wide-eyed. "Whatever you say."

Danae's last evening of freedom was slipping away, and all she wanted to do was to know where Kalin was and if he was all right. The dream the night before had really spooked her, but she had convinced herself that it was just the effect of an overactive imagination. However, all day and into the evening, every time she thought about him, she said a little prayer. There was nothing else she could do.

It hadn't taken long for the band members of Phoenix Rising to decide that Kalin would make the cut. They said good-bye to Jesse with a hail of "tell your mom we said, 'Hi's'." When Jesse walked over to Kalin, Kalin held his hand up and caught Jesse's topside.

"You take care of yourself on that plane, you hear me?" Kalin said.

"Thanks," Jesse said, and from the look in his eyes, Kalin knew he meant more than for just that comment.

"No problem, man. Hurry home."

With another wave to the rest of the band, Jesse headed out.

"Let's try, 'From the Ashes,'" Colton said, retaking the mic.

Kalin nodded, suddenly realizing that this was really happening. He tipped his neck one way and then the other. *Please help me remember, Lord. I may be in over my head here.*

The drum clicks behind him set his fingers in motion. They danced across the strings up the neck and back down. Held and then danced again. It was always awesome to play, but to play on an instrument that sounded like a dream was even sweeter. He was glad he had worn the lightest blue-gray T-shirt he owned because the room was getting hot. It could also have been that he was burning energy by the sackful as he played, but he didn't think about that. It just registered that sweat beads were forming on his forehead and starting to slide down through his hair.

He tossed them away with a flick of his head and dove headlong into Phoenix Rising's hardest rocking song. Colton started singing, but Kalin was paying more attention to the waves of music beneath that voice. They blended together into one cohesive harmony. Ducking and weaving through the lyrics, the notes intertwined so they formed a sort of substance of their own, carrying the lyrics along on top of them.

Then as the instrumental break hit, Kalin released the rein he'd had on his fingers and let them fly. His part was over in eight bars, and he backed his volume off for Adrian to saw the same melody out on the fiddle.

Kalin's smile couldn't be contained. This was just flat, all-out, no-holds-barred fun. It was more fun than he'd had in so many years, he couldn't count them all. Adrian finished, and Kalin took up the melody again just long enough to have it before he tossed it back to Adrian with a flick of the guitar neck.

At the last whine of the fiddle, Colton jumped in, and the lyrics again soared over the harmonies underneath. Adrian stepped to the mic to provide the back-up harmonies, which blended perfectly with Colton's. It sounded like they'd all been playing together for years.

The words flashed to a close, and with one more head-spinning trip up and down the neck of Kalin's guitar, the band hit the first stinger. The vibrato under Kalin's fingers sang out loud and clear as he turned to the other guys and with a downbeat of his head, they hit the final stinger, and the song was over.

Had there been a crowd of ten thousand in front of them, the band members couldn't have been more excited.

"Man, that was awesome!" Colton said, forgetting he was so close to the mic so that the statement echoed off the walls. They all laughed.

"One more time," Rob called, clicking the sticks together, and before Kalin had a chance to take a breath, the music was pouring through him again.

Yes, this was without a doubt more fun than any human being should be allowed to have.

The phone rang at a little after nine, but Danae didn't bother to pick it up. It would be for Tara anyway. It quit ringing, but she hardly noticed as she sat, reading back through Kalin's previous emails. Something was wrong. He would've written by now.

"Danae! It's for you!" Tara yelled from the bottom of the stairs.

"Got it!" she yelled back. She reached over and picked up the phone, still reading the email about stepping off into the darkness. Nothing in her was at all certain that tomorrow morning she would either step on something solid or learn to fly. From this vantage point, it looked more certain that she would crash mightily into a hundred thousand pieces. "Hello?"

"Tell me I didn't just get a phone call that you've thrown your life away," her mother said with all the histrionics that only her mother could add.

"Oh, hi, Mom."

"Don't hi Mom me. Joan just called me. Have you lost your mind?"

It was strange. Danae hadn't thought of Brandt since he'd walked out that door 28 hours before. "No."

"Well, it sure sounds like it to me. Joan said you gave the ring back. Why would you do something so stupid? You had him, Danae. In the palm of your hand. What could've possessed you to give that ring back? Have you completely lost your mind?"

"Mom," Danae said, cutting into the diatribe. "Look, I don't expect you to understand, but this is something I have to do for me."

"For you? Are you crazy? You had a great life right there…"

"No, Mom. I didn't. It wasn't the life I wanted."

"The life you wanted? It was the life every sane woman dreams about, Danae. The handsome guy with the nice bank account and good prospects. What more could you possibly want?"

"Love? Respect? Understanding?"

"Danae, he's a guy. He's not God."

Danae's gaze fell to the screen, and the words "me & God think you're the greatest" jumped out at her. Tears formed in her heart before she realized they were there. He was the greatest guy she'd ever met, and now she had no idea where he had disappeared to or how to contact him…

"Brandtly Emerson is the best thing that's ever happened to you," her mother continued. "Not to mention to this family. I will not let you throw that away for some silly little girl dreams of love and romance. Get your head out of the clouds. This isn't fantasyland. You've got to get practical here. Haven't I taught you anything?"

"Yeah, Mom," Danae said, but didn't mean it quite the way it sounded. She was looking at the email about going for X-Better. "Listen, I've got to go. I've got some things to get ready for tomorrow."

"By the way," her mother said, "why aren't you at home? I've called there and left messages for you to call me."

"Oh," Danae said, her gaze falling to the desk. "I'm... I signed up for some classes this summer."

"Classes? I thought all you had left was student teaching in the fall."

Danae could hear the screaming even before she said the words. "Yeah, well, I signed up for a few pre-med classes just to..."

"Pre-med?" her mother shrieked. "Danae Rachel Scott, what has gotten into you? This is insanity. You have a future—your future, and it's waiting for you. Stop acting like a spoiled brat and get on with it."

"With what, Mom? With the life you and everyone else planned out for me? What if that's not what I want anymore?"

"How can you know what you want? You're only 24-years-old, Danae, and look at you. By the time I was 24, I had two kids and your Daddy had bailed on us. Now, you listen to me. Love looks real pretty on the outside, but it ain't nothing more than a trick of some hormones. Don't waste your time looking for it. It's time to get practical. It's time to grow up and realize that life doesn't hand you these opportunities every day. You've got to grab them before they are gone."

"I'm not you, Mom."

"No, but you're about to make the biggest mistake of your life just like I did if you don't go apologize to Brandt. He's a nice guy, Danae. In six months he'll have his degree, and the two of you will be set for life. Now, please... could you get reasonable and call the poor boy? Joan says he's heartbroken."

It was difficult to picture Brandt heartbroken. He was probably out celebrating with Fagan and Dan.

"I'll think about it, Mom. Listen, I've got to go. I've got some other calls to make."

Her mother sighed. "Danae, please. I'm asking you to be reasonable. Call him. Say you're sorry. It won't kill you."

"Bye, Mom." Danae pulled the phone from her ear and held it long enough so that her mother didn't think she had hung up on her. Then she gently lowered it to the cradle.

Call Brandt and apologize? She would rather jump out the window with it closed. Her mother would never understand. Neither would anyone else. As that thought slid through her mind, her gaze caught on the screen. Knowing it was pointless, she clicked on the New button and put her fingers to the keyboard.

Sweat was pouring off his hair, which looked like he'd been standing in the rain for an hour, but Kalin didn't care. When they hit the final stinger for the last time on "From the Ashes," he knew life would never get any better than that. *X-Better*, he thought, and her face drifted through him. This was X-Better—at least.

"Well, I think that does it," Colton said, turning to the others. "Anybody got anything else they want to go through?"

All around heads shook no. It was clear that the others were as exhausted as Kalin was.

"Cool, then we'll meet at the Memphis Coliseum at four tomorrow to do sound checks. We go on at 6:30. Anything else?"

Again the heads shook no, and with that, the rehearsal broke up.

"Man, dude," Colton said, walking over to where Kalin was pulling the guitar off his shoulder, "where did you learn to play like that?"

Kalin shrugged as he looked around for the guitar case. "It was a gift."

"Well, the Man upstairs must've given you a double helping." Colton followed him around the amps where Kalin laid the guitar in the soft inner portion of the case and snapped the clasps together. "You're band's got to be crazy to even let us borrow you."

"Oh, well," Kalin said, not sure how much Jesse had told the others, "I don't think they'll mind, so long as I'm back by Thursday."

"Hey, Kalin," Rob said in that booming voice as he extended his hand. "Thanks for coming, man."

Kalin shook Rob's hand, wishing everything about him didn't feel so sweaty. "Thanks for letting me come. It was fun." He pushed his fingers through his hair and realized it was drenched as he felt.

Adrian walked around them and over to his fiddle case. "Ten to one Jesse hits the slots the second he gets off that plane."

"Would you blame him?" Colton asked.

"Didn't say that, I said I bet he does."

Colton laughed as he pulled a cough drop from his pocket, unwrapped it, and popped it in his mouth. "Our luck he'll hit it big and say to heck with all this."

"Well," Steve said, coming around the amps and into the conversation, bringing his large presence with him, "we'd be in good hands if he did. That was some mighty unbelievable playing out there." He clamped a large hand on Kalin's shoulder and squeezed, which buckled Kalin's knees.

"Thanks," he said, ducking out from under the hand. The guitar was safely put up. It suddenly occurred to him that he hadn't eaten in more than 12 hours. He even felt thinner than he had when he arrived. "I'd better get going."

"Yeah, thanks, Kalin," several of them said simultaneously.

He waved the hand that sported the band of leather. "I'll catch your acts tomorrow." With that, he strode out of the garage and over to his bike. Riding was almost not even necessary. The way he felt, he could fly home.

Danae had read every email twice, and the thought of him brought a knifing pain through her heart. He wasn't writing back because she'd told him she was engaged. That thought tore through her. If she just hadn't been so stupid to tell him, he wouldn't have left. The only thing that kept her from getting totally frustrated with herself for messing up their chances was the nagging thought that maybe something had happened to him. It was such an odd feeling, to know and yet not really know, that she didn't quite understand what to do with it.

As she crawled in bed, the daunting new life facing her when the sun arose again didn't even cross her mind. Instead, she said a prayer for him, for his safety, and then she hugged her pillow and fell asleep.

Kalin knew he should be sleeping. He was exhausted to the point of not being able to keep his eyes open, and yet there was a song drifting through him, playing dodge ball with his spirit. He would catch phrases here and there, but it wasn't any more than that.

He had done this before, laid in bed late into the night, listening to the music in his soul. And he knew that more often than not, the iridescent beauty of the music dissipated with the morning sunrise. If he didn't write this song down, it too would be gone like so many others before it. This one, however, was too important to let it slip into oblivion. He might not ever even get to play it for her, and yet he had to write it down—just so his own soul could remember their time together.

He didn't want to ever forget the moments he had been in her presence because he knew those moments were what had pointed him in the direction of the X-Better that he was living at this very moment. Sure it had to do with playing with Phoenix Rising, but it was much more than that. It was the feeling that it was not just all right to be the man God had made him to be, but that he was finally living the life God had meant for him from the very start.

The guitar strings hummed under his fingers as the phrases sprang to life through his voice. He shook his head at how incredible they felt coming out of his soul, and with everything that he had, he wished at that moment that she could be sitting there listening to his heart. It was the only thing that would take X-Better to X-Best.

Chapter 14

Monday flashed by like a dream for Kalin—between getting ready and then making the three-hour drive. It seemed he hadn't so much as taken a breath before he was standing with the other members of Phoenix Rising, ready to go on stage with more than 8,000 screaming fans anticipating their entrance. Okay, they were anticipating the entrance of the big name who came on after the band they warmed up for, but it was still 8,000 people.

Kalin's heart thudded like the gallop of a racehorse. It had been a lifetime ago since he'd played for so many people, and that time he didn't really appreciate it. This was more like stepping out into something totally new. As his mind thought that, it bumped into a face, and he smiled in spite of the nerves. *When you step out into the darkness...*

The lights in the auditorium plunged to black, and he and the others took the stage as the crowd cheered.

"Please welcome, Ace Nashville recording artists, Phoenix Rising!"

Rob's clicks ignited a fire burst from Kalin's fingers, and screams of appreciation flooded the auditorium as the lights flashed to life behind them. Adrian joined in on the fiddle, and in the next heartbeat they were flying.

"So, how was biology?" Tara asked as they sat at the dinner table over macaroni and cheese.

"Good."

Tara surveyed her as she chewed the soft pasta. "You don't sound too happy about that."

Danae shrugged. "It would be nice if everyone didn't think I was completely nuts."

"I don't think you're nuts. I think you've got a lot of guts."

Danae sighed and pushed the yellow concoction around the plate sullenly.

"So, are you going to tell me what's really bothering you or not?" Tara finally asked after the silence threatened to engulf the whole room.

With one glance Danae measured her friend's tolerance level. It was a given that her mother—not to even mention Brandt—would flip out if they knew about Kalin. Where Tara might stand on that issue was a whole other subject.

"Is it your mother?" Tara asked.

"Kind of." Danae looked at Tara squarely then, trying to decide. "Do you promise not to tell anyone?"

Tara laid her fork down obviously sensing this was big. "Of course."

Once again Danae sighed. "Remember that guy... the one who brought me home from the wedding?"

Tara's eyebrows shot up and then knitted in concern. "Yeah?"

With her fingers, Danae pushed her hair up and back. "Well, we were kind of emailing each other last week, and then he kind of disappeared."

"Dis..." Then Tara's gaze registered understanding. "When he found out you were engaged."

"Yeah," Danae said, wishing she hadn't said anything.

"Did you tell him you're not engaged any more?"

"I tried. But he won't write me back."

After a long minute, Tara sighed. "Well, I wish I could tell you he probably will, but..."

"Yeah. That's what I thought." Danae picked up her plate and stood. "I'm not very hungry. I think I'm going to go study." She took her plate to the kitchen and dumped her portion back in the pan. She could always eat it for lunch tomorrow after class. Once her plate was in the dishwasher, she walked back out, having no intention of continuing the conversation.

However, before she got halfway to the stairs, Tara said, "Does anyone else know about Kalin?"

Danae turned to her, and the knife of knowing she would never see him again slid through her heart. "No."

It was midnight before Kalin got back to his trailer. He wished with everything in him that he could think of an all-night something that would have an Internet connection. She probably thought he had totally forgotten about her by now. Of course, nothing could be further from the truth. What he wanted most of all was to tell her about tonight, to tell her how it felt up there on that stage, to share that with her.

He thought and considered and thought again, but he could come up with no way to get that message to her. Taking a last look at the clock lying on the table, he promised himself that tomorrow morning he was going to be at the library doors when they opened. This was too important to put off even one more day. "God, let her know I'm thinking about her, and keep her safe for me."

When Danae woke up Tuesday morning, she couldn't really explain it, but somehow she felt better. Peace had replaced a good measure of the depression, and she got her things together to head off to the campus for her 7:30 class.

Kalin had meant to leave by 8:30, but it was nearly 9 when he finally got on the road to the library. The wind whipping past him sent his spirit flying. The sunshine warmed every part of him, and one thought kept drifting through him—it was good to be alive.

At the library, he pushed through the second door, nodded hello to the lady at the counter, and climbed the stairs two at a time. The pull of those computers was incredible. They were like a giant magnet to his soul. He chose his favorite one, back in the corner, and went through the requisite steps to pull up his email. When it finally came up, his heart took a giant leap forward as the three messages from D_Scott flashed onto the list of incoming emails.

It took less than ten seconds to delete everything else. There wasn't another thing that he cared about. Excitement pounced on him when he clicked the first message. He sat forward to read it. The hand that managed the mouse wrapped around the leather wrist cuff on the other wrist. He twisted the leather band in anticipation of hearing from her again.

Dear Kalin,

Well, it was probably the hardest thing I've ever had to do, but it was something that I had to do. I gave the ring back.

Kalin closed his eyes for a long minute just to praise God for that simple intro. When he had absorbed that news, he opened his eyes and slid closer to the front of the chair as his gaze scanned back and forth trying to read faster.

If I had been honest with myself, I had known Brandt and I were doomed for a long time. He didn't see life the way I saw it, and I don't want to see it the way he does. Everyone is going to think I'm crazy. And you know what? I think am, too. I'm crazy about having the chance to find out what's real in my life. I've never been this excited (or this scared!).

I have to thank you so very much for giving me the gift of listening to my heart instead of to what everyone else was telling me to do. It means more than you will ever know. And just so you know, me & God think you're pretty great yourself! ;) Peace to you, Danae

Gratefulness and relief poured through Kalin as he sat back for one minute to give himself time to take in what he'd just read. So she had called it off. Good for her. It was another step toward real. He hiked himself up off the chair back, clicked Home, and then clicked her second message.

Dear Kalin, You're probably going to think I've totally lost it, but I have a real feeling that something is not right in your life. I had a horrible dream last night, and it really got to me. (And I'm not normally one who gets worked up about dreams) But this one was about you, and it wasn't at all comforting. Please write back so I know you're okay. Please... Until then, I'll be praying for you. Danae

Worry for her slid through his consciousness. Whatever she had dreamt wasn't good, that much he could tell from the terseness of the message. She even sounded scared in her words. But what kind of dream would upset her like that? He clicked back to the Home page, and his gaze scanned down the page to the date attached to that message. Sitting forward his hand went to his mouth as his head worked out the math details. It couldn't be.

However, every single time he worked back through the dates, he kept coming back to Saturday night. The feeling of standing in the rain, the hopelessness covering his spirit, washed through him. She had been praying for him? Even when she didn't know what was wrong. The air dissipated from around him, and his lungs had to work to find more.

He remembered the headlights of Rhett's car, and his heart flipped over. There was a reason Rhett had come back, and that reason was staring back at him from the depths of a computer screen.

He considered typing a reply right then, but his spirit simply couldn't wait to read her last message. It took three clicks to pull it up on the screen.

As expected the whole world thinks I'm crazy. My mom just called and told me I'm "throwing my life away," and that I should "stop being so silly." I can't tell you how much that hurts. I feel so alone right now— like there isn't one single person in the whole world who understands why I'm doing this. They don't realize this is the hardest thing I've ever done in my whole life. I keep thinking, What if I'm making a mistake? What if I should just go back and play it safe? It sounds like death itself, but I'm not sure I can do this on my own.

I know that you're mad at me, and I know that I don't deserve your friendship after springing the whole "I'm engaged" thing on you, but I would really appreciate it if you would write back—just so I know you weren't a ghost I dreamed up one night. Danae

Kalin's heart flipped over inside him. She thought he had abandoned her, that he hadn't so much as thought about her since their last conversation. He shook his head at that thought. Before one more minute went by, he had to correct that horrible misunderstanding.

Danae had an hour break between Biology and lab. The day before she had gone to the Student Union Building; however, it was too noisy to get anything meaningful done. So on Tuesday she chose the relative quiet of the computer lab. It was more like the library but much closer to the buildings her classes were in. She sat down at a computer and slid forward on the little mat.

There was reading to do, but as ridiculous as it sounded, she wanted to check her email just one more time. If he was going to write, today would be the day. It took more effort than normal because she had to pull it up from the server rather than her own inbox. Her mind worked through the steps, glad for something to do other than wondering what in the world had happened to him. It was like he had just dropped from the face of the earth. She was still saying a silent prayer that nothing horrible had actually happened to him when she finally got tapped into the server.

Her heart caught. She couldn't remember if his last message was on the bottom on her computer, but on the top of this list there was a message from him. Knowing that it wasn't new and yet hoping it was, she clicked on it.

Danae, I have not forgotten about you, nor am I mad. (Are you kidding?!)

She almost laughed out loud in joy and relief. He was alive, and he wasn't mad. It was too good to be true.

I'm so sorry I haven't written back. Like I told you, I have to get my email at the library and with gigs from Thursday through Sunday, I don't have a lot of time to get over here.

Of course, she should've thought of that. Weights that seemed to weigh thousands of pounds lifted from her soul. It felt wonderful just to breathe again.

You wrote that you thought about me Saturday night... Well, as insane as this sounds, I needed every prayer you sent up. I was really having a tough night, and then my car broke down, and it was raining, and all I wanted to do was find a way to make it all go away.

Danae's heart caught in her throat. "Oh, no."

But then a guy I know showed up and pulled me back from the hell I was staring into. At the time I thought I was lucky, but now I know it wasn't luck. My angel was watching out for me again ;)

Her heart soared as tears burst into her eyes.

Please don't ever think I've forgotten about you. Believe me, angels like you don't come along every day, and I'm going to hang onto this one God gave me for as long as possible! I've also got some more news, but I'm going to send this so it doesn't get too long. Take care of yourself for me. God bless! Kalin

Without hesitation her fingers were on the keyboard.

Kalin had just clicked SEND on his second message when he realized he had a new message at the top from her. In that instant he felt the connection to her snap together in his soul, and utter joy poured through him. He clicked on her message to read it.

Dear Kalin, I am so glad you're all right! I've been so worried. Believe me, you've had plenty of prayers coming your way because that was all I could think to do. As for me being an angel, well... I guess it takes one to know one. What's your news? I can't wait to hear. Danae

With two clicks and a twist of his wrist cuff, Kalin started typing.

Danae's spirit surged through her like a bolt of lightning when she realized he had written back. He was there. Somewhere in Nashville, he was sitting at a computer right now. That understanding did more to settle her concerns about him than anything else could have.

I'll tell you what... Your prayers must have a direct link to God because I've had the most amazing two days of my life! The short version is that I'm filling in for a guy I know with another band. They've been together quite awhile and have really made a name for themselves. It's only for two gigs (last night and tonight), but man, I had forgotten how much fun it is to really play. We're playing in Memphis, opening for a couple other acts. But it's just so awesome, being on stage again, kicking it with guys who aren't stoned out of their minds—or wishing that they were. It's hard to explain, but when I'm playing and I don't have to worry about who's about to screw something up, it's like the rest of the world just drops away... I know that sounds weird, but it's the only way I can describe it. I'm sending this now in case you happen to still be there.

~ Lucky ~

*Thanks for all the prayers... you will never know how much they helped.
Kalin*

When her message came into the library, Kalin read it like a hungry lion devouring the best meal of its life.

It's like you're flying. D

Happiness burst through him.

I couldn't have said it better myself! K

You did say it yourself—remember? ;) But I know exactly what you mean. Biology2 is like breathing. I have taken so many classes in the last two years that were like pulling my fingernails out with a scissors I had forgotten what I ever enjoyed about learning. It's so cool! D

That's completely awesome! It sounds like you're where you're supposed to be. K

Sounds like that makes two of us... D

Yeah, for one more night anyway. Then it's back to SM. Oh, joy.

Do you not think if God can handle getting you in with this other band, that He can handle getting you out of the other when the time is right?

Okay, good point. It's just that last night was so much fun! And then I look at going back, and ugh!

But maybe it will make you appreciate it more when you get out of ugh!

How did you get so smart? K

I don't know because last month I was in ugh too—except I was too dumb to realize it.

Sometimes it takes a trip out of ugh to know that we were meant for more.

Well, it's time for me to take my trip out of ugh... I've got Bio lab to get to. Please take care of yourself for me, and write back when you can. I guess I'll just have to learn some patience with this library thing...

Patience. What a concept! Peace out, Danae

Kalin read her message and then read it again because he knew there wouldn't be another one coming any time soon. He looked at the clock and knew he only had a few minutes himself. Colton had offered to drive him to Memphis, which meant gas money he didn't have to spend. Quickly he set his fingers on the keys and typed through the thoughts in his heart.

It was only the second day of lab and already they were cutting something up. To Danae everything about biology was just cool. The most amazing thing was how intricate and precise even a plant had to be to live. It had to have the right temperature of water, the right amount of oxygen, the right amount of sunlight, or its fragile little body would disintegrate.

As she worked dissecting the flower in front of her, her thoughts turned to how fragile all of life is. Every living thing has a life, and although she could learn the intricacies of it, it could never really be explained just by understanding how it worked. There had to be something there. Something that made it live. She smiled at how close God seemed all of a sudden. It was almost like He was telling her this was where she was supposed to be. She suddenly felt more alive than ever, and there was one person she couldn't wait to share that feeling with.

Kalin met Colton at his apartment across town. Although he never would've asked about riding with someone, he was really glad Colton had suggested it. Three hours on the road one way was not his idea of fun. Plus, his car was still sitting in the parking lot of Sevens so that meant making the drive on the bike for the second night in a row, which wouldn't have been a pleasant option.

Colton and Adrian were waiting for him when he pulled up although he was at least fifteen minutes early. He swung his leg off the bike, pulled off his helmet, and stowed it away. Checking himself once more to make sure he had everything, he strode over to the jacked-up, bright red, extended cab pickup where Colton and Adrian were leaning, obviously deep in a discussion.

"Hey, guitar-man," Colton said, holding up his hand when Kalin got close. "You ready to make some music?"

"Ready as I'll ever be." He shook Colton's hand upright.

"You take shotgun," Adrian said, yanking the back door open and climbing inside. Kalin considered protesting, but Adrian hadn't given him a chance to get anything out of his mouth. So he reached up to the handle and jerked his own door open. The climb inside was nothing to be sneezed at, and he wondered how Colton did it on a regular basis. The pickup itself wasn't overly new, nor overly nice, but it was about 50 steps up from his car—literally and figuratively.

Colton flipped his cell phone onto the seat as he got in. "I just talked to Jesse. He'll be home tomorrow night. He says, 'Hey.'"

Kalin nodded although the news pulled his spirit down a notch. He pulled his seatbelt across his body and snapped it. "That's good. So his mom's all right then?"

With a tug on the gearshift, Colton backed out and headed for the highway. "Yep. She's coming home tomorrow. Then he's got a flight back."

Again Kalin nodded. His hand slid over the leather wristband as his gaze took in just how high up off the road they actually were. The feeling of being out of place drifted over him. What was he doing here? He didn't even know these guys really. Colton with his hayseed quality. Adrian with his good looks and well-dressed nature. They were going to think he was some kind of a freak. He was sure, with their clean-cut appearances, that someone with his long hair and scruffy clothes screamed out on the edge, doing drugs, one half step from falling through the rabbit hole. It occurred to him that maybe he should've cleaned up a little more for this gig.

But then he heard the voices from so long before. "Oh, Kalin, this is so you…" "Your hair is too long, and those clothes have got to go…" It had been the first volleys in a war he ultimately lost. His spirit coiled around itself as he tried to banish the nagging memories.

Colton coughed twice and cleared his throat. "Stupid allergies." He reached for the air controls and readjusted them. "Oh, man, Adrian, have you heard that new song Ashton Raines just came out with?"

"The one with the fiddles?" Adrian asked, pulling himself forward in the seat so that he was leaning in between them. "It's awesome. And the harmonies…" He sang a few words, and his voice sounded like it had wings.

Kalin's attention turned from thoughts of himself to the conversation. Only instead of adding spoken words to it, he picked up the lead vocals like it had been written for him.

"Take my hand. Take my breath. Take my ring. Take my life…" The singing stopped as they mentally waited for the instrumental, and then Kalin picked up the lyrics as if the music was in fact backing them up. "I used to think that heartaches ruled the world. I'd played the game, made mistakes, got some breaks, and watched my life unfurl..." Adrian's harmonies blended right in to perfection. "Never knowing, never feeling, never hoping, never healing... Then you touched my heart and nothing's ever going to be the same... So take my hand..."

Colton's voice joined in—not as lead but supporting Kalin's as well. "Take my breath. Take my ring. Take my life..."

Memphis was sure to be the shortest three-hour trip of Kalin's life.

When she got home, Danae raced up the stairs, threw her books on the bed and dove into the chair without bothering to close the door. He had written. She knew it. A click and then another and the email was on her screen.

Dear Danae,

It took only that to make her heart jump with excitement and joy.

I could never tell you in words what your friendship has meant to me. It seemed like before I met you, I had all this stuff in my head—like God and wanting to live for Him, and wanting Him to be in my life—but I couldn't get it all straight because everyone else seemed to think I was crazy when I talked about it. So I finally stopped talking about it. Then I felt like a traitor to myself and to Him.

I can't explain it really, but since we've been talking, I don't feel the pressure to say or not to say whatever about God to everyone else anymore. I can just kind of have it as part of my life, and when it shows up, I know it's X-Better time. Maybe that's because I know there is one person who doesn't think I'm crazy. :) I honestly couldn't tell you where my life is going right now. Things just seem so chaotic and unfinished, possible and yet so far out there that I can't really see them, but I know He has a plan. I'm hanging onto that now. I'm even kind of excited to see what that plan entails. But what's really cool is having a friend to share my journey with, and having a friend who is willing to share her journey with me. Do you know how wonderful you are to me? If you don't, YOU ARE WONDERFUL, DANAE! Don't ever change! God bless & keep you,& may His dreams for you come true! Blessings, Kalin

They had sung until Kalin thought his head would spin with all the lyrics drifting through it. In Memphis, they pulled up in the back parking lot next to the trailers and buses for the main act.

"How can one person need so many people?" Colton asked in awe as they watched the myriad of roadies and crew milling about.

"Are the other guys meeting us here?" Kalin asked, looking around the parking lot as Colton parked.

"They're always late," Adrian said. "That's why we tell them we start thirty minutes before we actually do. That way they get here on time."

Kalin laughed. He'd tried that trick with his sister before. Careful not to sprain an ankle on the jump, he got out of the pickup and walked around the front. "So we're sound checking?"

"Yeah, after they get finished." Colton swung the heavy metal door to the Coliseum open. He choked back a cough and shook his head at Kalin as he put his hand to his throat. "That pollen is wicked."

They walked into the backstage. The music pouring from the speakers out front vibrated the concrete under their feet. Together they walked to the tiny dressing room with the masking tape label saying 'Phoenix Rising' on it.

Kalin's gaze snagged on that little label, and with everything in him, he wished that this wasn't going to end in four hours.

It was a mutual decision to stay until after the last act was over. Only then did they begin the arduous task of loading everything into the trailer. Stopping only to ask where they wanted things, Kalin dug into the task of loading. Guitars, cords, amps—it was unbelievable how much stuff the band had accumulated. Their next appearance would be at the end of the week in Kentucky. They were headlining the Thursday evening of a fair.

He kept himself from thinking about Thursday. It was just too depressing to know he wouldn't be on stage with them. When all the stuff was loaded and checked, the group split into their respective vehicles and headed back to Nashville in a tiny convoy.

"Wake me up when we get there," Adrian said from the backseat as he leaned his head against the window behind Colton and kicked his feet up on the bench seat.

For ten minutes after that, they drove in silence. Kalin's thoughts drifted back to the stage, and his fingers beat out the songs of their own volition. *How long do I have to wait, God? I want to be a part of this, with a band like this. I want to be around people who care about something other than getting high and making out. Why are you making me wait?*

Depression dropped over him. It felt like an anvil weighing down his tired spirit. He glanced back at Adrian who was breathing softly, obviously already asleep. Had it not been pounded into him that you do not go to sleep when someone else is driving, he might have joined Adrian. Instead he leaned back and tried to get his thoughts to settle on something other than the useless wishes in his heart.

Colton started to reach over into the glove box but then stopped. "Would you grab me a couple of cough drops out of there?"

Thankful for the distraction from his thoughts, Kalin popped the box open, dug through it, and handed Colton the entire package.

"Thanks. Man, I wasn't sure I was going to make it through tonight." He pulled two cough drops out and popped them into his mouth, a cough raking over his throat even as he did so. "I hate allergy season."

"I can imagine," Kalin said, feeling sorry for Colton.

They drove for another mile or so.

"You know, I hope you don't think this is a weird question," Colton said, cutting through the hum of the tires, "but how did you and Jesse end up in such different places? I mean from what he told us, you were both in the same band. You were both right there, ready to crest the top… what happened?"

Kalin thought back to that time, and his spirit dove further. Had it not been for the darkness surrounding the pickup, he never would've had the courage to answer. However, it gave him just enough distance to remember. "Jesse always had his head screwed on tighter than I did. He was one of the band. I was the one up front. The one everyone just knew was going to make it. When I fell apart, it fell apart—for all of us. Jesse had enough sense to get out before there was nothing left."

"Because you had to go back," Colton asked. The statement was punctuated with another sharp cough.

"No, because all the stupid things I was doing finally caught up with me," Kalin corrected. "Jess tried to warn me, but everyone else just wanted to get high and have fun. I just wanted to forget everything—the pressure, the loneliness. I wanted a way out. Jess finally had enough and quit just before it all went to hell." Kalin shook his head. "I wish I had gone with him."

The memory of Jesse standing at that door as Kalin cut lines on the little mirror played through his brain. They had been friends, but at that moment the only thing Kalin cared about was how high he could get how fast. The fact that Jesse was the only friend left in the friendship at that moment slid through his mind, and his heart snagged on that thought. He turned his face to the darkness beyond the pickup windows. It hurt to remember, to think of all of the people he had hurt in his obsession to get away from himself, away from the unrelenting understanding that nothing other than the drugs mattered anymore.

"Yeah, that stuff all looks so good from the outside. It looks like so much fun if you don't know the truth," Colton said. "But people don't see the fathers who come home drunk as a skunk with a bottle of whiskey in one hand and insanity in the other. Believe me, I've been there. I know. It's hell."

Kalin's gaze went over to Colton's face, but Colton didn't return the look.

"My dad was like that when I was growing up," Colton finally said as he reached down to adjust the heat. Then he unwrapped another cough drop and popped it into his mouth. "Everybody else thought he was so great. And you know, he really looked the part—dressed up nice, had a good job, kept it together, until he got home, man... I've never understood how somebody can be two completely different people."

"It's easy," Kalin said softly. "You're one person—that either you hate or that everybody else says isn't good enough—so you try to be somebody else, and pretty soon you're not even sure who that is anymore. Then the drugs or whatever you're doing to not see what's going on takes over, and you lose you altogether. You don't even want to know who you are anymore because being spaced out is so much easier... or at least that's what you tell yourself." He was having trouble breathing.

"But it's hell on everybody around you." The anger in Colton's words sliced through Kalin, and regret sifted through his spirit.

"It's hell on you too," Kalin said as his elbow found the window edge. He laid his chin in his hand. "But once you're there, once you've gone that far, the thought of having to dig yourself out of the hole you're in is even worse than the thought of losing yourself to the lies. Digging requires work, and if you were willing to do the work in the first place, you would've done what it took to stay out of that hole."

"But you made it out," Colton said. "Didn't you?"

It sounded more like a real question—as if Colton wasn't wholly sure that Kalin wasn't still in that hole.

"Yeah, but it was the hardest thing I've ever done in my life. And the real truth is, I didn't do it. I couldn't. It got so bad that I finally had to realize I couldn't do it by myself. I had to ask for help. I had to admit to myself and to everyone else that I was screwing up everything by trying to do it on my own. I had to let go of thinking the success or failure of me was about me. It wasn't. It never had been. It was about Him. Honestly, He was the one who got me out because if it was up to me, I'd probably still be trashed out in some ally somewhere. Either that or dead—which really isn't much different."

"Did you ever wish you were dead?"

"Every day. But really I was dead. I mean that's not life. I hated life. I hated everything about life. I wanted to get away from it so bad I did anything I could to get there."

"But Jesse said you had a contract," Colton said. He coughed again. It seemed he couldn't get more than a few words out without them choking him. "You had so much to live for, so much to be excited about."

Kalin shook his head. "But I didn't have me."

"I don't understand."

"When the whole world is telling you that you have to be something you're not… when you buy into the belief that who you are isn't good enough, that what you are has to be changed to something you don't even recognize, all the contracts, all the money, all the fame in the world don't feel like you thought they would. Rather than admit that, it's easier to make everyone think you're enjoying the heck out of it just like they think they would be if they had what you have. But that doesn't make you happy. It just makes you start looking for the exits—anything that will get you out of the misery of pretending."

Colton thought about that a long moment. "So you don't do drugs anymore?"

"No, I don't. I don't drink either—not because I'm trying to prove anything but because I know that's a dead end street with heavy emphasis on the word 'dead.' Not saying it's easy even now." Kalin sighed and looked at his hands that had fallen into the darkness on his lap. "I've got so many people around me right now who still think that stuff is everything there is. It gets tough to walk away time and again, to watch them get so excited about throwing their lives away. They just don't understand how fast the trip down is."

"You can't explain it to them?" Colton asked and then cleared his throat.

Kalin shook his head in resignation. "You can't save someone who doesn't want to be saved. Ask Jesse. God knows how hard he tried to save me. But they make their decisions. You make yours. Besides, a lie doesn't understand the truth anymore than fear understands faith."

Colton's gaze traced through the darkness over to Kalin's face. "Doesn't it make it tough when you've got more talent than half the town, and yet you're stuck with a bunch of idiots who are trying to drag you back down?"

"It's killing me." Then he sighed again. "But I know there's got to be a reason. Something I'm not seeing. I don't know what it is, but I know when the time is right, the next step will show up. Until then, I'm just practicing on the little steps." He shook his head, letting his hair gently sway under his jaw. "I just wish I hadn't messed up so many other lives along the way."

"Like?"

"Like Jess, and the other band members. They lost their shot because of me."

"They made their decisions."

"I still feel guilty. And then there's Zane, my manager. I could pay him back from now until the sun sets in the east, and I'd still owe him my life. I didn't deserve to have friends like them."

"Maybe you did, and you just didn't know it."

A face, fading with time drifted through his mind. He could still feel her hands in his hair, her breath on his face, her fingers on his skin. He wasn't sure they were real, but they wafted through his memory just the same. "It's a nice thought. But I made so many mistakes back then… not little ones either. I think sometimes that's why I am where I am, like God is punishing me because I hurt so many people."

"You don't think He's forgiven you?"

"Oh, no. I think He has. I mean I know He has, but when you've hurt so many people the way I did, I'm not sure how you can ever forgive yourself—or if you even should."

Colton looked over at him. "So it's not the drugs then?"

Kalin's gaze went to Colton's face, but he couldn't read the understanding in Colton's eyes. "Huh?"

"It's not the drugs and all of that junk that's holding you back. It's you. You don't believe you deserve it anymore."

Kalin's gaze drifted out the window. "I'm not sure I ever did."

Chapter 15

It was Friday before Kalin got up the energy to go to the library. Depression hung all around him like a thick, black cloud. Jesse was home. Phoenix Rising was back together, and he was back to Von and the others cavorting around. Thursday night at Sevens was pure torture. Nothing sounded right. Nothing felt right. In a way it was worse now. Now he couldn't tell himself that every band was like this. He couldn't hang onto the belief that without being high, every gig must be soul-sapping. Now he had gotten a fresh taste of life, and to go back to taking the poison of this world was like tasting death anew.

Fighting the nagging thoughts that the inbox was probably empty anyway, he climbed the library stairs. The computer in the corner was occupied, so he took the one two seats down against the wall. He pulled up his email, and a numb, sick feeling swarmed over him as he saw her new message. He wasn't sure how this had gone so far, how he had let it go so far. He thought about her as his gaze blurred on the words. She didn't deserve to be dragged through the muck of his life—past or present. There was just so much she didn't know about him, so much he couldn't tell her. Yet one tiny strand of hope made him click the message even as he distanced himself from it emotionally.

Kalin, You know, I have spent my whole life wishing that someone would realize that I wasn't just part of the scenery. At home, I was one more mouth to feed. With Brandt, I was "the girlfriend." I was never Danae. I wasn't allowed to be, and I never thought that was worth fighting for. You make me feel like it is, and I thank you so much for that.

Despite the thoughts that he shouldn't let himself get close to her again, the honesty in her words pulled him closer to the screen.

You have such a gentle spirit, and you care so much... I find it hard to believe that God loved me enough to send me you. It's something I've never had in my life. You have believed in me even when I didn't believe in myself. You've made me think that flying is possible. :)

A sad smile melted through him. He closed his eyes and wished that for her, that she would always take the chance to fly.

You gave me back so much that I hadn't even realized was missing—my faith and my hope. I will never be able to thank you enough for that. I'm sending up prayers tonight that your fondest wish will be granted, that what you dream will come true, and that every blessing God has in mind for you will be showered into your life—because you deserve the best He has to offer... X-Best! :)

I'm going now, but that doesn't mean I'm gone. I'll be thinking about you and praying for you... until the ether connects us again. Peace & Prayers, Danae

His heart hurt. How could she look at him and not see all the mistakes he had made? How could she think of him the way she wrote? Didn't she see? Didn't she know? He couldn't understand how she didn't see it because that's all he saw when he looked at himself.

Images from a blurry past washed through him. He had thought he had forgotten them in the haze of the mind-altering substances flowing through his system at the time. Yet when he really allowed himself to look, they were still there. Suddenly the memory of a beautiful blonde who had sauntered into his life and with one look sent everything else scattering crashed through him. In the next instant the void was filled with cascades of pain and regret.

"Rebecca," he breathed almost not hearing the name as his body fell back in the chair. His hand went to his mouth. He was shaking, though he didn't really notice.

He closed his eyes and fought the memory even then. He hadn't allowed himself to say even her name in nearly six years. It hurt too much. His breathing sounded like that of a drowning man as the memories, indistinct and fuzzy, played tag through his memory. He squeezed his eyes closed, trying to make them go away. The first night that neither of them probably even remembered 100 percent flowed right through the months they had spent together. Both had a habit, and both were glad to have a warm body around who wasn't trying to guilt them into quitting. It was a disaster from minute one.

He shook his head at the thought of her. That relationship was the very definition of "using someone." Had he not been on the lead mic with a guitar in hand and talent to burn, had she not had legs and a body he could lose himself in, had they not each been the other's worst ideal, life would never have played out the way it did.

He remembered her following the band, too high to even walk a straight line. The others worked around her, and him. They didn't have much choice. She was demanding, hyper and spoiled. He wasn't much better. The ensuing days were one, long, head-thwacking bash. When he wasn't on-stage, they were together. When he was on-stage, he knew she was waiting for him. It was such a good feeling that he had called it love and never really questioned that. Until...

At that thought he yanked himself out of the chair, clicking his email off even as he did so. Danae didn't need him in her life. He knew that even if she didn't. With that thought, he grabbed his jacket and raced headlong back to the shell he called a life. Danae was smart. She would figure it out.

As he got on the motorcycle, he vowed that he would not come back to check on his emails any time soon. More than that, he vowed that when he finally did, he would delete anything from D_Scott. He owed her that much.

Danae checked her email every day, thinking there would be a reply, but there hadn't been. There were moments when she thought it should bother her, but she didn't have time to worry about it. She would say a quick prayer for him and jump into the next project. A week later she was down to the final two pages of her Biology paper that was due the next morning when she heard the knock at the front door.

Tara answered it, and Danae heard the voices. Two females. Probably one of Tara's friends coming to study. However, after just a few seconds they stopped, and Danae heard footsteps on the stairs. That was strange. Tara never invited even her closest friends upstairs. Although her concentration should have been on her paper, her ear was practically pressed against the air at the door, as she tried to figure out what was going on.

"Hey, stranger," the voice at the door said, and when Danae looked up, dread crashed through her.

"Molly." She sat back in the chair. "What are you doing here?"

"Mind if I come in?"

"I... Sure. I guess so." Danae watched her friend come in and sit on the bed. Her sleeveless white sweater dropped perfectly off one shoulder, and with her hair in a ponytail at the back of her neck, she looked positively chic. "You look nice."

Molly looked down at herself as if she hadn't noticed. "Thanks. I just came from a job interview. I'm probably going to get the receptionist position at Dr. Benson's. You know, the dentist."

"Really? Cool. That's great." Danae had no idea what else to say or why Molly was there. Was this really just a friendly visit, or was there more? It didn't take long to find out.

"I talked to Mom this morning," Molly said, crossing her long legs.

Danae's gaze went down to her notes as she wound a piece of hair over her ear. "Oh, yeah. How are they?"

"Confused. Disappointed. Crushed." Molly waited for the answer that never came. "I don't understand, Danae. You had everything, and you threw it away for what? You shouldn't be up here studying. We should be out shopping for your wedding. What is going on with you?"

"Have you talked to Brandt?" Danae asked.

"I tried, but he just kept saying he had no idea this was coming, and he doesn't understand why you suddenly hate him, and why he's like a horrible person all of a sudden."

Danae debated her comment on this point. Saying it would mean trashing Brandt in his sister's eyes. Not saying it made Danae look even worse. Finally the truth won out. "Did he tell you about the wedding?"

The look on Molly's face narrowed. "That you called it off? Yeah."

"No, not our wedding. Your wedding. Did he tell you about Krystal?"

The look narrowed further. "What does Krystal have to do with any of this?"

So they didn't know. Not that Danae had expected him to tell them, but it did up the ante on why they wouldn't understand.

"Look," Molly said, cutting in before Danae had the chance to explain, "we all know about what your dad did, but you've got to let that go. You've got to realize that not all guys are scoping out someone to cheat on you with. Face it. Someday Brandt is going to have a secretary at work. You can't live your life suspecting and looking for reasons not to trust him."

Danae wanted to explode. Instead she sat there like stone and listened.

"What your dad did... walking out like that... I understand how something like that can make you believe that other guys can't be trusted, but Danae, you can't live your life like that. You've got to make peace with that, let it go, and move on."

In a strange way, Molly had no idea how right she was. For more than 22 years, Danae's very identity had been wrapped up in that single event in her life. Granted, Brandt wouldn't have been the one she wanted anyway, but that didn't mean that Molly didn't have a point.

"You know what?" Danae said with a real smile. "Thanks for telling me that. I think you're right."

Instantly Molly's face brightened. "So, you see that you were wrong to give the ring back."

"No, I didn't say that."

The brightness fell dark. "What do you mean? You just said…"

"Look, Molly. There are a lot of things about Brandt and me that you just don't understand, and that's not your fault. You think he's terrific, and that's great because he's your brother. I, however, have seen some things about him that aren't so great, and that's not so great. See, unlike you, who had no control over the decision of him being in your life, I do have to make that decision. Believe me, I tried to make the one everyone else wanted me to. It's just…"

"It's just what, Danae? You're talking in riddles, and I don't understand what you're trying to say."

"What I'm trying to say is: I've made my decision, and Brandt is not it. He's not what I want."

The look in Molly's eyes darkened. "Is there someone else?"

"There's everyone else. Don't you see that? I tied myself to him so early that I never had a chance to see my other options."

"When you've got a guy like Brandt, what other options do you need?" Molly's pitch was escalating dangerously out of control.

Danae took a long breath to calm down. The fact that she probably had already lost Molly's friendship didn't deter her from trying to salvage what she could. "Look, I know you don't understand, and I don't blame you. But can you please just try to accept that I need to do this for me?"

There was not a shred of compassion anywhere in Molly's gaze. "You know I never thought of you as selfish, Danae, but now I think I was wrong. I'm glad you broke it off with Brandt." Molly stood from the bed. "Because he deserves someone a whole lot better than you."

With that, Molly saw herself out the door. Danae closed her eyes when her friend was gone and tried to get a coherent thought through it. She had never thought of herself as selfish either. In fact, of all of her friends, she was the one most likely to drop everything the moment anyone needed anything. She couldn't count the number of times she had been up until the sun was peeking over the horizon trying to get her own things done because she'd been out helping someone else much too late.

And now, even when they didn't know all the facts, they threw "selfish" in her face. It hurt, but right behind hurt was anger. Her gaze traveled to the computer screen, and although he hadn't written, she needed someone to vent to. If for no other reason than if she didn't, her mind would never be able to work on the intricacies of how a giraffe uses adaptation methods in order to survive.

She let the anger flow through her fingertips and out onto the email. Kalin would understand even if none of them ever did.

By Saturday morning Kalin couldn't concentrate on a single other thing to save his life. Even music had lost its pull on his soul compared with the thoughts of the library. Sevens was livable—barely. And in the ensuing week, he had gotten enough distance from the memories to convince himself that just going to check that inbox wouldn't be a colossal mistake.

He climbed the steps as his heart thumped hard in his chest. He tried to tell himself it would be better if she hadn't written, but even he didn't believe that. He wanted to hear from her so bad, it was beginning to claw through him like a tiger-scratch. Back at his normal corner computer, he pulled up his email and was disappointed to see only one message from her. Stalling to make the moment of being with her last just a bit longer, he deleted the other messages—except for the one from his mom.

Quickly he pulled that one up and read it. Just suggestions for what to send for his dad for his birthday. Back on the Home page, he took a long breath and clicked on her message. For the second between the click and when it actually came on the screen, he closed his eyes, praying for her safety. When he opened his eyes and started reading, the joy of just being with her again cracked through him. Just reading his own name… It was completely without explanation what that simple act did to him.

Kalin, I know you are busy, and I know you don't have time to listen to me whine about my problems, but I just have to tell someone.

Worry pounced on him, and he sat forward in the chair.

As you know, most of my family and friends think I've lost my mind. The more I try to explain, the harder it is to explain. I mean if they don't understand that I'm doing this for myself, how many ways are there to say that? Worse, now they're mad at me. They are all taking Brandt's side in this—and by "all" I mean everyone except Tara and you—and Tara thinks this is about you so…

I'm getting more confused every time one of them shows up to talk. It really makes me mad that they can't for one second consider that maybe I can have a thought that someone else hasn't already laid out for me. I mean, why do I have to do everything they tell me I'm supposed to, and why does everyone get mad when I try to make a decision on my own? It's like they think I'm two again, and if everything isn't planned out to the last detail, we're all going to fall apart again.

~ Lucky ~

I hate this! I hate feeling like I'm one step away from everything falling apart on me. I'm not two anymore! Why does that keep following me around? It happened. I'm over it. Let's move on, shall we? Ugh! It's just so frustrating. Well, thanks for listening to me ramble. You can delete this now and go on with your life... Just me, Danae

  Deleting it was not even an option. She was in pain, and to him, leaving her there wasn't something he could ever do. He laid his fingers on the keys, thought for a moment, twisted his wristband to make it more comfortable and then began to type.

With her Biology final looming on Monday morning, Danae spent all of Saturday and most of the hours on Sunday with her study group. Eighteen weeks of class jammed into nine days had the effect of making one feel like there was no way to adequately prepare for the test. They had only taken one other test, and although she had studied hard for it, she had only come out with a high B. Pulling that grade up to an A with the help of her paper, which had already been turned in, and the final was the goal she was putting all her energy into.

  When the study session broke up on Sunday evening, she made a mad dash for church and managed to catch the last half—although with phylums, kingdoms, and classes swirling in her head, she had no idea what was said. By the time she made it back home, it was all her nervous stomach could do to heat a TV dinner and dive back into studying at the table.

  Tara came home, but Danae hardly noticed and wasn't even sure she said hello. She reread whole sections of the book because she didn't remember reading them in the first place. She reviewed charts of plant parts until they were criss-crossing her brain in no discernable patterns. When Tara came back down the stairs several hours later, Danae was still scribbling furiously in her notebook.

  "You don't have that memorized yet?" Tara asked when she came out of the kitchen with a glass of water in her hand. "You know, it's not smart to stay up all night before a test. You've been at this for three days straight. Why don't you give your brain a rest?"

  "Protozoa. Single-cell animals. Porifera. Sponges. Cnidovia. Jellyfish, like Porifera but has a nervous system. Bryozoa..."

  "What's that?"

  "The phylums. Mollusca. Clams, oysters... "

  "Danae."

  "What?" She looked back at the book, having lost her train of thought. "Arthropoda. Insects, ticks, mites..."

Tara walked around the table, took hold of Danae's arm, and pulled her up from the chair. "Go to bed. Get some sleep. Micromedinica will still be there tomorrow."

"Micromedinica? What's that?" Danae asked in horror that she had somehow missed studying something important.

"I made it up. Now come on." Tara pulled on her arm.

"I just…" Danae reached for the book, but Tara swiped her hand out of the way.

"No. No more studying. You need sleep." Never letting her go, Tara pulled her up the steps. Even at the door to her room, Tara didn't let go. At Danae's bed, Tara yanked the covers back and fluffed the pillow twice. "Now, lay down, and try to think of something nice… like the park in the summer or a hot air balloon."

Danae looked at her skeptically. "A hot air balloon?"

"I'm improvising, okay?"

"Oh, okay." She got into the bed, and she had to admit that it felt very good.

"Now, close your eyes and think happy thoughts."

Danae closed her eyes. "An A in Biology… An A in Biology."

"Not about Biology! Now go to sleep!" Tara walked to the door and pulled it closed. "That's an order. I'll see you in the morning."

Danae laughed. It was only when she rolled over to set her alarm clock that she really looked at it. 1:21 stared back at her. She was due in class at 7:30. Shutting off her mind before it had the chance to tell her how little sleep she was going to get, she lay down on the pillow, took a long breath, and was asleep before the clock said 1:23.

The fifty questions on the first test threatened to overload what few synapses Danae had left to concentrate with the next morning. Tired and stressed out, she worked through them diligently, hoping they wouldn't all be wrong in the fog of her brain. Tara was right. She should've gone to sleep much earlier. The extra studying had obviously not done anything to help her anyway.

She got all the way to question 43. She read it, reread it, but still couldn't quite understand the question. She looked at the answers, and panic began to wrap itself around her chest. None of the answers looked familiar, and she had no idea what a "transposable genetic element" was. Was that something they had studied? She fought to recall anything about it.

"Calm down, Danae," she whispered to herself as she closed her eyes and took a long breath. Trying not to remember that she had a second test for lab an hour after this one was over, she willed herself to concentrate. "Think. Transposable... Trans. Traveling. Genetic. It's going to have something to do with DNA..."

When she opened her eyes again and scanned the possible answers, there was one that incorporated those traits. She marked that one and proceeded to number 44.

Sunday had about driven Kalin's brain to the brink of insanity. He had done everything he could think of—even cleaned the trailer to some extent—just to have something to do so he wouldn't wish the library was open. He still wished it, and every time he thought about it, he sent up a prayer for her.

By Monday at noon, he could take it no longer. He had to know how she was. He wanted to drive to Knoxville, but he had no idea what her schedule was. There were only a few patrons milling about when he got to the computers, and he chose the corner one, sat down, and quickly pulled up his email. Frustration slid over him when he realized she hadn't replied.

Something was wrong. He knew it immediately. She always replied. She was better at this than he was. Concern flowed through his fingers as he set them in motion over the keyboard. The only thing corralling the disheartening thoughts was the prayer he started sending up instantly. "God, wherever she is, please be with her..."

Sitting in the sunshine on the steps of the Science Building, Danae sifted through her capacious notes. How was she supposed to keep all of this straight? Phylums, Kingdoms, Classes... all with names that would make Einstein weep. She closed her eyes to go through the list again. "Protazoa. Single-cell animals..."

Kalin finished that email and sat back. He put his elbows on the chair arms and stared at the computer, fighting to keep himself from checking to see if she had replied. His gaze went to the clock. One-fifteen. Where was she? He tried to remember what time they had connected the last time, but he couldn't be sure that any of those conditions would even be valid now.

After an agonizing three-minute wait, he clicked over to the Home page again, but there was nothing new. He sat back and tried to think of something else to do while he waited. Absently he stood and walked over to a bookshelf. His fingers ran over the titles although he wasn't really reading any of them. Then as if on their own, they pulled one book out.

He looked at it, read the title, and figured it was better than nothing.

For the seven millionth time, Danae pushed the hair out of her face wishing she had pulled it into a ponytail. Fighting it while trying to concentrate on a lab test was more than anyone should have to deal with.

"Count the yeast colonies on the following site grid," she read, and when her gaze went to the grid, she sucked in formaldehyde-laden air. They had done this like the third day for ten minutes. There was a trick to it, but what was that trick? Where you supposed to count all of the colonies in the whole thing? That didn't seem right. She searched her memory for how to do this. "Oh, God. Help me. Please. I don't remember this."

Even as Kalin's gaze scanned the book, his thoughts were on her. "God, wherever she is, please be with her. Clear the channels for Your love to be in her life."

One grid. The thought jumped into her mind. *Count one grid. You then extrapolate that to the others.* That was right. Her gut knew it even more than her mind did. Quickly but efficiently she counted the colonies and wrote down her answer.

The next question was about the Lagerstatten, and she smiled, clearly remembering the tar pits with the preserved bones. Why she remembered that so clearly, she couldn't be sure, but at that moment she wasn't questioning it, she was just grateful that she did.

For the last hour Kalin hadn't really been reading, more just trying to look busy and every so often refreshing the Home page to see if she had written. However, as the clock made its way through to 2:35, the clicking stopped, and he was reading. His gaze traveled over a sentence, then stopped.

Life is not about getting your life together and then giving it to God. It's about giving your life to God and letting Him put it together.

His mind drifted back to his conversation with Colton as it had several times since that night. "You don't think you deserve it anymore." Colton's words washed through Kalin. It was the truth. He didn't think he deserved it. There were still too many people he hadn't gotten straight with.

Air clogged his chest as his thoughts went to standing at that window. For nearly six years he had done everything he could not to think about that moment, about that decision, about walking away. The guilt ripped through his soul. The cool glass of the window seemed to press against his fingertips.

His gaze went back to the book, *Life is not about getting your life together and then giving it to God. It's about giving your life to God and letting Him put it together.* But how could he hand God such a mess? A mess that God had never done anything to make?

Pushing the memories back, Kalin clicked once more on the computer, and seeing that there was still no reply, he had to admit that she wasn't going to write him back any time soon. Standing stiffly, he walked over to the bookshelf and shoved the book onto it without taking the time to put it in the right place.

The middle of his soul felt disjointed and flat as he walked out of the library and climbed on the bike. His mind devolved into hanging onto the details of life lest it stumble upon the thoughts haunting the edges of it. It was selfishness that had let him walk away. Forgiving himself for that seemed the ultimate in selfishness. Giving it to God sounded like a nice idea, but it was his mess. He had made it, and now he was forever doomed to live in the chaos he had wrought in his soul.

Chapter 16

Danae trudged up the stairs of her apartment. To say she was worn out wouldn't have done the feeling justice. It was more like she was the walking dead. Her mind was no longer functioning. Her body was barely functioning, and how that was still working was beyond her. As she got to the top step and rounded her bedroom door, her glance settled on the two books stacked on the desk—Anatomy & Physiology and Genetics. Both were to start the following morning.

Without bothering to even straighten the blankets on her bed, which she hadn't bothered to make that morning, she dropped the books in her hands to the floor, collapsed on the bed, and promptly fell asleep.

When she awoke two hours later, the sun was three-quarters through its trip across the sky. Her eyes hurt. Her neck hurt. She lay there, trying to decide if she should get up or just go back to sleep. At first she decided sleep, but then she realized that her stomach was growling. Dragging herself up from the blankets, she put her feet on the ground and realized only then that she hadn't even bothered to take her tennis shoes off.

Slipping a toe into the heel of one, she forced it off. It clunked to the floor. In seconds the other one followed the first. Considering that she hadn't studied with her feet, she wondered why her ankles hurt so badly. She pushed herself up from the bed and stumbled over to the computer. With a thump, she sat down in the chair. She needed to check her schedule for the following morning. When it had come in, she hadn't had the time nor the memory space in her brain to devote to it.

Clicking over to her email box, she started to scan it for the schedule, but her breath snagged when she saw Lane_K at the top. She checked the date and tried to get it in the right slot to figure out when he had written, but her brain couldn't follow far enough to figure it out.

With a shove, she pushed the question out of her mind and clicked on his message.

Danae, First of all, if they love you, they should understand. If they don't, that doesn't mean YOU are wrong. It means THEY are wrong. Keep working. And remember, when you first start something new, everyone else will say you are crazy, then they will say it can't be done, then they will say well it can but not consistently. Finally they will hand you an award and say they knew you could do it the whole time ;) Just keep that in mind.

Besides, how can they know what you are capable of? They obviously don't know you at all. Right?

Finally, if you don't mind me asking, what happened when you were two? It doesn't really matter one way or the other, but it would help me know what to tell you if I knew what you were talking about. I'll be praying for you. Kalin

Her thoughts were no longer on studying and tests and plant parts. With that one message they had been transported to flying down a highway on the back of a bike. That seemed like so long ago, but it was strange how easily she could recall the feeling without so much as trying.

She considered replying but decided instead to read his next message.

Danae, I hope nothing is wrong. Don't stress out writing me back or anything. I just figured you would've written by now. But I know you're busy with school and everything. I hope that's all going great. You know I'm in your corner. Wouldn't know a frog leg from a jellyfish, but if you need a pep-talk, I'm here :)

As for my life... well, things are pretty much back to boring. Playing with PR was great. No, it was better than great. X-Best is close. I just wish I could find a band like them that wanted me because constantly going to play when I know all that junk is going to be there is getting really hard. Thursday night I thought Von was going to hog-tie me if I didn't join them. I don't know why it's so hard for them to get it that I don't want to do that anymore. Well, I do but...

But I've gotta tell you, playing with PR was just so much fun! It was so incredible to be on that stage, playing like that for 8,000 people. Ugh! I would give anything to get with a band like that. I know. Wait on God. I am. But what is taking Him so long?

Write back when you get a chance! Kalin

One more, she thought and she would type her reply no matter how much her stomach was revolting.

Dear Danae, I had hoped you would be somewhere around. It feels like it's been so long since we "talked." I'm thinking this email thing certainly has its drawbacks. If I knew you were around, I'd probably jump on my bike and come find you. But you're probably out studying, which I really understand (really I do). But that doesn't mean I'm missing you any less ;)

When you get half a chance even if it's just to say, "Hey, I'm still alive," I'd love to hear from you how things are going. Until then, take care of yourself, and know you are in my prayers. Peace to you, Kalin

It was amazing how different she felt after simply reading a few words from him. Life suddenly didn't seem like such an impossible climb anymore. For a long moment she rested her fingers on the keyboard just enjoying that feeling. Finally her thoughts wafted through her heart and out onto the keys.

Kalin forced himself to wait until Wednesday morning to go to the library. She was busy. He was sure of that. If he went and there was no reply, he would be too tempted to swamp her inbox with messages. So he had found and used every excuse in the books not to go. However, when the doors to the library opened on Wednesday morning, he was the first person through them.

He took the stairs two at a time, hoping and praying there would be something there. As he clicked on the computer, he sent up another prayer for her—only one of the thousands he had breathed since he'd last left the confines of the computer area. When he finally pulled the program up, all the hopes and prayers were answered, and a smile traipsed right across his heart and onto his face. He didn't even bother to delete the other unwanted emails before pulling hers up.

Kalin, It was so great to hear from you. I'm so glad your time with PR was wonderful. Don't worry. Someone very soon is going to notice you. God has a plan. Put it in His hands, and trust that it will happen the way it is supposed to happen, when it's supposed to happen. (I know you know this in your head... now you need to learn it with your heart. And yes, there IS a difference!)

Kalin's mind snagged on that comment. She was right. How she knew to say that, he couldn't clearly understand, but she was right. He knew about putting life in God's hands, but had he ever really done that in his heart? Before he kept reading, he closed his eyes, "God, Danae's right. I know You have a plan. Please let this work out the right way in Your time." He opened his eyes and kept reading.

As for my life... who hit the fast-forward button? I'm already through Bio 2 although at this point I'm not even going to say I passed. I just took my final tests in the class and the lab. Can you say UGH? Phylums and kingdoms and plant parts and cells and yeast colonies... Oh, yeah. It was lots of fun. The weird thing is, as overwhelming as it all is, it's so much easier than the stuff I was taking to teach. Social studies? Who cares! But this stuff is just so cool. I only wish I had more than a few days to soak it all in. I feel like a sponge in need of wringing!

Tomorrow I start Anatomy & Physiology. Oh, joy. I'm also taking Genetics this first summer session. The TA in bio lab was talking about it, and it sounds like a lot of stats and probabilities. Not too bad... I hope.

I do have to thank you though because my brain was on total meltdown mode when I got home today from those tests. But once I read your messages a couple of times, hope or something very much like it made it back into my brain. So, here we go! Wish me luck (even though I hope I don't need to much of it :)—maybe I'll store some up for when you can't get to the library... Then again, why don't you just plan on visiting that library every day for the next oh, six or eight years depending how long this takes me. I don't want to go too long without my lucky charm. Lots o' hugs, Danae

Joy danced through him. Kalin shook his head. How could she make him feel so good and not even be right there? Words paled so badly in comparison to what he wanted to do for her, but they were all he had to work with. He put his fingers to the keys to type his reply.

The first class of A&P turned out to be little more than handing out the syllabus. The TA who would be teaching Danae's lab had to fill in because the professor was sick. The TA assured them that the professor would be back the next day and advised them to use the time reading the first two chapters. Since it was a summer class, they would have to put their noses in the books and as he said, "forget that anything else exists."

Taking his advice, Danae went to the computer lab. Trying to read in the Student Union was a one-way ticket to insanity. She would be in class for Genetics in a couple of hours, and by the time she got out of A&P lab at 3:30, she wasn't sure her mind would be able to comprehend the reading.

She sat down at a station and opened her book. She read three pages.

"Excuse me," a young lady said, walking up to her, "but if you aren't using the computers..."

Danae sat up. "Oh, I was going to." She reached for the mouse for emphasis. The lady didn't look pleased, but she backed off. Knowing she'd better keep working on the computer until the lady found someone else to hassle, Danae clicked and pulled up her email server. She wasn't really expecting anything to be there, but when it came up and Lane_K was at the top, she closed the book on her lap and leaned forward.

When she clicked on the message, she noticed the time stamp and realized that it was possible he was still on the other side. Without reading his message, she clicked to New and typed a few words to keep him from leaving if he was planning to. With that, she hit send, clicked back over to his message, and pulled it up.

Jeez, girl! My brain would explode if I tried to take all of that. Are you trying to kill yourself, or is taking things slowly not in your vocabulary?

Actually I'm getting kind of used to the library. If it just wouldn't close all the time that would be even better. I've never been a fan of regular working hours. It probably doesn't help that I don't get in until 3 or later three nights a week. That has a way of messing with your sleep schedule. And in case you were serious, I'll be here for as long as you'll have me around. Just think, in a few years, I'll be able to say I know a real, live doctor! How unbelievable is that? You're in my thoughts and prayers. Keep yourself in one piece for me! Kalin

The fact that there was a reply in his box when Kalin clicked on it jumped on him like a hungry leopard. Quickly he pulled up her message.

Kalin, I hope I caught you and you're not already gone. I'm between classes. Just got out of A&P. How's everything going? D

She read one page before she clicked over to read his reply.

D, Things are okay. Wishing, hoping, and praying, but not much has happened. I feel like I'm doing the two-step in reverse sometimes, one step forward and two-steps back. It's frustrating.

Has your family come around yet? K

No on the family. Mom's supposed to be back this weekend. Not looking forward to that lecture. Molly, Brandt's sister, came the other night to tell me what an idiot I'm being... Okay, not in those words, but that was the gist. Thankfully Brandt is using everyone else to make me feel guilty. I haven't talked to him since I gave the ring back, but sooner or later I'm going to see him. It's not like I can hole up in this apartment the rest of my life—although I really wish that was an option. Is it? Danae

Oh, don't do that! The world needs you, D... and besides, you don't want to deprive the world of that wonderful, beautiful spirit of yours. That would be a true tragedy. K.

hahaha! Now that's funny! D

What's funny about it? I was being serious. K

I'm thinking your memory must be a little fuzzy. Beautiful? Wonderful? If I remember right, I had mascara all over my face, and I wasn't exactly scintillating company that night. D

Are you kidding? You were gorgeous! All the guys in the band were... well, let's just say they noticed too. You sure had my attention. K

Disbelief and embarrassment flooded through her as she reached for the keys.

What? You like the mascara look?

I liked you.

She had meant it to be a joke to diffuse how serious he sounded. However, the second she read it, funny stopped completely. She didn't know what to say to that. What exactly was he trying to tell her? Her gaze went to the clock, and she realized she would have to get to class. Quickly she typed a reply, clicked the email program off, and then stood and left the building.

Nothing had felt so right in days. Kalin's whole system was anchored to that chair, to that computer screen, to her. The comment about liking her hadn't been the most well-thought-out one he had ever written, but it was the truth. He twisted the wristband around his arm waiting and trying to decide if he should've been that honest.

When her message came back, he took a breath to steady his nerves.

:) I'm surprised. I figured you thought I was an idiot trying to navigate all those cables in heels! I should've known better. That one was pretty obvious... Then in the parking lot, that was bad. Really, REALLY bad. Ugh! Trust me, they do not write that one up in how-to-meet-someone handbooks... first, cover yourself in mud, then get your mascara to run all over your face... That was so awful. The very fact that you stopped and didn't run away screaming proves you're a great guy.

I am so darn lucky to have you in my life. I honestly don't want to think where I would be without you. The only thing that would make it any better is if you didn't live half-a-state away! The pics on the 'net don't do you justice AT ALL :) (BTW, what is up with that rhinestone jacket anyway? That couldn't have been your idea).

I'm not even sure my memory does you justice any more (and the more stuff I cram into it, the worse it gets). I do know, however, that what's the most awesome thing about you is not on the outside. It's that you have your values in place, that you know what's important, and that you're living your life—not letting everyone else live it for you. Just keep having fun like you seemed to be that night on stage, and I'm sure everything will work out.

I've gotta jet now. Class, class, and more class. I'll be back at the apartment about 4. If you're around, you know how to work the mouse! God bless! Danae

His gaze slid to the clock. Ten o'clock. He put his fingers to the keys even as he decided that when four o'clock rolled around, he would be right back here. Somehow talking to her, even in strange circumstances such as these, made his life make so much more sense. He wanted to hold onto that if at all possible.

The second Danae made it through her bedroom door, she threw her books on the desk and slid the mouse over the pad to bring the screen to life. She glanced at the clock and wondered if he was in fact going to be there. Happiness split that thought in half when she saw his name. A click and he was right there with her again.

D, You blow me away sometimes. You know that? Don't ever think you weren't beautiful that day. You were heart stopping. That's no joke. Then when I saw you sitting out there... ugh, you just have no idea how worried I was about you, how helpless I felt. I'm just glad I was there. You have no idea how many times I've thanked God for sending me out there. I'm not sure how much help I was, but if I helped at all, it was worth it.

No, the rhinestones were not my idea. Ugh! They were awful. How did you find those pictures? I should have burned them! That's when I was trying to be the guy everyone said I should be. DEFINITELY NOT ME. I assure you. I'm really glad God doesn't mind Lucky T-shirts and faded jeans because they are definitely more my style.

Have fun? Gee, that would be new. Most of the time these days I'm just trying to get through the night in one piece. Don't get me wrong... I love playing, it's just all the other stuff I could do without.

I'm thinking at some point here we're going to have to refresh each other's memories :) What are you doing this weekend?

I'll be back at four. Maybe we can set something up. Until then, study hard! Kalin

He wanted to meet? Her gaze jumped to her books, and she closed her eyes in frustration. Why now when she had so much to do? Why hadn't all this happened last semester when she was trying to find reasons to procrastinate? Aggravated at the timing of this request, she typed a reply, wondering if he would in fact show up at four.

Kalin nearly took out a street sign, two curbs, and a Jeep to get to the library by four, but it was worth it when he pulled the program up and her reply was there. He knew she would wait, so he pulled the message up and read it first.

Kalin, I wish I could say I'm as free as a bird. Unfortunately, I'm not. I've got all this reading to do before Monday. These summer classes are killers! It's the first day, and I've got four chapters to read TONIGHT! It's unreal.

That doesn't mean I don't want to see you though... Are you kidding? I'm just trying to figure out how to fit that into studying. We've got our first test in Genetics on Monday, and when I started reading through it this afternoon, let's just say... HELP! But please don't think that means I'm trying to find excuses. I'm NOT!

Let me know if you have another time to meet. Maybe we could hit halfway somewhere? I'm here--reading. Write back. Danae

Quickly he typed a reply and sent it. His insides were doing somersaults through the excitement.

Hey, don't apologize. It was just an idea. When the time is right, the time will be right ;) Until then, I'm just glad we get to talk once in awhile like this. K

* smiles * I am too! It's like sanity in the middle of all this craziness. God must really love me to have given me you. D

And I thought you were keeping me around for decoration. K

No, I'm keeping you around to keep me sane! And don't ever forget that. D

I'll try to keep that in mind.

Chapter 17

By Saturday their four o'clock email appointments were what Danae looked most forward to. Classes, although overwhelming, were going well. That was partly due to the fact that when she got home, he was waiting there on the ether to encourage her, to tell her that it was worth it, and to make sure she still thought she could do this.

She had spent all day Saturday studying, but now it didn't seem so much like cramming. There was only one more chapter in A&P to read and studying for her Genetics test to do, but it all seemed doable. At five-'til-four she clicked onto her computer. He would be there soon, but she wanted to have something in his inbox when he got there—so he knew she had been thinking about him.

Mischief wound through her as she set her fingers to the keys.

The second his email program came up at two after four, Kalin shook his head. She always managed to beat him here. He clicked on her message, feeling her presence on the other side of those lines. It felt better than it made sense to.

Well, hello there, Lucky! This is your afternoon wake up call. It's time to rise and shine. I know how good you are at that ;) Don't keep me waiting too long otherwise I might have to actually learn Genetics— scary thought. Been thinking about you. Can't wait to talk. Write back. Peace & Prayers, Danae

Joy wrapped around him like a warm blanket on a cold, clear night. Shaking his head at how she could make him feel so wonderful without even being there, he typed a reply.

The jangle of her email sent excitement scattering through her. She tossed her book on the desk and clicked to the message.

Hey, Sunshine. I'm awake. You sound happy. What's up? K

Of course I sound happy, I get to talk to you, don't I? That always makes me happy. Besides I need my daily dose of Kalin so I don't look at all this Genetics stuff and throw myself off a cliff.

Yikes. Sounds serious. But I'm just your cheerleader (and not a very good one at that). Don't put yourself down. You could do this stuff without me.

"Could" and "want to" are two very different things :)
How she could make him feel so needed, he wasn't at all sure.

I won't argue with that. If it weren't for you, I'd have probably already packed it in and gone back to Canada. Heaven knows I'm not making any progress here.

How do you know? Maybe there are pieces of the puzzle being put together even as we speak that you can't see.

Well, I wish they would hurry up. I don't have a lot of patience.

Then find something to do to stop thinking about how long it's taking.
The thought was intriguing although he wasn't totally sure what she meant.

Like what... knitting? :)
She laughed out loud at that comment. He was crazy.

No, ding-dong. Something productive. Do something nice for someone else—someone who maybe needs a thanks or better yet someone who can't do anything for you. Get creative. When you're thinking about them, you can't be thinking about you. D
Not thinking about himself. It wasn't something he had done in a long time—save for when four o'clock rolled around.

How creative do you mean? Singing I can do. More creative than that is a different story.

I don't know. Jeez! Do I have to do everything? :) Go to an old folks home and sing for them, buy a balloon for a kid at the park, give *someone something they weren't expecting. I used to do it a lot when I had time. Now, I'm just swamped... So maybe you can do something for both of us and tell me about it. D*

I'll think about it and see what I come up with. Is your mom home yet?

There's a fun topic. No. Not that I've heard. I'm sure she'll let me know the second she touches down. Oh, I've been meaning to ask—do you just sing and play or do you write stuff too?

The question danced over his mind as the answer waltzed out his fingertips.

I write, too. Mostly it's like 3:30 in the morning stuff. My brain works best then—or maybe it's that by then my brain has stopped working and something else has taken over.

I'd love to hear some of your songs sometime. I was never any good at that kind of stuff. Poetry. Yuck!

Oh, come on. Expand your horizons. What's really awesome is when a line comes out and you have no idea where it came from. That's totally cool.

So, what's the best line you've ever written?

He had to think about that a minute. Slowly he twisted the wristband over his arm as his mind slipped in and around the hundreds of songs he had written.

Toss up between: "Life ain't life if I ain't living it with you" & "She glides on angels wings, sailing through the devil's snare."

Cool. Are there whole songs to go with those?

Yeah. Those and about a hundred others—not that anybody will ever hear them.

Why not?

Are you kidding? I'm having a hard enough time getting people to come hear me sing OTHER PEOPLE'S songs. How could I get them to come listen to mine?

Not that there's anything wrong with other people's songs, but maybe they're like the rhinestones. They're nice for someone else, but they're not you.

Kalin sat back in the chair, and his hand went to his mouth as he thought about that comment. It made sense, but admitting terrified him.

What if they hate my stuff?

What if they love it?

He couldn't think of a reply. He started to type back, but the question lodged in his brain so that everything he considered sending back didn't sound right. Either it sounded conceited, or it sounded scared to death, which was closer. He typed a line, considered again and erased it.

Fear grabbed hold of him. He had reached for that life once and failed miserably. In fact, it had almost taken his life, and now here he was wanting it again? That was insane. But what if it wasn't just him and his stupid choices that had brought him down the first time? What if it was that life itself? What if he put himself out there again and found he couldn't handle it? What if he started looking for the escape hatch again? Maybe this time around he wouldn't be able to make it back out. Maybe this time it would take him down for good.

His mind was going faster than his body, and having absolutely no clue how to respond to her, he finally clicked back over to the Home page. It was then that he realized she had written again. He clicked on her message even as his spirit deflated. It was all just too hard and too overwhelming. How could he ever know it would be all right—that he wouldn't lose everything again? It would be so much easier not to try, to stay where he was, to convince himself that it wasn't worth it.

Kalin, Do you really think people will hate what you write? I don't. Why? Because IT'S REAL, and people can feel that. People are drawn to that. You are the most real person I've ever met. You don't do things so everyone else will love it. You do them because they come from your soul. You are so trusting of God and what He's given you. You see that, you understand that like no one else I've ever known. Do you really think after all you've been through, after all the things He's helped you through that this is suddenly more than He and you together can handle? Come on. You're sitting at X. What's stopping you from reaching for X-Better? D

P.S. I really want an answer to that question.

~ Lucky ~

He sat thinking about it a moment and then a moment more. Real. As he typed, he thought he had never been so real.

Danae knew they were in deep water. She couldn't quite decide why because from where she sat, it was clear that he was talented, smart, and most of all that he trusted God with everything else. So why not this? She had considered writing again when the email jangled.
Because I don't want to go through that again. I can't.
Her heart hurt at the desperation in those simple words.

The drugs?

Everything. I lost myself once. Thank God (literally) that He came along and pulled me out because I couldn't have done it myself. I don't know if I can go through all that again. How do I know that I won't screw up like I did last time? Because I think this time, I'm going to be on my own if I do. K

Ah-ha. So, you've stumbled upon an impossible something? Well, welcome to the club! I'm not being funny either. Man, do you really think I sit here reading about the significance of Plygenic Inheritance and think, "Oh, yeah. This is something I can totally do"? NO WAY! But someone who is much wiser than I am once told me that all things are possible <u>with God</u>. So the question then is why do you not think He's on your side with this one?

She knew so much, and yet Kalin knew all the things she didn't. He twisted the wristband around his arm. "Help, Holy Spirit. I don't know how to make her understand."

There are things that happened back then, things I'm not proud of, things that keep me up some nights. I try not to think about them, but they aren't leaving me alone. I keep thinking maybe that's because God is telling me it's too risky. That I don't deserve more. I've had my shot. Why should I get two when so many others don't even get one?

More than anything in the world, Danae wanted to be able to put her arms around him at that moment.

Have you ever considered that's just the devil's way of talking you out of sharing the talent God gave you with the world? You told me once not to throw away what God gave me because it would be easier. Well, I'm telling you that now. If you give up and marginalize yourself, that's exactly what the devil wants. He wants to take you out of the game before you get the chance to share with the world what you've shared with me. The worst part is, he doesn't even have to convince you. All he has to do is to confuse you. That's enough to get you to stop going for what God put you here to do. Are you going to let him win this round too?

Kalin read it once and then twice. Fear and confusion locked together tight and strong around his chest. Was he letting the devil win again by not taking the chance? That thought pulled defeat into him. It seemed like no matter what he did, he couldn't win. He reached up and typed very slowly. It took more effort than anything he had ever done.

I'm beginning to think the devil wins no matter what I do. K

Anger snapped through Danae. She anchored her gaze to the screen as the ugly face from the dream long before slashed through her. "Now, you listen to me, Satan. You cannot have Kalin. Jesus, please help me. Kalin needs you. What do I say to him?" A question she had never considered floated through her mind.

Do you believe that the Holy Spirit can fail?

Kalin thought that was an odd question.

No.

Have you put this dream in the Holy Spirit's hands?

He had said it so many times, that seemed obvious.

Yes.

Okay. If the Holy Spirit can't fail and you've put this in His hands... Then can you fail?

The fear in the middle of his chest jerked to a stop. He tried to start typing. However, the only word he could come up with was "But..." and he knew that too was an excuse, a lie created by the devil to keep him sidelined. It was then that he looked up at the clock and realized it was nearly six. Quickly he typed a reply, sent it, grabbed his jacket and left. He didn't want to, but life was calling.

For the first time in a long time, he felt like he could meet it head-on rather than dodging and weaving as he tried to stay in one piece. Living. It was a feeling he could get used to.

*You sure know how to level a good excuse. You know that? * smile *

~ Lucky ~

Well, I guess that means get off your lazy butt, Kalin. Stop making excuses, get to work, get out of the way, and let the Holy Spirit go to work for real.

Danae laughed at that. What a way to put it.

I think I have been doing that—blocking His efforts. Okay. I'm now officially taking your advice. I'm putting it in His hands. All of it. The excuses. The attempts. The successes. All of it. It's there. It's His. For better or worse. I just hope when I start to back down because of the junk, I'll see that's what I'm doing, or He'll smack me upside the head so I see it. :) You know, the devil's really good at this confusing you stuff. Funny. I'd never really thought about it like that, but that's exactly where I've been—confused.

Thanks for being there, Danae. You'll never know how much it helped. I'm off to share Him with the world! Wish me luck. Peace & Prayers, Kalin

Danae sat back and smiled. The world would never know what hit it. She sat forward, typed in a reply, and then went back to studying.

When Kalin stepped out of his trailer headed to Sevens later that evening, he was at his bike before he noticed the old man from the trailer next to his down on his hands and knees looking under the skirting of his trailer. Kalin had actually gotten on the bike before her words about helping someone out drifted through him. He looked up at the sky. "I don't have time for this."

But the feeling that he was supposed to help didn't leave. Reluctantly he pulled himself off the bike and strode over. His hands went to his hips. "Something wrong?"

The old man spun and squinted up at him. "It's my cat. She got herself tangled up in some wires. I can't quite reach her."

Kalin surveyed the situation, and his heart made the decision for him. "Why don't you let me try?"

The old man's eyes narrowed suspiciously. "You? Why?"

"Well, because it looks like I'm who God sent."

Slowly, reluctantly the old man backed up, and Kalin knelt down next to the skirting. He bent at the waist and then wound his frame down into the small hole as he looked inside. "Well, hello there, little miss. Looks like you got yourself into quite a predicament there."

The small gray kitten eyed him warily. She squirmed and let out a pitiful meow. However, the wires held her fast.

"You know, I've got a friend who knows all about getting hung up in wires like this." He reached in and slid one wire to the side and another the other way. "At least you're not in heels." In seconds he pulled the kitten out of the hole. Once back on the outside, he ran his hand down its soft gray fur and said a prayer for Danae. Then he handed the kitten back to her owner. The old man took her and rubbed her next to his face.

When he looked up at Kalin who had pulled himself to standing, there was gratefulness in the faded eyes. "Thank you so much. My granddaughter gave her to me this weekend. I could hear her, but I just couldn't get to her."

Kalin reached out a hand and carefully helped the old man to his feet. "I'm glad I could help." He walked over to the bike and got on, waving only once as he backed out and took off. "Now was that really so hard?" he asked himself with a smile.

The rest of the night Kalin's understanding-radar hit on all cylinders. Everything else about him was also. The songs flowed easily. His voice had never sounded better. He even started having fun with the crowd, smiling and arching an eyebrow at them in the middle of songs, which they responded to with cheers and hollers. By the time they broke at two, he was drenched in sweat and completely, joyously exhausted. The rest of Silver Moonlight might be hanging on by a thread, but he felt so alive it was like someone had plugged him into a light socket.

He stepped off the stage and found Zane standing there. He hadn't realized his manager was coming, nor had he seen him all night. However, his manager seemed almost ready to jump out of his paunchy skin.

"Zane? What're you doing here?" Kalin asked.

"This couldn't wait."

Concern dropped over Kalin. "Just a second, I'll get my jacket."

Zane looked like he might not be able to wait that long, but whatever it was, Kalin didn't really want the other band members privy to. He walked back stage where Von and the others were kicking back.

"Hey, Preacher Man," Von said with contempt dripping from the statement. "You finally comin' to join us?"

If you're with the Holy Spirit, can you fail? Kalin almost laughed out loud as the thought traced through him. "No, man, I've got better things to do than run into that brick wall."

Von's face dropped into a hard look of hatred. "You don't know what you're missing."

"That's just it," Kalin said as he pulled his jacket on. "I know what I'm missing. Nothing. See ya." With that, he walked back out into the bar where several young men milled about cleaning up. He strode over to where Zane was leaning against a black half-wall. "So, what's up?" He resettled the jacket on his shoulders even as he kept walking. "What's so important that it couldn't wait?"

He started for the door, and Zane followed him.

"I got a call awhile ago," Zane said, and excitement laced the edges of the words. He looked back into the club. "You really should be sitting down for this."

"I've got an appointment with my bed. Are you going to tell me or not?" Kalin pushed through the second door of the bar and out into the cool breeze of the late Tennessee night. He breathed in the air. It felt wonderful. A smile slid through him as he thought about her, sleeping somewhere he was sure. *Thank You, God for Danae.*

"Mitchell Coleman called me. He's Phoenix Rising's manager."

Kalin's steps slowed.

"They start their first national tour opening for Ashton Raines next month. The real tour, not just the local fill-ins."

"And?" Kalin was having trouble following. "What does that have to do with me?"

A look of pure disbelief carved its way across Zane's face. "Colton Hayes… Well, they thought it was just a cold, but…"

Concern ripped through Kalin, and it stopped his feet. He turned to his manager. "Is Colton okay?"

Zane shrugged, clearly surprised by the question. "He can't sing. If that's what you mean."

It wasn't what he meant at all. The memory of being in that pickup, Colton sucking cough drops like they were candy slid through Kalin. Allergies. That's what Colton had said it was, and Kalin had never questioned it. His brain lurched forward trying to figure out how he could find out how Colton was for real. The thoughts stumbled on Jesse and church the next morning. *God, please be with Colton. I can't imagine them telling me I couldn't sing.*

"Kalin, are you listening to me?" Zane asked, and annoyance scorched the edges of that question. "He can't sing. They need a singer. They called me."

Kalin was hearing every word. He just wasn't processing the flow of information. "Why?"

"Because. They want you."

Chapter 18

"Where have you been?" Danae's mother asked the next morning when Danae picked up the phone, just in from church and ready to devote her day to studying.

"I just got back from church. Is that a crime?" She wasn't in the mood to coddle her mother.

"Well, I'm having brunch over here in 45 minutes, so at least you're dressed and ready."

"For what?"

"To come over here of course. What did you forget about me?"

It would've been easier. "No, I didn't forget about you. I've just got a lot of studying to do."

"Oh, that's right. You're still living in la-la land."

"I am not, Mother. I resent that."

"You're wasting your time not to mention your father's money on this."

"It's better than wasting my life."

Her mother exhaled, clearly wanting to stop the escalating tension. "It's only for an hour. Maybe two. I haven't seen you for more than a month and a half, and we've got a lot of catching up to do."

Danae didn't want to even think about what "catching up" entailed. She sighed. "Okay, but I can't stay long."

Kalin hadn't slept a single wink the night before, and by the time he got to church, he was wired like he had never been in his life. The fact that the library was closed on Sundays was threatening to explode the energy coursing through him. Didn't they know how important it was for him to tell her? Surely the good people of Nashville could understand that. If he just had a way to ask them nicely, surely they would have pity on him and open the doors.

The smile on his face never left as his spirit flew through Sunday service. He didn't hear a word of it. It was like life was floating past him, and he couldn't quite grab back onto it. At the end of the service, he stepped from his bench and scanned the other parishioners. The one he was looking for was tall, with long dark hair. "Jesse!" he said too loudly, but corralling his voice seemed to take more effort than he had the sanity to muster.

When Jesse turned, his face lit up. "Hey! Where were you? I've been looking for you all morning." He held up a hand, which Kalin caught. Then he pulled his friend to him for a quick slap on the back. Kalin stepped back and fell into step with Jesse.

"So you heard, huh?" Jesse asked, his voice falling on the question.

"Yeah, how is he?" They walked side-by-side to the door. Kalin pushed out, and Jesse followed.

"Bummed." Jesse shook his head. "They said complete vocal rest for at least two months. Then they'll see."

"Man, that's tragic." And it was an honest statement. "But he'll be able to come back, right?"

"They don't know at this point. There's been some damage. They're hoping it's not permanent."

Kalin shook his head at the news and offered up a short prayer for Colton. No one deserved that.

"But they told you though?" Jesse asked slowly as they walked into the brilliant sunshine. "About filling in for him."

Somehow he had thought that part was just a dream. "Yeah, Zane told me last night."

"And?" Jesse asked, clearly not sure.

"And? Are you kidding me? That's like… Wow. But singing? Lead? I don't know…"

"You sing lead now."

"Yeah, but not for a national tour."

"We're just opening. Not head-lining."

Headlining couldn't have freaked him out any more.

"Yeah, but just stepping in like that," Kalin said, realizing even as he said it the excuse in that statement. Still he was too stunned to be able to accept it at face value.

"You were made to be up there," Jesse said as they stopped under a tree. "Even Colton said so."

That slammed Kalin to a stop. "Colton? What do you mean?"

"When we had the meeting and he told us he was out, he said we should call you."

Kalin's eyes widened. "But why me? I'm a nobody."

"They don't think so," Jesse said, but his gaze had slipped past Kalin out onto the street beyond.

The tone of the statement skidded through Kalin. When he looked at his friend, he knew the thoughts running through that head. "And what do you think?"

Jesse's gaze fell to the ground. "Man, I ain't going to lie to you. This is the biggest break I've ever had in my life…" The words trailed into oblivion.

"And I screwed the last one up for you," Kalin finished the sentence for him. Happiness and hope dropped into guilt.

An apology ran through Jesse's dark eyes. "That's bad, huh?"

"No." Understanding drifted through Kalin's spirit. "It's the truth." The next words threatened to rip him in two, but he had to say them. They wouldn't be square until he did. "You know I'd give anything for this shot. I mean it's like nothing I could ever have imagined." He exhaled slowly. "But it's not worth it to me if you're not cool with it. You've worked too long and too hard for there to be a chance that this doesn't work out, much less to know it won't going in."

Kalin slid both hands into his back pockets and closed his eyes. His head dropped, and he finally had to let the Holy Spirit say it for him because on his own, he simply couldn't get the words out. "If you think I'm too much of a risk, I'll tell them no, and you can get somebody else. No questions asked."

Surprise followed by concern slid over Jesse's face. "You'd do that?"

"Hey, I lost a best friend once because I was a selfish idiot. I'm not about to make that mistake again." The smile that danced across Kalin's face lifted his spirit as well. He couldn't tell what Jesse's answer would be, but as he stood there, the sun warming him through and through, he realized that whatever the answer was, it would be the right one. Whatever God had in mind, whether it was this or something else, it would be all right. He would be all right. He had finally let go of the future. It was in the Holy Spirit's hands now.

"You know that night I walked out?" Jesse asked, and Kalin nodded. Jesse's face said his mind was measuring the words carefully. "It was like walking out on the only thing I had ever really wanted in my life. We'd made it so far, and it took so much just to get there, and you were willing to throw it all away… I never understood that."

"Yes you did. You understood it better than any of the rest of us."

Peace flooded over Kalin. "Don't you get it? You made the right choice. You saw stupid for what it was."

"I should've done more to help you."

Kalin laughed softly at that. "You did more than anyone should've ever been asked to. Dang it, Jess. Don't beat yourself up because I was stupid. Look at where walking out got you. You're opening for Ashton Raines for Heaven's sake! Be proud of that. Be happy. Ninety-eight percent of this town would give their eyeteeth for what you have right now. And you got there legit. You didn't need all the crap to make yourself be something you weren't. You were just you. Don't let anyone take that away from you."

"Do you ever think about those times? Back then?"

Kalin sighed, and his head dropped. "All the time. I think about you and the guys and how bad I let you all down. I think about Zane and all the hell I put him through. I think about all the nights I could've made a different choice, and I didn't. I think about it, and I wish I could go back and change it all, but turning that sundial back isn't an option. You know? I've got to start here and try to use what I've learned to do it better this time." Kalin's gaze drifted backup to Jesse's face. "Lord knows, I just about killed myself to learn it in the first place."

"So, have you?" Jesse asked, and his gaze ensnared Kalin. "Have you learned?"

As he thought about that question, Kalin took a long though shallow breath. "Back then I was living for myself. Everything was about me. What I wanted. What I needed. What I could do or not do. What I wanted to do or didn't want to do. I, I, I…" He hooked a thumb in the front pocket of his jeans and leaned against the tree. "The choice was always there, and I chose myself every time—over everyone and everything else—even sanity. I didn't want to hurt, so I did whatever it took not to, and I didn't bother to think about the people I was hurting in the process. All that mattered was me." Serious contemplation dropped over his face. "The weird thing is the more I thought about me, the more I hated me, and the more I hated me, the more stupid, self-destructive choices I made. I can't explain it, and at the time I couldn't see it, but I see it now. And I regret every single second of it."

Jesse looked at him for a long moment as if truly appraising Kalin for the first time. "You've changed."

"God, I hope so," Kalin said, regretting the man he was back then more than he ever had before. "I was one sick duck."

"That's not what I mean."

The self-hatred slammed into uncertainty. "How's that?"

"The Kalin Lane I knew would never have stopped long enough to say he was wrong. He would've made you feel like it was your fault instead of his and then gone on doing whatever the distraction of the month happened to be."

"And he would've never looked back to see the hurt he'd caused," Kalin added. He thought about that, shook his head, started to say something, but then breathed instead. Finally, he ducked his head. "He thought the world owed him something—happiness, a good time, something to entertain him so he wouldn't see how desperately miserable he was."

Jesse tilted his head quizzically. "I got to tell you, I thought I was seeing things that first day I saw you here." He lifted his chin to indicate the church. "I guarantee I never thought I'd see you inside a church."

"Yeah, well, when He's all you've got left, your choices get real simple."

The dark eyebrows lifted for a second. "So, it's real then?"

Kalin's gaze pulled up to his friend's face. "What?"

"You. Being here. It's not just for looks, to make someone else think you're all saved and cured and healed."

"No. It's not for anyone else. And I am saved… He saved me from myself, and let me tell you, that took some doing."

Jesse's gaze narrowed on him. "And what happens when the other stuff starts being an option again?"

"Starts?" Kalin asked with a laugh. "Jeez. I'm so sick of being offered, I could scream. I've been begging Zane to find me someone sane to play with for months now. I know he's tired of hearing it."

"And it doesn't bother you—being around it? I mean you're not tempted?"

"If you mean do I ever think that would be fun to go back and try it again? No. If you mean is it ever offered? Yes. Hourly, and sometimes more often than that. To hear Von tell it, you'd think I've been a straight-laced, never so much as colored outside of the lines, goody-two-shoes my whole life." He closed his eyes and shook his head. "I'm sick of being called Preacher Man and feeling like the only sane person in a room full of people running their lives into the ground. It really gets old." The complaints rolled to a stop, and he opened his eyes. "But, for whatever reason, this is where The Big Guy wants me, so I'm doing my best to learn the lessons He's giving me right now. Everything else is up to Him."

"And you're not mad about that?"

Kalin shrugged. "What good would that do me? It would just make

Him think I needed more time to learn this lesson, and believe me, the less time it takes for me to get it and move on, the better." X-Better floated through his mind, and he smiled.

Jesse considered that for a long moment. "So, you doing anything now?"

Kalin's consciousness jammed into the present. "Now? No. Not that I know of. Why?"

"What do you say we pick up something quick to eat and go over the new stuff. We're due in the studio next week. That doesn't give us much time to get Phoenix Rising's newest lead singer ready."

Danae and her mother had just sat down at the small, round, glass breakfast table. Nothing about this visit felt normal. It was almost like this was the first time she had ever been in this house, which was strange because it was where she had lived sixteen years of her life.

"The rolls look good," Danae said as she spread strawberry jelly on one. "We haven't had these in forever."

"I remembered they were your favorite," her mother said, primly spreading her napkin on her lap.

"They're really good," Danae said when she had chewed a bite and swallowed it. "So, how's Nikki?"

Her mother opened her mouth to respond, but at that moment the doorbell rang. Danae started to stand as she was closer to the door, but her mother patted her hand. "I'll get that."

With a slight shrug, Danae resumed her seat. The rolls really were good. She took another one off the plate. Midway through smearing jelly on this one, however, she stopped as her ears picked up the two voices coming from the front door. There was her mother's yes, but the other… As understanding plowed through her, she knew she had stepped into a trap. Her legs pushed her up out of the chair just as her mother and Brandt rounded the corner.

"Oh, Danae," her mother cooed. "Look who came over to join us."

Dread and anger splashed through her; however, she pushed that down. Slowly she put her knee on the chair but didn't sit down. "Oh. Hi, Brandt."

"Hi, Danae," he said barely getting the words across the room to her. Then he remembered something and swiped a bouquet of not quite fresh flowers from his side and held them out to her. "Here. These are for you."

"Oh, look, Danae. How lovely," her mother said, fawning over the flowers. "Aren't they just lovely, dear?"

"Lovely," Danae repeated with no enthusiasm in her voice.

"Here, I'll just go find a vase for these." Her mother took them and disappeared around the corner.

Danae's gaze traveled heavenward. Could her mother be any more obvious? Exhaling, she sat back down. Like he wasn't sure he wouldn't be shot, Brandt took a step and then another over to the table.

"I hope you don't mind..." he started, but her mother bustled back into the room, cutting through his statement.

"These will make the perfect centerpiece." She set the vase and flowers on the table right in front of Danae. The only thing good that she could say about them was that they would block her view of the seat across from hers. Wickedly, she thought that she hoped he sat there.

"Please, help yourself, Brandt," her mother said. "We have plenty."

Because you were cooking for more than two, Danae thought, but she said nothing. Brandt filled himself a plate and sat down at Danae's right rather than across the table. She knew she couldn't get that lucky.

"So, Brandt, what are you up to this summer?" her mother asked.

"Oh, I'm interning at a firm downtown."

"Interning. How exciting. Isn't that exciting, Danae?"

"Thrilling."

Danae wasn't at all sure how long her mother planned to keep this up, but just because she had been set up, didn't mean she had to play along. She answered every question about how wonderful Brandt looked, how smart he now was, how accomplished he had become. The drone of the conversation wafted by her. It sounded like a rusty wheel, grinding to the point of tedium. It was strange because she had heard this conversation before, but she had always been a participant until now. As she listened, she wondered at what point anyone would notice that she was even in the room anymore.

After a full 20 minutes of Brandt this, and Brandt that, Danae had had enough. "You know, Genetics is so interesting," she said, breaking into whatever inane magnificent thing they were talking about at that moment. She took a bite of sweet roll. "DNA and how family traits are passed down. It's fascinating."

Brandt looked at her like she'd grown an extra nose.

"And that whole polygenic inheritance theory in general is just incredible. But you know, it really makes you wonder how someone can take all of the environmental and genetic causes that should lead to one thing but come out with something so totally disparate that it looks nothing at all like the factors that produced it."

Both faces at the table were awash in incomprehension.

Danae smiled at them both. "Could I get some more eggs, please? These are really good."

"Eric, our producer, has been really great about helping us put this thing together," Jesse said as they sat over a bucket of supermarket chicken and two guitars. "We're pretty much down to laying the tracks and/getting the harmonies down. The whole Raines thing threw us into a panic though. They had this solo act booked, and then at the last minute…"

Jesse's statement trailed off as he looked at Kalin.

"And the circle is complete," Kalin said softly. "What do you say, we start at one and work our way down?"

"Sounds like a plan."

"Well, as much fun as this has obviously been," Danae said when the dishes were washed and it was time to head into the living room for an afternoon of utter tediousness. She knew the routine. She had lived it too many times. However, since their last get-together, she had added some new steps to this dance, and it was time to try them out. "I've got a Genetics book calling my name."

"You're not staying?" her mother asked in horror.

"Can't. Homework." Danae walked to the front door and took her jacket off the hook as like puppy dogs, they followed her.

"But we could play cards or something," her mother said.

"Sounds fascinating," Danae said. She reached over and kissed her mother. "Some other time though." She smiled a half-smile at the young man standing awkwardly by the wall. "Brandt, it was nice seeing you again."

"Yeah," he said, more breathing the word than saying it.

Before either of them could mount a suitable protest, Danae opened the door and stepped into the sunshine beyond. Halfway down the walk, she realized that both Mr. and Mrs. Emerson were in their front yard, planting flowers.

"Hi there," Danae said, waving to them. "Isn't it a beautiful day?"

When they caught sight of her, at first they smiled, and then their smiles fell.

"Danae, wait!" Brandt said, rushing through the door and down the walk to where she stood. When he got close enough to touch her, he stopped. Gently he reached down and took her hand in his. "Can't we talk about this?"

Only part of the incomprehension she gazed at him was fake.

"About what?"

He glanced over his shoulder toward his parents, and he swallowed hard. Then he looked back at her but never really met her gaze. "About us. You don't have to leave. I get it. I was wrong."

Even if no one else did, she saw through the statement. "Wrong about what?" It wasn't a challenge. It was a question.

"About..." He glanced around again. "Us. Please, Danae. Give us another chance. You don't know what it's been like without you."

No, but she knew what it had been like without him. When she smiled at him, it was in sympathy. "Brandt, what we had... us... it wasn't real. We were playing house, and not doing a very good job of it either. I don't want to play anymore. I want real. I want better... X-better."

Questioning concern traced through his eyes.

"I don't expect you to understand," she said as compassion for him slipped into her heart. "But I'm not who you thought I was, and trying to be her isn't fair to either one of us. I hope someday you can understand that."

However, it was clear that he didn't understand it then. Tiptoeing, she reached up and kissed his cheek.

"Good luck with everything," she said. With that, she pulled her hand out of his, strode to her car, got in, and drove off. She was sure there were four open mouths gawking at her departure, but for the first time in her life, she didn't care what everyone else thought. This wasn't about them. It was about her and what God wanted for her, and now more than ever she hoped that X-Better had a guitar strapped to his body and talent coming out his ears.

A smile drifted through her. He would've been proud. "God, please let Kalin know how wonderful he is... wherever he is right now."

"We've been looking for a ballad," Jesse said as he flipped the pages to another song. "The rest of the album feels really balanced and right, but every ballad we've looked at is just not us."

Kalin hesitated for a moment. He was here to fill in. It wasn't his band. It wasn't his place. Then a second before he let the moment slip by him, he reached around his guitar and pulled the melody out of it that had been flowing through him for a month. Jesse's movement stopped, and he watched the chord progression once again. Forgetting the papers, his full attention went to Kalin.

Watching someone critique the words was too hard, so Kalin let his eyes fall closed as the words poured from his soul. "Because of you, I'm lucky to be me..."

The only thing that would've made getting home any better would've been if there was a message waiting in her inbox. She knew there wasn't, but she checked anyway. It wasn't so much disappointment at not having a message as in not being able to connect with him today. Her gaze went to the clock, and she wondered if he realized what time it was. Four o'clock was now set in her body.

As she sat down to study, she breathed a quick prayer for him. "Wherever he is, whatever he's doing, please be with Kalin even though I can't be."

The last strums sounded on the guitar, and with embarrassment haunting him, Kalin pulled the guitar forward and back on his knee. "It's just something I've been working on," he said, not really looking at Jesse.

Jesse sat without moving, and Kalin's awkward meter zoomed off the charts. He grabbed the wristband, twisted it, and then let his gaze traipse up to the clock on the wall. Despite knowing he had just poured his heart out to someone who thought he was insane now, a smile spread through him as he realized it was four o'clock. *God bless Danae.*

"So, do you hear the background too?" Jesse asked, breaking into his thoughts.

"The background?"

"Yeah, for... 'Lucky.' Do you hear the background?"

Kalin was trying to figure out what train they had gotten on. "You mean the instrumentals?"

"Yeah," Jesse breathed.

Wishing he hadn't bothered to play it, he rubbed his hand over his face. "Yeah. Some... why?"

"Show me."

Thinking that was an odd request, Kalin laid his fingers on the guitar and added the accompanying notes drifting through his soul. It wasn't difficult. It was more like it was a part of him. The only hard thing was putting it out there for someone else to hear. As he played, Jesse set his fingers on his guitar and began picking his own way through the song. Finally they fell into rhythm together, and Kalin couldn't stop the smile.

As they hit the place for the lyrics, Jesse's voice blended in with the harmony. "Because of you, I'm lucky to be me..."

Again, Kalin was grateful for the gift of her in his life. He closed his eyes and let the words take him to that place where he was with her.

Chapter 19

Kalin climbed the stairs without the need for effort. He was 20 minutes early for their Monday email date, but he didn't care. All he wanted to do was share his news with her, hear about her day, and connect with her for another moment in time.

At the computer the clicks were swift and sure. He had time to twist the wristband only once before his inbox was up. Instantly he leaned forward as excitement burst through him. He clicked on her first message, wishing she was right there with him rather than 120 miles away.

Dear Kalin, You know, I have thought I was a failure so long. Maybe because I was trying to be something I wasn't. Maybe because I was trying to do it on my own. I don't know. Either way, it wasn't working. I have to say thanks for helping me see that I can't but HE can. Thanks also for not taking the easy way out in life. You've taught me so much! God bless you! Danae

He would never be able to tell her what a few simple words could do for his soul. It was impossible to put it into words. How could he tell her that it was she not he who had drastically altered the thoughts running through his life? How could he explain that when he was with her even through words on a screen, he felt like he could do anything? It was just too overwhelming, too big to explain.

A click back to the Home Page, and he clicked on her second message.

Dear Kalin, Don't know where you are or what you're doing. It's four o'clock on Sunday, and I'm sitting here thinking about you. May God's abundant blessings be in your life now and always. Danae

How could she do that? It was like she knew even without being here. Shaking his head in disbelief, he set his fingers on the keyboard.

Danae was five minutes later than normal on Monday afternoon, and by the time she got to her computer, her heart was threatening to beat out of her chest. The second she clicked on her Inbox, she saw his new message. With no other thought, she clicked on it.

Dear Danae, I know you're busy. I am too. But I have to see you. There are just some things that can't be said over the computer. I'm here. Let me know. Kalin

Danae sat back as her mind and heart slid into and through those words. The Genetics test was over. The first A&P test wasn't until Thursday. There had to be more to life than studying, and besides being excited by the prospect of seeing him again, the "some things" comment had her intrigued.

What do you have in mind? D

Excitement and panic smashed into him.

Do you know where Kingston is? What do you say we meet there in an hour? We can leave your car at the little gas station on the east side of town. You interested?

Interested? She laughed out loud. That was the understatement of the century.

Race you! D

Kalin laughed. She was crazy. He typed a quick reply, clicked out of the program, and headed out to his bike.

Danae switched out her drab gray T-shirt for a red spaghetti-strapped tank top, grabbed her jacket, and carefully ran a hairbrush through the tangles at the back of her head without bothering to take the front sections out of the clip at the top. She must be completely insane to be this excited, but the butterflies were crashing into each other in her stomach. Just before she pulled on her flip-flops, an email jangled into her inbox. She looked up, and joy shot through her.

Hopping as she put her other shoe on, she clicked on his message. It was a single word.

Go.

Kalin had to be careful all the way to Kingston so as not to speed. It would've been easier than not the way his heart was racing. The bike under him seemed to be in as big of a hurry as he was to get there, and he had to consciously slow down several times lest the police delay him even further.

The sun-drenched earth held the beauty of life around him. Everything was green and alive. It was like flying through heaven.

When he pulled into the little gas station, he scanned the parking lot, trying to remember what kind of car she drove. The memory wasn't there, he finally realized with frustration. He should've thought to ask. He pulled into a parking space and stabilized the bike. His mind worked to calculate the time she might have left versus the distance she would've had to travel to get there. If she drove 70, how soon would she have gotten there in relation to the amount of time it took him? Just before he came up with a plausible answer, his gaze caught on the lithe figure walking hesitantly toward him, and all the numbers flew out of his head.

Praying he wouldn't crash to the ground with the bike on top of him, he pulled the helmet off, swung his leg over the back, and stood. She was more beautiful than he remembered—smaller and more fragile. Not one thing about her could be called big. Delicate and graceful fit much better. He swallowed hard and was only barely sane enough to pull the sunglasses from his face. It was like standing in a dream.

Her light brown hair flitted across her face, dancing in the gentle breeze. She seemed not to even notice it. The closer she got, the slower she walked until with only a few yards to go she was almost not moving at all. Her hand was tucked in the back pocket of her dark denim jeans, and her gaze kept falling to the concrete. His heart filled with the sight.

"Looks like you beat me," he said as his own gaze fell. Staring was all he wanted to do, and yet just looking at her seemed to heighten the nervousness of her movement. His gaze traced back up to her as she approached, and he took a half step backward so she wouldn't feel as threatened as she seemed to.

"Yeah, I got out before rush hour, or it would've been midnight before I got here," she said. He noticed how her soft voice matched her soft face to perfection. She dug her hand further into her back pocket wrenching her shoulder upward as she stepped off the curb into the parking space next to the one his bike occupied. Her head tilted to the side as her gaze swung around the parking lot nervously. "I wasn't sure I would find it. I'm not that great with directions."

He smiled softly, taking in the full effect of her beauty now that she was only a couple feet away. "Well, there's only one, so I figured it wouldn't be too hard."

She nodded as her gaze fell again. She wound her wayward hair over her ear.

"I was surprised you didn't have to study," he said, wishing this was easier.

Her shoulders lifted. "Finished one test this morning. I've got another one Thursday, but…" She looked at him for one half second, and then her gaze fled across the parking lot again as if she was concerned that someone she knew might drive up and catch them there.

Kalin looked back at the bike and questioned the wisdom of this arrangement. "Umm, this is kind of weird, so if you don't want to, I'll understand, but there's a little place over by the river. I thought maybe we could go and talk."

Her hand dug deeper into her pocket. "Oh, okay." However, she never moved. "On your bike?"

"Is that a problem?"

The hesitation was evident as was the tentativeness of her half-smile. "I guess not."

He wished he hadn't asked. However, going back now didn't seem to be an option so he handed her the helmet, which she proceeded to put on. Rather than watching her, he backed into the details of his own life. He replaced his sunglasses, mounted the bike, and backed it out of the space. Once he was ready, he turned to her and offered her his hand. The barest touch of her hand sent his alert system screaming.

In two heartbeats she was once again on the back of his bike. He lifted his feet, and they were off. How he was really here and this was really happening, he couldn't be at all sure. How he would stay sane enough to not mess it up was even less sure.

Danae had never been more panicked in her life. He wasn't just nice-looking as she had told herself so many times she had begun to believe it. He was incredible. Not really much taller than her, he had a rock-solid air to him that said he was ready to take on the world. The sunglasses almost did her heart in, but when he had taken them off, the heather gray-blue of his eyes threatened to undermine every admonition she had given herself from Knoxville to Kingston. Those eyes just weren't fair to a girl who was trying to keep herself from falling for him. His shag cut blonde hair fell in perfect proportion around the face that radiated surfer-style carelessness. His incredible had nothing to do with conventional and everything to do with living carefree and relaxed.

Had she seen him in a crowded room, she would've taken more than a second look, but why he had taken a second look at her was beyond her understanding. Now here she was on the back of his bike—again. Holding onto him and hoping that it would never end. It made absolutely no sense. She had always gone for conservative. Button-down shirts. Nice slacks. Ties. Definitely not stonewashed, boot-cut jeans with a rip in the knee.

And that didn't even touch the slight dusting of whiskers on his jaw line or the silver earring dangling from his left ear. The farther she went through his style, the farther from conventional she got. Still her arms were around him, and they were racing through the warm sunshine, and nothing she had ever done had felt so right.

They turned onto a gravel road, and the bike picked up speed. The fact that they were now miles from even the tiny town of Kingston was not lost on Danae's awareness. It was the fact that she really didn't care that was throwing her under waves of panic. She had never been the kind to not worry—about every detail of every minute. So where had the Danae that she had known suddenly gone? Why wasn't she here protesting that they should've stayed in town, that this was insane, that she should be more sensible? Where had practical gone?

The gravel road deteriorated into a dirt road and then into a dirt trail. Had she had any sense left, she should've been questioning the fact that she was on a bike that was digging its way up a rocky hill with a guy who three months before she would've run the other direction from. She should've been, and yet she wasn't.

As they crested the hill, her lungs sucked in air so pure it felt like one-hundred percent oxygen. It made her dizzy, and the sight suddenly stretched out before her wasn't helping the headiness wafting through her. A wide finger of water seemed to meander from one side of the world to the other in front of them, undulating across the landscape in a lazy arc, teasing the tall grass at its edges. The brilliant sunlight sparkled off the water making it glint like a field of diamonds. As the breeze drifted across the tops of the grass, the water played the bottoms making it weave and dance peacefully all along the river's edge.

Danae felt Kalin's body stabilize the bike as they started down the embankment to the river's edge at the lowest point of the gentle slope. In seconds they were parallel to the river on a small trail just wide enough for the bike's front wheel. Stopping here would've been perfectly fine with her, but he didn't seem to be stopping, so she simply let the scene around her cascade into her consciousness and down into her memory. The feel of him. The whitewash of the water. The sunshine pouring down over all of it. It was in that moment that she remembered again what really living felt like.

Just when she thought they would continue to ride forever, Kalin slowed the bike and leaned to the right in a gentle turn as they approached a meander in the river that had formed a slight embankment before winding in the other direction, creating a sort of beachfront. Near the embankment, Kalin braked the bike, put his feet down, settled the bike, and then hit the ignition, plunging the air around them into a stillness that was astonishing after her ears had become so accustom the roar of the bike. It took several moments for the peaceful lull of being at the water's edge to fully enter her consciousness. Besides that and the breeze, there was no sound.

"Here," he said, and his accent traipsed across her heart. Funny how email didn't do his accent justice. "Careful. The ground's kind of soft." He reached back for her arm, and she let him help her off. Her legs wobbled beneath her when she was again on solid ground, and she wasn't at all sure if it was because of the ground or him or the day or just that she was obviously no longer in control of herself.

She reached up and pulled the helmet off as he disentangled himself from the bike. He made the last few checks of the bike and then turned and took the helmet from her. She raked her fingers through her hair, wishing she had more than just the small clip at the top of her head to hold it back. The breeze caught several strands and sent them skittering across her face. With a toss of her head, she brushed them back, watching him anchor the bike to the embankment. Finally he turned to her, and if he could've looked any more heart stopping, she wouldn't have known how. It was downright criminal.

He seemed to remember the sunglasses and swept them off his face before stowing them in the helmet. When he turned back to her, she dug her hands into her back pockets, wondering what came next, and so excited about whatever it was that she was about to jump out of her skin.

"So." His left hand twisted the thin brown wristband on his other arm. "What do you think?"

Her gaze slipped from his out to the river beyond. "It's amazing." She tossed her head again to get the hair out of her face. "Beautiful."

For a long moment it seemed that neither of them knew what to do next. Finally he turned his gaze up the trail. "Want to walk?"

She shrugged, and together they stepped back onto the trail. Her steps swerved in time with his as they walked with the sun to their backs parallel to the river rushing in the other direction. After moments that seemed to hold the world around them in their hands, Danae's gaze chanced over to him simply walking with her down a trail in the middle of nowhere. What he had to say and why he had brought her out here suddenly lost their meaning. She didn't care why anymore. The fact that they were together was enough for her.

"You know," she said as they walked slowly side-by-side, "I never got the chance to thank you."

"Thank me?" he asked in confusion. "For what?"

"For making me important again."

The confusion in his eyes deepened. "You are important."

She shook her head as her hands came out of her pockets. She let them sway at her sides in time with her steps. "No, I wasn't—not to me anyway. I didn't want 73rd, but I had convinced myself I did—for them." She breathed the admission in. How many years had she lived that lie? "I didn't think I could have what I really wanted until you showed up. I thought it was too much, too hard to even try for. They still try to tell me that, but it's easier not to listen now."

When his gaze found her face, she couldn't return the look. "Why now?"

She considered the question as she continued to walk. "Because now I have someone who doesn't think the real me is stupid and worthless."

She felt the traces of anger and worry in his gaze as it surveyed her face although he didn't reply immediately.

Finally his gaze dropped to the dirt at their feet. "Anybody who says that what you love is stupid and worthless doesn't understand that you didn't choose it. God chose it for you. He gave you what you love. It was a gift. How could anybody say that was stupid and worthless?" He shook his head in annoyance. "That just drives me crazy. The whole world is running around trying to be what the world says they should be instead of being where God put them for the reasons He put them here. It takes so much energy to keep that up. To me, that is stupid and worthless, but we keep telling each other that's what's real. It's not. But we buy into that, and we think, 'Yeah. They're right. I can't have it. Why even try?' And we talk ourselves out of even trying for it. Ugh. Just drives me crazy sometimes."

She hadn't expected that outburst, and she looked at him skeptically. "You mean I'm not the only one doing that?"

"Hardly." He laughed. "Jeez, I don't think there are many people out there not doing that. But everybody's so scared to be honest that nobody sees we're all living trying to be what we think everyone else thinks we should be—rather than being what God meant us to be."

"Unless you're you."

"Or you," he said with a smile, and when he swerved his steps into hers to bump her shoulder, she had to smile as well.

"Yeah, well, we're working on that." Her hand was swaying at her side, but suddenly it wasn't swaying by itself. Tenderly he caught hold of it and twined her fingers through his. The heat from his hand sent her other senses scattering through her, and she didn't have enough sanity left to decide if she should protest. By the time she decided, it was too late.

His gaze drifted out to the river beyond as they walked hand-in hand. "I've got news."

She couldn't stop the smile that was bursting from her soul. "Yeah, seems like I remember that." She looked over at him, but he was still looking at the river. After a long moment, her heart slid into seriousness when he didn't say anything. "So, are you going to tell me, or am I supposed to read your mind?"

Still he said nothing for several steps. Finally he exhaled a long breath. "I'm going on tour."

Her feet made the decision for her, slowing to a near-stop in a breath. "On tour? Wow! Really? That's awesome!"

His steps slowed too although he didn't look nearly as excited as she thought he should. "Yeah. Remember Phoenix Rising? They asked me to be their lead."

Happiness was jumping through her like acrobats gone mad. However, his face registered only pensiveness.

"That's great, right?" she asked, willing him to look at her so she might have a chance at reading his eyes.

"Yeah… yes," he said, looking up but his gaze never quite made it to hers before it fell between them again. "Of course it's great."

The river and the beauty of the day was forgotten in the concern washing through her at the look on his face. "Then why doesn't it sound so great? I thought that's what you wanted."

"It was. It is." He glanced at her, and then his gaze fell to the grass at their feet. "I don't know. It's all just happening so fast."

"Fast? Are you kidding? You worked your tail off to get here the first time. Then you did it again to get back here. You've climbed every wall they've put in your path—and a lot of walls no one else had to climb. That wasn't easy, and it didn't just happen. And it certainly couldn't have seemed fast."

With that his steps stopped completely. When he let go of her hand to sit down on the grass, she suddenly felt very cold. Her hand reached up to rub across the top of her other arm. She looked at him sitting there, and although she couldn't be sure why, she knew his world was spinning in chaos.

Carefully, gently she sat down next to him, and for all the peace of the little meadow, concern was all she felt. She watched as he took the hand that had been hers for one brief moment in time and wrapped it around the brown leather wristband of his other hand. Absently he twisted it back and forth, looking at it but clearly not seeing it.

"You know, I really can't read minds yet," Danae finally said when she had done her best to do just that. "So are you going to tell me what's really going on, or am I going to have to pound it out of you?"

He smiled but only barely. Then he shook his head. "It's just... Why do I get a second chance? There are so many people out there who want this, who've worked so hard... why me?"

Words rushed through her and right back out before she could catch them. He was the most together person she knew, and yet right here, standing on the cusp of his dream, his spirit was screaming doubt and fear. Gently her hand traced through the air over to his, which was still twisting that band until she couldn't figure out how he didn't have a carpet burn. She didn't question the gesture, just let her spirit guide her body. Her fingers wrapped through his and pulled them from the wristband. "Maybe it's because you gave me my second chance."

Surprise and incomprehension jumped into his eyes, which were suddenly fixed only on her. "I didn't do anything anyone else wouldn't have."

"Oh, yeah?" she asked. "Do you know how many anyone else's I've known in my lifetime? A lot. And not one of them ever gave me what you did. Not one. Don't you get that? You gave me the courage to chase what I really wanted. And when you give something like that, you're going to receive. That's the way life works. Now maybe all of those people out there wishing they could make it are so focused on themselves, they don't even see other people who need help. But you did. You stopped. You helped. You did it. That means something."

Her words stopped, and her gaze fell to their fingers lying on his knee intertwined. Her thoughts continued running through her head although they were no longer finding the air between them. God knew her better than she knew herself. She would never have opened herself to this relationship had He not cracked her open and laid it in front of her.

"Sometimes," she said softly, "God knows what we need better than we even know ourselves. Sometimes we think only one thing is a possibility, but He has other ideas—options we've never even thought of, options we don't think are even possible." She tossed her hair out of her face as she looked back to Kalin. "X-Better, remember?"

That, finally, brought a real smile to his face. His gaze was still anchored on their hands clasped together. "Even when you don't deserve it?"

"It's not about deserving it or not deserving it," she said. "It's about letting go and being open to it—whatever it happens to be."

"But I've taken so much for granted in my life," he breathed, the words barely making a dent in the sound of the waves. "I didn't appreciate what I had, what He had given me until it was gone. Now, things are happening so fast, I'm afraid they're going to be gone before I have a chance to appreciate them."

"Then start right now," she said softly. "This minute. Look around you, and be grateful for what's here. I know I am."

She squeezed his fingers lest he not comprehend the full meaning of her words. When his gaze wrapped around hers, she had never been more grateful for anything in her life. In a way she had never before experienced, she knew he was leaning toward her, not taking but asking for her to come to him. Head-spinning desire flooded through her as she let go of caution and tilted herself into the invitation of his lips.

Like falling onto a feather-soft pillow, her lips touched his, and every thought of why this would never work evaporated. In fact, any thought other than how he could feel so good faded into oblivion as well. The first kiss melted into a second as without her directing it, her body twisted until she sat with her back next to his thigh.

His arm wrapped over her shoulders, pulling her backward and cradling her in his embrace as his other hand slipped up to her jaw line. The whisper-soft touch of his hand on her neck just under her ear sent chills of delight spiraling through her. Wanting nothing more than to never stop, she felt him pull back, and with her back leaning on his knee, she opened her eyes to the realization that his were only a heartbeat away.

The disbelief in his smile and his eyes wafted through her.

"What?" she asked, gazing at him, aware that she was totally at his mercy and yet knowing with perfect trust that he would never try to take anything she wasn't ready to give.

"You," he breathed. "I don't know how this happened."

"God gave us another option." In a wash, gratefulness and joy spread through her. She let her fingers wind through the locks of golden hair glinting in the sunshine at his neck. "X-Better anyone?"

"Man, you blew X-Better out of the water way back there," he said, gazing at her with undisguised astonishment.

"Me? I didn't do anything."

Seriousness dropped over the teasing in his face. "Then why do I feel like I'm flying?" He lowered his lips to hers again, and love so strong that it hurt clutched the middle of her chest. She never wanted this to end. Wrapped in him she felt safe, like the world out there could never touch her—could never touch them. Like nothing other than this even existed. When his lips left hers again, she let herself get lost in the dream of just feeling how he was holding her. It was like being weightless. If this wasn't real, she never wanted to go back to what was.

Sitting there on the soft grass with the sun beginning its downward trek toward the horizon in earnest, Kalin watched her. There was a placid trust not just on her face but drifting through her body as well. She never opened her eyes, even as his gaze took in the arch of smooth white skin on her neck as it plummeted down to the brilliant red jersey material at her breastbone. He traced a finger down it simply wanting to memorize the feeling of it, the feeling of this—of being with her, of having her in his arms. He never wanted to leave.

"So tell me about this touring thing," she said never really coming back to reality. "What're you so scared about?"

His finger stopped, and he turned her gently so that her back was leaning against his chest. He wrapped his arms around her shoulders and let them trail down until they crossed at the wrists at her waist. "We're opening for Ashton Raines in Indiana on July 3rd. It's a national tour, so we'll be on the road from then until it's over in May.... at least they will be."

She arched her neck to be able to see him, but it didn't work very well. "Who's they?"

"Phoenix Rising. I'm just filling in for the lead singer. It's not permanent."

"Oh," she said softly. "Well, it's a step, and God knows the next one, so…" Her finger traced up and down his forearm as she gazed out at the river. "You know I keep thinking about what happens come August. Do I keep going with the doctor thing, or do I go back to teaching?"

Instantly he let his shoulder drop so that she was again cradled in his arms, looking up at him. "Are you kidding?"

She didn't meet his gaze. "Well, I haven't withdrawn my name yet."

"Danae…"

"I know. I know." She pulled herself to sitting and put her back to him. "I just keep thinking what if I wake up and all of this is a dream, and I'm on my own again."

His hands reached up and laid themselves on her shoulders. "Is that a possibility?"

She tossed the hair drifting over her face onto the wind. "I don't know. Is it?"

His hands fell from her shoulders back to his ankles. He didn't want it to be. He wanted to grab on and never let her go. But she had her life, and he had his. Making this work would take both of them wanting it more than anything else in the world.

"Believe me, I know what it's like to wake up one day and realize the person you thought you could count on is just gone," she said as the river swept the words away.

Concern slid through him on her tone. He wanted to reach out to her, but it was clear that she was putting distance between them so she could get the words out. The name coiled anger around him. "Brandt?"

She shook her head, sending her hair in a thousand directions at once. Her fingers were playing with the grass at her feet, and her gaze was stuck to them. She took a shaky breath that ripped through him. "My parents."

He heard the sniff, and trepidation trounced its way through him. He slid six inches to the side so he could see her silhouette in the blinding light of the sun.

"My dad walked out when I was little. Just left. One day he was there. The next day he wasn't." The words sounded like they were going to strangle her. "I've never understood that, you know—how you could love someone one minute and then just leave the next?"

Pain he hadn't seen coming rammed into his chest, and his gaze fell. "Sometimes it's not that simple."

"He walked out. Seems pretty simple to me." The ache in her words tore through his gut. "The thing I never could figure out is that he never came back. Not once. Not for birthdays or Christmas. And he knew where we were. He knew, and he didn't care to even come see us. It was like he was just some ghost in some old pictures Mom had hidden in the closet. I mean, what did I do that was so bad he had to leave and never come back?"

"No, Danae." Despite the demons snapping at his spirit, Kalin reached up and put his hand on her arm. "Don't do that to yourself. It wasn't you."

There were tears in her eyes when she turned to him. "Then why did he leave like that?"

He wanted to stop the hurt in her, but he didn't know how to do that. "I don't know why he left, but I know it wasn't about you. It was about him. Maybe he thought he didn't have enough to give to you."

"All I needed was him. That's all I needed. That would've been enough." With that, she leaned into Kalin's chest and let him hold her. His mind drifted back to that first night by the tire as he bent forward and kissed the top of her hair. So much had changed, and yet it seemed that nothing had.

He wanted to make her world better, but his was in so much chaos that helping anyone else seemed impossible. Finally, she sniffed again and pulled back, wiping her eyes.

"I'm sorry. I don't know why I said that. It's dumb. I mean it's over. Get over it already, Danae. Everybody else has."

"Hey," Kalin said, coming to her defense reflexively. "Don't do that. This isn't about everybody else. It's about you." He put a finger under her chin and turned her gaze to meet his. "And to me, that's never dumb. Got it?"

She smiled a half-smile and dropped her head to her shoulder. "It was just so long ago. I don't know why it still bothers me so much now."

A thought traced through Kalin, and his mind recoiled at it. However, he had to ask. "Have you thought about contacting him?"

She sniffed and ran her hand under her nose. "How much postage do you put on a letter to Heaven?"

The thought had never occurred to Kalin. Then he realized what she was telling him. "He... died?"

"My freshman year of high school," she said. "Mom wouldn't let us go to the funeral. Nikki wanted to, but..." The statement trailed into oblivion.

"And you?"

"Brandt said it was better if I didn't."

"What did you think?"

She shrugged. "I don't know. I didn't even know him, you know? It seemed kind of pointless."

"So, you didn't want to go?"

"I didn't go if that's what you're asking."

Exasperation exploded through him. "No, that's not what I'm asking. Jeez, Danae, at what point does what everyone else think stop and you start?"

She turned on him, anger flashing through her almond-brown eyes. "What do you want me to say? That I've been mad ever since I was little that the other girls had daddies and I didn't? That my mother drove me nuts trying to make me be the woman she wasn't so I could hold onto a man? That I let them drive every piece of me out in favor of someone they said could hold onto somebody, and I let them do it because I didn't want to be alone? Is that what you want to hear?"

"Is that honest?"

The tantrum fled, and her shoulders collapsed around her bowed head. "Yeah."

"Then that's what I want to hear."

When she looked up, pain and confusion swathed her features. "Why?"

"Because I want to know you... the real you. Not the you they made up, but the real Danae. Who she is. Who she was. Who she wants to be. That's who I want to know."

That statement ran across her face and pulled her head back down. "How do you know she's even worth getting to know?"

How she could even ask that question was beyond him. Gently he reached over and pulled her chin up so his gaze embraced hers. "Because she's the best thing that's happen to me in a really, really long time. Do you have any idea what you've done for my life?" He waited for her to answer, but she didn't. "Do you?"

Her gaze searched his but held only confusion.

"Every time I pull that email up, and there's something from you, I could just float right out of that chair. You make me see what's possible. You make me remember that God's on my side. You challenge me, and you make me want to share what I'm feeling with you with everyone I meet. Jesse keeps saying I've changed, and he's right. I have. And you helped me to do that. Not just in words like I was doing but in here but for real." He pressed his other hand to his heart. "With you, I want to be a better man than I've ever been before. I want X-Better, because I believe it's out there now. You've made me believe that. And I want to be X-Better for you, too. So that you'll be proud of me, proud to be with me—so that you'll want to be with me. I don't just want to be some guy who happens to play the guitar and sing. I want to be the best Kalin I can be every single minute because I know you deserve no less."

She wanted to say something. He could see it in her eyes, but the words never made it to the surface. His hands fell back to his ankle.

"That's why I want to know the real you because the real Danae is someone who makes me glad to be alive, who pushes me to be me, who I get up every day and just want to be around. Jeez, don't you get it? I love you..." The words were in the air before he had really thought about them. They were true, but how she would take them was another story entirely.

Her gaze fell. She sat there without saying anything for a long moment, and then she tossed her hair back when she picked her gaze up to meet his. "So does that mean I get free tickets to your concerts?"

He laughed at the 180-degree turn they had somehow made. Skepticism poured through him. "I don't know. Do you want free tickets?"

There was only teasing in her face when she looked at him. "Yeah. And I'm thinking I'd better get them now because they're going to be impossible to get in a month." Letting the rest of the serious conversation go, she spun slightly and leaned back into him as the sun reached for the horizon opposite the river.

"Yeah? You just want to see Ashton Raines," he said, pushing the possibility of what she could be telling away from him.

"No." Her finger traced down his arm, sending electricity corkscrewing through him. "I've heard Phoenix Rising has this hot new singer all the girls are going to be crazy for."

Throwing his head back, he laughed out loud at that. "And how do you know that?"

She arched her neck and smiled up at him. "Because I'm already crazy for him, and I've got really good taste."

He shook his head slowly as he bent his lips to hers. Crazy was the least of his worries.

Driving back to Knoxville long after the sun had relinquished its hold on the sky, Danae replayed the evening in her memory. Never had she felt more loved. The fact that he had actually said it was just icing on the cake. A laugh drifted through her when she thought about the preacher's cake analogy. Kalin certainly had the right ingredients—faith, solidity, trust, love… He wasn't just icing like Brandt. He was real.

She exhaled on the thought. "Thank You, God, for putting Kalin in my life. Help me to be the Danae that he can be proud of, the Danae You made me to be, and help us to be more together than we ever were apart."

When he got back to the little trailer just after eleven, Kalin crawled into the bunk over the hitch and lay with his hands clasped on his stomach. She was more than he ever could've imagined God would put into his life—much more than he deserved. His thoughts slid to her growing up without a father, and then of their own volition, his thoughts drifted where he had never allowed them to go before.

Tears of regret stung his heart as his fingers ticked off the years in the darkness. Five, he finally decided as he ran his fingers through his hair and held them there. She would be about five by now. The tiny baby face he had stared at through that hospital glass was no more. It was older now, in a young-little-girl kind of way. He wondered what color hair she had. He searched his memory, but there was no indication from those few brief moments. The color of her eyes, whether she was tall like her mother—they were all no more than mere guesses.

"Oh, Lily, baby girl," he said to the darkness. "What did I do?"

Chapter 20

Kalin had warned Danae that without a map of every library in every state in the nation, he might not be able to keep their email dates, which had morphed into eight o'clock appointments as life got more hectic for both of them. That didn't make missing the first one the night they left for Indiana any less heart-rending. As they crossed from Tennessee into the night-darkening sky of Kentucky, all he could think about was how much he missed not being able to talk to her.

With rehearsals and studio appointments running almost simultaneously during the last month, his time had been sucked down a black hole, and that was doing nothing for his hold on life. He sat in the back of the lighted but not-near-state-of-the-art tour bus the band had rented, picking aimlessly on the acoustic guitar Colton had loaned him and thinking through the path his life had taken. Even after their time by the river, the conversations with Danae over the 'net had gone right back to where they had left off. There was no mention of the fact he had said he loved her—just how was life, what was up, and what projects and plans were coming up next.

He wondered about that at odd moments. How she seemed not just willing to overlook that little detail but like it was important to overlook it. As his fingers drifted over the strings without any real direction from him, his thoughts ran smack into why again. It was clear that love had walked out on her once, and she was afraid it was going to do so again.

In reality, he couldn't blame her. As much as he wanted this time to be different, he couldn't deny that he had a track record with these things that wasn't stellar. Granted she didn't even know about that, but there was such a thing as a woman's intuition, and he wasn't discounting that. Besides, she was too busy with her own life to worry about how quickly she could tie hers to his.

As June turned to July, Genetics and Anatomy I had melted into Anatomy II and Biochemistry. They talked about her school some, but he could barely say the names of the classes much less keep up with what they entailed learning. It seemed he knew as much about biochemistry as she knew about music—which wasn't much. Once or twice she had mentioned the free tickets again, but they both knew it was a joke. She was locked into being in Knoxville indefinitely. Two years of pre-med, then med school, internship, residency… They didn't even talk about that. It was too far away and implied too many things about their future to even mention.

"Sounds good," Jesse said, indicating the music emanating from Kalin's guitar with a nod as he dropped into the seat next to Kalin. "New song?"

"Oh," Kalin said, pulling his fingers from the strings. "I don't know. Wasn't really paying attention."

Jesse shook his head. "Wish I could play like that without paying attention."

Kalin shrugged the compliment off. Talent and hours of practice guaranteed nothing. When he sang with Phoenix Rising, it was too easy to believe it was real, that it could go on forever, and yet, he was smart enough not to let that hope take hold. They had four concert dates between now and the time Colton would be released. Four times on stage, living the dream. What came after that was anybody's guess.

"They said the concert sold out in two hours," Jesse said, pulling his knees up onto the seat in front of him. "Verizon Wireless—the vaunted Deer Creek. Should be a good one."

"Yeah," Kalin said as he put his thumb to the side of his mouth and stared out the window, the words of all the Phoenix Rising songs seemed like mush in his brain—there and yet all jumbled together in a hopeless tangle of lyrics and chords.

"You nervous?" Jesse asked.

Kalin pulled his attention back into the bus. "Trying not to be. You?"

"As a Mexican Jumping Bean. I'm just hoping once we get there, it's going to feel like all the others, so I don't totally freak out, you know?"

"Yeah," Kalin said, having only a few others to go by that he actually remembered. His fingers went back to the strings, and he plucked out the melody to Lucky for no other reason than he wanted to be with her right then so badly it was making the middle of his chest ache.

~ Lucky ~

Jesse picked up the memory of that melody as he watched Kalin's fingers. "Too bad Eric brought that other song in," Jesse said. "I really think the guys would've killed for that song."

"Wasn't the right time," Kalin said as his wrist worked back and forth on the neck of the guitar.

With a shake of his head, Jesse looked at Kalin in perplexed annoyance. "Man, I've never known anybody like you."

"Lucky thing there."

"No, man. You act like everything's handled, taken care of—even when stuff doesn't go your way. It's like it's no big deal. I don't get that."

Kalin shrugged. "What's not to get? I'm not in control anyway. If I tried to be... well, we both know how well that worked."

"Yeah, but you act like everything's perfect in your life, but you live in a rat hole, you've got a car that belongs in a junk heap, a career that's hanging by a thread, and pending a doctor's decision that you have no control over, you could be right back there, and yet here you are—not grasping and trying to hold on, just being... well, here. How do you do that?"

Kalin thought about the question for a long moment and then took a deep breath. "When I tried to run things, no matter how it worked out, it was never enough. We got the booking, but I wanted it to be bigger. We got the perfect song, and then someone came out with a better one. We ran around grabbing and wishing and praying for what we wanted never realizing that God might have something better in mind." Kalin laughed slightly. Even when she wasn't here, she was. He smiled. "X-Better."

"X-Better?" Jesse asked in confusion. "What's that?"

The notes rang out from the strings. "It's just something a friend of mine and I say. Reminds us to take our hands off the wheel and let Him drive."

Curiosity drained over Jesse's face. "And this friend... is someone from Canada?"

"No, she's from here. Well, Knoxville really." The guitar was singing as if it had a voice of its own. "We met at a wedding."

"Really?" The question was a slow drawl. "And this friend is..."

Kalin exhaled, knowing Jesse well enough to know that within the six hour drive he would find a way to drag out the whole story no matter how much Kalin tried to hide it. It was easier just to tell him. "Her name is Danae Scott. She's pre-med at Tennessee University. We met at a wedding in April. We've been emailing..."

"Emailing?" Jesse asked incredulously.

Kalin shrugged. "We've both got lives we couldn't just drop." The music stopped as his spirit plunged into the darkness of being without her tonight. He wondered where she was. It was almost 9:30, and he felt every second as it passed without her. His gaze slipped out the window into the night beyond. He missed her more than he could ever put into words. "Well, at least we did until…"

"Until…?" Jesse asked with concern.

Shaking his head, Kalin planted his gaze back in the bus. "The tour. I had to tell her last night I didn't know when things would work out so I could send her anything else. She understood, but…"

Jesse's face fell in confusion. "You didn't bring your laptop?"

Kalin laughed at that. "Hello. I don't have a laptop. I live in a rat hole, remember?"

"You can't call her?"

He laughed softly. "I don't even know her number. I couldn't afford the minutes, and so I never really asked." He shook his head as the music resumed, sadder this time although he didn't do it consciously. "I've been using the computers at the library, but now…"

"Well, good grief, man. What are you sitting here driving yourself crazy for?" Jesse stood up. "Hey, Adrian!"

"Yeah?" Adrian called from the front of the bus where he was playing Gin Rummy with Steve.

"Where's your laptop?"

"With my stuff in the back seat."

"You mind?" Jesse asked as Kalin sat, looking up at him, trying to figure out how to tell him it wasn't that important without tearing his soul to shreds.

"Have I ever minded before?" Adrian asked without looking up from the game.

Jesse stepped to the back and dug through the pile. In seconds he was back with the black plastic case. "Adrian's like the techno wizard. He's set up on a wireless—national something or another." As he talked, Jesse sat back down, opened the computer, turned it on, and clicked the IE icon. "We all use it. He's used to somebody needing to check something by now." He spun the laptop. "There you go."

Between the guitar and the laptop, Kalin didn't have enough hands.

"Here." Jesse settled the confusion by taking the guitar from him. He played a few notes but gave up. "I don't know how you do that."

Kalin watched him stand with the guitar. "Be careful with that."

"Always." Jesse took it with him to the front where he sat down and started strumming.

~ Lucky ~

The hazy blue light of the small computer screen pulled Kalin's gaze back to it. If only she was there...

The first BioChem test was in ten hours, and Danae knew she should be studying. However, all she could think about was Kalin. She wondered where they were by now, how things were going with the guys, if he was ready for his big debut the following night. It wasn't fair that she had to be here—studying. She wanted with everything in her to be there.

At her desk, she tried to focus on nucleic acid & enzymes, but they weren't holding her attention. In front of her, her computer jangled with an incoming email. She looked at the black screen in annoyance. That was just plain cruel. It wasn't him, and it wasn't going to be him. Drilling her gaze into her book, she willed herself to understand the intricacies of enzymes—or even to care. She should care. She needed to care. This was important.

After only a few more seconds, she gave up and flipped to another topic that would be on the test. She had studied for no more than a couple of minutes when the email jangled again, and she stared at the computer. spam and more spam. It was bound to drive her crazy before she got any kind of a message that she wanted to get. Tapping her foot on the ground to keep from thinking about it, she re-read the part about the structures of the Mycoplasma genitalium and Mycoplasma pneumoniae, wishing they made any sense at all. When the email jangled again, she exhaled audibly. With annoyance, she grabbed the mouse and moved it. Shutting the thing off was the only way she was going to get any studying done.

She clicked on the email program and was a half-click from shutting it down when her heart jumped into her throat. Her gaze narrowed on the sight. Three new messages? How was that possible? Trying not to analyze it too much, she clicked on the first one that had come in.

Testing one, two, three. Is this thing on? Tell me you're there and that this is working because I'm going crazy here not talking to you. K

Joy jumped into her. He was alive, and he was sending messages. It was for real. Quickly she clicked back and onto the second one.

Danae! Hello. Where are you? Speak to me... I'm sitting on a bus that's driving through the middle of nowhere, wondering where you are. Where are you? Write back if you're there.

Two more clicks and she had the third message up.

Please tell me you're there and not off studying with some hunky pre-med guy who actually knows what biochemistry means. Write back. I've got six hours to talk—provided they don't steal the laptop back between here and Indianapolis... K

Books forgotten, she typed a message.

Kalin checked the Home page, liking the feeling of having the world to himself as he typed. Sure the guys were up front, but there weren't other people walking around looking at him. This was far more private and much, much nicer. Now if only... He clicked on the Home page and sat up straighter in the seat. It was too good to be true. He clicked on it.

No, no hunky pre-med guy... They can't sing. How's it going? Where are you, and how is this possible? I thought you said weeks. (I'm glad it wasn't. Hours was making me nuts!) D

So she was as lost as he was. Funny how important those words on a screen had become.

Thank Adrian. It's his laptop. Jesse stole it from him and said I could use it. I think he felt sorry for me sitting back here all depressed because we were leaving. K

Who's Adrian? Thank him for me! You were depressed? What are you thinking? You're going for your dream, what's there to be depressed about?

Because you're not here. : (I know. I'm a sap. So sue me. I just kept sitting here thinking about how long it was going to be before we could do this again, and it was killing me. Adrian's the fiddle player. Real nice guy. You'd like him. Anyway, he had the laptop, and what was I going to say when they gave it to me? No, I enjoy being miserable without her?

Danae smiled at the compliment.

Well, that would make two of us—except you were actually getting something done—going to the concert. Me? I was just sitting here looking at a book I've got a test in tomorrow that was making NO SENSE!

Uh-oh. Maybe I'd better let you go if you've got studying to do.

Call it the break I've been wishing for. So are you all ready for tomorrow night?

Ready? Probably not. Scared to death would be a much better choice of words.

Worry crept into her. She set her hands to type back.

Well, scared to death is not such a bad place to be. Believe me, I've been there before, and it means you are finally taking a chance and going for something that seems impossible.

Yeah, but what if I can't do it? What if I get up there and 3,000 people think I'm the worst singer they've ever heard? What if I let the guys down...?

What if you don't? What if it's wonderful—the best night of your life? What if those 3,000 people are the start of something amazing in your life? What if your dream is within your grasp again?

What if I screw it up again?

You won't.

How do you know?

Because I know you, and I know that you know now not to try to do the impossible on your own. You can't, but HE can—remember? With Him it's possible. Don't try to do it yourself. Let Him do it through you... funny, seems I've heard this from someone before. :)

Kalin almost laughed through the fear clutching him. His reply was on its way in seconds.

It's weird. I look into tomorrow, and I can't see it. I can't see it working out and I can't see it not working out. It's like it's this black hole and anything can happen.

Danae smiled as true peace dropped through her.

When you get to the end of everything you know, and you're about to step off into the darkness. One of two things will happen. Either you will step on something solid, or you will learn... to fly. I know you. You will fly. Trust that. Trust Him. It will be what it is meant to be. Let go and trust that. It's the best advice anyone ever gave me.

For the first time in the conversation Kalin didn't hit the reply key immediately. Instead, he put his elbow on the armrest and his thumb to his mouth. One thing was for sure. He was at the end of everything he knew. What wasn't so sure was if he could really fly or not. However, when he closed his eyes and breathed in her words, he knew she was right. Whatever happened on the Deer Creek stage was meant to be. Good or bad. God had a plan, Kalin's job was to trust that.

Finally he put his fingers to the keyboard.

That's why I wanted to talk to you so badly.

Why's that?

You give me so much peace—even when I'm freaking out. You know what to say to get my focus back where it needs to be. I'm not worried anymore. Thanks.

Tears sprang into her heart at the honesty of his words.

Just repaying a favor. Well, my work here is done, so I'd better be getting back to studying. UGH! Wish me luck!

Luck. Not that you'll need it. I'm sure you'll do awesome just like always. But I'll be praying anyway because that never hurts. I might not get a chance to write tomorrow night, but I will write as soon as I can. Know that I'm thinking about you and praying for you—and being grateful for you! God bless and keep you until we talk again. Kalin

The peace he had felt talking to Danae stayed with Kalin until ten minutes before show time the next evening. The cool breeze that drifted into the backstage where the members of Phoenix Rising stood getting ready to go on stage should have felt good on his hot skin, but he barely felt it. The royal blue cotton shirt unbuttoned to the third button down shouldn't have been hot either, but he was frying. The turmoil in his gut began to form a tight knot in his chest and throat, and he picked the collar of his shirt up off his shoulders as if that might help keep him from melting with nerves and heat. It didn't help at all.

"Well, this is it," Jesse said, turning to the others who looked about as calm and cool as Kalin felt. "What do you say we huddle up?"

The others took Jesse's suggestion and formed a tight circle around him. Kalin let his collar go and joined the group between Jesse and Adrian, wondering how in the world he was ever going to make it through the next hour. They each put their arm around his shoulders. It was the first thing that made him feel like he wasn't walking out on this limb alone. He was grateful for that small reminder.

"Dear Lord," Jesse said very softly. "Please be with us on that stage tonight. Thank You so much for giving us an awesome crowd. Be with us as we play. Thank You for all the blessings in our lives, and for letting us see where they come from."

The prayer stopped, and for a moment Kalin felt Jesse's gaze turn to him.

"And show us what X-Better looks like tonight."

Kalin couldn't stop the smile. The peace, the solid understanding that God was at that moment with him slipped into his spirit. He took a breath and said a soft amen with the rest of them. When they broke, Jesse was looking at him with a smile he had never seen before.

"Take your hands off the wheel," Jesse said softly as he winked at Kalin.

As Kalin nodded, there were no nerves left. He could do this. With God and the great members of Phoenix Rising by his side, he could.

"It's time," the stagehand called.

Purposefully, Kalin walked over to the wall where the sea foam green electric guitar stood. He picked it up, settled the strap over his shoulder, and ran a hand over the soft smooth polish. Closing his eyes, he memorized that feeling, and let the worry drop away from him. Just beyond the door where he stood, he could hear the crowd, and he let the sound of their excitement wash over him in waves. The other band members took their places in front of him.

When the lights in the arena dropped off into darkness, Kalin looked down and suddenly realized he couldn't see his feet. He felt the others walking forward, taking the stage in front of him, but his cue wouldn't come for another minute or more. He took his gaze off his invisible feet and looked out into the darkness punctuated by swaying spotlights. It was dizzying.

"The Verizon Wireless Event Center is proud to welcome… Ace Nashville Recording artists… Phoenix Rising!"

Rob's drumbeats were nearly drown out by the screaming crowd, but in seconds on the wings of the music the band dove into the first song as the backlights came on, illuminating them not as individuals but as silhouettes. Kalin looked down at his feet still swathed in darkness, and there was no stopping the smile.

"When you get to the end…" he whispered. With that, he took a hard breath, looked up, closed his eyes, and let his fingers jump onto the strings and slide down them in perfect time with the other music. He heard the crowd's reaction and felt his spirit lift from the earth. With the push of God's palm, he stepped out onto the stage as six spotlights slammed onto him.

It was a good thing God was leading because at that moment Kalin couldn't see a thing. Dancing in time to the music just because he couldn't help himself, his feet kicked into the rhythm as his fingers continued through the notes at breakneck speed. His steps finally got him to the microphone. Six more notes and the lyrics fell into place through him and around him.

"Up from the ashes... of a heart crushed and burned. Up from the ashes... a way in, a way out. It's one for the money, two for the show, three to get ready, and four to GO!"

Joy took over then, and he danced and played—a spirit cut loose from the bounds of reality. It wasn't that he was conscious of it. It was just that at this moment, truly living was right under his fingertips, and he wanted to feel every second of it from top to bottom. He was moving to the music, singing, dancing and playing without so much as trying.

At the instrumental break, he drifted back across the stage toward Jesse who stepped forward and snagged the guitar riffs from the middle of the melody as the notes Kalin played swerved in and out of Jesse's. They stood shoulder to shoulder, making music and having the time of their lives. When their part ended, they looked across the stage at Adrian who with only a step forward brought every girl in the first three rows toward him like a magnet. His bow danced across the strings in and out of the drumbeats behind him. Then he tossed it back to Kalin who took the final guitar solo and stepped back to the mic.

Had he thought about the 3,000 people wrapped in darkness beyond, the overflowing confidence powering through him might have left. So he didn't think. He just lived, and it was better than anyone could've ever explained.

When they bounded off the stage into the back area, Jesse caught Kalin before the others could.

"Man, that was incredible!" Jesse fell into step with Kalin who still felt like he was floating. "Wow! Woohoo!" Despite the fact that the whole band was right behind them, Jesse jumped in the air and did an impromptu jig. "That was so cool! Let's do it again!"

"I'm right there with you," Adrian said, coming abreast of them. "That place was rocking. I've never seen people go that nuts before."

"Yeah, I thought those girls in the front were going to pull you guys off the stage," Steve said.

"If they'd have gotten a good hold on Kalin, they would have pulled him out there that's for sure," Adrian said, laughing. "Woohoo! Missouri, here we come!"

Chapter 21

"Did you see this yet?" Jesse asked three weeks later as the bus crossed from Texas into New Mexico. In just under two days the dream Kalin had been living in for the past two months would be over. Colton had called twice, saying things looked very positive and the doctors were optimistic that he'd be able to rejoin the group by their San Diego concert. That left only this one at Albuquerque's Journal Pavilion, and as much as Kalin wanted to be out on the road with the guys, he couldn't bring himself to pray for that to happen. Colton had worked too hard for Kalin to be selfish.

"What's that?" Kalin tilted his head to the side to try to read what Jesse was handing him. He took it and scanned it. *Phoenix Definitely Rising* blared back at him from the headline. Feeling Jesse sit down next to him, Kalin started reading. It was a review from their last concert written in the Kansas City Star.

Phoenix Rising kicked it up a good 40 notches with the addition of new lead singer and guitarist, Kalin Lane. Lane's adroit guitar stylings are matched only by his deft vocals, which seem to caress the Phoenix Rising repertoire in ways that make the lyrics come alive. The question that keeps coming up is: where have they been hiding this guy?

Kalin breathed a short laugh, scratched his eyebrow in embarrassment, and handed the paper back.

"They love you, man," Jesse said as his gaze went to the article. He seemed to think for several seconds about his next comment. "So, what happens to you when Colton comes back?"

It was the same question that had been on-loop in Kalin's brain since Zane had called the week before to say that Silver Moonlight had cut Kalin loose in favor of a young buxom blonde torch singer. He hadn't told the others, and it was only after Danae threatened to come and pound him that he told her. She didn't have a great answer for him, but it was nice to be able to tell her anyway.

"I don't know," Kalin said as the weight of the question crashed on him. "I guess I go back to Nashville and start scrounging around in garbage cans again."

Jesse's foot kicked the seat back in front of them. "You're better than that, Kalin. You are. Look at this." He lifted the paper. "You shouldn't have to be scrounging around anything."

"It's not my call," Kalin said, shrugging. "I took the shot. If it's going to end, I guess that means there's something better coming."

"X-Better," Jesse said but didn't sound very pleased.

Kalin nodded. "I'll be okay."

Jesse shook his head. "I wish there was something I could do."

"You already did."

They would be onstage in less than two hours, and Kalin was trying to get okay with that in his mind and his heart. He couldn't really tell how he was going to go out and rock the house when his spirit felt like it was being stepped on. Finally as he sat in their dressing room, his gaze went over to Adrian, and he knew he had to ask.

"Hey. You don't happen to have your laptop around, do you?" Kalin asked, trying to make it sound off-handed.

"Sure," Adrian said. "It's over in my stuff. You know where the on button is."

It had taken only one time to figure that out, and by that point there had been far more times than one. Kalin went over to Adrian's neat pile and pulled the black plastic case out. He went over to the rounded, padded blue chair, pulled it into the corner, and sat down. It took a minimal amount of effort to get the computer going, and as he waited for the connection to latch onto the web, he put his hand to his wrist and twisted the brown leather band there.

Finally the computer beeped, and he worked the built-in mouse, which had gotten easier with all of the practice. He put his fingers to the keys and wrote what was in his heart. Had she been standing right there, he wasn't sure he could've said it, but on the ether there was enough distance to make it feel safe.

Danae had taken the night off from studying. She only had her two finals left—one on Monday and one on Tuesday, but she also had Saturday and Sunday to devote to studying for them. So she was busy cleaning her room when the email jangled in. Instantly she dropped the dust rag on the little shelf that held a myriad of tiny trinkets she had accumulated over the years. At the computer she ran the mouse back and forth to get it to come to life. She'd been waiting and worrying and praying all day. It was his last concert, and from their last two conversations, she knew it was killing him.

Her breath caught when she saw his message, and she clicked on it, feeling his presence on the other side of that modem.

Dear Danae, Hate to bother you AGAIN, but I'm really struggling here. I know they all deserve better than I feel up to giving them tonight. I just keep thinking about this being the end, and I don't want it to be, and I'm so dang scared about what happens when I get off that plane in Nashville I can't think straight. There's nothing waiting for me there. I don't have a job. I don't have a band. I don't have anything. Help! I feel like I'm drowning here, and I don't have the strength to keep swimming! Please write back if you're there. Please...

Like he had to ask.

He checked the Inbox once, twice, three times as he ran his hand over his mouth. If only she had been there. Then on the fourth time, there was a message. He clicked on it feeling like he was grabbing for a life preserver.

Dear Kalin, It's not the end. I know it's not. But since it feels like it is, then make this the concert to end all concerts. Live it like it's the last concert you will ever give. Give them the show they will still be talking about when they get to Heaven :) As for what happens when you get off the plane, remember, you will still have the three things that matter most... God, yourself, and me. Everything else we can handle. D

Tears trounced through his heart. He sat back and ran his thumb over his bottom lip as he re-read the message. There was no doubt any more that God had sent him an angel.

Danae, Do you have any idea how special you are? I've been trying for a week to get right with this, and it was still about to kill me. But with myself, you and God waiting for me when I get off that plane, I know everything will be all right. Know that I'll be singing the love songs for you tonight ;) I've gotta go. All God's exceedingly abundant blessings to you—my good luck charm. Kalin

Danae shook her head when she read the message. She hadn't done anything for him that he hadn't done for her. She clicked the Compose button to tell him so. She knew it would be the message that he would read after the concert—when the end was really the beginning. Feeling the heaviness in her heart that he would feel when he read it, she typed out her heart and then went back to cleaning.

The songs flowed through Kalin like they had been written for him. He didn't have to think about the words. He just had to be and let the music take care of itself. It wasn't until the last song, "Come Again," that the memory that this was all ending jumped on him, clawing through the well-disguised ache he'd been hiding for days. He fought it as it rose in him. He willed it to go away for just one more song. Then it could take him wherever it wanted to go. The lights dimmed around him as they had the previous three shows, and a hazy blue backlight illuminated the stage from his back.

On the neck of his guitar, his hand shook with the emotions assaulting him. He had never been so grateful for one moment even as he so wished that it never had to end. The last time the dream ended, he hadn't seen it coming. This time all he could do was stand there and sing while he watched it steam toward him. There was no way to stop it, and in that moment it was all he could do to stand there on those tracks as if nothing in the world was wrong.

"Live this moment as if it's your last," he sang on wobbly pitch as he fought with his fingers to find the strings. He swallowed hard and closed his eyes—knowing the audience couldn't see him. Somehow he had to get through this. "Live today for it won't come again. Life is a balance of holding on and letting go, and you only get one chance…"

The rest of the band joined in behind him as the spotlights once again flared to life. The song was supposed to be upbeat and happy, but he was struggling. It was like life was swimming in patterns around him, and he couldn't quite grab on. The center of him ached, jamming memories and wishes into his throat so that it was all he could do to get the words out.

"Give each day your best. Take it with the rest. Live it, breathe it, love it, leave it for it won't come again…"

Behind him Adrian backed off the harmony, sensing the weakness in Kalin's voice. Kalin tried to make his feet dance, but they felt like lead. Every word seemed to take the breath right out of him. His only prayer was that the song would get to the end before he actually passed out center stage from lack of oxygen.

"Life is a balance of holding on and letting go," he sang as the final lyrics rounded the bend. "And you only get one chance…"

The music behind him continued for a few more measures, and then it was over. Applause and screams of approval burst through the crowd.

~ Lucky ~

The front four rows surged forward. He tired to smile, but even that hurt. Pulling the ache into him so that maybe it wouldn't be written all over his face, he stepped back, removed the guitar from his shoulder, and set it in the stand. Then he took his place between Jesse and Adrian for their bow. When he stood again, he realized he still held the pick in his fingers. Without really thinking about it, he flicked it forward with his wrist. It flew into the crowd, and a group of fans lunged for it. Following Adrian, he strode off the stage.

The second they trailed into the backstage area, Kalin felt the speechlessness of the others. They knew how hard he was fighting to keep it together. He put his head down and choked the emotion back into his chest. How he was ever going to walk away from this, he didn't have a clue. At that moment, Jesse stepped up next to him and clapped a hand over his shoulder.

"God's got a plan, man. God's got a plan."

"That's what I'm hanging onto."

In the little hotel room, Kalin opened the laptop for the last time. He would miss this privacy when he was back to using the library again. The guys had all turned in early. They were due to head out at 6:30 the next morning. More than that, it was clear that none of them knew what to say, so rather than say more than "Thanks and good luck," it was easier to just go to their own rooms.

The hazy blue light of the computer screen illuminated the little area around the desk. On the bed across the way, Jesse lay, ostensibly sleeping, although Kalin could tell he wasn't. Slowly, deliberately, Kalin worked the mouse and pulled up the email. Melancholy surprise jumped into him when he saw her message, and then he smiled and shook his head. Of course she had written. He clicked on the message.

Dearest Kalin, The end of one thing is always the beginning of another. You are where God put you. Be there. Be where you are right now, and bless it for what it's teaching you that you couldn't have learned any other way.

He pulled his gaze away from the screen, put his head down, and squeezed his eyes closed against the ache. All he wanted to do was cry, and she wanted him to bless that? It hurt to even think that way. His breathing was shallow when he looked back at the screen.

I know. You think that's impossible. But someone very special to me once said that all things are possible <u>with God</u>. He was right then, and he's right now. Let go, and believe that God has a plan for you. Scary, I know. Believe me, I'm taking BioChemistry for Pete's sake! But it's real.

Trust it.

The breath he took carried peace into the turmoil in his soul. As hard as it was to keep it with him, she was right.

Funny thing, Tara was telling me that today a friend told her about a class where they had made an acronym of the word LIGHT. When she told me what her friend had come up with, I thought of you. When you live in His light, "Luck Is God's Help Trusted." Trust that His help will be there, and know that no matter what I will be there for you too! Peace and prayers as you begin your new life, Danae

How she knew, he would never be able to put into words, but she did. He typed a short message and then closed the plastic case. She was already sleeping. It was after all, long after midnight in Tennessee. Quietly he went over to the unoccupied bed and slid onto it. He lay on his back on top of the covers, crossing his feet at the ankles. It was nearly a sure bet that he wouldn't be getting any sleep anyway, so it was pointless to crawl between the sheets. He twined his fingers together and put his head on them as he looked up to the ceiling somewhere above him.

"I take it she wasn't there," Jesse said from the middle of the darkness on the other side of the room. He had obviously become used to his roommate's late night laptop chats.

"I'm sure she's sleeping."

There was silence for a moment.

"So, does she know?" Jesse finally asked as if he was talking to the shadows.

Kalin thought about the question and swallowed. "About before?"

"Yeah."

"Yeah." The thought twisted through Kalin's consciousness. "Well, most of it anyway."

Jesse didn't say anything for a few seconds, and then he exhaled softly. "Does she know about Rebecca?"

Kalin raked in a thick intake of air. He knew the question deserved an answer, but it took more than a moment to get one out. "It's been a long time."

"Does Rebecca know you're back?"

It was a question Kalin had never really considered. "I don't know."

"So you haven't called her then."

He couldn't get the answer out. Guilt, fear, hurt, shame, remorse. One after another they tramped across his chest making it hard to get in a good breath much less to get any words out.

Jesse rolled to his side and then onto his elbows. "You know she called me after you went back."

Kalin's attention snapped to the statement as that thought wound through him. "She did?"

"Yeah, she was pretty bad off. She wanted to know how to get in touch with you. I didn't know what to tell her. I mean it wasn't like you left forwarding information. I guess I could've gone to Zane..." The words trailed off as Jesse contemplated an option he had clearly never considered before. "But I was so hacked off at the time, I told her I really didn't care where you were."

Regret ripped at the tattered edges of Kalin's spirit. "It wasn't your problem."

For a long minute Jesse said nothing. Then he exhaled hard. "Is it yours?"

Kalin's brain stumbled through that question. "What does that mean?"

"Well, you're back now. Right with the world and everything, you know? So why haven't you tried to contact her, or were you just planning to go on with your life like it never happened?"

Guilt seared through Kalin's chest and brought anger into the void. "Kentucky's a big state. She could be anywhere by now."

"It's not that big as states go. You haven't even looked? Don't you think you owe it to her and to..." Jesse was obviously searching for the name.

"Lily," Kalin breathed into the darkness. He closed his eyes on the ache as the name scraped over his heart. "Man, they don't want to see me. What do they need me for? I walked out on them. Took off and kept going. Now, what? They're going to welcome me with open arms? I don't think so."

"I didn't say that. I just said there's a little girl and a woman you said you loved out there somewhere. They may very well tell you to get lost—or worse, but shouldn't that be their call rather than yours?"

The whole question tangled its way around and through Kalin's brain. In a way he had hoped everyone had forgotten, so that he could in fact go on with life as if the past had never happened. However, as he lay there in that moment, he knew with perfect certainty that this was the block that was holding his spirit hostage. This was the reason he always felt less than worthy of any good thing that came along.

He thought and breathed and breathed and thought. Then, the decision formed in his gut. "Do you think Adrian knows enough about the computer to do a search?"

Jesse never moved. "Maybe. I don't know. Why?"

Kalin sat up, and his equilibrium tilted dangerously on the suddenness of his movement. "Because if I don't do this right now, I'm going to lose my nerve, and I may never get this chance again." He stood from the bed and paced to the end of it where he stopped and turned. His whole spirit felt like it was in a battle for its life.

Jesse pushed himself off the mattress. "We could always ask."

Adrian had been working the keys for more than half-an-hour while Jesse and Kalin paced the room in front of him.

"Would you two please stop that?" Adrian asked as he sat, concentrating on the screen. "You're making me nervous."

Jesse had filled Adrian in on the basics, and although it didn't thrill Kalin to hear the sordid details of his life story laid out like that, he knew it was good to have friends who would help and not judge.

"Sorry." Kalin sat down on the bed, but his knee started jumping up and down like an out of control piston. "What're you doing anyway?"

"Scanning the newspaper files for a lead," Adrian said. "The white page searches are getting us nowhere." Then he stopped. "Ah."

"What?" Kalin jumped up from the bed and strode across the room in three paces. He stepped up behind Adrian as at the computer Adrian's gaze narrowed on the screen.

"Rebecca J. Bennett, right?" Adrian asked.

"Yeah," Kalin said, unable to read the screen because Adrian was in the way and unable to breathe because this might really be happening.

"Did she live in London, Kentucky?"

"Yeah, that sounds right," Jesse supplied both because Kalin couldn't get out the words and because he couldn't remember that many details.

"Oh, man," Adrian breathed as he leaned closer to the screen. "Parents: Mel and Cathleen?"

"I don't know," Kalin said, his nerves about to jump from his skin. "Why?"

"And a daughter, Lily Mae."

Kalin's breath snagged as he looked over at Jesse who looked as stunned and frightened as his gut felt.

"That's in there?" Jesse asked, looking at Adrian uncomprehendingly. "In the newspaper?"

Adrian looked up at Jesse, not daring to look at Kalin. He nodded. "In Rebecca's obituary."

Chapter 22

Danae couldn't wait for Tuesday. Besides wondering where Kalin was and what he was doing, the fact that she would be out of school for five whole days was all she could think about. She had considered going to Nashville to surprise him, but she wasn't sure where the line was that said what she could suggest and what she couldn't. When she clicked on her computer on Sunday morning, a smile slid through her spirit. How could 26 letters arranged in different patterns on some ether make her feel like she was going to float off the planet?

Danae, The more I see, the more I'm thankful for you. If I'm sane at all by this point, it's because you haven't let me lose it. Thanks for the note of encouragement. I needed to hear that. I'll try to get back online Monday or so once I get back to Nashville. No promises though. I'm just trying to make it through the next minute at this point. Any extra encouragement you've got would be much appreciated. Gotta go. Kalin

Her heart hurt at the ache in his words. She wished she could put her arms around him and tell him it would be all right. However, 120 miles wasn't making that any easier. She put her hands to the keyboard and typed a reply not at all sure he would get it in time to make a difference but hoping he might all the same.

It had been 48 hours since Adrian had uttered those words, and still Kalin couldn't get his mind all the way around them. It wasn't like Rebecca was old. She was younger than Kalin if he remembered right. Back in his little trailer, trying to find a reality that had somehow spun from his grasp, he tried to put the past into some timeline. It wasn't easy.

There were so many pieces missing—like when they met and how. It was as if one moment she wasn't there, and the next she was. The partying. He remembered that. But beyond that, it was all just one big, fuzzy picture with no definition to anything.

Standing over the scrambled eggs cooking in the little skillet, he let his gaze slide out the window to the world on the other side. If Rebecca was in fact dead, then what had happened to Lily? Did someone adopt her or what? The question slashed through his heart. He wanted to know, and yet he didn't. Somehow not knowing gave him enough distance to believe that everything had worked out for her and that the last thing she needed was for him to show up.

The sizzling on the stove brought his attention back, and instantly he realized the eggs were scorched on the edges. He grabbed for the metal handle and yanked the skillet off the burner, flinging it across the stove where it crashed into the timer that had never worked since it had been his.

"Cripes!" He picked his singed fingers up to his mouth and sucked on them. "Ugh. What is wrong with me?" With one hand he wrenched the burner off as with the other, he repositioned the skillet carefully. Depression flowed through him as he stared at the blackened eggs. He put his hand to his forehead and pressed as hard as he could. "I can't even make eggs anymore."

There were nine more in the carton in the little refrigerator, but he didn't dare use them. He'd spent 22 dollars on groceries the day before, and he was determined to make them last as long as possible.

The knock on the door yanked his attention toward it for a second, and then it returned. If he just didn't answer it, maybe they would go away. Quietly, carefully he picked up the skillet with the towel and grabbed a fork. Without bothering to put the eggs on a plate, he forked some of them out of the skillet and into his mouth. The knock sounded again. Louder this time.

"Kalin! Son! You in there? It's Zane. Open up!"

Confusion and dread traced through Kalin as he stepped across the trailer with one footfall and snapped the door open. He didn't bother with a greeting. His mind was too wrapped up in feeling sorry for himself.

"Are you trying to scare the living daylights out of me?" Zane asked. Anger streaked across the question. He took one step up, then the second, and he was in the trailer.

Kalin couldn't clearly recall if Zane had ever actually seen the trailer, but at that moment that question just joined the others in the slush pile. He stalked over to the little bench seat, sat down with his back to the hard steel, propped a foot up on the other side of it, and continued eating the eggs that crunched with each bite.

"I see you didn't blow that advance they gave you on housing,"

Zane said, looking around at the trailer.

"I might need it to eat next week."

Zane scratched the folds of the side of his neck. "No wonder you look like no one feeds you. Do you always Cajun-style your eggs?"

In annoyance Kalin looked up at him. "Did you come here to critique my cooking?"

"No." Zane closed the door and motioned to the little fold out chair next to the embarrassingly small table. "May I?"

Kalin shrugged.

"I came because somebody forgot to turn on his cell phone... again." Zane sat down and leveled his gaze at Kalin. "I've been trying to get a hold of you for three days now."

The eggs were starting to solidify in Kalin's throat. He stood and walked over to the cabinet to get a glass of water. "It's probably not even charged any more." He filled the glass and took a long drink, fighting not to taste the acridness of it. Bitter tap water. Why should he expect anything more in this rat hole? He took another drink and forced it down. Then he wiped his mouth with the back of his wrist, grabbed the skillet sans towel, and stalked back to the bench seat. "So what was so all fire important that you had to come all the way out to the sticks to track me down?"

"Oh, nothing," Zane said, the spite dripping from the words. "Just that every major player in town has been beating down my door to talk to you."

Kalin snorted and forked another mound of eggs into his mouth. "Yeah, right."

"What? I'm serious. Do you know how many calls I've gotten in the last week? McGraw, Shania, Chesney, Raines. The word's sure spread fast about you."

Zane's words were sliding in and out of the stack of emotions Kalin had been fighting for the better part of a week, making it difficult to comprehend what his manager was saying. "Why would they want me? They've all got bands."

"Not for their bands, dummy, as a feature guitarist for their upcoming albums."

Kalin shook his head trying to figure out if he was somehow just asleep and dreaming. "Why me?"

"Because from what I hear you kicked some serious booty out there with Phoenix." Zane pulled some papers out of his gray jacket pocket. "I've also got half a dozen bands that have called too…"

Slowly Kalin stood, walked to the stove, and laid the skillet on it.

He laid his hands on either side of it, searching for a clear answer for what all this meant. "They want me?" he breathed.

Zane smiled, clearly not sure Kalin was happy about the turn of events. "Yep, looks like you're gold again, kid."

Gold. It was an interesting concept. Cold and hard. Unfeeling but worth a fortune in the world's eyes. As Kalin rode to the library on Tuesday afternoon, he wondered if he wanted to be gold again. He and Zane had spent the better part of the morning sorting the offers, and there were some that made his heart stop. Most of them were offering more money than he had made in the last two years put together.

But the question nagging him was if he could really be worth all that money. He climbed the library steps as if they were Everest. He needed to talk to someone. Someone sane. Someone who still lived in reality. He pulled up the chair at the first computer he came to. As he waited for the computer to process his request, he twisted the wristband slowly.

The second he saw her new message in the heap of other emails, his spirit relaxed for the first time in four days. He clicked on it.

It sounds like you could use a hug. I know someone who would like to give you one. You doing anything this weekend? Saturday or Sunday maybe? After tomorrow morning's BioChem test, I'm out until next Wednesday. It's just a thought. Let me know. D

A thought was all it took.

Danae made it back just after the test to find a message from her mother taped to her door. "Came by. You weren't here. Call me. Mom" It didn't bode well. Danae took the post-it note down, unlocked the door, and climbed the steps on eight bounds. Surely he knew he was driving her crazy not writing. Surely by today there would be something.

She slid into her computer chair and clicked the computer on. It seemed to take an eternity for it to whir to life. Praying that he wouldn't just flatly refuse, she watched the emails stream into her box—seven of them. When they had downloaded, her gaze surveyed the list and clicked on the only one that mattered.

D, So much has happened it's hard to know where to start. I got back, and there are gigs lining themselves up in my path.

Her heart jumped with excitement for him, and she sat forward.

I think I'm going to take an offer from Ashton Raines and maybe one from KC. They want me to play on their upcoming albums. Don't ask me why because I think they've all lost it. But apparently they are crazier than I am. Anyway, I'm in pre-rehearsals most of the week. I do think I could swing Sunday though—if that works for you. Let me know. K

She looked up to the time stamp, and hope surged through her. Quickly she typed out a response.

He was glad he had waited.
Dear Kalin, Woohoo! It sounds like things are really taking off for you! Sunday would be super-fantastico with me. What time and where?

How about I come there? The river can get kinda nuts on Sundays in August.

Sounds good. What time?

Ten or so? We could go out for lunch somewhere. I might even be able to pay this time—what a concept. K

Lunch sounds good, and what happened to women's lib?

It's called chivalry. Besides, it can be a congratulations you're going to be a doctor lunch.

I haven't officially made that decision yet.

Well, what in the world are you waiting for?
It was a good question.

Yeah, what am I waiting for? Okay, then. It will be a Yeah Kalin is doing awesome and a Yeah Danae is actually going to go for it lunch.

I'm there! K

When they were talking about it, the whole thing had sounded so simple. So, so unbelievably simple. Then he had to leave, and Danae remembered her mother's message. Feeling like she was about to get bitten by a poisonous snake, Danae picked up the phone and dialed the number.

"Well, it's about time," her mother snapped when she realized it was her younger daughter. "Where have you been?"

Danae's spirit dove for the ground. "Studying. Taking finals."

"Oh, that. Well, I hope you got that little fantasy out of your system."

"It wasn't a fantasy, Mom." Danae pulled herself up in the chair as if preparing to defend herself physically. "In fact, I'm going tomorrow to make it official."

There was a pause. "To make what official?"

"I'm changing my major to pre-med and dropping out of student teaching."

There was an audible gasp. "Have you completely lost your ever-loving mind? We've talked about this. Pre-med is…"

"What, Mom? Hard? Well, let me tell you it's a lot more interesting than learning the correct way to set up a classroom. Besides it's what I love, can't you see that?"

"I don't know why you're being so stubborn about this. I talked with Joan the other day, and they just can't understand what possessed you to break up with Brandt."

"Oh, come on, Mother. We're not going to go through that again, are we?"

"You are throwing away your future, Danae. What do you want me to do stand by and say, 'Way to go, darling. Here, let me help you trash it some more'?"

"I am not trashing anything. I'm making my own decision for a change."

Her mother sighed. "Well, you're not making very good ones."

"Was there a point to this phone call, or can I hang up now?"

For a long moment there was no reply. "Yes, there was a point. You haven't been over here since… Well, since you walked out the last time. I was really hoping we could get together for brunch."

Fear jumped onto Danae. "Brunch?"

"On Sunday. Unless you are too busy with your own life to come see your mother for an hour or two."

Yes! Danae's spirit screamed. I'm way too busy! No! No, brunch. Not lunch. Not dinner. Not even a to-go salad! "Could we make it Saturday?"

"No, Saturday's out I've got that shower for Sally's daughter."

Danae thought about the question for more than a minute before she asked it. "Can I bring someone?"

Thrilled would've been at the far other end of the spectrum of what Kalin felt when she gently explained what had happened via email on Thursday afternoon. She had even given him the opportunity to back out, which he had seriously considered. However, the fact that he was desperate to see her again had won out over the fear.

And so when he arrived at her apartment on Sunday morning, windblown from the two-hour ride, his nerves were hopping like sparks in a fireplace. It wasn't until she opened the door on his knock that he knew he had made the right decision. Truth was, Danae Scott was worth a trip through burning hot coals to be with.

The black swoop-necked sweater set off her dark hair, which was pulled to the top of her head and then cascaded down the sides of her face like a dancing waterfall. He took in a breath as his gaze surveyed her.

"You made it," she said, barely breathing the words.

"I did."

She stepped back. "Please, come on in."

After all their conversations Kalin hadn't expected the awkwardness. It was like they were two strangers instead of two people who had told each other virtually everything. He crossed in front of her with his head down. She shut the door, and he turned just as she took a step in his direction. Suddenly standing there, ten inches from her, his senses picked up the scent of her perfume, which sent the rest of him skittering.

His gaze found hers, and it was as if she was visibly trying to keep herself from letting the words in her heart spill out. He saw so much in her eyes, so many of the same things that were in his heart. Love and gentleness for her overtook him. "So where's that hug you promised me? Or was that just a bait and switch tactic to get me to come?"

In the next second she was in his arms. He closed his eyes to keep the emotions flooding through him in check. Every curve of her body fit perfectly with his. It was as if they had been made to fit that way. His hand slid down her back to her waist and then back up to her shoulder blades again—memorizing every piece of the journey.

"I missed you so much," she whispered, the words strangling out of her.

He pulled her tighter. "Not half as much as I missed you." If staying right there forever had been an option, he would've gladly taken it. However, it wasn't. So with one more squeeze, he released her enough so she could look at him. His gaze searched the depths of hers, and it was clear she was hiding nothing from him all the way into the center of her soul. He couldn't fathom the trust he saw there, the completely lack of fear. He had never seen anything like it.

"Do you know how beautiful you are?" he asked, the question being the only way his mind could explain the effect she was having on him. However, he didn't wait for her answer. His arm tightened around her as he bent forward and his lips found hers. The moment his lips touched hers, fire flashed through him, and suddenly it was like everything would never be enough. For a split second in the middle of the kiss he realized that she was not backing up, not running, not breaking it off.

No, she seemed as hungry for his kisses as he was for hers. Desire for her threatened to overtake his sanity, and just before it slipped completely away from him, he pulled back and came up for air. His head was spinning, and nothing other than one small piece of his brain wanted to stop. But one of them had to, and at the moment as much as he hated to be the one, it looked like it was up to him.

She laid her head in the crook between his shoulder and his neck, and that feeling alone was enough to make him question why he had stopped.

"So, what are we celebrating today, Ms. Scott?" he asked, breathing and trying to put some distance between them and the intoxicating idea of going through a guardrail.

"That's Pre-Doctor Scott to you," she said as her finger traced up his arm.

Happiness surged through him, and he kissed the top of her hair. "Way to go, Danae. Now was that so hard?"

She jerked her head up to look at him. "It was the hardest thing I've ever done."

Respect for her flowed through him. "But you did it? You stepped off into the dark, and now you're flying?"

"Yeah," she said with a challenge in her voice. "Want to join me?" With that, she put her fingers in his hair and pulled his lips down to hers.

After only a short kiss that he knew was dangerously long, Kalin pulled back and laughed. "Hey now, I thought we had to be somewhere."

"I'd rather stay here," she said, and for the first time a shadow drifted through the trust in her eyes.

"Yeah, so would I, but there are things you get to do, things you want to do, and things you have to do. Unfortunately, this is one of those have to do things."

Annoyance flashed across her features as she let go of him and shook her head. "Okay, but don't say I didn't warn you."

Praying. It was what Danae had been doing about this moment since her mother had said the word brunch. She watched Kalin get out of her car and walk around to her side. He reached for her hand, and her fingers drifted through his. She tried to breathe, tried to tell herself that together they could do anything, but it still felt like she was about to feed him to the lions.

At the front door she stopped and turned to him, loving everything about him, but knowing what her mother would say. "This is it."

His smile touched her heart. "It's going to be okay."

She took a hard breath to try to convince herself of that. "Yeah." With that, she turned to the door and popped it open. "Hey, Mom! We're here!"

From the opposite corner of the room, her mother strode toward them. Her chestnut brown hair fell in hair-sprayed curls down the sides of her face. "I was beginning to wonder what happened," she said. "You said you'd be here at 10:30."

Instinctively, Danae tightened her grip on Kalin's hand to keep him from running.

"We got stuck in some traffic," Danae lied not really sure why. She turned slightly and looked at Kalin who stood rooted to the spot. "Mom, this is Kalin Lane. Kalin, this is my mother."

He let go of Danae's hand to offer it to her mother. "It's nice to meet you, Mrs. Scott."

"You too," she said, and Danae heard the judgment and saw it in the full-once over that her mother trained down Kalin. After the handshake, no one moved for an eternity. "Well, brunch is ready. Why don't we go eat?"

Pushing her feet to start moving, Danae grabbed Kalin's hand so they could follow her mother. The warmth of his hand bled through her shivering spirit. She tried to smile at him, but it didn't feel at all real even to her. His smile looked much more genuine.

"There are eggs and bagels," her mother said, indicating each kind of food spread on the bar. "I've got coffee and orange juice, or if you would rather have milk..."

"Coffee is fine," Kalin said as he followed Danae through the food choices.

"Cream, sugar, milk?" her mother asked.

"Black is fine," he said.

With every fiber of her being, Danae hated this. She hated putting him through this. She should've just told her mother no and spent a nice, relaxing day with him. Why hadn't she done that? As if on autopilot, she selected a few things and spaced them out on her plate so it looked like she had gotten something. Plate and glass in hand, she turned to the little breakfast table. *Please God, make Mom be nice to him.*

Kalin pulled the chair out next to Danae and sat down. He felt like meat on an inspection line, and he knew he wasn't making the grade.

"So, Kalin," Mrs. Scott said as she set a cup of coffee on the table in front of him, "what do you do for a living?"

"Thanks," he said, nodding at the coffee. As hard as he was trying, he couldn't get the fear in his chest to dissipate. "Oh, I'm working in Nashville. I play guitar."

"Uh-huh." Her mother sat down with her own cup of coffee, never bothering to get any food. "So, you're with a band then?"

"Well, I was." Kalin struggled to figure out how to eat and carry on a conversation without being impolite in some form or fashion. "I'm kind of free lance right now, doing studio work on some albums."

"He's working on one with Ashton Raines this week," Danae said, and the pride in her eyes when she looked at him carried his nerves away from him.

"So you just do studio work then?" Mrs. Scott asked, and the disapproval in her voice crashed his spirit back to earth.

He swallowed the bite of roll that jammed in his throat. "For now. I did do some work with a group last month on the road, but it was only temporary."

"On the road," Mrs. Scott said, making that sound even worse that being in the studio. "Uh-huh." She took a sip of her coffee.

He was failing this test miserably.

"Oh, Mom," Danae said, yanking her mother's attention over to her and away from Kalin. He was grateful for the reprieve, and he fought not to exhale too loudly. "I was going to tell you. I dropped out of student teaching. I start pre-med next week for real."

By the look in Mrs. Scott's eyes, Kalin knew that Danae had just taken a bullet for him. At first her mother's face went ashen, then very slowly she shook her head as contempt rained over her features. "So, you are really serious about this then?"

"Yes, I'm serious, and I'm excited too. I've got 16 hours lined up for the fall. I even went and talked to the pre-med counselor the other day. She said it'll only take a year or so for me to complete the pre-med degree plan because I picked up so many science electives when I was undeclared that will count. Of course, then I'll have actual medical school, and an internship and residency and all, but..."

Mrs. Scott stood from the table and walked over to the sink without bothering to hear the end of the statement. Kalin had the feeling that if he hadn't been in the room, there would've been an audible explosion. His gaze slid to Danae's face as he ate food that he couldn't taste. Danae's chin was lifted, and she looked like she was ready to joust a champion and come out on top. He had never been more proud of her.

"So, how were your finals?" he asked, clearing his throat in mid-question.

"BioChem wasn't too bad, but that A&PII one was a monster," Danae said. Her gaze slid from her mother's back to his eyes, and in one second it was as if their partnership was solidified. "Have you heard anything from the guys?"

"I talked to Jesse at Zane's the other day. Colton's back, and things look good for them. They're playing Seattle... well, no, they played there last night I guess. Next week it's somewhere in Montana." His gaze went to his cold eggs. He couldn't even look at them.

"So, now you never told me, how do you know Jesse anyway?" Danae asked, and it was clear that except for her mother eavesdropping at the sink, they were the only two in the conversation.

He had wanted to get to talk with her so long that it suddenly occurred to him how in the fear of her mother he had almost let that opportunity slip away. "We were in a band together before..."

"When you were here before?" she clarified, and it was obvious that she, too, wasn't going to let her mother ruin this.

So, he let the bizarre nature of where they were and why slide away from him as he told her about meeting Jesse again, and how cool Jesse had always been. He made sure to tread lightly on the gory details, but besides that he told her most of everything else.

They had been talking for almost an hour. At some point her mother had left the room. Danae wanted to apologize, but the subject never came up. There were just too many others things to discuss. By the time they had eaten, washed the dishes, and put everything away, she was a regular Kalin Lane trivia buff. How close he lived to Vancouver in Canada, his family, growing up, how he found music... They were all fair game.

He hadn't left too many questions out regarding her life either. She told him about high school and waitressing at the local hangout on weekends. Nothing major and yet everything her life had been built upon. It was only when the kitchen was clean that she realized they had a decision to make. Going in and watching television didn't seem like the worst idea in the world. She would've given anything for him to feel comfortable in the house she had grown up in, and yet there was a nugget of not-quite-right about the whole situation.

"What do you say we ditch this and go back to my place?" Danae asked. "We're not making any headway here anyway."

He was leaning on the counter next to the solid black double oven, watching her fold the last kitchen towel. "I'm really sorry. I guess I should've…"

Instantly she stepped over to him and put her arms over his neck. "No, you're perfect just the way you are. If she can't see that, that's her problem, not yours."

His hands went to the sides of her waist as he shook his head. "But she's…"

Danae looked at him as he clasped his hands around her waist. "Don't. Okay? That's why I've been twisting myself into a pretzel for years—trying to get her to be proud of me. It's not worth it. If she's going to be like that, it's her problem not ours. Okay?"

He looked at her and fought to get the word out of his mouth.

"Okay?" she repeated, a challenge tingeing the word this time. "I don't care what she thinks because I know what I think."

"Oh, yeah?" he asked, picking up the teasing tone. "What's that?"

Teasing drained out of her face. "I think I love you."

The words stunned him, and for a moment they pulled questions across his heart.

"You, Kalin Lane, are the best thing that's ever happened to me," Danae continued. "And if you ever leave me, I'll hunt you down and drag you back."

His gaze tripped past her to the empty doorframe. "But what about…?"

With a flick of her hair over her shoulder, she looked at the doorway and shook her head. "This is about me. Not her." She looked back at him, and peace flowed through her eyes. "She chose fear, but I choose love. And from here on out, I'm making my own decisions."

He smiled although there were warning shots being fired in remote portions of his heart. "So you've made your choice then?"

Nothing had prepared him for the look of hope and trust and tranquility in her eyes. "Yep. I choose you."

"Then I must be the luckiest man alive." Knowing they were in her mother's kitchen, and knowing her mother could walk in at any moment were not strong enough protests to keep him from pulling her to him. Their lips met, and he felt her relax into him. At that moment the past swiped at his happiness, and trying not to alert her to the fact that something was wrong with this picture, he broke the kiss. "What do you say we get out of here?"

"Where are we going to go?"

"Does it matter?"

She smiled. "Let's go back and get your bike."

Surprise jumped through him. "Are you serious?"

"Just for a little while."

They left the house without saying good-bye to her mother. Danae knew she couldn't avoid the confrontation with her forever, but for one perfect day, she was willing to believe that she could. By the time they made it back to her apartment that evening after sightseeing, the sun was already dipping toward the horizon. She wished he didn't have to go, but she knew he did. Hand-in-hand they walked into her apartment and over to the couch where they sat down. She snuggled into him, breathing in the scent that always made her feel so safe.

"Oh, hi, you two," Tara said, coming down the stairs. "I thought I heard someone."

Danae sat up as the feeling of being caught slithered through her. Under her, Kalin straightened as well.

"No, no." Tara waved them back down. "Don't get up on my account." She walked over to the chair, grabbed a throw pillow, and sat down. "I don't think we've ever formally met." She extended her hand to Kalin who reached over Danae to shake it. "I'm Tara Morgan, Danae's roommate."

"Kalin... Lane."

"Well, it looks like you two had a good day," Tara said, smiling at them. "I take it you made it out of the she-devil's lair in one piece."

Shooting a warning glare at Tara, Danae frowned as she snuggled back up next to Kalin. It was just too inviting not to.

"It wasn't so bad," Kalin said, and surprise jumped through Danae. He hugged her to him. "Besides, it was worth it."

Embarrassment drifted through her right along with the happiness.

"So, Danae tells me you play out in Nashville," Tara said.

The warmth of his arms covering her from both shoulders down her arms tugged sleepiness into Danae's consciousness, and she fought the yawn.

"Mostly free lance stuff right now. I've got a couple offers to feature on some albums though."

"Really?" Tara asked clearly impressed. "That's awesome. Anybody I would know?"

"Oh, maybe. Chesney and Ashton Raines..."

Tara's eyes widened. "You're kidding."

"No, it's been pretty cool lately."

The conversation faded out around Danae as warmth, security, and safety all dragged her eyelids down into them. She fought their undercurrent for as long as she could. Then she gave up and let them take her. She was in his arms. Everything else could take care of itself.

"Danae, hey," Kalin's voice said softly as if it was coming from some other realm. "Hey, baby, wake up."

She pushed through the curtain of black as the realization that she had actually fallen asleep crawled through her. She yawned, stretched, and finally opened her eyes to find him gazing down at her with the most peaceful smile she had ever seen.

"You do too much sightseeing today?" he asked.

"Too much something. What time is it?"

"About nine-thirty."

"Oh my gosh." She sat up, but the movement made her head swim, and she had to grab onto the couch cushion to get it to stop. "Where's Tara?"

"She said she's got some stuff to do early tomorrow. She just went to bed."

The time crashed through her understanding. "You've been talking for two hours?"

"Something like that. She's really nice."

Danae moved to the end of the couch as she shook her head. "I'm sorry. Jeez, what a great host I turned out to be."

Kalin slid over to her. "Are you kidding? I got to hold you for two hours. Life doesn't get any better than that."

Even when she messed up, with him, she still felt like a success. She wasn't sure why that was. "So does that mean I'm not fired?"

He leaned toward her and traced his finger down the side of her hair. "Like that's a possibility."

She laughed. "It's not?"

"Not if I have anything to say about it." His lips brushed hers, and even flying on the back of a bike took second place to that feeling.

When he moved backward, he gazed at her and took a long breath. "Well, I'd better be going."

"Yeah." She stood with him, and they walked to the door, their hands connecting their spirits.

"Well," he said, turning to her at the door and gathering her back into his arms. "You take care of yourself for me. Okay?" He kissed the top of her forehead, and happiness spread through her.

"You, too, and let me know how things go this week."

His hug danced across her heart. "Always."

With two more kisses, he finally made it out her door. She waved once when he got to the outside door, and sadness mixed with gratefulness twined through her. She shut the door quietly and climbed the steps to her room. Her computer snagged her attention, and she sat down to type. He wouldn't get the message until at least tomorrow, but she needed to tell him nonetheless.

She had typed only a couple minutes when Tara appeared at her door.

"You got a minute?"

"Sure." Danae kept typing. "What's up?"

Tara sat down on the bed. "I just wanted to tell you not to let your psycho mother talk you out of going with Kalin. He really is sweet."

The typing slowed.

"He told me about what happened today... at your mom's."

The typing stopped. "He did?"

"Yeah. He said he didn't think she was too thrilled with your choice."

Guilt for putting him through that rained through Danae.

Tara shook her head seriously. "She's wrong, Danae. She is. If she would've given him a chance, she would've seen that. Don't let her talk you out of being with him. Okay? He deserves better, and so do you."

Danae let that advice flow through her. "He is great, huh?"

"Great?" Tara asked skeptically. "Well, duh! I'm thinking I should try the mud and mascara thing if you can get a hunk like him to fall for you."

With that Danae swiveled in the chair in disbelief. "He told you about that?"

"I asked."

"Oh, great. What else did you ask?"

For two hours Kalin's brain had battled until what was right and what was wrong were fuzzy replicas of themselves. The trust he saw in her eyes made him ache to be the man she thought he was. And yet, he knew the second that he told her, that trust and all that went with it would be gone.

His brain said he should just forget about the past and make a new start with Danae. However, he, of all people, knew the past had a way of catching up with you. He had told her once that he wanted to be the man she deserved, and no matter how hard he tried to tell himself that he was, he knew differently. By the time he climbed the two steps into the little trailer, he knew it was pointless to keep running from it.

He had messed up, and until he at least tried to make it right, it wasn't going anywhere. So sitting down on the little bench seat, he pulled the yellow legal pad and pen from the shelf. It was a shot in the dark. He only had the address Adrian had conjured up to send it to, but he had to try. For her, for him, and for Lily.

He flipped to a clean page and took a long breath to settle the swirling thoughts. "Dear Holy Spirit," he whispered. "I need the words."

His gaze went to the blank page, and the words began flowing through his spirit.

"Dear Mr. & Mrs. Bennett,

I know this is the letter you never thought would come and maybe never wanted to come. I know how easy it would be to simply burn it—or to pretend you never got it. But I'm asking you please, for Lily's sake, please give me a chance to do what's right, to do what I should've done five years ago.

"I know how trite that sounds now. Where have I been for five years, and what gives me the right to be any part of her life now? Maybe you're right. Maybe I don't have the right to even ask, but I'm asking anyway because I can't let there ever be the possibility that Lily would somehow think I don't care. Because I do. I always have."

He had to stop and breathe and wipe his nose. His chest hurt with the memories, but he forced himself to go on.

"Walking out of that hospital was the dumbest, most selfish thing I've ever done. It's a decision I will regret the rest of my life. But the boy who walked out of that hospital is no longer here. I make no excuses for him because he made every decision that led us all here. I ask only that you try to understand that he was lost and scared and overwhelmed, and he did the only thing he could see to do at that moment. He believed he had nothing to give to Lily or to her mother, so like the coward that he was, he took off and left you to pick up the pieces. You didn't deserve that. Rebecca didn't deserve that. Most of all, Lily didn't deserve that. She needed a daddy. She needed me, but I thought more about myself than I thought about her. I'm not proud of that, but it's the truth.

"You've probably stopped reading by now, but in case you haven't, I first want to ask for your forgiveness. I do not deserve it, nor do I expect it. But I ask anyway because I think asking is the first step to something better for us all, and it's a step, however small, that I know needs to be made.

"Secondly, I'm not at all sure where Lily is, but I'm guessing that you have contact with her. So I would like to ask you to forward the enclosed money to be used on her behalf. I know it's late, and I should've been doing this all along, but I would like to begin supporting my child from this moment on. I know that money doesn't make up for the lost time or for all the pain I caused. It's not meant to. I'm only hoping that it will be a start to show you that I'm different now. That I've grown up—for what that's worth."

Kalin's heart lurched forward at the thought of the next words. He closed his eyes and willed himself to calm down. Finally he opened his eyes and put the pen on the paper again.

"Finally, if and when there ever comes a time that you see fit to give me the chance to meet my daughter and to be a part of her life—as small or as big as you see fit—know that I am here, and that I am ready. But I will leave that decision to you and to God. I know you will make it wisely.

"Please know that I have loved that little girl since I knew she was coming. But my heart and my head were in two different places back then. I have learned to see when I will regret not doing something my heart is telling me to do. That's why I'm writing to you today because I know I will regret it forever if I don't. It's a chance I feel that God is asking me to take—no matter what happens as a result.

"Whatever comes, whatever you think of me, please know that I only want what's best for Lily—whatever that is. I will abide by your best judgment on her behalf. When you hug her the next time, please give her one from me too. I realize now how many hugs I've missed giving her, and I promise if I ever get the chance to put my arms around her, I will never take it for granted.

"In searching for Rebecca and Lily, I found out about Rebecca's death. Know that my heart goes out to the two of you for her loss.

"May God be with you both as you consider my requests, and may He forever watch over and guide my little girl so that she always knows for certain that God and I love her beyond all measure.

Sincerely,
Kalin Lane"

He didn't even re-read it. If he did, he would lose his courage. He simply tore it out, folded it in thirds, and laid it by the door so he could mail it the next day when he went to the library.

Chapter 23

The fact that there was a letter floating around the world that could change everything about his life forever attacked Kalin at odd moments. Like when Ashton's family showed up at the studio to check on things. It was clear how much his three little girls adored their father, and the sight made Kalin's insides ache. They had only been in the studio for a few moments when Kalin retreated into retuning his guitar so he wouldn't have to watch. It just hurt too much to see what he had given up.

He had moved out of the trailer into a little green house with white shutters on the corner of a back street. It had a real shower and more than a four-foot seat to sit on. The furnishings were kept at a bare minimum. It was as if he was planning for the floor to drop out from under his dreams even as he built them. The money had begun to show up in earnest and regularly. He'd even started a checking account and a savings account. The bi-weekly checks to Lily's grandparents had continued although he hadn't heard so much as a single word from them.

Sometime in late October when he realized he had a desk to set one on, the money to pay for one, and Adrian coming into town for two days to help him set it up, he bought a laptop and a landline. The near-daily trip to the library was getting old, and with her schedule, there were times that the only time she had to get online was after nine when the library was closed. To have a secure connection to her was more than worth the hassle, the money, and the time.

Adrian showed up on his doorstep on a chilly Tuesday morning, a small pack of tools in hand.

"Hey, there," Kalin said, opening the door although he was still in his gray muscle A-shirt and sweatpants from sleeping. "I didn't think I'd see you until at least ten."

"Nope. We've got final tracks to lay down this afternoon, so I figured I'd better get over here and get this done first." Adrian stepped into the little house. "So I'm guessing you got everything."

"I tried. I got everything on that list you gave me."

Adrian walked over to the little desk sitting next to the wall in the tiny living room. He looked the equipment over and got down to work.

Feeling useless, Kalin sat down on the couch to watch him. "So, how's it been going?"

"Great. The album's supposed to be out for Christmas, and they're releasing the first single next week. How about you?"

Kalin nodded. "I finished my part on Chesney's yesterday. I've had a couple offers from bands, but they just haven't felt right yet. I've got another studio gig next week for some new girl. We start today. She wants me to play on the video too, which is kind of freaky…"

"I hear you there. We've sat down with the director for ours like twice now, and it's just 'Would someone please make a decision about what we're doing here?'" Adrian ripped into a box. "So have you had any luck tracking down your little girl? Jesse said you'd tried."

Kalin scratched the back of his head. "Ten letters, no reply. I think they're burning them."

"That's tough."

"Yeah. So, how's Colton?"

"Ugh," Adrian grunted when the screwdriver he was using slipped off the screw. "He's hanging in. It's tough though. All the rehearsals and stuff. We've got to be real careful and not overload him."

Kalin nodded as worry snaked through him.

"How's computer girl?" Adrian asked as he snapped a connection into the computer. "I take it this is for her?"

The smile slipped through Kalin's heart. "She's good. Studying like the world might end tomorrow, but good."

"She lives in Knoxville, right?"

"Yeah."

"She come here? You go there?"

"Some," Kalin said, exhaling. "Not as much as we'd like. We're both pretty busy."

"Understand that. My wife and I were on the phone every night for a year before I finally got up the nerve to pop the question. The phone company got rich off of us."

"I guess she's happy you're back for the break."

"Oh, yeah. It's tough sometimes, but when it's right, you make it work. You know?"

"Yeah," Kalin breathed.

"Done." Adrian slipped the computer onto the desk and held up both hands. He went around to the chair and sat down. "Now. Let's see what this puppy can do."

Danae had done her level best to steer clear of her mother ever since the infamous brunch. It had worked wonderfully until the second day in November, which was a Tuesday. It was her birthday, and the day hadn't been the greatest. Through emails she had learned that Kalin had a big rehearsal scheduled for that day, so she didn't mention the fact that it would be her birthday. She figured that she and Tara could hang out and eat ice cream. That would have to be celebration enough for the quarter-century mark.

However, when she got back to her apartment after classes, she found the post-it note stuck to the door. "Came by for your birthday. Call me. Mom." She tore the post-it down as her spirit plunged. She tramped into the apartment and up the stairs, debating on whether or not she should call. However, before she got the chance to even make the decision, her phone rang. She picked it up. "Hello?"

"Hey, Danae, how's it going?"

Her throat tightened on the sound of that voice. "Brandt? What are you calling me for?"

"Jeez! Can't a guy call and wish you a Happy Birthday without getting his head bit off?"

Danae sank into the chair and sighed. "Sorry. Thanks." She flipped the post-it onto the desk, looked over at the computer, and moved the mouse. There was no message, but it was something to do.

"Listen, I was thinking, since it's your birthday and all, maybe we could get together—for old times. I could come pick you up. We could do the movies. It would be fun."

Fun. That was a word she wouldn't have used.

"Come on, Danae. I know things got kind of messed up between us, but your mom said…"

Anger slammed into her. "My mom? Did she put you up to this?"

"Did she… ? No. I mean, well, we just talked, and she said maybe we could get together and work things out… I mean…"

"Thanks for the call, Brandt, but I'm not interested." Very gently she hung up the phone. For a minute she thought about not typing, but she needed someone. Trying not to think too much, she let her fingers say what her heart was feeling.

At just after six, Kalin walked back in the door. All day while he was playing for Tamara's album, shadows had been sliding over his spirit. There was something wrong with Danae. What it was or how he knew that, he couldn't really tell, but he didn't even bother to take his coat off or sit down before he clicked on the computer and pulled up the email program.

Concern traced through him when he saw that in fact there was a message.

Dear Kalin, I know I shouldn't tell you this or you'll feel guilty, but it's been a really rotten day. Today's my birthday, and...

Concern layered over the concern. It was her birthday? Why didn't she tell him that before this moment?

my mom came by. I wasn't here, but she wants me to call her. And then Brandt just called, and he wanted me to go out... If you're there, please write back. I need some sanity. d

He typed only two words and headed out the door.

At 7:30 Danae trudged up the stairs. Even her plans with Tara hadn't worked out. She hadn't remembered that Tara had a night class on Tuesdays. It was becoming clear that this day was a complete bust. When she had figured out it would only be her until after ten, she had opted for her baggy, fleece pajama bottoms and her pink "It's Your Lucky Day" T-shirt. There was no one to impress anyway. Just as she walked in her room, the phone rang. She considered not picking it up, but things were so rotten, she didn't know how they could get any worse. "Hello?"

"Well, it's about time." Her mother sounded irritated, and it transferred to Danae through the phone line.

"Hello to you to," Danae said as her face and spirit fell even further.

"I take it you're ignoring me."

"Rude deserves rude, right?" Danae asked, spitting the words she had learned from her mother back at her.

"What's that supposed to mean?"

"You're kidding, right? You invite us over, and then you disappear making Kalin feel like an outcast."

"First of all, I didn't invite him, you did. Second of all, open your eyes, Danae. That guy has serious trouble written all over him."

"Why? Because he has an earring?"

"The long hair, the earring, the clothes, the tattoos. It's not like he's trying to hide it."

"That's icing, Mom, and you didn't bother to look beneath that to see what's really there. If you would have, you would've seen what I see—a really great guy who treats me better than anyone else ever has."

"He's a *musician*, Danae. That's not stable or steady. That's nothing that you can build your life on."

"It's what he loves."

"What does that have to do with anything?"

Danae exhaled hard. "It means everything."

"You're not being practical, here. You're dreaming pipe dreams about a guy who will walk out on you just like…"

The end of the sentence never came, but Danae heard it anyway. "Just like Dad? No, Mom. Kalin is nothing like Dad. He's got his life together. He's got his feet on the ground. He knows who his is, and he's making his dreams come true. That's something. More than that, he loves me—not the me he wants me to be, but the real me…"

"What? The you who thinks being a doctor is a good idea?"

"That's part of it."

"Let me tell you something. Life is not lived on dreams. You have to play the cards you're dealt—not the ones you wish you had got."

"Is that what you're doing? Is that what you did?"

"I did what I had to do."

"Yeah? Well, now I'm doing what I have to do. If you understand and support that, great. If you don't, it makes no difference. I'm going for it anyway."

"And what happens when your dad's life insurance money runs out?"

"I haven't blown any of it. I've worked through the math, and I think it's doable. But if I get to the end and it's not, there are other options."

"But you could have life right now. Why do you want to wait?"

"It's not about waiting. I'm living right now. This minute. This is my life. This is the life I want. It just took me 24 years to figure that out." Getting bored with the conversation, Danae let her hand fall on the mouse, and she moved it not really hearing her mother's words. She clicked over to the inbox, knowing he had been out all day and that the possibility of a message was nil.

"…I know about guys like him, Danae. They talk a good line. They pull you into the dream, and then when it blows up in their faces, they take off. Suddenly you're left with two kids, no job, and three lives to support. Is that what you want?"

As the inbox snapped to the screen, Danae looked down at her ring finger, which was still missing a ring, and for the first time she realized something she hadn't thought of. They had been together several times now, but not once had she felt like he might try to take advantage of her. There was no ring there to protect her. There was no need for one. She couldn't explain that. She could hardly grasp that. But she knew at that moment it was the truth.

"...Brandt is solid. He's got a good future. Why would you want to throw that away on...?"

"He cheated on me, Mom," Danae said, seeing the new message from Kalin, wanting to click on it, but holding off.

"What?"

"At the wedding, Brandt cheated on me with the maid of honor."

"Danae, don't be such a drama queen. Brandt wouldn't..."

"I found them in bed together." Danae sighed, but there was no hurt in it only acceptance. "That's not my idea of love or stable, Mom. You can think what you want about Kalin, but before you judge him, you really should at least give him a chance." She shook her head. Talking was getting them nowhere. "I've got to go."

"Oh," her mother said, barely breathing the word. "Okay."

Danae said good-bye and hung up. Her mother didn't understand. And even if she got over setting her up with Brandt, Kalin would never be good enough in her eyes. It was a given. Sitting forward, Danae clicked on his message, and her face contracted.

Don't move.

What did that mean? At that moment, there was a knock on the front door. Confused, she stood and tramped down the stairs. At the door she stopped with her hand on the knob and looked through the peephole. Concern drained through the confusion as she jerked the door open. "Kalin? What in the world?"

His right hand was on his hip just below the leather jacket. "Do you have a phonebook?"

Her eyes widened. "A phonebook?"

"It's short notice, I know, but you didn't give me a whole lot of choice. Do you have a phonebook?"

"I..." She put her hand up to her hair, which was wrapped and clenched at the back of her head in something resembling a hideous pagoda. "Umm, there's one in the kitchen I think."

"Okay, good." He breathed a sigh of relief, and she stepped out of the way to let him in. Just as he stepped past her, he seemed to remember something, and he stopped. "Oh, by the way, happy birthday." He kissed her—if it could be called that. It was more like a quick a peck that missed her lips and landed on her cheek. Then he was gone, striding into her kitchen as she stood there with the door still open.

Slowly she closed it and walked in the direction of the kitchen.

When she entered, he was flipping through the phonebook, his cell phone in the other hand.

"You never told me you had a cell phone," she said, her mind still working through the fact that he was actually here as she pulled herself up onto a cabinet to watch him.

"I never have it on. Why?"

"I don't know. A phone number would be nice."

"You never gave me yours."

She couldn't argue.

He dialed the number and glanced over his shoulder. "Meat lovers okay?"

"Fine."

"Pepsi?"

"Mountain Dew."

She watched as he placed an order for pizza delivery. Then he looked over his shoulder again. "Address?"

"Oh, uh. 1616 N. 57th. Apartment 4."

He relayed the information. "Okay, great. Thanks." With that he hung up and wrote something at the top of her phonebook. "There's my number—if you ever need it." Then he closed the book and turned to her with a look of intense concentration. "Do you have a blanket that's not attached to a bed?"

Her eyebrows shot up.

"Work with me here. I'm improvising," he said as if he was in an all-out panic.

Obediently she slid off the cabinet and went to the little storage chest in the living room. She pulled out a blanket. "Will this work?"

"Like a charm." His accent still did funny things to her knees. He took the blanket from her and walked over in front of the couch. There, he threw the blanket onto the couch, grabbed hold of the coffee table and dragged it over into the corner. Then he stood and swiped the hair out of his face. "Whew. Is it hot in here, or is it just me?" He pulled the leather jacket off his shoulders and threw it onto the chair.

The only thought that ran through her mind was that it was definitely him that was hot. Yes, definitely him. A black T-shirt stretched nicely across his shoulders showed off the muscles of his back and arms when he turned and began spreading the blanket on the floor. Danae was having trouble comprehending anything.

"Okay," he said, standing again. "Do you have...? Oh, there we go." He walked over to the bookshelf and pulled the two candles standing there down. "You mind?"

Danae couldn't find a no anywhere in her. He took the candles and surveyed the layout. Finally, he set them on the coffee table and dragged it back just a little bit.

"Better," he said, nodding. Then he looked at her. "Matches?"

"Top drawer in the kitchen," she said, pointing.

He stepped past her again, brushing a warm hand across her waist, and went into the kitchen. It was like she had stumbled into a whirlwind that had sucked her will to move into it. In seconds he was back, and in his other hand he had the vase of dusty fake flowers that had been sitting on the kitchen cabinet since she had moved in. Danae almost laughed out loud as she watched him. He had just lit the candles and set the flowers down on the coffee table when there was a knock on the door.

He looked up at the door in bewilderment. "That was fast."

Danae never moved as she watched him stride to the door, his hand pulling out the wallet that was attached to a silver chain on his jeans. It was only when he had the door opened that shock hit her like a truck. Standing there was not the pizza man. It was Brandt.

"Oh," Brandt said as his face plummeted when he saw Kalin. "Umm, is Danae here?"

She saw the muscles in Kalin's back tighten like a lion that was preparing to pounce as his movement stopped, and then he turned to her. "Danae? Someone's here to see you."

On legs she couldn't be sure would hold her up, she stepped around the couch and walked to the door. "Brandt? What're you doing here?"

"I came by so we could talk." He looked into the living room, and the lit candles and blanket registered on his face. "You didn't say anyone was going to be here."

She pulled her chin up. "You didn't ask."

"Oh. Well..." He looked over at Kalin, and it was clear he was concerned for his own neck. "Could we... umm... talk? For a minute? Out here?"

Danae crossed her arms in front of her. "About what?"

Brandt looked at her. "Please...?"

She looked at Kalin, whose expression said he was there no matter what.

"You've got three minutes." She stepped past Kalin, brushing his stomach with her hand. Out in the hallway, she pulled the door but didn't quite close it behind her. "Make it quick."

"Danae," Brandt said as if he was talking to a child. "You don't have to do this. This guy. Come on. I get it. Okay? You don't have to

~ Lucky ~

throw him in my face for me to see how much I care about you."

Stunned. It was the only thing she could feel. "Get it?" She laughed. "You don't even kind of get it, Brandt. You may not like it. You may not even understand it, but I'm with Kalin now, and I'm happier with him than I ever was when I was with us. So, get over it already. I know I have." She moved to the door just as Brandt reached out and grabbed her forearm. His grip tightened until it sent knifing pains through her.

"Danae, come on. Him? He's gutter trash. Surely you can see that."

With a determined yank, she twisted her arm from his grip. "Look in the mirror, Brandt. That's gutter trash. Now if you'll excuse me, I've got a date to get back to." She pushed into the door, and before he could say another word, she stepped in and shut it behind her. It took a moment for her eyes to adjust to the dimmed lighting.

"How's loverboy?" Kalin asked with spite dripping from the words, and she realized he had gotten plates, silverware, and glasses out and was setting them up on the blanket.

How she deserved Kalin, she would never know. Peace flowed through her. "The man who loves me is just great."

In surprise, Kalin looked over at her. Without hesitation she stepped across the room until she was standing right in front of him. Lifting her arms, she laid them over his shoulders, and her gaze locked with his. "He's the best thing that ever happened to me."

For one second it was as if Kalin didn't understand what she was saying.

"I didn't know what love was until you showed up," she said, her voice dropping on the seriousness. "But now I'm thinking I must be the luckiest girl in the world because you're here now."

The smile went through his smoky blue eyes first and then slowly slid to his mouth. His gaze took in her face, feature by feature. Slowly his picked his hand up and traced his finger across her forehead, pushing the fall of bangs to the side. "No. I'm the lucky one."

She smiled as his gaze locked again with hers. "Thanks for coming."

"Happy birthday." His hands were on her waist before she realized it, and their warmth pulled her effortlessly to him. His lips brushed hers, and joy crashed through her.

At that moment there was a knock on the door, and Kalin pulled away. "Don't move."

Like that was a possibility.

Tara had taken the last of the pizza upstairs with her when she got home. She had conspicuously made herself scarce, which Danae thought was kind of funny—usually she wouldn't leave when Kalin was there. Sitting next to Kalin on the floor next to the couch, his arm draped over her shoulders, Danae shook her head at the memory of him showing up.

"What?" he asked, turning to look at her.

"You." The fact that he was there made her heart ache with gratefulness. "This is the best birthday I've ever had."

He raised his eyebrows skeptically. "Pizza on the floor? I don't think it would be a stretch to get better than that."

"You cared," she said softly. "You cared enough to show up." She took in a breath and let it out slowly. "I've been waiting for 24 years to have a man in my life who loved me enough to show up on my birthday because I was more important than whatever else he was doing. Tonight it finally happened." She leaned forward away from his arm, but the warmth of his hand found her back and traced down it anyway.

"Your dad?"

The tears were in her eyes before she knew they were in her heart. She nodded, sniffing the pain away. Then she threw her head back and looked back at him. "I think it's finally going to be okay. I'm finally going to be okay."

Kalin's smile was filled with compassion. "Well," he said, sitting forward on his feet and grabbing one of the candles. "Then I think it's time for you to make your birthday wish."

He pulled the candle over to her. It was down to nearly nothing on the holder. She looked at it for a long moment as all of the hurt drained away from her. Then she sighed and looked back at him. That face, those eyes—she couldn't have loved him any more had she tried. "I don't have to."

Confusion jumped to his face. "Why not?"

"Because my wish already came true." She leaned toward him, and her heart said that he was every wish she had ever whispered.

Long after he was home in the little green house that night, Kalin lay on the bed, his hands clasped on his stomach. He had to tell her. He had to. Going on, pretending he was someone he wasn't would only hurt her worse in the end. The only question was: would she hate him when she found out as much as she hated Brandt now—or more? Still, she deserved to know. He closed his eyes and breathed a long prayer that didn't end even when the sun came up the next morning.

Chapter 24

All day Wednesday the words had tangled and untangled in Kalin's brain. He had finally come to the conclusion that there just was no good way to say it. As he sat at his computer, a plate of half-eaten macaroni and cheese sitting next to it as the clock wound around to nine o'clock, he went through them again. There had been a message waiting for him when he got home at six, telling him how thankful she was, how much his visit meant to her, how she couldn't wait to see him again—the words carved the guilt through him like a dull knife.

For minutes upon minutes, he sat there, staring at the blank screen, twisting the leather band back and forth on his wrist. The words twined through his brain pulling the guilt and regret up into his chest and lodging them there.

Finally, as if they might explode if he didn't get them out, he put his fingers on the keys and began to type. He wrote and rewrote, considered, erased, and wrote some more. When he signed off, he stopped before hitting the send button. His finger bounced up and down on the left mouse button as if playing chicken with his soul.

Then, he closed his eyes, whispered a prayer to the Holy Spirit to be with her when she read it, and let his finger click it for him. The second it left, ache slashed through him. He sat back and put his hand to his mouth knowing it was the beginning of the end. There was no doubt that he had just trashed the best thing that had ever happened to him.

The jangle of the email brought Danae up off the bed as excitement flowed through her. He was there, and although she had to study, all she had thought about all day was when they would get the chance to be together again—even if the miles said they weren't. She clicked on his message as she pulled her foot up in the chair with her.

Dear, sweet Danae, Last night was the best night of my life too, and I'm so glad we got the chance to be together. You are the kindest, most wonderful person I know, and no matter what happens from here out, know always that I do love you with all my heart.

Strange, she thought, it sounded like he was breaking up with her.

Ever since we first met, I've wanted this to work more than anything I've ever wanted in my life. But there are things about me I haven't been honest with you about. There are lots of reasons why—excuses really— but even when I try to run from them, they don't go away. As much as I want us to work, I know that keeping things from you is not the best way to do that. So, right now, before we go any further, I have to be honest with you. Please know that I never meant to hurt you, and that it's killing me to have to tell you this...

She wanted with everything she had to stop reading right there. If she just didn't finish it, she could hold onto the man she knew him to be. However, her gaze betrayed her and kept reading.

You know about the drugs and the other stupid stuff I did in the past. What you don't know is that I was involved with someone else back then.

Not one part of her wanted to keep reading. This was a break-up letter. Her heart twisted on that understanding.

Her name was Rebecca, and we went through every guardrail there was. I didn't think about the consequences back then. I didn't think about her. All I thought about was myself and how I could use her to stop hurting—or to forget about hurting for a while. Right before everything fell apart with the band, Rebecca gave birth to a little girl—my little girl.

Danae raked in a breath that tore through her lungs. It hurt too much to keep reading. Still even through the tears, she couldn't stop.

Her name is Lily. She's now about five-years-old.

"No," she whispered, feeling like the world was crashing down on her. As tears of hurt and anger poured out of her soul, she simply couldn't keep reading. She put her head down as the serrated edges of his admission ripped through her heart. Her hand came up to her nose and then slid up to her eyes. Why was this happening? Why now? What had she ever done to deserve this? When she pulled her head up again, it was all she could do not to click off the message.

The day Lily was born, I went to the hospital to see her. Rebecca and I had had a fight about something... life in general I guess, and as I stood there at that window looking at Lily in the nursery, I knew there wasn't a single thing I had to give her. I was bankrupt—emotionally, physically, spiritually. She deserved so much better, and so I did the stupidest thing I've ever done in my life. I walked away.

~ Lucky ~

Anguish tore through Danae. She grabbed for the mouse as tormented anger streamed through her. She clicked off the message with a snap. Banging the mouse into the desk, she fought to breathe. How many times had she trusted him with how much her father had hurt her, and he had sat there and never said a thing? Pain sliced through her, ripping sanity and breath away with one swipe. "Way to go, Danae. Your stupidity strikes again." She pressed her palm to her forehead to try to stop the tears.

Tears were useless anyway. What could they change? What minute could they rewind? Not a single one. He had lied to her. Over and over again, he had lied. He had made her believe he was something he wasn't. She uncoiled from the chair and ripped her book up from the desk. If every single person in her life was going to let her down, then she had only one left to count on. Herself. The Cell Biology test was tomorrow, and she would ace it just to show the world that she didn't need any of them.

Every thirty seconds or so, Kalin clicked on the Home screen, refreshing it and praying that she would write back. He didn't blame her, but as ridiculous as that sounded all he wanted to do was to put his arms around her and comfort her, to help her through this. But this time it was he who had driven the knife through her heart.

He clicked on the Home page again, but still there was nothing. Finally, with the last energy he had left, he reached up and typed one more email. As soon as it had left the program, he knew life as he had wished it would be was over.

The email jangled in, and Danae looked up at it with narrowed eyes. She didn't want to hear it. She didn't. She never wanted to hear that sound again as long as she lived. Anger yanked her up off the bed and walked her over to the computer. She didn't even bother to sit down. Instead she swiped at the mouse and closed out every program that was open. By the time she hit the Turn Off button, she was crying again, and that even made her mad.

Not one more tear would they get out of her. Not one. That was it. She was through with trusting, through with believing their lies. They could find another girl to rip apart. She had already been shredded.

By Friday evening when Kalin checked his email, he had to admit she wasn't going to write back. It was over. As much as he hated that, he didn't blame her. She had been hurt enough. She certainly didn't need more from him.

He walked into the kitchen and looked through the cabinets. Nothing looked appealing. Nothing sounded good. His stomach wasn't feeling good at all. He closed the cabinet just as his cell phone rang. Granted, it had lain right here on the counter all day, but at least he was getting better about leaving it on. Trying not to think too much about anything, he hit the talk button. "Hello?"

"Kalin, where have you been? I've been trying to get a hold of you all day!" Zane had a way of upping the drama quotient in less than 20 words.

"I didn't take it to the studio," Kalin said, transferring it to the other ear so he could rummage through the refrigerator. "What's up?"

"Ace called this morning," Zane said, his voice dancing over the lines. "They made you an offer."

Kalin stood up straight, and the refrigerator door shut on its own. "An offer? What does that mean?"

"It means they want you. They're sending over a contract for us to look over on Monday! Isn't that great?"

Kalin fought to get a word out. Any word would've been good, but nothing was coming.

"Did you hear me? They want you to sign a solo deal!"

Pain was tumbling over the happiness. "Are they serious?"

"Man, they don't call if they're not."

"Well, well, if it isn't Ace's newest solo act," Jesse said the next Sunday morning as he fell in step with Kalin who was walking slowly out of the church. He had hoped church would help. It hadn't.

Kalin looked at him and tried to smile. "Looks like it."

Jesse cocked an eyebrow. "For someone who just signed a major, life-changing deal, you don't look too thrilled."

Trying not to, Kalin sighed. They skirted past the minister and out the side door. The weather was holding although the mid-November sunshine wasn't doing much to get the temperatures over fifty degrees. Kalin pulled his jacket closer to him.

"Okay, so what's up with you?" Jesse asked when they had walked all the way to the trees without a word.

Closing his eyes against the pain and the cold, Kalin shook his head. "Everything's all out of whack. I don't know. The deal is great. Better than I could ever have imagined. I'm working, which is good. I love it. Tamara even elevated my back-up vocals to a duet, and now they're going to release it as a single and do a video…"

"So what's the problem?"

"Life," Kalin said vehemently as he kicked the tree with the toe of his boot. "Life is the problem." He leaned back on the tree and was glad that for the moment at least he didn't have to hold himself up. That was getting harder and harder with each passing second. "I told Danae about Lily."

Jesse let his head go back in understanding. "Uh-oh."

"I knew it was going to be bad. I just didn't think it was going to hurt like this."

"She broke it off?"

"I guess. She won't even answer my emails. I haven't heard from her in over a week. I don't know what to do." He ran his thumb under his nose. "And I haven't heard anything from Lily's grandparents either. I've been sending letters and checks for three months now, and nothing…"

It was clear that Jesse wanted to make everything better, but he couldn't quite figure out how to do that.

"I guess I just screwed up so bad, I can't go back." Kalin thought for another minute and then realized he would drown in the waves if he didn't find another place to look. "So, how's everything with Phoenix Rising?"

Jesse's gaze said he noticed the change of subject. "We're hanging in. I just hope Colton can make it to May. There are times I think he's holding on by a slim thread. But he says everything's fine, so what are we supposed to do. You know?"

Kalin nodded, wishing he could make life better for Jesse, too.

"We've only got two gigs, and then we break for Christmas, so we're crossing our fingers and hoping the break will get his legs under him again."

"Well, good luck with that." Kalin looked out to the motorcycle. "I'd better get going. I'm supposed to be at the studio bright and early tomorrow to lay down the tracks for Tamara."

"Yeah. I've gotta get, too. Take care of yourself, and I'll send up some prayers that everything will work out."

Kalin smiled. "Right back at you." In the parking lot, he got on the bike and roared away. However, once he was home, he wished he had prolonged the meeting with Jesse. It was so lonely in the little house. He tried to watch football, but he didn't care. He called his parents, and they talked for a little while, but that couldn't last either. Finally he let his heart lead him where it wanted to go—to the computer.

He sat down and ran the mouse around the screen. After pulling the email program up, he scrolled down to the first few messages, marveling at how many they had exchanged.

And just so you know, He does hear you, but sometimes you're praying for X when what He really wants to give you is X-Better. So be sure to pray for what He wants instead of praying for what you want.

A smile dipped in tears drifted through him. He really had lost an angel. His gaze fell from the screen as pain screeched through him. "God, I know I have no right to ask this, but if You're listening, I need her more than I need the next breath. Please, if there is any way..."

The enchiladas Danae had spent most of the afternoon making tasted like cardboard. She stabbed her fork into them but then just pushed them around the plate. If she kept this up, she would lose every one of the freshman fifteen she had managed to acquire plus some by Christmas. Nothing tasted good. Nothing looked appealing. She was studying for no reason other than she had no other option. Anything beyond that had been relegated to maybe later.

"I thought I smelled enchiladas," Tara said, coming down the stairs. "Why didn't you call me?"

"I don't know."

Tara went into the kitchen and came back with a plate heaped with food. "I am starved. I've been eating those freezer burned peas for a week." She dug into the food, took a bite, and closed her eyes. "Oh! Now that is good." She had taken two more bites before she looked over at Danae, and concern slid over her. "You still didn't write him back?"

Danae swiveled in the chair uncomfortably.

"Everybody makes mistakes, Danae. He's not perfect. So what? He loves you."

"But he lied to me."

"Have you asked him why? Have you given him a chance to explain?"

Danae's gaze never lifted from her plate.

"He deserves that much."

Setting her face into stone, Danae stood. "I've got studying to do."

Tara watched her go. "What's new?"

Kalin spent Christmas with Adrian and his wife. They were nice, but it was depressing. The harder he tried not to be depressed, the more depressed he got. He prayed constantly, sometimes in his dreams even. But still no answer seemed to come. New Years passed without so much as a nod, and before he knew it so had January. He was working now.

Every waking hour and some sleeping ones seemed to be taken up with the music.

There was so much to do. They wanted to get going on the new solo album, but choosing a band was about to snap his already frayed nerves. He couldn't tell if it was him or them, but somebody was not in sync. As the first day of February turned into the second, he parked the bike at the curb next to his house, grabbed the mail from the box by the door, and stomped inside, shaking off the bitter cold. He would be glad when spring decided to get sprung.

Without really thinking about it, he looked down at the two letters. A credit card application, which he fired into the trash, and then his gaze snagged on the second. His address was hand-written in carefully made cursive letters. Puzzlement pulled him up short. He turned it over and ran his finger under it.

Inside there was a single piece of paper. He opened it and began to read, wondering even as he did so what this was going to be.

Dear Kalin, I'm sure you thought you would never hear from us.

His gaze jumped to the bottom as his knees buckled, landing him on the couch. *Cathleen Bennett* stared back at him. He swallowed hard and put his hand to his mouth. Forcing his gaze back to the top, he kept reading.

I figured that Lily was an idea you would get tired of pursuing sooner or later. I guess I underestimated how much you must have changed. To be honest, I was also so hurt that I couldn't see how much you might be hurting over all of this. When we got your last letter, Mel and I decided we couldn't keep ignoring you. Anyone who is trying that hard deserves something of a second chance. Just so you know, Mel and I do have custody of Lily. We have ever since Rebecca relapsed the last time. I'm sorry. I don't talk about that much. It was a really bad time—for all of us. Anyway, Lily will turn six in September, and she will start kindergarten in the fall. I'm sure you've got a million questions, but we think it's important that we take this slow for Lily's sake. Please understand. We are the only parents she has ever known. I don't want to topple her life, but if this has a chance, I think she deserves for us to take it. That said, I will wait until I hear back from you before I send more. Sincerely, Cathleen Bennett

He grabbed for the pen and paper so fast he knocked the pen to the floor. A response he could do.

The phone rang just before 8:30 in the evening on February 2nd, and Danae looked at it over the top of her book as she sat at her computer.

Tara would get it, so she went back to reading. Just as she found her place again, Tara's voice ripped through the stillness. "Danae, it's for you!"

In annoyance she picked it up. "Hello?"

"Danae Scott?" the voice she didn't recognize asked.

"Yes?"

"This is Evelyn, your mother's boss."

Danae sat up at the tone in the woman's voice.

"Honey, I hate to tell you this, but your mother is on her way to the emergency room."

She slid the book to the desk. "Why? What happened?"

"We don't know. She was working late, and she collapsed at her desk. We called 911, and…"

"Which hospital?" It was then that Danae first noticed Tara standing at the door, her arms crossed and concern etched on her face. Evelyn relayed the information, and Danae thanked her. When she hung up, it was like her thoughts were moving so fast she couldn't get her body to move at all. "My mom," she finally said.

"You want me to drive you?"

All Danae could do was nod.

On the way to the hospital, Danae called Nikki from Tara's cell phone. Nikki immediately went into hysterics. The gist of the conversation as far as Danae could tell was that Nikki couldn't leave. John wasn't home. Belle, one of the twins, was sick, and it was just a matter of time before Chad caught whatever it was. Before Nikki had the chance to completely melt down, Danae told her she would handle it, and she would call her later with the details as soon as she knew them.

When she snapped the phone off, she put her head back on the car's headrest in exhaustion.

"It's going to be okay," Tara said, looking over at her. Danae nodded, wishing helplessness didn't feel so bad.

The hours slid by as Danae sat in the waiting room. It was a good name for it she finally decided. Waiting. That was about all she could do. The doctors had confirmed a heart attack. As Danae listened to the one who had come out to explain what was going on, all she could think was how young her mother was. Forty-seven. It wasn't ninety. A prolapsed valve that no one had ever diagnosed gave way without notice. But, according to the doctor, her age was a good factor that would work in her favor. She was strong, and when they got her stabilized, she would have a much better chance of getting through the surgery.

BioChemistry, Anatomy & Physiology, Genetics, MicroBiology they were crashing together in Danae's brain making it hard to follow anything. There was the word new valve and surgery and ICU. She really hoped Tara was getting all of this because she certainly wasn't. Finally he told her there were some papers to sign and that the nurse would bring them in as soon as they got them together. Danae nodded, letting it all soak in. He patted on the arm gently and left.

She turned unseeing eyes to Tara who took her by the arm and led her over to the chairs. Medicine had never seemed so frightening.

It wasn't until the clock wound around to eleven-thirty that anything resembling reality dawned on Danae. Tara had been at the nurse's station, and when she returned, she gazed at Danae with overflowing sympathy.

"They said she's resting, and we might as well go on home."

Instantly fear snaked through Danae. "No. I'm not leaving."

"Danae, there's nothing you can do for her tonight. She's resting. She's in good hands. We'll come back in the morning for the surgery. There's nothing you can do now."

They were the worst words she had ever heard spoken.

Sleep had long since given way to dreams when Kalin heard the cell phone bleep in the kitchen. Bleary-eyed consciousness slapped him awake, and he lay there listening to make sure that's what it was. His head rolled to the side, and he looked at the clock. It was nearly one in the morning. For one more minute he convinced himself it was the wrong number, and when it stopped ringing, he was sure of it. He rolled over and closed his eyes.

Just as he was beginning to relax, it rang again. In annoyance, he rolled back over, ripped the covers off his body, and swung his legs off the bed, which pulled him upright. On the way to the kitchen he scratched the back of his head and yawned. If this was Zane… He picked up the phone and looked at the number. Unknown shone back at him. He clicked the talk button. "Hello?"

"Kalin?"

Concern slid through him although he didn't recognize the voice. "It is."

"Kalin. Oh, good. It's you."

He heard the sigh, but it did nothing to calm the concern.

"This is Tara, Danae's roommate."

Alarm jumped on him. "What's wrong? What happened?"

"Don't panic. It's not Danae. Well, it kind of is, but…"

"Tara, slow down. What happened?"

"Oh, she'd kill me if she knew I called you."

"You did the right thing. What's wrong?"

"It's her mom. She had a heart attack tonight."

"Oh, no." Kalin's eyes fell closed on the news, and he shook his head. His hand went to the top of his hair then slid over his head and down to the back of his neck.

"I'm sorry. I know, you're not together anymore, but Nikki can't come, and they're doing surgery tomorrow, and I didn't know who else to call…"

Plans started running through his head. "Where's Danae?"

"She's sleeping. We got home a while ago, and I made her take one of my sleeping pills. She didn't even want to come home…"

"But you're there with her. At the apartment?"

"Yeah."

"Okay. I'm going to throw some things together, and I'll be there."

"Tonight?"

"It'll take me a couple hours, but I want to be there when she wakes up."

He heard the sigh again. "Okay."

"You sure you're all right?"

"Yeah, I'm better now."

The apartments were bone-chillingly quiet when Kalin stepped inside the hallway just over two hours later. He only hoped that Tara would in fact be awake. Quietly he knocked, and after only a few seconds, the door creaked open. One look at Tara was enough to confirm that it was a good thing he had come. She looked near tears as she stepped into his embrace.

"It's okay," he said softly. "It's going to be okay." He only wished he felt as sure of that as he sounded.

Chapter 25

Her head felt like someone had used it as a punching bag for 14 rounds. It throbbed forward and back with the weight of a million bricks when Danae pulled herself upright the next morning. Then, reality took a swing at her, and she closed her eyes, fighting back the tears and praying for the strength and the wisdom to get through the day in one piece. She dragged her legs off the bed and grabbed her robe.

Her thoughts went to her mother, lying on a cold, white bed across town. Did she know what had happened? Did she know that Danae had come last night? There were no answers to those questions—only more questions. The best she could do was get through the day, and then maybe she would get the chance to tell her mother what she was feeling. She tramped down the stairs, fully prepared to eat Frosted Flakes and whatever else she could find that wouldn't require effort to make.

However, the further down the steps she got, the more the space smelled like eggs. The second she turned the corner at the bottom of the stairs, her eyes widened on the scene. She grabbed for the edges of her robe and pulled them around her tightly.

At the table talking with Tara quietly stood Kalin, and when Danae stopped short, he looked up. There were so many emotions written on his face, she couldn't clearly decipher her own.

"Morning," he said softly, and the gentleness in his tone and on his face drifted through her.

The bleak numbness that had been wrapped around her since the phone call the night before faded into confusion. However, before she had the chance to so much as ask what he was doing there, he walked over to her and pulled her to him. In the next second she was in his arms, and it was better than she remembered. He was warm and solid. She grabbed onto his shoulder, hoping he wouldn't leave again and not really caring why he had left the first time.

The tears of fear she had been fighting broke free from her heart and slid down her cheeks, but she hadn't even noticed them until she tried to breathe but couldn't. She gasped for air, fighting to find it again.

"Shhh." He smoothed down her hair. His arm supported her as his hand rubbed across her back. "Shhh."

Even the sound of his voice was comforting. Finally she shook her head and pulled back from him. "How did you…?"

His gaze was steady and strong. "Tara called me."

Danae thought about that and considered getting angry, but even that took too much effort. She nodded and pulled all the way out of his arms. However, his hand stayed on her back, drifting there like it belonged nowhere else.

"We've got some scrambled eggs and toast, but if you want something else…"

She shook her head, fought to smile, and ducked her head. Then she pulled her gaze up to meet his. "I'm starving."

Neither of them asked any questions. They just survived one moment to get to the next. They took Danae's car to the hospital, and halfway there when she sniffed, he reached across the seats and twined her fingers through his. His only goal in life at that moment was to be there for her—whatever she needed. The future and what came next didn't enter his consciousness. Only this moment mattered.

At the hospital they went up to the eighth floor, and he held back a half step while she consulted the nurses. Then they went to the waiting room until the doctor could come and brief them. As they sat there, he realized her hand wasn't in his, so he reached over and traced his finger across the back of her hand. She looked over at him in exhausted gratefulness and turned her hand so his could mesh with hers. He leaned back into the wall. It was all he now asked of life.

By the time the surgery was over and her mother was cleared for a single, brief ICU visit, Danae didn't think she could even stand long enough to get to the room. She pulled herself to her feet and took a step before she realized he hadn't moved.

With concern, she turned. "Aren't you coming?"

There was only serenity in his eyes. "Do you want me to?"

"Yeah." It was the most honest word she had ever spoken.

He stood and took her hand, and together, they walked down the stark white hallways and into the ICU unit. At the round nurse's station, one of the nurses stepped forward and led them to a room lined with glass. At the door Danae squeezed his hand, and when he squeezed back, she knew he wasn't going anywhere. They walked in, and the sight swept her breath away.

In a tangle of wires and tubes lay her mother. Pale, and thinner than Danae remembered, she looked like she was hardly breathing. The myriad of machines beeping and humming in the room did nothing to settle her nerves. She took a hesitant step forward and willed herself to keep moving. At the bedside, she looked for some part of her mother's body that wasn't hooked to something else. Finally she released his hand and laid hers gently on her mother's forearm.

"Mom, it's Danae." The breaths in her lungs lodged at the top of her throat, and she sniffed to get a free path for the words. At that moment she felt his hand on her back, drifting up and down, giving her his strength. "Kalin's here too." She glanced back at him but didn't really get even a glimpse. He was there. That was enough. "The doctors said you did really well. You'll be up and out of here in no time." She couldn't think of any more words, so she just stood there rubbing her mother's arm gently and wishing she could undo every bad moment between them. It was as if for this one moment their spirits touched across some vast horizon, one connected to the other connected to the other. And the worst of it was, she had no guarantee that this moment would bring her to another with her mother.

His hand was the only thing keeping her standing, and even as she touched her mom, she reached back and wound her arm around his waist. Leaning into him, she looked back through the tubes and the wires at the face her heart knew she could never walk away from. When her mother came out of this, Danae would find a way to explain how much Kalin meant to her. Until then, she would just hang onto him and soak his strength into her soul while she prayed for the wisdom to some day make her mother understand.

"They said not to stay too long," he said, and the gentle lilt of his accent danced across her heart.

She nodded and with one more touch, let him lead her from the room. The warmth of his hand wrapped around hers, and suddenly the world didn't look nearly so frightening or overwhelming. As they walked, she leaned into him, and he put his arm around her. It was all she now wished of life.

By the time they made it back to the hospital the next morning, her mother was awake. She still didn't look strong, but Danae's spirits lifted on the sight of those eyes. "Hey, Mom."

"Danae," her mother whispered, her voice hoarse from the tubes that had been down her throat the day before.

Careful not to jar any of the remaining tubes, Danae leaned over the bed and gave her mother a hug. The returned hug was weak, but it was a start. When Danae stepped back, she realized her mother's gaze had traveled behind Danae's shoulder. Seeing but not really understanding the look, Danae took a step back and then understood. She reached over and pulled Kalin to her side.

"Kalin," her mother said in that same raspy voice. Then, slowly she held her hand out to him, and ducking his head, he stepped forward and took her hand. "Thanks for being here... for Danae."

His gaze slipped from her mother's face to Danae's. "I wouldn't be anywhere else."

Two trays of hospital cafeteria food sat between them along with issues that seemed like boulders. Kalin knew they needed to talk, but he wasn't at all sure how to broach the subjects or if now was even the right time.

"So, you're not working," Danae said as she pushed her mashed potatoes around in circles. "What's up with that?"

He leaned back in the chair and draped an arm over the chair next to him. "You needed me."

"Yeah, but you're not... in Nashville."

"I probably should be getting back soon." His gaze went to the hardly eaten food on his plate. He exhaled slowly, blowing the air through a small hole in his mouth. "We've got to get a band put together or the solo deal is going to fall through."

Her gaze jumped to his, questioningly. "Solo deal?"

He sat forward, leaned his forearms on the table, and cleared his throat. "I... Umm... Well, I signed with Ace Nashville in December. As a solo." He felt the confusion in her gaze.

"You're... really?"

"Yeah, I was pretty shocked, too. We've been working on the logistics of putting an album together, but we can't find a decent band to save our lives." He shook his head. "You would not believe how many flashes in the pan there are in that city."

Her gaze fell, and it was clear she was sorting through the new layout of his world. "So, it's real then? It's really happening?"

He nodded, but he wasn't sure of anything—least of all what her reaction to that would be. She seemed to absorb the information for a few seconds, and then she laughed softly.

"What?" he asked, her reaction pulling him forward.

She looked up with wonderment in her eyes. "You. I'm just so blown away by you."

He smiled softly. "The feeling is mutual."

Kalin waited until the next day when her mother looked to be on the road to recovery before he made the decision that he had to go back. He didn't want to. In fact, standing in the parking lot next to his motorcycle, the only thing he wanted to do was stay. However, Zane was about to have a meltdown over the band choices, and Kalin knew it was time to go.

"You know where I am," he said as he memorized the feeling of her hand in his.

"I do." She closed her eyes seeming to form the words carefully before she spoke them. "Thanks... for everything."

With that, he took her in his arms, praying it wouldn't be the last time he would get that chance. "You take care of yourself."

She squeezed him to her once more and then stepped back. "You, too."

Seeing no way to prolong the moment, he let go of her, stepped over to the bike, swung his leg over it, put the helmet on, and backed it out. She waved and then ran her hand over her arm. It was all he could do to hit the starter and drive away.

Danae watched him long after he was gone. If her heart could hurt any more, she didn't want to know how. A few minutes and then a few minutes more, and then she had to face the fact that he had really left. She turned and trudged back into the apartment building. When she walked into her own, Tara was sitting at the table.

"Kalin leave?" Tara asked, looking up.

"Yeah." It was all she could get out. "I'm going to go..." She didn't even finish the sentence, and Tara just nodded. On legs of lead, Danae climbed the stairs and tramped into her room. Wanting only to be near him again, she sat down at her computer and clicked it on. She pulled her foot up into the chair with her and clicked on the last message he had sent. The one she had never even opened.

Danae, I'm so sorry. I know you're mad. I won't bother you any more. If you need me, I'm here. I love you, Kalin

She sniffed the emotions flowing through her away. The palm of her hand slid under her nose as she tried to corral every skittering thought. She took the mouse and clicked back to look at the other messages. With a heart that felt like it wasn't even beating anymore, she clicked on the message that had ripped her world apart. She re-read it all the way to the point where she had stopped.

I did the stupidest thing I ever did. I walked away.

Fighting the tears and the ache, she forced herself to keep reading.

I kept telling myself it was better for her this way. But that was a lie. It wasn't better for her. It was better for me. At least I thought it was. I see that now. That and how selfish and horrible it was. But that's honestly where I was—until I realized how much it was going to hurt her... if not now, then in the future. That's why I started searching for her a couple months ago. I don't know that I ever thought I would find her, but with Adrian's help, I did. Now I have no idea if I will ever get the chance to tell her what an idiot her father's been, but I'm writing her letters, a couple a month... hoping and praying that some day she can forgive me.

I know this explanation is too little too late. I know I hurt you just like the others did, and for that, you will never know how sorry I am. I also know that I don't deserve for you to forgive me, but I'm asking anyway. I love you more than life itself, Danae, and no matter what, I want what's best for you. If that's not me, I understand, but please, I ask you... try to understand that who I was then is not who I am now. That's not an excuse. It's a fact. May God give you X-Better—whatever that turns out to be. Sincerely, Kalin

She felt like an emotional dishrag. She hadn't thought there was a single tear left in her, but as she read, they came again. In the span of two messages, he had backed off completely, no pressure, no questions. Yet when she needed him, he was there again no pressure, no questions. As she thought about that, her heart wrapped around the fact that life without him wasn't life anymore.

Yes, he had messed up. Yes, she was furious about that. But there was no doubt he was indeed trying to make up for the mistakes he had made and trying to do it better this time. Swiping at the tears, she laid her fingers on the keyboard and typed the first message she had sent him three months.

The cell phone that was still connected to the wall plug on the cabinet was beeping when Kalin walked in his front door. He stalked over to it and punched the button without bothering to see who it was. "Hello?"

"Kalin, man, it's Jesse. Dang, where have you been?"

"Knoxville."

Jesse breathed in that information and then dove forward. "Listen, man. I called Zane, and we've already talked with Ace…"

~ Lucky ~

Kalin's thoughts swerved from her standing in that parking lot for the first time since he'd ridden away. "Ace? Why? What's going on?"

"Colton's out. He can't finish the tour. It's the throat thing again. The doctors are worried he really messed up his chords this time. But we're supposed to open tomorrow night in Houston, and now we've got no lead. Are you available?"

"Me...?" The idea sent his hand to the top of his head. "I don't know. We're trying to get a band. What about...?"

"I know. I said, we already talked to Ace. They've got too much riding on this tour for us to back out now. They can put your album on hold for a couple months until we can get through this. All they need is your okay."

Kalin leaned against the cabinet and pulled lungfuls of air in.

"So, what do you say? Will you do an old friend the favor of his life?"

It took only a moment of thought, and then Kalin laughed. "Paying back a few favors? I like the sound of that."

Jesse detailed Kalin's next 24-hours. A flight overnight to Dallas and then a short hop to Houston the next morning. He would meet them at the hotel just before they left for the Houston Rodeo and Livestock Show. They would play tomorrow night, and then they would deal with what came next. Kalin took down the information. After signing off, he dialed Zane who was beside himself with worry.

"For the love of Pete, Kalin, would you please take that thing with you?" Zane practically yelled. "I do not need another ulcer here!"

"Okay. Okay. I'll take it with me. I promise." They worked out the few details that needed solidified, and Zane said he would be there to take Kalin to the airport in an hour. When he hung up, Kalin knew there were 75,000 other things he needed to be doing, but before he did any of them, he went over and turned on the computer.

He sat down, praying for her even as he did so. When he pulled up the email program, grateful disbelief slid through him. She had already written. That fact alone threatened to untether his soul. He clicked on the message as anticipation rose in his chest. He leaned forward to read her words, twisting the wristband, and then laying his thumb on his bottom lip.

Kalin, Although I almost wrecked us over it, I am glad you told me. I know that wasn't easy. Also, thanks so much for coming when Mom got sick. I don't know how I would've made it without you. I wish I knew where "this" is going, where we're headed, and how we're ever going to get there, but seeing you leave tonight, I realized I can't keep lying to myself that I can live without you. There seem to be so many obstacles between us—the miles, our lives, my school, your music... But no matter how hard I try, I can't convince myself that life can ever be life if I'm trying to live it without you. Please forgive me for jumping off the deep end when you told me. I just really wasn't prepared for that at all.

I see now that you are Kalin, and that if I love some of you, I have to love all of you—the past, the present, and the future. I have to say I admire you for trying to correct the past even though it might mess up your present. I know there are times it looks impossible right now, but God's good at impossible. I know because you are reading these words, and two weeks ago, I would've considered that impossible. :)

He has a plan for you. Trust that. Everything else will fall into place.

Please know how much I love you. We can work this out. We have to. I need you too much to ever let you go again. Peace & Prayers, Danae

The middle of him ached with joy as he read the words. He didn't have time, but he put his fingers to the keys and typed a reply anyway.

Danae had been reading for two hours. Catching up after missing nearly a week wasn't going to be easy. When the email jangled, she slid the book to the bed next to her, got up, and walked to the computer. Gliding the mouse across the screen, she saw his message. She sat down and pulled her foot into the chair with her. Excitement and fear tangled together in her chest as she clicked on his message.

Dear Danae, How can I even put into words what I'm feeling right now? You don't even have to ask for forgiveness. I completely understand. Don't think for even one more minute that what you did was wrong. It was what you needed to do. I'm just glad you are going to give me the chance to prove that I've changed. I have. There's no question about that. And you have no idea how much of that is because of your love and faith in me. It means more than I can ever say.

And now, I'm going to jump off yet another cliff. Jesse just called, and it looks like I'm headed out to help them finish the tour. Colton's too bad to finish. It's like life is throwing pieces at me that don't even seem to fit together, and yet in a weird way they kind of do. My album is on hold until after the tour. Weird because a week ago, I thought I knew where all this was headed, and now everything has changed. I know. Take my hands off the wheel. Believe He knows X-Better. It's just that I feel like I'm on a chain that's going, "Okay, now we're going to go THIS way" jerking me around. I'm starting to get whiplash :)

Anyway, that's the long way to say that the next time I write, it will be from somewhere in Texas. (When did life get so crazy?) Know that my thoughts and prayers are with you. Tell your mom I'll send some her way too. Don't study too hard. Write back. Those emails in my box do more to keep me going than you will ever know! Peace & Love, Kalin

Peace and love. They floated through her. She thought about how right life suddenly felt. "Dear Lord, If I'm ever stupid enough to let him go again, would You please slap me?" Then she laid her fingers to the keys and let her happiness flow though them.

When Kalin made it to the hotel in Houston before the band was ready to go, he had one mission on his mind. After throwing his stuff in Jesse's room, he walked down the hall to Adrian's where he knocked.

"Hey!" Adrian said, throwing his arms around him in greeting like a long-lost brother. "Hallelujah you made it!"

Kalin smiled. "You can say that again. Hey, you don't happen to have your laptop, do you?"

"Danae?"

The smile widened. "Who else?"

Adrian let him into the room. "It's all yours."

"Thanks, man." Kalin sat down at the little desk and went through the motions. He didn't have much time. Getting ready was nudged out only to this in the priority category. He clicked on the email program, and his heart danced at the sight of her message.

Dear Kalin, By the time you read this you will probably be in Texas. Know that my heart, my soul, and my prayers are with you as you begin this chapter of your life. You will be in my thoughts until we are together again... I love you. Danae

Overwhelming gratefulness wrapped around him. He exhaled slowly and then set his fingers on the keys.

Three hours later as the arena plunged into darkness, pure, unadulterated exhilaration burst through Kalin. As he stood in the wings the guitar hanging from his shoulder, he could hardly breathe for the anticipation twining through him. He felt the other band members step past him to take their places.

"And now, the Houston Livestock Rodeo and Show is proud to present Ace Nashville Recording artists Phoenix Rising featuring Ace's newest recording artist Kalin Lane!"

The introduction surprised Kalin. He looked up into the darkness and shook his head in disbelief. Had he been asked to explain how he got here, he never would've been able to—save that it was by the grace of God.

Rob clicked the drumsticks, and the pounding beat poured through the huge speakers. At the back of the stage, the lights swooshed up, illuminating Phoenix Rising in outlines of black, and the crowd screamed their approval. Ten seconds, five, and then from stage right Kalin's fingers went into motion on the guitar. There was no uncertainty, no fear as he strode onto the stage. Spotlights fell on him from every direction.

On a wave of screams the front rows surged forward, and he smiled at them, which brought a fresh surge. A thousand hands reached out to him as he spun on the heel of his boot, his fingers sliding down and back up the neck of the guitar. Kick-dancing to the beat of the music he stepped to the microphone.

"Up from the ashes... of a heart crushed and burned. Up from the ashes... a way in, a way out. It's one for the money, two for the show, three to get ready, and four to GO!" He kicked away from the microphone, and his right leg caught him as he leaned back into the music pouring through his fingers on the guitar raised only by his hip. The navy blue shirt, unbuttoned to the third button and rolled at the sleeves, slid back and forth over his skin as he rocked in time to the rhythm.

He pulled himself back up to the microphone, his whole body seeming to flow with the beat. "You never gave me reason, you never told me why, just waltzed out my door, and I thought I would die. But I'm a survivor, now baby that's true. And from what I see, I'm doing more than making do. Yeah!" Six notes and he leaned into the mic. "Up from the ashes... of a heart crushed and burned. Up from the ashes... a way in, a way out. It's one for the money, and two for the show, three to get ready..." He ducked away from the microphone and let the crowd finish it.

"And four to GO!" they screamed.

Spinning in circles on the pivot of his right foot, Kalin pounded out the sixteenth notes that streamed through his consciousness into his fingers and out through the speakers. Every other detail of life other than standing right there on the stage playing his heart out for those fans disappeared into the brilliance of lights and the soul-lifting sounds pouring out around him.

With two tests on Monday, Danae had spent much of the evening at the library with her study group. Her mind was ninety percent on the tests, but there was always that one part of her that was anchored on him.

When she finally made it back to her apartment a little after ten, she sat down at her computer. Sure enough there was a message.

You Believed In Me
I don't know why. I don't know how.
But you believed, and there's no doubt
That I wouldn't be here without you there
So don't you ever think about leaving, don't you dare
'Cuz I'm right here, and I ain't goin' nowhere
Because You Believed in Me
So now I can believe too...

Danae's heart wound around those words as she let them slide through her a second time. They unleashed her soul in a way that nothing before ever had.

I've been thinking about us, Danae, and although I have no idea how we're going to make two such opposite lives fit together, not making it work is no longer an option for me either. Like my song says, "Don't ever think about leaving, don't you dare!"

So it was a song, she thought with a smile. At that moment all she wanted to do was hear the music that accompanied it.

And in case you're wondering, I wrote that while I was sitting in the terminal at the Dallas-Fort Worth airport this morning. I think the lady next to me thought I was high. I was... high on you! Being with you is the most incredible feeling in the world to me, and tonight when I step onto that stage, I know your spirit will be singing right in time with mine. There is nothing else that I ask for on this earth. God bless you for everything you have given to me. I will spend the rest of my life wondering how I got so LUCKY! God be with you when I can't be. Peace and Love, Kalin

Danae shook her head and then had to put it down to corral the tears she suddenly felt stinging the backs of her eyes. This was for real. How it had happened, she had no idea, but they were together—in spirit and in life. She was indeed lucky.

Three weeks later as March edged closer to middle of the month, Kalin was finally falling into the rhythm of the road. He had just settled back into the seat on the bus that was traveling to Seattle when his cell phone bleeped to life. He pulled it from the case at his hip and punched the on button. "It's Kalin."

"Kalin, hey. Glad I caught you," Zane said. "I went to your place yesterday to make sure everything was cool, and I picked up your mail. Bills, which I'll handle here, but there were three letters that look kind of personal. What do you want me to do with them?"

His body sat him up straight. "Is there a return address?"

"Yeah, something Bennett from London, Kentucky?"

"They wrote." Kalin couldn't get that twisted into his consciousness. He had continued sending his every-other-week letters, but the thought that they would write back again hadn't occurred to him. "Can you overnight them to the hotel? I can pick them up when we get there."

"Sure thing."

Sleeping on the bus, traveling all night, pit-stopping only at hotels, it was a rhythm that Kalin had finally caught hold of. When he dragged his bags up to the fourth floor of the hotel and threw them on the bed in the room he always shared with Jesse, he said, "I'm going to run down and see if the letters have made it."

"K," Jesse called from the inside of the closet where he was working to get his bags unpacked.

It took mere minutes for the letters to be in Kalin's hands, and he carried them back up to the room as if they were the crown jewels. He sat down on the bed oblivious to his two bags still lying there and examined the letters. They were, indeed, from Cathleen. He grabbed one and opened it. A photograph floated to the floor, and he reached down and retrieved it, spinning it to the white side in his fingers as he began to read.

Dear Kalin, We're glad to know you finally got help. Rebecca would be glad too. She always talked about you—how talented you were, how you were going places. It seems that is finally coming true. I miss Rebecca every day of my life, but the gift of Lily is one I will forever be grateful for. She is a little ray of sunshine in our home. I am sending a picture of her. This was taken at her birthday party in September. God bless you as you go forward in life. Sincerely, Cathleen

It took a long moment for Kalin to get up the courage to turn the picture around. This was it. The moment he had waited so long for. Slowly he flipped it over, and his heart dropped into his shoes. The little girl standing there in her party hat and carnation pink dress stole his heart with one look. Light blonde hair with curls so numerous God would've had a hard time counting them flowed down to her shoulders. The little face was awash in joy. A wide smile danced from her eyes to her mouth and back again. Happiness personified, he thought, closing his eyes on the sight to keep the emotions from overflowing their banks. After a minute, he opened them again and couldn't quit staring at it. He leaned forward, holding onto it as if it might disappear.

"That her?" Jesse asked, breaking into Kalin's thoughts.

"Yeah." He handed the picture across the bed to where Jesse stood.

Jesse's gaze took in the picture, and then he looked over at Kalin with sadness in his eyes. "She looks like Rebecca." He handed the picture back, and Kalin took it and looked at it anew.

"Yeah, she kind of does." The problem was he couldn't get a clear picture of the child's mother in his head no matter how hard he tried. "Man… this is unbelievable."

Wordlessly, Jesse smiled. Kalin looked down at the other two letters, picked one up, and ripped it open.

Dear Kalin, We got your letter and your check today. We are putting that money back for Lily's college. I hope you don't mind. She is such an undemanding child. You take her to Toys 'R Us, and she just walks the aisles looking. When I ask if she wants this or that, she'll say, "Oh, you don't have to." Such a beautiful little spirit. Kind and generous. Patient and loving.

I sat down with her last night, and we had a talk about you and her mother. Not that I was surprised, but she wants to see you.

Kalin's heart jumped in joy and terror.

I know you're out on the road now, so when it works, it will work. Until then, know that Lily has added you to her list of prayer people at night. Here's our number, so when you get this, you can call and we can make arrangements. God bless you. Sincerely, Cathleen

Grabbing the other letter, he tore into it.

Dear Kalin, I think our letters must be passing in the mail, so I wanted to give you our number again in case you didn't get the last one. I thought you would like to have this drawing that Lily gave me yesterday. Stick people, I know, but I think you'll get the idea. On the stage, that's you. In the clouds, that's Rebecca, and in the little house off to the side, that's us and Lily. Such understanding from someone so young. Please call. Lily asks every day when you're coming now. Sincerely, Cathleen

"You think Adrian is set up yet?" Kalin asked as he surveyed the small drawing that threatened to yank tears from his eyes.

"It's Adrian. He was set up when he was born."

Kalin stood and went over to Adrian's room. On the knock Adrian opened the door. "I was wondering what was taking you so long."

Ducking his head, Kalin held up the letters. "From my little girl."

A slow smile spread across Adrian's face. "Good for you."

"You mind?"

"It's all yours."

Kalin sat down at the computer, wondering how he was going to tell her. He clicked on the email program and hadn't really thought about there being a message from her, but there was. He clicked on it.

Hey, there, Lucky! hahaha I went to Mom's today. We had a nice, LONG talk. She says she's sorry she misjudged you. It's not her blessing, but it's a start.

If you wouldn't mind, send up some prayers for me. Statistical Methods is about to eat my lunch. I've got a low A, and I really need to keep it if at all possible. Prayers and good thoughts might just tip the scale. Then there's studying for the MCAT, which is probably going to eat what's left of my lunch. (More prayers, please) Besides that, things are good. Tara is wondering when you're coming back. She said you've really got to come when you can stay and talk awhile. I told her there's no telling when you'll even come within a 100 miles of this place again, but we're keeping our fingers crossed. Well, just wanted to check in and see how things are going with you. Peace, Danae

Kalin laid his fingers on the keyboard and typed a reply. Then he stood and stretched. "Hey, Adrian?" he called into the bathroom where Adrian was shaving.

"Yeah?"

Kalin walked over to the bathroom door, which was open. "When's the next time we'll be within a hundred miles of Kentucky?"

"We're in Cinci at the end of April. Is that close enough?"

"Do you know the date?"

Adrian closed one eye concentrating on either the shaving or the schedule. "Umm... the 22nd, I think? It's that Friday—whatever the date is."

"Cool." Kalin pushed himself up from the doorpost. "Thanks."

"No problem."

Kalin went back to his room, sat down on the bed, and pulled the cell phone out. He stared at it, praying for the courage to make the call. "Oh, dear Lord, please give me the words." He looked down at the letter and punched in the numbers, then put the phone to his ear, and listened to it ring three maddening times.

"Hello?"

"Oh, umm." He cleared his throat. "Hi. Is this Cathleen?"

"It is." She sounded guarded.

"Hi, Cathleen, this is Kalin."

He had thought it would be hard, that talking to her would rake his spirit over the coals. However, her voice registered only genuine happiness. They talked a little about the letters, a little about how surprised they each were about the whole thing, and quite a bit about Lily. When he asked the question that was tugging at his consciousness, Cathleen's kindness never wavered. Within minutes they had the meeting scheduled. Before he hung up, he asked if he could call again, and she said any time. That one simple invitation sent his heart soaring.

Danae was hanging on by her fingernails for Spring Break. With two projects and a paper due the Friday before, she was up to her nose in work, but she took a break to check the email. The smile was there the second she saw it.

Danae, We just made it to Seattle, and I really should be getting ready for the in-store meet and greet, but I had to tell you... I got a picture of Lily today! You should see it. I never would've guessed how just a picture could make me want to see her for real even more. I'm going to call Cathleen and set something up to see her. I can't wait now. But I know in God's time. Pray that it will all go smoothly. I'll let you know what happens when I get a free minute here. Things are crazy. We're supposed to be at the radio station at six tomorrow morning to do another interview. I'm nervous—as usual—but I'm praying for X-Better and seriously beginning to like flying :) Heaven knows I've had enough practice stepping off cliffs this last year! Take care, and know that my thoughts and prayers are with you always. Love, Kalin

Danae said a quick prayer for the meeting with Lily and then dove into her projects. One simple email. It was amazing.

Chapter 26

The emails flew back and forth as Phoenix Rising toured the Western states, following Ashton Raines, but picking up a following of their own as they went. Sales of their CD was skyrocketing, and Ace Nashville was considering giving them a short headline tour to finish out the year as soon as their new album was finished.

The only problem was that no lead singer had materialized. In truth, however, the only time that was even a problem was when they weren't on stage with Kalin. But he felt their apprehension anyway. He heard the conversations that stopped when he walked up, and he knew they were trying to figure out what to do with their future. As for his future, it seemed to be coming up on him with fearsome speed. As the April showers ushered in the Spring, his thoughts were more and more on the 22nd. He now had several pictures—each as soul-tugging as the first. He had called a couple of times, and even that was getting easier. Somehow he was keeping up, but it was like being in the middle of an out-of-control three-ring circus.

The night they finished up in Cincinnati, he stepped from one ring into another as he settled into the rental car and headed to Southern Kentucky. He knew Danae was praying. He was praying too. His hands worked the wheel, guiding it down I-75, as his mind traced back over the years that had brought him to this moment. A dim memory floated up, and at first he didn't recognize it. Then it flashed across his mind with greater intensity.

It was his apartment from his first go-round in the states. He squinted into the on-coming headlights as the memory drifted into his consciousness and then out again. He tried to grab it and then realized it was better to just let it come on its own. The hum of the road lulled him to the point that his consciousness let go, and a deeper part of him took over.

He was at the apartment, and even from this distance, he felt the unreality of being under the influence. He also felt the anger and deep-seeded hate snake through him as it had that night. It was fury tinged with a wanton desire to destroy everything that hadn't already been destroyed in his life. He saw himself ripping, tearing, and dumping anything he could get his hands on as he flung himself around the apartment like a cyclone gone mad. It was like anything that was in one piece had to be smashed and fed to the rage pulsating through him, and his hands and body obliged.

Paintings, furniture, curtains, everything on the desk, anything he could grasp or throw became fair game to be ripped, broken, and shattered. The memory of the pounding on the door followed in the next instant by the hands of people trying to restrain him reverberated through his soul. He remembered screaming at them—what he had said was no longer recorded on his mind. Even their faces were hazy, but the looks of horror on them were not. He felt those looks piercing through him even now.

At that moment, he knew exactly how utter shame felt. It had been all he had left by the time he got back to Canada, and with a vengeance, it reached up again and grabbed him in its tight fist. Not one time had he ever gone back to that apartment since he had torn himself free of the grasp of those fighting to keep something intact. Thinking about it as he drove, he realized someone must have picked up that mess, someone must have paid to restore what he had destroyed. Probably Zane.

Utter exhaustion crashed over him, pulling his spirit down with it. He didn't want to remember any more, but not remembering was eating him from the inside out. It hurt to even think about it. It hurt to go back there, but back there would be with him forever if he never did. His hands spun the wheel, and he took an exit he didn't even see. He had to stop if only for a moment to get his bearings back under him.

As the car wound around a narrow road leading off into the darkness, he pulled to the side of the road and into the ditch where he jammed his foot on the brake. He threw the gearshift into park, and gripping the wheel, he sucked in a long, slow breath to settle the storm raging in him. "God, I know there's something there. Something I've never let myself see…"

A bright light flashed through his mind, and he blinked at its intensity. The memories overtook him then like a giant wall of water, knocking him back in his seat. His scream ripped through the night. "Oh, God, help!"

Danae's body jolted forward as if it had just been struck by lightning. "Kalin." He was her first thought. "God," she said, yanking the covers off her legs even though she had no idea where she was going, "I don't know why, but Kalin needs you. Please, please be with him. He needs you."

Through the fog of time, Kalin saw the dark, low-rent apartment. It was all a sick brown color. He could feel the scratchy couch underneath him, and he knew that wasn't the first time he had sat there. From the middle of his being, he felt the clawing, digging, overwhelming need for his chosen mode of escape. He could see the lines already cut and ready on the glass in front of him. The memory of leaning forward and pulling a line in over the pain of walking away surged through him.

He beat back that memory, willing it to go away. But it clung to him. Past and present merged into one in his mind as he felt himself fall back onto the couch. He knew that T.J., his supplier, was there, but he wanted to forget even that. He wanted to forget everything. He leaned forward again and dragged more white powder into his system.

Something had to stop the hurt. If he did enough, maybe it would take him out for good. Even that had to be better than feeling like his insides were on fire with the understanding of how horrible he had somehow become.

"Jeez, man. Slow down," T.J. said, and in the present Kalin's mind stumbled over how familiar that voice sounded. Before he had time to sort out why, T.J. continued, "Don't worry about it, man. I mean how do you know the kid's even yours? It might be Caleb's for all anybody knows."

That stopped his headlong, reckless escape plans. He turned to look at T.J. who seemed to waver like vapor in front of his drug-blurred vision. "What's that supposed to mean?"

"Aw, come on, dude." T.J. sat back on the couch and laid a bony arm over it. "Even you can't be that blind. Those two have been doing each other since he first figured out you liked her."

Kalin turned all the way around to face T.J. "What're you talking about?"

"Man, wake up and smell the coffee. Caleb's main in with the ladies has been you from day one. You pick 'em, and he steals 'em right out from under you. That's how his game works. Everybody knows that. Okay, so this one just happened to be less careful than the others. Doesn't make the brat your problem. Only reason she pinned it on you was because you've got the dough to keep up her lifestyle. So what's the big deal? You dump her and the brat, figure it ain't your problem 'cause she was stepping out on you anyway. She sure as heck ain't going after Caleb. He's so broke, nobody can fix him. You're all in the clear, and we all go on with our lives."

Agony tore through Kalin, and he let out a moan that filled the car. He pulled his arms over his chest, fighting to get the memories to stop, but they gushed forth convulsing him over the seat. In the midst of the memories, he felt himself grabbing for something. He watched in horror as in the memories, he sat forward and dragged two more lines in without pause. At that moment the sight of the door opening tripped through his mind.

Revulsion filled him as for the first time since the moment it had happened, he looked up and saw Caleb. Wan and horridly skinny, the drummer for the band that had lifted Kalin to stardom's doorstep stood there, peering in with abject horror etched on his face. The betrayal from one Kalin had thought of as a friend sliced him to the core.

His chest filled with stale, hate-filled air. The desire for revenge ripped through him, and as the memories rolled forward, he stumbled off the couch, hurling the table, the glass, and the white powder in all directions with a tremendous crash. He heard the string of curse words flow from him as he lunged at Caleb who didn't even have time to move. Kalin's hands caught the top of the young drummer's shirt, and they both toppled out into the hallway, crashing into the wall.

"No, man!" T.J. screamed as Kalin smashed a fist into Caleb's nose.

Again and again, his fist connected, cocked and connected again. Caleb tried to fight back, pushing and struggling to get away from Kalin's wrath. Their battle careened them into the wall and then rammed them down into the hardwood floor.

"Kalin! Stop it, man!" T.J. yelled, gripping the back of Kalin's shirt and trying to pull him off of Caleb. "He ain't worth it, man! He ain't worth it!"

With a final shove, Kalin let T.J. yank him away. He crashed a knee into the hardwood floorboards, and then with one hand reaching for the wall, he stood and staggered away without a look back. It was only then that he realized he was covered in blood—his, Caleb's... He couldn't really tell, but his hands were stained with it, his shirt covered in it. His soul was soaked in it, and it had been there ever since.

Sitting in the darkness on a lonely Kentucky side road, he could still feel the hate bleeding through him, and it occurred to him that had there been a gun or a knife within reaching distance, Caleb would not have made it out of there alive. A fresh wave of self-loathing attacked him. He would've killed someone in cold blood had that been an option. It was a side of himself he didn't know existed. But pushed to the limits by drugs and shame and grief, jealousy and rage, there was a moment that a guardrail of steel couldn't have saved him from going over the edge had the circumstances of that moment been altered just slightly.

As the memories continued to attack him, he laid his head on the steering wheel and quit fighting to forget.

Struggling to stay on her feet, Danae stumbled through the darkness down the stairs and into the kitchen. She had never called him before, but her spirit was screaming that this was an emergency. She flipped the light on and blinked back its intensity. Grabbing the phonebook and the phone in all-out panic, she punched in the numbers, her hands shaking furiously. "Please, God, please, let him answer."

The cell phone on Kalin's belt bleeped, and his thoughts crashed back into the present. He grabbed it, wiped his eyes with his wrists, and tried to rake in a good breath. "Hello?" he asked as his lungs let out the air in short, mini bursts. Cold enveloped him, and he shivered.

"Kalin, where are you?" The panic in Danae's voice ripped through his consciousness.

"Danae, what's wrong?" he asked, sitting up straight.

It was clear she was having trouble breathing.

"Is it your mom?"

"It's you," she gasped. "What's wrong? I just had the most horrible feeling that you were going through a guardrail."

Kalin tried to take that information in even as the memories continued to twist through him.

"Where are you?" she asked.

He looked out the window into the darkness. "Somewhere in Kentucky." He closed his eyes and ran a hand over them to calm his spirit. "I don't know if she's mine."

"Wh... what?"

"I don't know... I don't know if Lily is mine."

That seemed to stop her panic. "What are you talking about?"

"There was this other guy... my... I thought he was a friend. They were sleeping together behind my back." On that thought, Kalin jammed his head back into the headrest three times. "I was so stupid! How could I not have seen what he was doing?"

The confusion was in her voice. "How did you find this out?"

"I knew… a long time ago… back then. But I didn't want to remember. I couldn't…" Hate for himself and every stupid choice he had ever made bled through him. He whacked his head back into the headrest trying to give himself exactly what he deserved. "I was so stupid!"

"Okay. Okay. Calm down." She sounded terrified as if he might do something really stupid. "Tell me where you are exactly."

A weird, parallel-universe kind of calm crept back him, and he looked out the window at I-75 running next to where he sat. "I just got off I-75. I'm… I don't know. I went through Richmond a little while ago, I think."

"Do you know what the next town is?"

He fought to get his short-term memory to take over again. "It starts with a B… Umm… Bear? Brady? Berea? Yeah, that's it. Berea."

"Okay. Then don't move. I'm coming."

The laugh jumped from the middle of him although nothing in him felt like laughing. "Danae, it's the middle of the night. You don't…"

"This is not a discussion. Now, leave your cell phone on. Plug it in if you have to. I'll borrow Tara's, and when I get on the road, I'll call you…"

"Danae…"

"I said, 'Don't move.'" And with that, she hung up.

Reluctant exhaustion seeped through his entire being as Kalin hit the off button and put his head back on the headrest. Why couldn't life just leave him alone?

Tara was as panicked as Danae by the time the story had made the transfer. In less than ten minutes Danae was out the door, cell phone in hand. She hated to, but she waited until she got to the I-75 on ramp to call him back. Driving and directions had never been her forte. "Come on, pick up."

"Hello?" His tired voice barely made it over the airwaves.

Her heart turned over for him. "You sound horrible. Want to talk about it?"

A moment slipped into the next.

"I just… I don't want to drag you through this."

"You're not dragging me through anything. You're in trouble. You need a friend. I'm a friend. So tell me what's going on."

Then, one memory at a time he started at the beginning, and over the course of the next two hours he told her all of it. She was glad for the distraction of the road at times because at some points his story yanked the tears right out of her eyes. The pain, the grief, the desperate need for an escape, she could feel it all as he talked.

"I talked to Cathleen the other day," he said softly as her gaze went to the sign that said: Berea 8. When the sign was no longer in front of her, she realized he hadn't gone on.

"And...?"

His exhale hurt her lungs. "I just feel so guilty. I mean, choices are choices. I know. We all make our own, but I just keep thinking if I hadn't been so out-of-control, maybe Rebecca wouldn't have gotten in so deep."

"The drugs?"

"Yeah, Jesse told me she called him after I left. She must've been pretty bad off. She was looking for me, but I was already gone. Then the other day, Cathleen told me about the end..."

Danae waited, wishing there was a way to make him wait to finish until she could hold him.

"She was by herself," Kalin continued, his voice hollow with the words. "She had a bottle of whiskey and who knows how much coke. She died like that... all alone in some dump. Nobody there. Nobody to save her or to make her see that it didn't have to be like that." He took a ragged breath. "She didn't deserve that. Nobody does."

A prayer for Rebecca wound through Danae. "Well, sometimes you can't see what could've been until it's gone."

The town of Berea slid past her window, and she retrained her thoughts to her present mission. "What're you driving anyway?" she asked, narrowing her gaze to the other side of the road. After two hours on the phone with him, it felt like his voice was a part of her now.

"It's a white... I don't know... something. Little," he said. "I'm off I-75 on the access road."

The headlights from a car going the other direction illuminated the access road just long enough for her to see his car. "I see you. Hang on. Okay? I'll be there in a minute." With that she snapped off the phone and negotiated the bridge to get going in the direction he had been. In five minutes she was pulling up behind him.

She jumped out of her car and ran to his door just as he pulled himself out of it. Throwing her arms around his neck, she hugged him like she'd never hugged any other person. "Oh, thank God you're okay."

He seemed to soak in her hug through his arms slung around her waist. "You didn't have to come."

"Yes, I did." She sniffed as she pulled back from him. Fatigue, guilt, and sorrow were in his eyes. Gently she took his face in her hands. "Never again. You hear me? You do not have to do it alone. Ever. I'm right here… a phone call away. Day or night. Any time. You got that?"

Gratefulness overtook the other things she saw in his eyes. He smiled tiredly and then nodded. His head ducked into her shoulder, and he clung to her. She didn't question it. She just stood and held him for the space of time he needed. When he finally took a breath and pulled back, she surveyed him. "What do you say? We'll drive back to Berea and ditch your car for today. We can take mine."

He looked like he wanted to argue, but instead he nodded.

Although he felt badly about imposing on her, Kalin was grateful when once he was in her car, she told him to put his head down and rest. Sitting there in her passenger's seat, her hand in his, his spirit finally stopped replaying the memories and settled down. By the time he woke up again, it was after five-thirty, and he found Danae sitting next to him asleep. He looked around to find they were sitting at a gas station with a Welcome to London, Kentucky sign plastered along its side. He did some figuring in his head and decided that sleeping awhile longer was a good option. As he settled back into the seat, he looked across the seat at her. Eyelids closed, her features peaceful, he knew at that moment what real love felt like.

The sun was shining into the driver's side window when Danae woke up. She opened her eyes and found him lying there looking at her. "What time is it?"

"A little after eight. How's my guardian angel?"

"Fine. How are you?"

"Better."

"I'm glad."

Danae waited until they were in the tiny eating establishment that was the first one they found to begin to figure out what came next. "So, have you decided what you're going to do about today?"

The question pulled his head closer to the pancakes on his plate, and she felt bad for even asking. After a moment he picked his head up and looked out the window. "She's mine."

He took a breath that she watched as she tried to discern his meaning.

"She has been ever since Rebecca told me." His gaze traced over to Danae's face, and there was quiet acceptance in his eyes. "And she deserves to have a father who loves her, who has loved her from the very first moment he knew about her—even if he had a sick way of showing it." He looked down and stuck a fork in his pancakes. "I'm not walking away again. I can't."

"You're not even going to question it? I mean there are tests…"

His gaze stopped her statement. "I know it in my heart. I do. Besides, they don't know about any of this. Cathleen has already talked to Lily. She already told her I'm her father. I can't do that to her again. I can't put her through more turmoil than I already have."

As Danae looked at him, a smile crept onto her face. She laid her hand across the table, and it landed on his forearm. "She's lucky to have you for a dad."

It was the first time she had seen real happiness in his eyes. "Yeah, well, I'm lucky to have her."

Nerves were the only thing left in Kalin when they parked in front of the tan house on Cedar Drive.

"You want me to come in with you?" Danae asked, looking at the house.

He was looking too—a dizzying array of possibilities winding through him. "I think I should go up first."

She nodded. "Okay. Well, I'll be right here if you need me."

His smile barely touched his lips. He exhaled hard, let his hand slide down his leg slowly, and then he reached for the door handle. Willpower carried him all the way to the front door where he twisted the wristband once and looked back at the car. She was watching him, and somehow that settled his spirit and gave him the courage he needed. He reached up and rang the doorbell.

For a full minute nothing moved, and then a lady just older than his mother appeared and opened the door. About his height and thin, she had short, light brown hair that blended with the gray making it look a dark blonde. She smiled slightly. "Kalin?"

He nodded. His voice failed him.

"Hi. I'm Cathleen. Please, come on in."

He followed her all the way in to the little living area, digging his hand into his back pocket the whole way to keep himself from running.

"Lily went out with Mel for eggs," Cathleen said. "I thought it would be better that way."

Again he nodded and searched for a place to put his gaze that didn't threaten to send his nerves careening over the edge. "I really appreciate you giving me this chance. I know it isn't easy… I mean things didn't exactly happen the way I'm sure you would've liked for them to."

Cathleen shook her head. "Sometimes life takes detours we didn't see coming." She sat, looking at her hands for a long moment. "I want you to know, I know how much courage it took for you to write that letter, to contact us. It couldn't have been easy. But I know what a difference you can make in her life, what a difference you've already made. She needed that... that connection, that bond."

He sat down on the tan ottoman, and his hands twisted over themselves. "I know," he said, and he really did. He heard the back door slam, and his attention snapped to the sound. He shook the hair out of his face, wondering if he should stand. However, in the next second a tiny angel appeared in the doorway, and all thoughts other than her escaped from him.

"Lily." Cathleen reached a hand out to the child. Lily walked to her grandmother's side, but her gaze never left Kalin who sat on the opposite side of the room. "Lily, this is Kalin, the one we've been talking about."

Had he wanted to move, he couldn't have. "Hi, Lily."

"Hi," she said softly, never moving from her grandmother's side.

"I really like the pictures you drew for me," Kalin said, grabbing for something to say. "Especially the first one—the one with me on the stage. You must have worked really hard on that."

The little head nodded, the curls around the shoulders gliding up and down. At that moment a man the size of a mountain stepped into the doorway. Swallowing the fear that gripped him, Kalin stood and extended his hand. "Kalin Lane."

"Mel Bennett," the man said. He shook Kalin's hand.

Awkward descended around them.

"Lily," Cathleen finally said. "Why don't you take Kalin out to see your flowers?"

For a second the little girl didn't move. Then slowly she took a step toward him and extended her hand. Kalin's heart jolted forward with the gesture. He smiled at her although she had her gaze down and didn't see him. His hand met hers, and when they were together, he knew he had made the right decision.

A full hour passed as Lily led him by the hand around the backyard that was alive with spring flowers. Apparently she and her grandmother were quite the flower lovers. She led him to the flowerpots and showed him how to count to ten as she put water on the plants. Then she took his hand to lead him to the next one.

After all of the plants were sufficiently watered, he sat down on the grass, and she sat next to him. She had his hand in hers again only this time she bounced her fingers on the tips of his. "You've got hard fingers," she said questioningly.

"That's from playing the guitar." He turned his left hand up so she could see the calluses.

Her face corkscrewed into thoughtfulness. "You play a lot, huh?"

"All the time."

"Did you play when you knew Mommy?"

The question rang through him like a shot. "Yeah, I did. She came to see me play a lot."

"Am I going to get to see you play?" Lily's hazy blue eyes looked up into his, and he smiled.

"I hope so. Someday—if you want to."

"I want to," she said, putting a stamp on the statement with a nod of her head.

"Then we'll have to see what we can do about that." He couldn't stop himself. He reached over and ran his hand down her tiny back, wishing he could hug her but knowing that had to be her decision.

She tilted her head to the side and looked up at him. "Can you play a song for me?"

Surprise jumped through him. "Now?"

"Grandpa has an old guitar. Please... Please!"

How could he say no to that? "Well, okay, if you'll help me up."

She was on her feet in a flash, and she pulled him up as if she really could. Hand-in-hand they walked into the house. "Grandpa, can we borrow your guitar?"

The mountain of a man looked up from his coffee setting on the table in the kitchen. "That old thing?"

"When you get a request, you do what you can," Kalin said, shrugging. Lily led him into the living room, and after a few minutes, Mr. Bennett came in carrying a case with several years of dust on it.

"It's probably not in tune any more." He unlatched the case and lifted the guitar out. It was no more than a starter guitar, but Kalin took it and sat down on the ottoman. He bowed his head over it and began plucking the strings to find the place where it would be in tune. Lily sat at his feet gazing up at him, and he smiled down at her.

He got the strings as close to tuned as he could. It wasn't perfect, but it would have to work. He started strumming just letting the music flow through him. He moved his foot slightly, repositioned the guitar, and started again. "This one is for Lily." The notes he'd been hearing for a month only in his head ran under his fingers.

"Lily, when I see your face, I fall in love again. You set my spirit free. Oh, Lily... God's great gift to me, and for eternity, I will love you..."

He looked down, and Lily's face radiated pure love back at him. His fingers stopped on the strings as his thoughts snagged on the one who had literally brought him here. Gratefulness for her love gripped him. He would never be able to repay her for giving him this moment. He looked across the room to Cathleen. "Umm... I have another song, but it's for someone I brought with me. Would you mind?"

Confusion snagged on Cathleen face. "Who?"

He tried to hold her gaze but couldn't. "Well, I wasn't real sure about today, so she agreed to come with me. Umm, she's... well, I guess we're kind of together. I mean, it's kind of weird because she lives in Knoxville, and I'm on the road all the time, so we don't get much chance to be together..."

"Where is she?" Cathleen asked in concern.

"Out in the car. She said she would wait."

"You've been here an hour and a half!" Cathleen jumped up and headed for the door.

Kalin followed her up and leaned the guitar next to the chair. "I know, but I wanted to spend some time with Lily..."

Cathleen opened the door and stepped out onto the porch. He saw Danae notice the movement and look their direction. With one hand Cathleen waved to her, and Danae waved back sheepishly.

"Well, go get her already," Cathleen commanded, reaching back, pulling him forward, and then pushing him off the porch steps. "Don't leave her sitting out in the car."

Kalin stepped off the porch and motioned for Danae. She seemed reluctant to get out, and so he was halfway to the car before she actually opened the door. She stood and ran her hand over her hair clearly wary. She closed the door and walked very slowly to where he stood. When she met him on the sidewalk, love burst through him. He took her hand. "They want to meet you."

"Me? Are you sure?" She looked past him. "I don't want to intrude."

"You're going to love Lily." His hand intertwined with hers, and together they walked up to the porch where Cathleen stood with her arm around Lily. Kalin let Danae's hand go as he stepped up the first porch step. He reached for Lily. Pulling her forward gently, he bent down so he could look at her at eye level. "Lily, I want you to meet someone. This is Danae Scott."

"Hi, Lily," Danae said, extending her hand.

"Danae brought me here to see you," Kalin said, looking at Lily.

The little hand went out, shook Danae's, and dropped back to the child's side. "Hi."

When Kalin stood, he reached out and took hold of Lily's hand. "I was just giving Lily a little impromptu concert, and I thought you'd like to join us."

"Oh." That sent Danae's wary level to new heights. "Okay." She put her hand in her back pocket. Together they turned and started up the steps.

At the top step, Cathleen extended her hand. "It's nice to meet you, Danae. I'm Cathleen. Kalin didn't tell us you've been sitting out in the car all this time."

"Oh, it was okay. I took a little nap. That driving all night thing will get you."

Kalin didn't miss the look of surprised concern that Cathleen gave Danae.

"You're from Nashville then?" Cathleen asked as they went back into the living room.

"Knoxville. I'm a student at UT."

"Oh, really? What are you studying?"

"Pre-med," Danae said, grabbing for Kalin's free hand as they walked from the entry into the living room. She looked positively petrified.

"Pre-med?" Mel stepped into the living room. "That's a tough field."

Danae's fingers tightened on Kalin's as her gaze jumped to the man standing there. "Well, when it's where God wants you, tough is relative."

"Are you going to play again?" Lily asked, pulling on Kalin's other hand.

Kalin looked down at her. "Do you want to hear more?"

She nodded, making the curls bounce around her shoulders. "Lots more."

"Okay." He led the two of them to the floor in front of the ottoman and let their hands go, feeling like he might float right off the ground when he did so. He picked up the guitar, and the only song that was streaming through his brain was the one Phoenix Rising had never gotten the chance to record. It was appropriate because at that moment with the two of them gazing up at him, he had never felt so lucky. G wound into C, and C into D.

"Because of you, I'm lucky to be me," he sang as the words and music wound through him. "Never before have I been so free. To do what I feel, to be who I am, to be the man I was meant to be... to be the man I was meant to be."

Lily giggled and leaned in closer to Danae, who put her arm around the little girl.

"So leave the penny on the street, give the horse back his shoe, I don't need no rabbit's foot… All… I need… is you." Enraptured by the moment, Kalin gazed at the two of them, and for a split second too long, the picture they made wove through his heart. Reaching up with his wristband, he wiped a hot tear from the edge of his eye.

"And because of you, I'm lucky to be me…" If life could get any more perfect, he didn't know how.

Chapter 27

"So, how are you?" Danae asked, glancing over at Kalin who had sat wordlessly in her passenger seat ever since they'd left the Bennett's ten minutes before. For the last five of those minutes, she had been praying for him to start the conversation, and when he didn't, she finally started praying for the right words to help him through this.

"She's great, huh?" Kalin asked softly in reply to her question.

"Beautiful."

His gaze dropped to his hands as one pushed on the other aimlessly. "They're all so nice. They make me feel like it's a good thing I showed up."

Concern traced through her at his tone. "It is a good thing, isn't it?"

"I don't know." His gaze flipped to hers and then dropped again. "Is it? I mean, look at me. What do I have to offer her? I'm on the road all the time. My past is a horror story. I screwed up her mother's life as well as my own. I don't have any idea what my future holds. I'm running night and day just to keep up with right now…"

"Excuses," Danae said, cutting into the string of statements.

His gaze swung to hers defensively.

"Those are all excuses, and we both know it." She glanced over at him. "So, do you mind telling me what's really going on?"

He put his head down and never said anything although she waited as long as her spirit would let her.

"So, how long are you going to keep beating yourself up about what happened back then? And at what point do you let that go and start really living now?"

He shook his head as his eyes fell closed. "But I hurt so many people, and they didn't deserve that."

"And wallowing in the guilt now is going to help them how?"

That stopped him. "Well, it's not, but..."

"Okay, here's what I think. I think you don't think you really deserve anything good to happen now because of what you did back then. I think you're bound and determined to punish yourself for those decisions no matter what you risk losing by not living today to do it."

He didn't look at her. It would've been easier and far less risky to just shut up, but she couldn't leave him there. He was too important.

"It's not true, you know?" she said softly. "It's a lie just like all the rest of it. We all make mistakes. We all make bad decisions. We all act out of fear rather than out of love, but that doesn't give us the right to give up and quit."

"But I just keep thinking about back then, about what I could've done, what I should've done, how messed up I was... I just keep thinking if I hadn't been so stupid..."

"And what does that do for you? Lift you up? Make you better now? No, it keeps you where you were then. Don't you see, you're holding on to all the bad stuff and by holding on to it, you're letting it hold onto you. Let it go. Release it. Give it to God."

"But I've done that, and I know He's forgiven me, but it's still there."

"Well, have you ever thought about forgiving yourself?"

His head fell further, and for a long moment he said nothing. Then he shook his head. "I can't do that."

The statement knifed through her, and she knew he would never be whole until he did. "Then you're going to live right there forever. Is that really what you want?" He didn't answer. "Is that what you want, Kalin?"

"No," he finally said, and there was anger in the syllable. "It's killing me."

"Then why hang onto it?"

"Because if I forgive myself, that means I think it's all right, and it's not."

Love and patience drifted through her spirit. "No, if you forgive yourself, that means you choose love over all the pain and the lies and the heartache. You choose love over fear now. You realize that you were hurting, and you did things to try to stop the hurt that didn't help at all. You love yourself enough to see you were in pain, and rather than add more pain to that by beating yourself up about it, you choose to love and bless rather than curse and regret. Punishing yourself now only keeps you in that hurt. It holds you there until you decide to let it go."

"But how do I do that? It's so big. I don't even know where to start."

Danae exhaled and prayed for the words. "Ask to be willing. Ask Him to help you to be willing to forgive yourself. Ask Him to change how you see that time so that you see the lessons you learned because of it." She glanced across the seat. "And if you can't do it for you, then do it for Lily because in that little girl's eyes you are Superman."

His gaze snapped to hers and held.

"She loves you, Kalin. So do I, and so does God. In fact, the only one not on your team right now is you. It's like you know how to give all of us love, but you won't let yourself accept the love we're giving you. But that's the other half of the equation. One without the other doesn't work. Right now, you're doing everything you can to give yourself reasons not to accept it. It's time to forgive yourself and start believing we could love you in spite of the past, or maybe because of what the past made you today."

Long after they had parted ways, Danae going back to Knoxville, Kalin back to Cincinnati to catch up with the tour bus, he thought about her words. Had he been asked to do it for himself, he never could have brought himself to so much as breathe the words. But because of those who loved him, his life had taken on more importance over the last year, so this wasn't just about him anymore. It was about them, and for them, he was willing to do even this.

"Dear Lord," he breathed as he lay in the hotel room that night, "You and I both know I don't think I deserve this, but You and I both know I have to find a way to get past it. Please, please help me find a way to be willing to forgive myself. I want to choose love. I'm tired of choosing fear."

As he prayed, he heard the words begin to take root in his soul. "I choose love, and I forgive myself. I choose love, and I forgive myself. I choose love, and I forgive myself..." He fell asleep to their gentle lullaby.

For three weeks, Kalin had been praying that prayer nearly non-stop. At first it seemed silly. Then it seemed monotonous. Finally, it just felt like him. More and more he recognized the love that was finding its way to his doorstep. There were the letters back and forth to Kentucky, not to mention the emails back and forth to Knoxville. The band members, the fans, his family... The list of love was growing by the day, and for the first time in what felt like forever, he was beginning to let himself feel it.

"You busy?" Jesse asked one afternoon as the drone of the bus rolled under them. Michigan, their last stop on the tour, was fast approaching.

"Not really." Kalin pulled his attention back into the bus. "What's up?"

Jesse sat down in a heap, and it took a long moment for him to even move again. Concern slid through Kalin as he looked at his friend.

"I've got to ask you a question," Jesse finally said slowly. "And I don't want you to say yes right away. I want you to think about it, and I mean really think about it, okay?"

Uncertainty crawled through Kalin. "O—kay."

"And promise me you won't just say yes out of pity."

"Good grief, Jess, what is it?"

For another second Jesse said nothing, and then his dark gaze slipped up to meet Kalin's. Fear and worry trounced through Jesse's eyes. "Well, we've been talking about it... me and the guys, and we don't want to find somebody else. We want you."

The statement hit Kalin like a brick. In two weeks he was supposed to be in the studio, recording his solo album. Zane had half a dozen bands waiting for him to interview the second the tour was over. "I... Jess..."

"No, please. Let me finish." Jesse took a long breath, which did nothing to calm Kalin's racing thoughts. "We're not asking you to give up on your dream. We just... well, we want to join yours."

Kalin shook his head. "I don't understand."

A short breath and Jesse closed his eyes. "You need a band. We need a singer. One without the other isn't going anywhere in this business. And we want to be your band on your solo album and for the tour when there is one." He nodded three times as if he was trying to get the words out of his soul. "You have such an unbelievable talent, and you connect with people—with the fans—like nobody I've ever seen. It's like they're drawn to you. Besides that, when you're up there, you make me believe what you have is possible, that life's worth living." He threw his head back. "Jeez! I sound like a stupid self-help book. This wasn't supposed to be this hard."

"You're serious," Kalin said as if realizing that for the first time.

"Yeah." Jesse's gaze fell to his hands. "I keep looking at it, and I've been praying like mad trying to figure out what to do. And I just can't shake the feeling that this could really work. Adrian and I talked while you were gone after Cinci, and he thought it would work too. Then we talked to the others..."

"What about Ace?"

"It's not a done deal," Jesse conceded, "but we needed to know what you thought before anything went forward." He looked over at Kalin. "Just think about it, okay? Whatever you decide, we'll understand." He stood, giving Kalin all the room he needed. "And no matter what, you know I'm in your corner." With that, Jesse left.

Kalin felt the mantel of responsibility fall onto his shoulders. If he accepted, his success or failure would trickle over and become his friends' success or failure. What if he couldn't do it? What if he couldn't pull it off? What if…? For one second it all seemed to overwhelm him, but with a snap, the thoughts stopped. In his mind, he looked up, and he could see the light, shining over the gray-green waves rolling at his feet.

"This is right, isn't it?" he asked softly, feeling it in his soul even as he asked the question. Peace poured over and through him. It was meant to be from the first moment he and Jesse had met in the church nearly a year before, and maybe even from the very start of their friendship. Slowly, one step at a time, the Holy Spirit had been guiding them to this spot. Kalin let out a breath. "No more what if's, okay? I'm tired of the past deciding the future. I lay all the what if's to rest right now."

Doubt and fear seemed to flow with the breath out of his chest. He leaned back in the seat, put his head on the headrest, and closed his eyes.

"Okay, God. This is it. From this moment on, I choose love, I choose You—not the past. The past is the past, and I choose only to hold onto the good things that got me to here. The bad, I let go of forever. Guide my steps from this point on. I put them all in Your hands. Holy Spirit unclench fear's hold on my life, and as You do, I lay it down right here and move forward in You knowing You can take even the mistakes and make them victories."

It was like nothing he had ever felt before, and he grabbed onto the armrest so as not to float right off of the seat. "Oh, God, forgive me for all the time I wasted."

But even as the thought went through his mind, another one overtook it. "None was wasted for it brought you here."

His spirit smiled, and then he actually laughed. "Okay. I get it. No more beating myself up. I bless it—all of it. Every single thing that happened for what it taught me." He felt like standing up and shouting his happiness to the world. Instead, after another minute, he pulled himself to his feet, walked to the front of the bus and sat down in the midst of Phoenix Rising. "Okay. I'm in. How do we make this happen?"

There was never a shortage of excitement between the two of them. Either he had an album, a video, a concert, rehearsals, or promotional events coming up or she was cramming for some kind of a test—Microbiology, Biochemistry, Organic Chemistry. At least every other month one or both managed to get away long enough to go see Lily, and those were the times Danae knew she would remember most about this chapter in her life.

It was like watching a flower open as Lily and Kalin's lives fused together. Danae never felt left out, but still there was something special between the two of them that made her spirit smile. Watching him with Lily made Danae love him even more. He was learning to be a good dad even though he couldn't be there every second. They had even come up with their own secret code for letters so no one else who intercepted one might be able to decipher it. And every time she was with Kalin, it was clear he was finally living X-Better.

In late March, nearly three years after they first met, Danae was engrossed in studying for Epidemiology. All that remained for the word Doctor to be placed before her name was her internship in the fall. Residency after that would keep her here, but it was now a goal—not a dead end. The little efficiency apartment that afforded her the privacy to study also got very quiet on nights like tonight. She wondered how Tara and Michael were doing now that their trip down the aisle had made it official.

Being a bridesmaid had been so different this go-round, and she smiled at how touched Tara was when Kalin agreed to sing the first song at their dance. Granted, he didn't have Phoenix Rising to back him up, but how could anyone beat having Kalin Lane sing "Lucky" at their wedding? It had been his first real break out song, and with its success had come his as well.

Missing him had become a way of life, and Danae knew she would never get used to that feeling. Just as his absence traced through her, the phone rang, and she reached for it. "Hello?"

"What, were you sitting on that thing?" he asked, and love mixed with a generous portion of happiness burst through her.

She sat back in the chair and slipped her pen behind her ear. "No, just waiting for you to call as usual. What's up?"

"Well, the new tour schedule came out today, and I had to call."

In three years that accent hadn't lost its magic spell on her sanity. She sat forward as her heart fluttered ahead of her. "Oh, yeah? Well, I'm glad you found a reason to call. I'd hate to waste time talking for no reason." A smile traced over her heart as the hours they had spent on the phone just listening to one another breathe wound through her memory. "So what's so special about the schedule?"

"Well, I've been thinking about it, and I think I owe you something."

"Owe me something? Like what?"

"Like I seem to remember some free tickets you asked for a long time ago."

She laughed outright. "Was I psychic or what? I said you were going to have girls all over you."

His laugh made her grin stretch wider. "Yeah? Well, one is all I need."

It took him a moment to continue, and although she knew she should protest if out of kidding than of nothing else, the words wouldn't come through the ache of missing him. A long exhale was all that kept the emotion from flooding through her.

"We're coming to Frankfort, Kentucky in September, and I was thinking maybe we could take Lily out for her birthday. I've been telling her if we ever got close…"

Danae's own excitement was drowned only by her excitement for Lily. "Oh, my gosh. You will send that child into cardiac arrest when you tell her. You know that, right?"

"And you?"

"The concert's great," she said, her voice falling, "but the best part is I'll get to see you again. I miss you so much."

"I know that feeling," he said, his pitch matching hers. "We're really going to have to do something about that."

"Like what?"

"Well, there are hospitals in Nashville, aren't there? Surely there's a residency program you can get into there…"

"But you're on the road anyway. What would that help?"

He breathed. "Do you think there's an X-Better in this situation?"

"I don't know. Maybe…"

"What do you say, we start praying for X-Better and let Him take care of it?"

She couldn't argue. "Okay."

X-Better had yet to show up, but that was the last thing Danae was thinking about in early September when she picked up Lily, who had turned eight the week before. Somehow the little girl had talked her dad into letting her bring a friend along. Bribed, cajoled, and groveled was probably more like it, but after he had consulted with Danae to make sure it was okay, Kalin had relented. The two girls sat in the back of Danae's car, singing along to the CD that had been on perpetual play ever since he had given it to her the year before. How she would ever decide which to listen to when the new one came out in October, she couldn't quite tell.

Looking in the rearview mirror, Danae smiled. They knew every word and had even made up movements to the songs.

"Hey, you two," Danae said, breaking into their spontaneous concert. "Grandma Cathleen said you need to practice a little for the Spelling Bee next week."

"Ahhh!" they both moaned.

"Fifteen minutes of spelling, and then we'll listen some more." She reached down and turned off the music.

Lily sat forward, her curls bouncing with the bob of her head. "Do you think Dad's ready to see us?"

Danae smiled. "I'm sure he can't wait."

"Where are they?" Kalin breathed, looking out his ninth story window.

"Danae said they'd be here. They'll be here," Jesse said from the bed where he was flipping through a magazine.

"But I wanted them to ride over with us."

"Kalin, man. Calm down. They'll be here."

He paced away from the window and then back to it. He peeked out the curtain again.

"You're going to drive yourself crazy doing that," Jesse warned.

"I'm going to go crazy if I don't!"

Jesse smiled. "You really do love her, don't you?"

"What was your first clue?"

Jesse shook his head. "Then what are you waiting for?"

The curtain fell from Kalin's hand. "What do you mean?"

"Da-da-da-da…" Jesse sang, approximating the Wedding March as he swung his arms as if conducting a symphony. "We've got a pot going, you know, and if you don't hurry it up, I'm going to lose my fifty bucks."

That stopped Kalin. "A pot?"

"Yeah, Adrian and me are the only ones left. Everybody else got axed months ago. Steve figured you'd already be hitched and have a kid on the way by now."

Fear tackled Kalin. "But she's in…"

"Doctor school. I know, and then she'll be in her internship and then in residency and then in her first year of practice… If you're waiting for perfect, I don't think it's coming. Besides, it's not like you won't be on the road half the time anyway. At least if you make it official, she'll be waiting at home when you get back."

His mouth was suddenly devoid of any moisture. The knock on the door yanked his attention to it.

"I can see you're busy," Jesse said as he rolled off the bed and stood, "so I'll just get that." He went to the door and peeked in the peephole. "Well, look who's here..." With a flourish, he opened the door, and a wave of happiness gushed into the room.

The first one in his arms was Lily who looked much older than he had remembered her being in July. The second was Danae, and when she buried her face into the crook of his neck, Jesse's question ran through him. What was he waiting for?

Danae and Victoria, Lily's guest, had gone to the lobby to secure their room which would be just down from his for the evening. Every moment he watched her, the question ran through him again. She was it. The one he had been waiting his whole life to find. Denying that, putting off being together was making less and less sense the more he looked.

"So, did you have fun coming with Danae?" Kalin asked Lily as she stood brushing her hair at the floor to ceiling mirror on the closet.

"She's great," Lily said. She looked at him then sitting on the bed behind her, and her head tilted to the side. "Victoria asked if you guys are married."

He scratched the back of his neck as he chuckled self-consciously. "Oh really?"

"I told her no, and she said why not."

Kalin couldn't take a real breath as he sat there looking at his daughter.

Her gaze traced to the carpet as the brushing slowed to a stop. "It's not because of me, is it?"

Love he hadn't seen coming flooded through him. Gently he reached over, took her arm, and pulled her to where he sat on the bed. He sat her on his leg and put his arms around her. "The fact that Danae and I aren't married is not about you. It's about us. Okay? We're just busy... We've both got lots of things going on."

"But Grandma and Grandpa have lots of things going on, and they're married."

Kalin sighed. She had a point. "Well, we were kind of waiting for the right time."

"When's that going to be?"

He began to see that this wasn't a passing fancy with Lily. "You like her, don't you?"

Worry clouded the little face. "Yes. Don't you?"

He laughed. "Yeah, I do. I really do."

"And she loves you, too. I know because she was all excited today when she picked us up."

Her honesty was quickly eroding his objections. Finally he looked at her.

"You know what? I think you're right. I think it's time, but I don't want to just ask her any old way. That wouldn't be special enough, and for Danae, this has to be really special."

Lily nodded solemnly.

A plan began to form in his head. "Hey, you wouldn't want to help me, would you?"

Lily bounced up and down on his knee.

"Okay, but you have to promise me you won't tell Danae anything about this."

The little head full of blonde curls nodded for all it was worth.

Everyone else in the front rows was screaming and pushing to get to where he stood on the stage. To Danae just getting to watch him was enough. Fluid and confident. Handsome and heart stopping. He sang as if he was having the time of his life. She couldn't take her gaze off of him, and when he looked down at her with a just-between-us smile in the middle of the song "Lucky," she melted. That smile. Those eyes. That spirit. They had captured her heart so completely it didn't take anything at all for her to see why he had accumulated such a fanatical following of rabid fans.

An official website and half a hundred unofficial ones, a second CD, three videos, a new tour, whispers of a headline tour after that... It was hard to grasp that he was the same Kalin who called her every other night, the same one who still sent emails that gave her the strength to go on. He was amazing. Her focus honed in on the ease with which his body seemed to do everything. He danced like gravity had no hold on him. He sang like an angel. His fingers seemed not to have to so much as listen to messages from his brain they played so fast. And she hadn't missed the fact that it was the songs that he wrote that got the most response.

By the time he left the stage, she had no desire to wait to see the headliner. She bent down to Lily's ear. "Do you want to stay?"

Lily's eyes looked as mesmerized as Danae's spirit felt. "Can we go see Dad?"

"Yeah, let's go."

"Hey, look who I found," Jesse said, ushering Danae, Lily and Victoria into the backstage dressing room.

"Hey," Kalin said as the two of them ran into his arms leaving Victoria standing with Jesse. He kissed Lily on the top of the head, and without letting her go, kissed Danae on the forehead. "So...?"

"Oh! That was awesome!" Lily bounced from foot to foot. "I want to be able to dance like that." She pulled her body back and simulated playing a guitar.

"It's not hard," he said, hugging Danae to him again. "Just takes a lot of practice."

Danae's arms were around his waist, and she wasn't moving although he was drenched in sweat.

"What do you say we get out of here and find somewhere quiet?" He kissed Danae's forehead again as she leaned into him, closed her eyes, and nodded.

They had stopped to eat on the way back to the hotel, and with the girls talking 90-miles-an-hour, the two of them had been swept along just enjoying the gift of being close enough to touch one another again. It wasn't until they neared the hotel that Danae realized the non-stop conversation had begun to have long, intermittent pauses. With him driving, she looked back into the backseat, and the girls were about ten seconds from crashing for good.

"We'd better get them in bed," she said softly. "I think their adrenaline finally ran out."

He glanced over his shoulder, then at her and nodded, but she couldn't quite read the look in his eyes. Without saying a word, he reached over, picked up her hand, raised it to his lips, and kissed it gently. "It was so great having you out there tonight. You have no idea how many nights I've wanted you there."

Her smile barely made it to her lips as she felt the quiet begin to pull at her eyelids as well. "You're unbelievable."

"How could I not be? I've got a God who loves me... you, Lily, my parents, the band, the fans... I must be the luckiest guy in the world."

"And because of you, I'm lucky to be me," she sang softly, laying her head over onto his shoulder.

He picked up the harmony which would've thrown her off had she not listened to the song ten cagillion times already. "Never before have I been so free. To do what I feel, to be who I am, to be the man I was meant to be... to be the man I was meant to be..."

Danae helped the girls get into their pajamas and into bed while Kalin went to his room and took a shower. By the time he made it back to her room, she too was in her sweatpants. Thankfully he had the same idea because when she opened the door, it was clear that his gray T-shirt and black sweats didn't scream going out partying.

"Hey," he said softly.

"Shh. They're asleep."

"Already?"

She nodded.

"Okay," he said as he followed her in. He walked over to the little refrigerator that she had been too busy to inspect and opened it. "You want something?"

She went over to the couch in the sitting area opposite from the space occupied by the table and chairs where he stood. Spent from making it through the day, she collapsed onto the couch. "Sure. What you got?"

"Hmm." He examined the options. "Coke. Pepsi. Sprite. Water…"

"Water sounds wonderful."

He pulled two waters out, walked over to the couch, handed her one, and opened his. Then he spun around and sat next to her before putting his foot up on the coffee table. He leaned back and closed his eyes. His still shower-damp hair fell back and away from his face exposing his unshaven jawline to the light. He took a drink without opening his eyes.

"Quiet?" she asked.

His head relaxed to the side, and he looked at her. "Peace." Another two drinks, and he set his water bottle on the coffee table. He took hers out of her hand and set it next to his. Then he put his arms around her and pulled her down with him so that he was lying with his back on the couch, his head resting on the throw pillow. Her back was pressed flat against the back of the couch, one leg traced down his and the other knee lay on his thigh.

He sighed deeply, and she felt his chest rise and fall under her temple as he relaxed. Her head was on his chest. His arms wrapped around her. It was the safest feeling she'd ever known.

"You know something?" he asked softly.

"What's that?"

"I can't believe how good things are right now. The music, the tour, my family back home, Lily, you… But it's all going so fast. I'm afraid I'm going to miss something."

She propped her chin up with her hand to be able to look at him. "Are you missing something?"

Love slipped into his smile when he looked at her. "Not any more." He pulled her back down onto to him, ratcheted his shoulders twice to get comfortable and fell still. It was the best moment of her life to that point.

The next morning Danae was fighting with herself not to break down completely at the thought of leaving him. The girls were back to chattering away, but today it was more annoying than exciting. At breakfast she noticed Kalin looking over at her with concern, and with everything she had she wanted to put on a happy face for him. However, the mere thought of smiling made her want to cry. In two hours they would be leaving again. It hurt to even think about that.

Midway through breakfast, Lily suddenly had a thought. "Oh, Danae, I was going to tell you. Dad and I were talking last night, and he's going to come on Thursday for my birthday. Do you want to come?"

She felt his soft gaze trace over her face. "You already had your birthday."

"I know, but y'all weren't there to celebrate it with me."

Tears stung the backs of Danae's eyes even as she smiled. "Of course, I'll come. I wouldn't miss it."

Chapter 28

Reading, studying, writing papers, even helping to set a broken bone—those were all things she could now do with confidence. However, by the time she had the ingredients out on the counter, Danae was convinced that baking a cake was not one of those things. She surveyed the box, reading for the third time that it took two eggs, a third cup of water, and oil for each cake just to make sure.

It was a given that she was going to screw this up. It was too important for it to come out right; and therefore she would find a way that it wouldn't. Biting her bottom lip between her teeth, she carefully dumped the first then the second cake mix into the bowl and one-by-one added the other ingredients. She pushed the stray strand of hair out of her eyes and glanced back at the oven, which was going through the pre-heating process. Her gaze chanced on the clock. He would be here in less than an hour and a half. All day long she had begged anyone who happened to be listening to convince her attending supervisor to let her go early. Of course she was almost thirty minutes late when she finally walked out.

Digging into the preparations, she whipped the mix as fast as she could. Then she grabbed the two round cake pans, and made sure she had sprayed them. Carefully she dumped the cake first into one and then into the other. The oven beeped behind her making her jump which almost landed the bowl on the floor. When the bowl was securely back on the counter, she took the two pans and set them in the oven, turned the timer, and closed the door. She stepped back and brushed the hair out of her face again; however, she felt something cold and wet slide across her forehead as she did so. In annoyance she reached up and wiped at the spot, realizing that she had transferred unbaked chocolate cake mix to her forehead. She licked her fingers tiredly. "That was good, Danae."

Leaving the kitchen, she went to take a shower. It was a rush from that moment until she was back in the kitchen, and she barely beat the timer. She pulled her hair into an impromptu ponytail and then anchored it over the shoulder of her polished-cotton, light blue, button-down shirt. She grabbed the potholders, pulled the pans out of the oven and tested them. Perfect.

Something about letting them cool ran through her mind, so she went back to the bathroom to finish up her make-up. When she glanced up into the mirror, the reflection snagged her attention, and she stopped. Happiness glowed back at her from those eyes, and the smile in her heart shone from them. She stuck her tongue out at her reflection and laughed. Quickly she finished her make-up.

As she went back to the kitchen, she glanced at the clock. If he was late, she might make this work. If he was early, she was toast. Grabbing the two containers of ready made icing from the cabinet, she set them on the counter and stood over the two cakes trying to figure out the best way to accomplish the next part of this undertaking. She took the plate she was going to use to transport it to Kentucky out of the cabinet, set it next to the cakes, and surveyed the job.

Seeing no great way to do it, she finally laid the plate over one cake pan and flipped it. When she lifted the cake pan off, she smiled in victory. "See, Danae, that wasn't so hard." She opened the icing and commenced smearing the sweet concoction over the cake. However, when that one was done, concern traced through her. She couldn't do the plate thing again to get the second cake. She surveyed and considered and thought, but finally decided her best bet was just to flip the cake pan up on top of the already iced part and hope for the best.

However, just as she flipped the pan, there was a knock on her door. Her attention swerved from her mission one second too long, and when she pulled the pan up, it wasn't quite square. The top cake slid to the side of the bottom one and stopped—half on, half off. "Oh, you've gotta be kidding me!"

There was another knock. She considered trying to right the cake, but the knocking was fraying her nerves. Finally she left the cakes and went to the door, where she heaved one breath to settle herself and swung the door open.

"Jeez. I was beginning to wonder if you were standing me up," Kalin said with a laugh.

"Now would I do that?" she asked, turning and heading back for the kitchen.

He stepped in, closed the door, and sniffed. "Smells good."

She was again standing over the cake in the kitchen trying to figure out how to get the top cake back up on top. "Yeah? Well, it looks worse."

Stepping up behind her, he looked over her shoulder. "Getting kind of daring there, aren't you?"

"Well, I was until that happened." Finally she reached in the drawer for two spatulas. She angled them over the cakes first one way and then the other, trying to figure out a good entry point.

"Would you like some help?"

"I think I need a lot more than help."

"Here." He took the spatulas from her, and she stepped to the side. Slowly he pushed them through the icing under the top cake. Before he moved anything, he looked at her. "Where do you want this?"

"On top of the other one preferably."

Sliding it gently he repositioned the cake, and remarkably it didn't look too bad.

"Fab," she said gratefully. "Okay. Now, I've just got to get this iced, and throw my shoes on, and then we can go."

He shrugged and backed up. "No rush. Lily said to be there about 7, so we've got time." Leaning on the cabinet behind her, he dug his hands into his back pockets, and watched her finish icing the cake.

It was then, as she was transferring the icing from the jar to the cake that the preacher's words from so long before came back to her. *If we're not careful, we choose our friends based not on the ingredients they have chosen to include in their lives but on how the cake looks on the outside. We base our decision on the icing when sometimes all that icing does is mask that they've made their cake with the wrong ingredients.* It was so true she had to put her head down to keep from laughing.

"Thank You, God for helping Kalin be more than icing," she said under her breath. Two more swipes with the knife, and the cake was finished. "That's as good as it's going to get."

All the way to Kentucky, Danae was sure this had to be some kind of dream she had wandered into. They talked about her school, how much longer she had interning, where she might have her residency, how long that would take, what she wanted to do after that. Then the conversation swung to his current schedule.

Although she had thought he had this week off, he'd actually been in the studio working on Faith Hill's new album. It seemed that Ashton had been so impressed, he had talked Tim and his wife into using Kalin as well. By the following week he and Phoenix Rising would be on the road again, promoting the new CD, which was to hit stores in late October.

"Oh, I have something for you," Kalin said as they neared the Kentucky line.

"What's that?"

He reached under the seat and pulled out a CD case. "Hot off the press."

Her heart jumped as he spun it to her. "The new one?"

He nodded. "I hope you like it."

She held it as if it was her favorite present of all time. "Can I listen to it now?"

He laughed. "If you want to."

"I want to." She worked the CD player like an expert, and in no time she was listening to him sing fresh love songs to her—on the speakers and in person. She felt like she was flying on an angel's wings.

They pulled up to the little house at just after 7, and Danae climbed out and opened the back door to retrieve the cake. It was only then that she saw what had happened to her beautiful masterpiece. "Oh, no."

"What?" he asked as he got out of the other side. He joined her at the backdoor but said nothing as they both stood, staring at the cake. During the ride, the top half had slid forward, smooshing into the plastic wrap. The toothpicks that were supposed to keep the plastic from touching the icing were either stuck in the fallen layer or sticking out in weird directions. The cellophane was all that was holding the entire thing from sliding right into the floorboard. It looked like a double-decker bus that had just smashed into a bridge.

Seeing no other option, Danae reached in and tried to push the top back onto its perch, but instead of righting it, she put a big dent in it with her hand. "Dat-gum-it!" She stomped her foot in frustration.

"Here." Kalin pulled her backward and picked the cake up with its now smooshed and dented side coupled with its Leaning Tower of Piazza façade. "Maybe they won't notice."

She looked at him in furious annoyance.

He shrugged. "Hey, you tried. Lily will love it because she loves you." He held the cake, grabbed her hand, and kicked the door closed.

Unwilling acceptance drained through her. Short of leaving the thing in the car, there weren't many other options. Halfway up the walk, the front door burst open, and Lily came streaming down the sidewalk until she jumped into the arm he had barely released from Danae's hand, very nearly knocking the cake to the ground.

"Hey, girl! Happy Birthday." He pulled her to him and kissed the side of her head

The little girl barely got anything out through her excitement. Instead she grabbed his now free hand and Danae's hand and pulled them with a hard yank up the porch steps. "They're here!" she yelled for everyone in the entire neighborhood to hear.

"Oh, good," Cathleen said, coming around the corner and into the entryway.

Kalin handed her the plate of cake so he could take his jacket off and help Danae with hers. "Danae made Lily a cake, but it didn't travel very well."

"Oh, dear." Cathleen spun the cake slowly as she examined it. "Did you let it cool before you frosted it?"

"I tried," Danae said, knowing Cathleen was going to think she was a horrible cook.

Instead Cathleen patted her on the back softly. "Happens to the best of us. Don't worry. I'm sure it's still edible."

It was all Danae was praying for by that point.

"Please, come in," Cathleen said, and Danae caught the look Lily and her grandmother exchanged.

"Yes," Lily said formally as she unfurled her arms to indicate the hallway. "Do come in. Your table is ready."

Kalin looked at Danae who glanced at him skeptically. Lily took his hand and then reached back for Danae's. She led them down the hallway to the living room door, which had dark material hung on it.

"What's this?" Kalin asked with concern.

"You'll see," Lily said mysteriously.

Kalin glanced over at Danae with a look she couldn't quite read. At the doorway, Lily pulled back the material. "Table for two, for Lane."

"What did you do?" Kalin asked her, but she was decisively in maitre de mode.

"Right this way please." She led them over to the only table in the room, which sat right next to the fireplace. A quiet gas fire danced on the other side of the glass, and soft music hummed through the speakers hidden somewhere in the dimly lit room.

"I thought we were here to celebrate your birthday," Kalin said as it became clear there were only two chairs at the table.

"Please, have a seat," Lily continued as if she hadn't heard him. Staring at her, they both took their seats. "Tonight we have our chef's specialty—Trout in Lemon Sauce, Bread Knots, and green beans. Would you like a fresh salad to start off with?"

Kalin looked at her for a long minute with his eyebrows raised. "Sure."

Lily nodded. "I'll be right back… I mean, please enjoy your dinner." And she traipsed off to the kitchen.

Danae looked at him warily. "What is this about?"

"I have no idea," he said as his eyes got wide. "But it looks like they went to a lot of trouble, so just play along."

At that moment Lily reappeared with a tray of two salads and several kinds of dressing. Instantly Kalin jumped up to help her as it looked like it might all go crashing to the carpet at any moment.

"I got it," Lily said as she struggled under the tray. Despite her protest, he helped her remove the salads and the dressing. When the tray was empty, she tucked it under her side. "Would you like tea or water?"

"Tea would be fine," Danae said.

"Tea," Kalin confirmed as he sat back down.

She nodded and left.

"You think Cathleen set her up to this?" Danae asked quietly as she leaned across the table.

"I don't know," he said with a shrug. "You know Lily."

They had polished off the salads, the appetizer, and the meal, and it was clear that Lily was having the time of her life playing restaurant. Finally she came out, walked over to Kalin, and ducked in close to him for a private consultation. She whispered something. He whispered something back. Then she nodded and went back to the kitchen. Danae took a slow drink of her tea trying not to be nosy but wondering just the same.

Kalin looked over at her and smiled although it wasn't the happiest smile she had ever seen.

"Something wrong?" she asked.

"Oh, uh, no. Everything's fine."

Lily reappeared with two small dishes of chocolate cake that had obviously been pieced back together and cut. She set them down in front of Kalin and Danae, and then she looked at Danae solemnly. "Thank you for making my cake. It really is good."

Incomprehension dropped over Danae as she looked down at the cake in front of her. "But—" When she looked up, Lily had already turned and was walking out. Danae's gaze went to Kalin. "I wanted to put candles on it and everything."

"It's okay." He reached across the table to lay his hand on hers. "It's the thought that counts."

"Well, that's original," she said in a huff as she picked up her fork and cut into the cake. On the first bite, however, she had to admit that it was surprisingly good. "Hey, that's not half bad."

"Yeah," he said slowly, "I guess it doesn't really matter what it looks like on the outside, only what's really in it that counts."

Her thoughts snagged on that, and she knew he was talking about more than the cake. She ate three more bites and then gave up. "I'm stuffed." She reached for her tea and took a drink. "I don't think I'll have to eat for a month."

"We'll have to give our compliments to the chef," he said, and she noticed that he wasn't exactly breaking speed records on how fast he was eating either.

She glanced back at the kitchen. "Cathleen is a good cook. Wish I was this good."

"Yeah." He thought for a moment, and the effort seemed to tax his response circuits. "I can scramble eggs."

She laughed. "Well, I'm a little more advanced than that."

Finally he finished the last of his cake and put his fork down. He wiped his mouth with his napkin and laid it on the table. Then he sat for a long moment just staring at the napkin. Concern slid through her. Just before she got the words to her mouth to ask what was wrong, his gaze drifted up and locked with hers. That question and everything else flew away from her.

He blew out the air in his lungs in a short surge, then reached over and slipped his hand under hers. His gaze fell once more then retook hers. "When I came back to Nashville, I thought the only dream that mattered to me was getting back to the big time. That's all I thought about. That's all I cared about. Well, I'm back now, and the more I look around, the more I realize that all of that means nothing if you're not there to share it with me."

"Kalin..." she started to protest, but he stopped her.

"Please, let me finish." His gaze fell to her half-eaten cake still lying on the plate. "You know, we're kind of like your cake. We don't look perfect on the outside. You're here. I'm there. We're both running around trying to get all these other dreams to work out." His gaze caught hers and held. "But that's not what's real. We're what's real, and it doesn't matter how it looks on the outside, or how it looks to anyone else. All that matters is what we know to be the truth, and what I know to be the truth is that I don't want to live another minute without you with me..."

He reached into the pocket of his jeans, and when his fingers came back to hers, she saw the ring. Disbelief crashed into her, and she put her fingers up to her nose.

The longer he went, the more confident he sounded. "Danae, everything else in the world means nothing to me if I can't share it with you." His gaze dug into hers. "Will you marry me?"

For a moment she didn't think she could ever get anything out. Her breathing wasn't cooperating. Her heart was ramming into her chest with hard thumps. For an eternity she just sat there, staring at the ring.

Finally, not trusting her voice to do anymore than squeak, she nodded. His smile lit him from the inside out.

"Really?" He sounded as if he wasn't sure she would say yes.

Her eyes beat back the tears, but they were too many and too adamant. Slowly her hand fell to the table in one long, shaky trip. "Yes."

She watched as he gently reached over and took her left hand. His hand smooth and graceful held hers, and she remembered the first time he had touched her hand. From the very first, he had been there, guiding her out of a tangled life she had no idea how she had gotten herself mixed up in. Her other hand slid back to her nose as she tried to keep the tears from falling. However, they were already sliding down her cheeks as she fought for breath.

His fingers slipped the ring onto her finger as his smile embraced her. "I love you so much."

"I love you, too."

He stood and somehow she did too. His arms caught her in a hug that she never wanted to end. She squeezed her eyes closed and diligently etched that moment in her memory. Whether it made sense to anyone else in the world or not, she knew they were made to be together. When he pulled back, she wiped her eyes and laughed. "They're going to think I'm nuts."

"No," he said as his spirit touched hers through his gaze. "They're going to think you're beautiful, just like I do." His lips found hers, and what breath she had left evaporated. She melted into him, pressing him next to her. She never wanted to let go again for as long as she lived.

The look on her face, the passion of her kisses, the feel of her next to him awakened emotions Kalin had thought were buried forever. It took all the sanity he had left, but finally he pulled her away from him. "So, you want to tell them or should I?"

She laughed and brushed at the tears still glistening on her eyelashes. "You can tell them. I might not get anything out."

His arm wrapped around her waist, and he looked over at the kitchen door. He wanted to scream it to the world, so he did. "She said,

'Yes!'"

Instantly Lily burst into the room, jumping up and down and racing for him as her excitement overflowed its banks. "Yes! It worked! It worked! They're getting married!"

Danae's gaze went to him. "What does she mean 'it worked'?"

Sheepishness drifted over him as he ducked his head. "Well, see... me and Lily were kind of talking, and..."

She whacked him with the palm of her hand. "You set me up."

He leaned away from the attack. "I didn't expect them to go to these lengths."

"It was Lily's idea," Cathleen said, stepping into the room with Mel right behind her. "She wanted it to be all romantic and everything."

"She's been working ever since she got back from Frankfort," Mel said. "She even went with me to pick out the fish."

"Eeewww," Lily said, her face scrunching in revulsion. "Fish is gross."

"Well, it was good, you." Kalin laid his arm around her neck and squeezed her into his thigh. Confidence slid away from him as the love poured into him, over him, and through him in gushing torrents from all sides.

Danae felt his certainty sliding, and she looked over at him. She laid her hand on his chest, and he squeezed her to him once more.

He looked around at all of them. "Thank you all, so much. This was so special..." He reached up and wiped the side of his eye with his wristband.

"A special night for two very special people," Cathleen said. "Thanks for including us." She stepped over and hugged Kalin who had to let go of Danae to return the hug.

Before Danae realized it, Mel was by her side. His smile spoke of sadness and acceptance. "Welcome to the family, Danae."

They were the best words she had ever heard.

Epilogue

On a windswept beach overlooking the Atlantic Ocean, in early April, with their friends and family looking on, Kalin reached out and took Danae's hand from Mel who had filled in for her own father. Mel looked at him with a gaze that would've melted steel. "Be good to her."

Kalin nodded his understanding and then tucked her arm under his. He took a breath and looked at her. "You ready for this?"

She smiled. "Try and stop me."

With joy in his heart, Kalin walked with her forward to where the preacher stood. His gaze snagged for a second on Lily, who stood just to the left of Danae. In the soft breeze, she gazed at them with perfect serenity. He swallowed and retrained his gaze on the preacher.

"The marriage of two souls is something God has given us to remind us of His love for us and to give us a soul mate—one who will be with us in good times and in bad, in sickness and health. This soul mate is to be our sounding board, our help, and our safety net. Kalin and Danae have come here today to pledge their love for one another in the sight of God and their friends and family. That love is to be cherished and encouraged and supported by all those present. So if anyone knows of a reason why these two should not be married, please speak now or forever hold your peace."

Danae's gaze drifted from Kalin's out to the assembled guests. It took only a moment for her to find her mother, and only a moment more for the slight nod to tell her that stepping into the future without the baggage of the past could really be happening.

"Since there is no objection," the preacher intoned. "May I have the rings, please?"

To Kalin's right, Jesse reached into his pocket and handed the rings over. Danae breathed a silent prayer of thanks for Kalin's road family. Their support and encouragement never ceased to amaze her.

"Bless these rings and those who wear them, Father. In the name of the Father, and of the Son, and of the Holy Spirit. Amen." The preacher handed Kalin her ring.

Kalin looked down and placed the ring halfway onto her finger. The breeze was the only sound as she watched his gaze find hers. He shook his head slightly, which sent the ends of his hair dancing about his head, and he smiled. It took one more breath for him to begin speaking.

"I don't really know how we got here," he said, and several guests laughed softly. "I certainly didn't see you coming. That's for sure." He put his head down, and it was clear he was having trouble getting the words out. When he looked back up, she saw the emotion in his eyes, and her spirit took on a placid, serene feeling as she willed her strength into him. "Sometimes what you think is possible is only a glint in God's eye compared with what He really wants to give you. Danae, you taught me to pray for X-Better, to really believe that all things are possible with God, and standing here right now…" His gaze traced up to the blue sky above them and then dropped back to hers. "I know that's true. It has to be. Because you never gave up on me. I promise you now, from this moment forward, I will honor you and cherish you, I will hold you and keep you… in sickness and in health, for richer or poorer, for better or for worse until death do us part." He slid the ring the rest of the way onto her finger.

Softly she smiled at him as she mouthed, "I love you." Then she turned to get his ring and had to brush the hair that skittered across her face from her eyes. The preacher handed her Kalin's ring. With a toss of her head, she embraced his gaze with hers.

All while he was saying his vows, she had thought he made it look hard. Now she knew why. It wasn't the words. It was getting them out for anyone other than the breeze to hear that was the problem.

"Because of you, I'm lucky to be me," she said, her voice a bare whisper, and his soft smile didn't help. "You wrote those words for me, but I live them every single day of my life. I look at you, and I think, 'How did I get so lucky?' Not because you're a gorgeous guy who plays a phenomenal guitar but because of who you are in here." She took her hand from his and pressed it to his chest. After a moment, she let it drop back into his. She had to swallow the emotion to be able to continue. "You let me be me. You taught me to be me. You believed in my dreams, and you encouraged me to chase them… even when they seemed impossible. Whatever I accomplish in this life, I know it's because of the love and the support and the encouragement of the man I love more than life itself. And so today, I promise that I will love you, and I will honor you with my heart, my body, and my soul. I will forsake all others from this moment forward, and I will be yours until death itself parts us."

She slipped the ring onto his finger, and several quiet cheers went up, but Danae hardly noticed. She was lost, staring into the forever in his eyes.

"Kalin and Danae, by the powers vested in me, I now pronounce you husband and wife. Kalin, you may kiss your bride."

Their gazes never broke as she leaned into his arms. Past and future ceased to exist in that moment. All that mattered was the present they had been given. X-Better felt better than it ever had.

She heard the door close behind Kalin with a snap, and Danae turned toward it. With the light off, she couldn't really see the suite he had acquired for their special night. Suddenly her chest throbbed from not letting go of the breath in her lungs. She felt him walk toward her, and with every step, the air vanished from the room. He laid the warmth of his hand gently under her ear.

Her head spun from lack of oxygen. She tried to look at him, but that only made breathing that much harder. Finally, in desperation, she closed her eyes and said what her heart was screaming. "I'm scared."

The gentleness of his touch never wavered. She opened her eyes, and having had time for them to adjust, she now saw his eyes clearly.

He smiled at her softly. "So am I..."

She brushed that off as she turned. "No, you're not. You've done this before. I haven't."

His hands wrapped around her arms, and with only the barest of tugs, he turned her back to face him. "I haven't either."

Questions ran through her, but the solidity in his eyes never faltered.

He shook his head slowly. "I've never made love to a woman that I loved with everything I am. Don't you think that's a little scary? It's kind of like jumping off a cliff in the dark."

The fear left her then, and her spirit soared free. She reached up and adjusted his collar. "Well, you know what they say about that, don't you?"

Amusement traces through his eyes. "What's that?"

There was peace in the gaze she leveled on him. "When you get to the end of everything you know, and you're about to step off into the darkness, one of two things will happen. Either you will step on something solid or..."

He closed his eyes and leaned toward her. "You will learn to fly..."

*When you get to the end of all the light you know
And it's time to step into the darkness of the unknown,
Faith is knowing that one of two things shall happen:
Either you will be given something solid to stand on,
Or you will be taught how to fly.*

Author's Note: I love this poem; however, as sometimes happens with very powerful and profound sayings, the origins have become befuddled and the wording slightly altered depending on who heard it where, when, and from whom. Such is the case with this poem. Just as Kalin did, I heard it on Oprah during a show with Iyanla Vanzant, and it went into my favorite quotes file in my brain. When Kalin said it in "Lucky," I knew I would have to track down the author, which proved not to be very easy as it is attributed in various forms to various people. To the best of my research, one of the following three people actually penned or said this quote the first time... Barbara J. Winter, Edward Teller, or Patrick Overton.

About the Author

A stay-at-home mom with a husband, three kids and a writing addiction on the side, Staci Stallings has seen three Inspirational Romance novels "The Long Way Home," "Eternity," and "Cowboy," and one collection of short stories "Reflections on Life" in print. Stallings has also been a featured writer in the "From the Heart" series, in "Chicken Soup for the Body and Soul," "Soul Matters," and in numerous inspirational, spiritual, and family-oriented ezines across the Internet. Although she lives in Amarillo, Texas and her main career right now is her family, Staci touches thousands of lives across the globe every month with her newsletter, "On Our Journey Home," which is featured at her website, www.stacistallings.com Come on over for a visit. You'll feel better for the experience!

Also Available from Staci Stallings

THE LONG WAY HOME
City-bred Jaxton Anderson thinks he knows more than the "country hicks" in Kansas ever will. However, one intriguing farm girl, Ami Martin, who is about as welcoming as the thorns on the rosebushes in her garden, and a grandfather Jaxton hasn't seen in years soon convince him that he doesn't have as much figured out as he thought. The harder Jaxton tries, the worse he makes things until a series of crises force him to reevaluate himself and the ideals he has always held to be important in this life.
Winner of the WordWeaving Award for Excellence

ETERNITY
Aaron Foster is in a bind. His fiancée has dumped him and moved out. Then to Aaron's horror, his new roommate, Drew Easton, unwittingly comes home with her. To save Drew's heart, Aaron conspires with his best friend, Harmony Jordan to break up Drew and Mandy by setting him up with Harmony. Unfortunately for Aaron, the plan works better than he could ever have imagined. Now with the tables turned, Aaron struggles with regret while remaining hopeful that somehow Harmony will come to want him as much as he now realizes he wants her.

REFLECTIONS ON LIFE
Fifty-two stories to encourage you on your journey. This book will compel you to look at each challenge in life as an opportunity to observe a miracle. It will encourage you to allow God to transform your ordinary life into an extraordinary one. It will remind you to reflect on your own life experiences and learn from them.

COWBOY
Cowboy is a grace-filled story about the power of giving everything to God and how a simple act of compassion can change lives forever. Emotional, soothing, and heart-wrenching, Cowboy is infused with the message that no matter who we are and no matter what life has thrown at us, we never have to walk alone.

Spirit Light Publishing
www.lulu.com/spirit-light
or
www.stacistallings.com